A SUNLESS HEART

broadview editions
series editor: L.W. Conolly

Photograph of Edith Johnstone from *The Sketch*,
12 Sept. 1894: 377

A SUNLESS HEART

Edith Johnstone

edited by Constance D. Harsh

broadview editions

Library and Archives Canada Cataloguing in Publication

Johnstone, Edith, 1866-1902
    A sunless heart / Edith Johnstone ; edited by Constance D. Harsh.

Includes bibliographical references.
ISBN 978-1-55111-741-6 (pbk.)

    I. Harsh, Constance D., 1960- II. Title.

PR4826.J66S85 2008   823′.8   C2008-902550-4

Broadview Editions
The Broadview Editions series represents the ever-changing canon of literature in English by bringing together texts long regarded as classics with valuable lesser-known works.

Advisory editor for this volume: Jennie Rubio

Broadview Press is an independent, international publishing house, incorporated in 1985. Broadview believes in shared ownership, both with its employees and with the general public; since the year 2000 Broadview shares have traded publicly on the Toronto Venture Exchange under the symbol BDP.

We welcome comments and suggestions regarding any aspect of our publications— please feel free to contact us at the addresses below or at broadview@broadview-press.com.

North America
Post Office Box 1243, Peterborough, Ontario, Canada K9J 7H5
2215 Kenmore Avenue, Buffalo, NY, USA 14207
Tel: (705) 743-8990; Fax: (705) 743-8353;
email: customerservice@broadviewpress.com

UK, Ireland, and continental Europe
NBN International, Estover Road, Plymouth UK PL6 7PY
Tel: 44 (0) 1752 202300   Fax: 44 (0) 1752 202330
email: enquiries@nbninternational.com

Australia and New Zealand
UNIREPS, University of New South Wales
Sydney, NSW, Australia 2052
Tel: 61 2 9664 0999; Fax: 61 2 9664 5420
email: info.press@unsw.edu.au

www.broadviewpress.com

Typesetting and assembly: True to Type Inc., Claremont, Canada.

PRINTED IN CANADA

This book is made of paper from well-managed FSC® - certified forests, recycled materials, and other controlled sources.

Contents

Acknowledgements

I would like to thank the following for their assistance to my work on this edition: Stirling Central Library, Peter Clapham of the Stirling Archives, the National Library of Scotland, the British Library, and the New York State Library. I am grateful to Colgate University's Research Council for its support, as well as to Colgate's Division of the Humanities. The members of Colgate's Interlibrary Loan office, and in particular Ann Ackerson, deserve special mention for their help. Thanks are due as well for the suggestions made by the following people: the members of the Central New York Victorian Studies Group; the readers of my proposal to Broadview Press; and Jennie Rubio, the copy-editor for Broadview. I am indebted to the following individuals for their advice at various stages of this project: Susan Cerasano, Margaret Darby, Lynn Staley, D. Kay Johnston, and Margaret Maurer.

Introduction

A Sunless Heart does not comfortably fit either of the most common rationales for reconsidering a forgotten novel. While it has power, it is not a lost masterpiece. While it connects with the most heated debates of its day, its position in them does not exemplify its own age's thinking or anticipate ours. Yet this idiosyncratic book has a claim on our attention. Its main topics—grief, poverty, women's work, homoeroticism, and sexual abuse—continue to interest us today. Its approach is original, for these subjects were not all equally acceptable to Victorian tastes, even in the exploratory climate of the 1890s. Readers with some experience of *fin de siècle*[1] literature will find familiar elements here, most notably the touches of naturalism, the interest in exploring emotional states, and the concern with women's expanding roles. It may be surprising, though, that Edith Johnstone handles these elements in conjunction with an unapologetic exploration of what she calls "what women may be to one another"—what today looks a great deal like lesbianism. This is an unconventional subject for the period, and Johnstone seems uninterested in making concessions that would bring her characters firmly within the bounds of traditional womanly roles. Johnstone's sexually traumatized *femme fatale*, Lotus Grace, stands as a heroine despite her inability to feel love, even for her own daughter. Neither condemned nor brought back into the role of wife or mother, Lotus finds salvation only through the love of another woman. The novel's boldness makes its initial reception one final element worthy of our attention. Despite its unconventionality, it received considerable popular and critical success upon its publication in the summer of 1894. To reconsider *A Sunless Heart* is to gain a more nuanced understanding of how late-Victorian culture functioned, particularly how culturally suppressed experiences could find expression in a palatable form.

---

1   "*Fin de siècle*" is a term used to refer to the end of the nineteenth century. It often conjures up the atmosphere of decadence and modernity that characterized much literature of the period. Naturalism is an approach to fiction that had particular currency from the second half of the nineteenth century through the early decades of the twentieth century. It is notable for its unidealized descriptions of everyday (often lower-class) life, and it tends to see people's lives as largely determined by heredity, society, and their own physical natures.

The woman who wrote this novel is an elusive figure. Public records can reveal the outlines of her life, but without her correspondence or any mention of her by contemporaries we have limited access to her personality. From the evidence of the heroines she created, she knew what it was like to have a difficult temperament—a headstrong, discontented nature that could be selfish and sometimes even cruel. Her poetry and this novel suggest an almost extravagantly emotional sensibility. In her only surviving letter, she is so forward in asking for literary advice that the publisher William Blackwood has scrawled a note at the top instructing his staff to turn her away when she visits his office. Yet other literary men supported her aspirations, at least for a time. She was either conservative enough or devoted enough to live with her mother and sister, at least until she inherited money from the husband to whom she was married for less than three weeks. And she had enough vanity that her age is understated on her census, marriage, and death records. All this is implicit in the hard evidence that we have.

Edith Johnstone was born in Belfast, Ireland, on 23 November 1866, the daughter of Charles Crockley Johnston and Margaret McIver Johnston.[1] The Johnstons were a family of well-established landowners in County Down; Charles himself had come into a considerable inheritance from his maternal grandmother, including Viewfield Lodge, a villa on four acres in the burgh of Stirling in Scotland. His elder brother William, who inherited the Irish estate of Ballykilbeg, was an MP and fiery Orangeman who made a name for himself by opposing the Party Processions Act of 1850.[2] William's son Charles would become a leading Theosophist writer and friend of William Butler Yeats.[3]

---

1 The variable spelling of this name is common. While this birth record gives the family name as Johnston, other public records show the family moving to the spelling "Johnstone" over time. As all Edith's autonymous books are published under the name Johnstone, I have consistently used this spelling for her name.

2 The Act prohibited public parades: in Ireland, these had become disruptive displays of sectarian allegiance, particularly by Protestant fraternal organizations such as the Orange Order, of which Johnston was a member.

3 The Theosophical Society was founded in 1875 as a mystical, non-dogmatic religious organization with a particular interest in spiritualism. William Butler Yeats (1865–1939) was one of Ireland's greatest poets (and himself a Theosophist).

Charles Crockley Johnston acted as agent and farm manager for his brother, although he typically gave his occupation in public records as that of an officer in the 5th Battalion Royal Irish Rifles, a militia unit that likely required fairly undemanding service. (An 1884 squib in *Punch*, identifying the uses of the militia, listed "As a Peace Association" first, followed by "As a Local Lawn Tennis Club.") Charles's work for his brother was hampered, according to William's biographer, by "one trait [they had] in common—both were totally incapable of managing financial affairs" (McClelland 9). This incapacity would have implications for Charles's own affairs: he borrowed sums against the Viewfield estate and finally in 1885 went through the Scottish bankruptcy process (called "sequestration"). The precise effect of Charles's improvidence on the lives of Edith and her siblings is uncertain. Charles may have been as irregular a figure in their lives as the ne'er-do-well Sir Gaspar O'Neill in *A Sunless Heart*. While the Stirling newspaper columnist "Atalanta" observed that "the greater part of Miss Johnston's girlhood was passed in Stirling," Charles seems to have lived at Viewfield only sporadically; the Census of 1881 finds him with his family in lodgings in Edinburgh, but in 1891 and 1901 he is alive but not living with his wife and children. At the least, Charles's difficulties with money would have imposed on the Johnstone girls the necessity of making their own way in the world.

If her father's fiscal mismanagement lent some instability to her early years, Edith's brother Charles Herbert may have been an emotional anchor. Atalanta notes in 1894 that in Stirling "she and the brother, to whom she was so fondly attached, were several years ago familiar figures." It was this brother to whom she dedicates *A Sunless Heart*, emphasizing their close imaginative bond: "We sought together ever for an Ideal Land. So painfully we searched!" So it was clearly an occasion of great grief to her when he died at the age of nineteen in 1884. As in the case of the novel's Gaspar O'Neill, the cause of death was long-standing tuberculosis accompanied by the expectoration of blood.

When Johnstone first enters the world as a writer in early 1889, it is appropriately enough with a poem that is expressive of tremendous sorrow. She and her younger sister had enrolled in the University Extension course offered at Stirling by Professor W.S. McCormick on the English poets of the nineteenth century.[1] A poem of Edith's that McCormick had distributed to the class made its way into the pages of the *Stirling Journal and Advertiser*. "My Dead Hope" is an intensely lugubrious effort, somewhat along the lines of "My City of Refuge" in *A Sunless Heart*. It explores the state of mind of one lamenting a serious loss, although it is unclear whether it is a beloved person or something more abstract that has died. The poem elicited both criticism and praise, inspiring five letters to the editor, including one that condemned the author for not holding out the promise of religion to the mourner. In Edith's first experience of encountering conventional opinion as an author, there is no indication that she or her partisans backed down. To the contrary, McCormick was quoted in one letter to the editor as telling his class that the most severe critic was an "ignoramus." This local brouhaha may have taught Johnstone that public opinion could be safely braved.

The census of 1891 found Johnstone, her occupation "Teacher," living with her mother and younger sister Flora in lodgings in Edinburgh. A *Times Literary Supplement* review of a posthumous collection of her writings, perhaps shading her age by a few years, states that she "took up kindergarten work energetically at twenty." There is no independent confirmation of this fact, but it is interesting to note its ideological plausibility for the author of a novel that celebrates female education: as Kevin Brehony has pointed out, in the English context "the struggle for women to receive a secondary and higher education and the Froebel [kindergarten] movement became inseparable [...]" (63). The *TLS* review asserts that Johnstone "gained recognition from Edinburgh publishers quite early in her teens." This claim too is unverifiable; it is grotesquely inflated if it refers to the abortive correspondence with William Blackwood in 1892.

By this time Johnstone had published, under the pseudonym "Miss E. O'Byrne," two children's books with the Glasgow firm of Blackie and Son: *Gladys; or, The Sister's Charge* (1889) and *Daphne: A Story of Self-Conquest* (1890). Appearing in series

---

1 This was only the second University Extension Course offered in Stirling. Like the University Extension Movement in other cities, this modestly priced program sought to bring the educational advantages of university study to those who were unable to become conventional students. Those who passed a final examination would receive certificates of satisfactory completion, which might in time be recognized by Scottish universities "as something in the nature of higher local examination certificates" ("University Extension Scheme").

designed to inculcate good values in children, both deal with spunky, unconventional girls who have neglectful parents. The eponymous heroine of *Gladys* saves the day by informing her aunt about the bullying that her younger brother experiences at school; she receives the reward of being allowed to live with a sympathetic friend of the family and growing from an unattractive and "gypsy-like" (20) girl into a beautiful young woman. *Daphne*, a somewhat more complex story, focuses on the difficult temperament of the title character, who is irascible and selfish, but also imaginative and energetic—clearly far superior to those around her. As Daphne does eventually succeed in gaining self-control, this is for the most part a familiar tale of female acculturation, in which a rebellious girl becomes a dutiful woman. But the novel is consistently sympathetic to Daphne, seeing her temperament from the inside rather than the outside: its emphasis is on the difficulty of her self-conquest rather than the distastefulness of her unconventionality.

Johnstone would publish one more children's novel with Blackie: *The Girleen* (1895). This book must have enjoyed some degree of popularity, since it is extant in several editions; it is indeed the only one of Johnstone's works that is regularly available in online used book stores. This is certainly the most interesting of her other novels for the reader of *A Sunless Heart*. If the morals of *Daphne* and *Gladys* are evident if rather flaccid, the moral of *The Girleen* is almost imperceptible. The title character, more formally known as Amini De Warren, is the next-to-youngest daughter of a retired army officer who has an English house and an estate in the West Indies. Like Johnstone's other child heroines, Amini is a wild girl who loves to frolic in the outdoors. But this protagonist has a devoted adult friend, the former slave Cassius Brutus, who accompanies her everywhere. This episodic novel includes an adventure with some unsavory Jesuits, the return home of the Girleen's eldest sister Natalie, and a journey to the West Indies, where Cassius Brutus is reunited with his long-lost wife and child. Natalie, who shares Amini's Creole coloring and impetuous temperament, has become a pious Christian through her love for an Evangelical minister. As Natalie turns her attention to bringing the unruly Girleen into Christian orthodoxy, a moral seems to loom on the horizon. But before Amini can lose her girlish vitality, she is killed in a slave rebellion along with Cassius Brutus and his family. It is an oddly bloody conclusion to a children's story, a happy ending only if one is glad to see the Girleen escape adult womanhood. Readers of *A Sunless Heart* will find familiar elements here in the use of passionate Creoles and climactic slaughter.[1] But even more notable is the novel's freedom from conventional pieties about the qualities that girls ought to possess.

Johnstone moved to London sometime in the early 1890s, becoming the protégée of W.T. Stead, the well-known publisher and social crusader (Waugh 95). Stead seems to have made a habit of befriending women authors. His biographer Frederic Whyte mentions his friendships with Sarah Grand and Elizabeth Robins, and (perhaps more to the point) his early support of Annie Holdsworth, whom Stead bankrolled for a year until she achieved success with *Joanna Traill, Spinster* (II:59–62). Stead's special knowledge of *A Sunless Heart* is evident in "The Novel of the Modern Woman" (see Appendix B)—he can discuss the novel before it is published, and he can produce a communication from and photograph of its anonymous author. Johnstone found another advocate in Coulson Kernahan, a well-established literary man who was the literary advisor to Ward, Lock, and Bowden (Waugh 95). It is unknown whether Kernahan continued in his support for her. But Stead would commission Johnstone to edit *The Canterbury Tales* for Stead's Masterpiece Library of Penny Poets, and she may have worked for him anonymously as well—the *TLS* review asserts that she "did much work, with her sister, for Mr. Stead."

In July 1894 *A Sunless Heart* was published and widely reviewed; it sold sufficiently well to warrant a second edition in September and a cheaper one-volume edition the following April.[2] Ward, Lock, and Bowden had announced it with some fanfare in the *Athenaeum* on 30 June, declaring that "If ever a woman put her heart into a story, one has done so in this story. It is a Novel of very unus[u]al power and singular intensity, and is likely to attract exceptional attention and curiosity." As the material in Appendix A indicates, most reviewers found the book to have merit, although some objected to its gloominess, emotionalism, and uncertain construction. On the whole, it was a

---

1   There is a possible biographical explanation for Johnstone's interest in Creoles. The mother of the great-grandmother who left Viewfield Lodge to the family was a native of the West Indies, the illegitimate daughter of a British officer (McClelland 4). Johnstone may have felt that she herself was partly Creole.

2   The first two editions were published anonymously; the one-volume edition carried Johnstone's name.

mixed but largely encouraging reception for a literary newcomer.

Presumably around this time, Johnstone met Walter Ruding, the man whom she would marry. *The Douce Family*, Johnstone's final novel, has a dedication to him with the unexplained date of February 1895. Ruding, born in 1870, was the only child of John Clement Ruding (1823–81), a bank manager who had also edited *The Whitehall Review*. After attending Christ's Hospital School in London, Walter matriculated at Corpus Christi College, Cambridge, in 1889,[1] but left before sitting his exams (Young 25). Little else is known about Ruding, and there is some unseemliness in speculating about him on the basis of a single novel. But when that novel is entitled *An Evil Motherhood*, and when it is dedicated "To my own dear mother [...] in love and honour," the temptation to speculate is strong indeed. The novel is emotionally centered on the protagonist's ambivalence towards a powerful mother, a feeling that Ruding himself may well have shared. Despite its intriguingly decadent tone and evocative frontispiece by Aubrey Beardsley,[2] *An Evil Motherhood* (1895) is not an accomplished work of fiction. It is a disjointed piece that seeks unsuccessfully to claim disjointedness as a literary virtue. Its put-upon protagonist, wrongly confined to a lunatic asylum by his avaricious mother, cannot make anything of his life even after his release because of his uncontrollably morbid temperament. Using the language of romantic love rather than filial piety, the novel envisions a possible happy ending in which the hero will reunite with his mother and redeem her. The book represents something of a plea for a sensitive but impractical nature from an author who seems to have worried a good deal about the diagnosis and treatment of mental illness.

---

1 The official College history remarks of this period in its life, "Undistinguished socially, the College also continued to be undistinguished academically" (Bury 99). For an account of one undergraduate's experience at this time, see John Cowper Powys, *Autobiography*, ch. 5. Powys entered in 1891.

2 One may literally get a picture of Ruding from this image, which Aubrey Beardsley drew after John Lane objected to Beardsley's initial use of "Black Coffee," a drawing Beardsley had originally done for *The Yellow Book* (Samuels Lasner 55–56). The second frontispiece operates almost as a commentary on the novel. A young man with flowing hair sits sullenly in an easy chair, a book unregarded on the floor to his left. Behind him towers a woman looking down at him, a kind of maternal ghost ship under full sail. Is she real, or has he imagined her?

The dedication page of *The Douce Family* provides evidence that Ruding may have been an emotionally fragile person. After the statement of dedication, there come two unattributed epigraphs: "L'expérience du monde brise le coeur ou le bronze,"[1] and eight unattributed lines from "I blame thee not, a broken heart my lot," James Thomson's translation of two Heinrich Heine poems. The poem's speaker, addressing a melancholy beloved, declares "[I] saw black night within thy soul supreme,/And saw the worm still fretting at thy heart." Suggestively, the last two lines here are full of foreboding: "Until death's peace concludes our fatal lot,/My love, we both must ever wretched be." Johnstone implies that Ruding was a man doomed by his own personality; given her own long-standing sympathy with unconventional temperaments, these quotations may show the basis of the affinity between them.

Johnstone and Ruding were married on 23 November 1895 at the parish church of Stoke Newington in London. The couple's married life would be short. Within a few days Walter fell ill; he died on 12 December 1895 of typhoid fever of sixteen days' duration. There are some grounds for believing that the family dynamics of this death were complicated. Ruding did not die at the home address that he had given just nineteen days previously, but rather at the home of his maternal grandmother, attended by his aunt. He lies in his family's plot in West Norwood Cemetery, London, but Johnstone does not. There is no mention of his wife in the memorial notice that his mother placed in the *Times* on the first anniversary of his death. Ruding died intestate with an estate worth £1542, a substantial sum: to put it into the context of *A Sunless Heart*, it is roughly five years' income for Lotus's household, or fifty years' income for the impoverished Gaspar and Gasparine. As his widow, Johnstone would presumably have received half of this amount.

In November 1896, before Ruding's estate was settled, she published one more novel, *The Douce Family*, this time with T. Fisher Unwin. It is a slight piece that shows some interesting developments in Johnstone's concerns. Some elements are familiar: a Scottish setting, a high-spirited young woman, another woman with a crush on her, and a vague concern with women's

---

1 French: "Experience of the world either breaks the heart or hardens it." This seems to be a misquotation of an aphorism by Nicolas de Chamfort, "En vivant et en voyant les hommes, il faut que le coeur se brise ou se bronze."

emancipation. But *The Douce Family* reads like a less highly colored version of George Egerton's *Keynotes*: the nominally liberated heroine, whose saucy charms the novel insists upon, has an affair with a caddish married man that ends badly. Despite his boorishness, the man clearly has an alluring virility that overshadows the foolish romantic devotion of the heroine's female admirer. By the end of the novel, the heroine learns to give way to the power of social convention, represented by the stultifying bourgeois family of the title. The novel represents a move towards a subject (transgressive heterosexuality) and a manner (strained cleverness) that had become commonplace by the mid-1890s. It is "advanced" in a fairly conventional way.

The end of Johnstone's life is largely a mystery. She had had a fairly active literary career since publishing her first children's novel in 1889, but there is no record of any publication after *The Douce Family*. Perhaps she had already begun to suffer from the heart disease that would kill her. Her whereabouts after 1897 until her death are unknown. Johnstone died of "valvular disease of heart [with] syncope" in the seaside resort town of Herne Bay, Kent, on 1 May 1902. Her death certificate indicates that she was a widow "of independent means" and that her mother was present at her death. In 1915, her name would reappear briefly in an unlikely context—the pages of *The Matron*, a London-based magazine chiefly devoted to fashions for middle-aged women. Her sister Flora, who was on the staff of the journal, published some of her sister's literary remains in its pages; later she would collect them in a pamphlet called *Thoughts of To-day and Yesterday* (1916). But then Edith Johnstone vanished from literary history, regaining some visibility only in the 1990s as critical studies of the New Woman novel listed her among the contributors to the genre. Even in this era of renewed interest in 1890s fiction, *A Sunless Heart* has been largely overlooked because of its unavailability.

A Sunless Heart exhibits some of the typical concerns of New Woman fiction. Like many of them, it deals with the sexual exploitation of women. Johnstone's interest in a specifically female sensibility allies this work with George Egerton's studies of feminine psychology in *Keynotes* (1893) and *Discords* (1894). Her heroine's frozen emotions are like those of the heroine of Iota's *A Yellow Aster* (1894). And her heroine's university education is shared by one of the protagonists of Eliza Lynn Linton's *The One Too Many* (1894). Even its examination of a woman's abortive effort to pursue a career in art has analogues in Ella Hepworth Dixon's *The Story of a Modern Woman* (1894) and Sara Jeannette Duncan's *A Daughter of To-Day* (1894). As the materials in Appendices B and C indicate, this novel connects to contemporary discourses about the proper role of women in literature, art, and public life.

Nonetheless it would be misleading to consider *A Sunless Heart* solely in light of its literary affinities. Part of the appeal of *A Sunless Heart* comes from a kind of ingenuous nonconformity. Johnstone does not seem to be trying to position herself within the literary marketplace by working within established parameters. Certainly she is not like most novelists who took the New Woman as a subject. The majority of them wrote from a smugly conservative position, exploring advanced ideas only to conclude comfortably that traditional gender arrangements are best. But neither is she, like the more progressive novelists Ménie Muriel Dowie and Mona Caird, writing to advance a carefully devised agenda. Johnstone has a commitment to following emotions wherever they take her. She is self-aware enough to know that her novel has unconventional elements, but in the book itself she does not make concessions to popular taste or try to reason her reader out of old-fashioned beliefs. She seems to hope that the authenticity of her vision will carry her through.

Before considering the shape of the novel in more detail, it is worth glancing at one of those unusual elements. At the heart of the novel lies a sexual secret: Lotus's abuse from ages twelve to sixteen at the hands of her future brother-in-law. This is not a common subject in the period. While 1890s literature eagerly explored such subjects as prostitution and adult extramarital affairs, it did not take an interest in this form of illicit sexuality. It is not that Victorians were entirely unaware of child sexual abuse; as Louise Jackson notes, they "had a clear concept of inappropriate sexual attention that constituted abuse of power [...]" (2–3).[1] Nevertheless, this topic receives very limited literary treatment. While Victorian fiction may, as James Kincaid has argued, abound in eroticized children, it does not examine the psychic after-effects of childhood sexual exploitation. Even W.T. Stead, who called attention to child prostitution in *The Maiden Tribute of Modern Babylon* (see Appendix D), embraced a narrative of vio-

---

1 The nineteenth century saw changes in the English legal definition of the age of consent, which rose from 12 to 13 in 1875 and to 16 in 1885 (Jackson 3).

lated virginity and ruined prospects, not one of traumatized personality. In this respect *A Sunless Heart* appears nearly our contemporary in its analysis of Lotus's quasi-incestuous experience. Lotus confesses to Gasparine that "that wicked and unnatural outrage dried up with damning fire each natural and womanly impulse, turning my child-heart to stone, my mother instincts to gall" (157). Diana Russell, along with others, has identified one of the after-effects of incest as "feeling emotionally cold, callous, hard, or frigid as a result of the sexual abuse" (140). Johnstone is exploring new ground here in a fashion notably free of conventionalized horror or prurience.

Johnstone's two apologies show some self-consciousness about subject matter, but they also make two different claims to truthfulness. The first justifies the depiction of Gaspar and Gasparine by declaring, "Their reality is their only *raison d'être*. I submit them to the mercies of a public, that is often unexpectedly kind" (36). This might have served as a calm and modest defense of the grubby setting of Book I, except that it follows the extraordinarily sentimental "Dedication" to her late brother Charlie. In context, the first apology becomes a claim that the first book's story of a sister's love for her doomed brother has an emotional truthfulness rooted in biographical fact. The second apology offers a more developed ideological content and greater emotional distance. Explaining a threefold aim, Johnstone promises to give voice to those who are uninvolved in "the passion of love between man and woman," to reveal the wrongs "women have silently borne," and to show "what women may be, and often are, to one another" (90). Here is a more abstract justification by authenticity, one with a stronger sense of social and artistic purpose. But this, like the first apology, roots the novel's reality in its access to true feelings.

When seen in light of the two books they introduce, the apologies help underscore the unifying principle of an apparently heterogeneous novel. As some reviewers noted disapprovingly, *A Sunless Heart* is oddly constructed, with its chief interest transferred from Gasparine to Lotus roughly halfway through. It also has an inconsistent literary texture. Book I, "The Brother and Sister," mixes gritty descriptions of impoverished gentility with mawkishly sentimental exclamations. Book II, "Lotus," initially reads as a kind of fantasy, in which the protagonist is rescued from despair by the intervention of a beautiful angel who lives in a lovely suburban house on £300 a year. Seemingly the second book explores scenes and issues vastly different from the first. Yet there is a continuity between the two books that becomes evident as Gasparine begins to see what lies beneath the surface brilliance of Lotus's life as an ideal modern woman. Lotus's malady, her "sunless heart," demonstrates the novel's consistent commitment to emotional intensity as the highest form of human experience. Gasparine, whose emotional bond with her brother the novel has celebrated, experiences tragedy when she loses him; but Lotus experiences the greater tragedy in being unable to feel what Gasparine feels.[1] Lotus locates her own potential cure in an act of superlatively intense devotion, "when some one [...] wraps me in a boundless and perfect love that does not question [...]" (132). While Gasparine's own impassioned dedication looks extravagant enough to fit the bill, even it will not suffice. Gasparine is disqualified from the office of savior by her lack of courage years before, when she failed to seize the opportunity she had of comforting the young Lotus in her time of greatest need. All the truths that this novel seeks to reveal have a connection to human sentiment: this novel's highest value is emotional responsiveness.

In her second apology, Johnstone indicates that her focus is on those in whose lives conventional romantic love plays little part. Yet this statement only hints at the novel's thoroughgoing revolt against heterosexual romance. Its strongest emotional ties are those between brother and sister or friend and friend. Lotus's family group in Stirling is eccentric even before Gasparine joins it, consisting as it does of Lotus, her illegitimate daughter Ladybird, and Lotus's former employer. The novel problematizes marriage. Lotus, herself the product of an extramarital affair, experiences the hypocrisy of the institution of marriage when her sister weds her fiancé even after learning that he has sexually abused Lotus. Gasparine's eventual marriage, well after Lotus's death, is described in aggressively prosaic terms: acting as housekeeper for her father, she "found her little husband—the smallest and ugliest of the three clerks who did Sir Gaspar's work [...]" (197). The consolations conventionally offered to women have

---

1 The subject of the woman whose greatest failure is emotional frigidity is not new. One thinks, for instance, of Estella in Charles Dickens's *Great Expectations* (1860–61). I have already suggested that unfeeling women figure in such novels as *A Yellow Aster*. But it is noteworthy that Lotus is an object of sympathy rather than judgment, and that her occupation and advanced ideas are irrelevant to her psychic plight. Her professional life is an unproblematic ideal, not a source of pathology.

little significance to Gasparine. Her husband has no sexual magnetism, and her children are unsightly. Her most meaningful experience comes while she is in emotional thrall to Lotus. More significantly, heterosexual love is brought to trial and found wanting when Lionel Raymond nearly proposes to Lotus but is won away by Mona Lefcadio's unwitting physical allure. As Lotus contemplates his apostasy, she pointedly questions the nature of masculine devotion: "is he, like all other men, in love with the *woman*, not the soul?" (186). Not only is Raymond not her "salvation"; Lotus wonders whether any man could fill this role.

The narrative solution to Lotus's malaise, appropriately enough, does not come from marriage to a good man, but from a more unconventional source. It might seem surprising that Mona Lefcadio should prove to possess what Lotus needs, for the novel has delineated her many faults of temperament. In her first appearance, Lotus temporarily banishes her for making a callous remark about Gaspar—"The stupid fellow gets consumption—he lies in there" (102). Mona's feverish jealousy makes her hate both Ladybird and Gasparine as rivals for Lotus's affection. In an ordinary Victorian novel, we would know to compare her unfavorably with the more mature, emotionally controlled Gasparine. But Mona exemplifies the values of *A Sunless Heart*. Mona has an inborn fire that marks her as special: she is "a creature of flame and water, genius and strung nerves; a mad, lovable thing; a West Indian heiress, who owned a pitch lake in Trinidad" (101). Mona's racial otherness, which is defined in conformity with the cultural preconceptions visible in the material in Appendix E, seems to guarantee the richness of her emotional nature. She continually protests her adoration for Lotus, who often brushes her off savagely out of a disbelief in her sincerity. She assures Mona that her devotion is just a dress rehearsal for heterosexual love: "At present you yearn for sentiment, emotion, passion. I am your lay-figure. In a few years you will find man is the right and legal object of these hysterics—you would have found it out long ago, but your beauty has made you proud and scornful. It will come, however, rest content" (107). Even later, when Mona returns after a period of absence to assert her claim on Lotus's companionship, Lotus is skeptical, judging her feelings to be "a passionate desire into which your imagination has crowded your life. It will pass" (178). So, although the narrative identifies Mona positively as a "sweet woman" whose "tender heart was [...] full of its noble, idealising love" (178), there is reason to believe in the transience of her feelings and the ultimate triumph of heterosexual romance.

But Mona's love proves enduring, and her reunion with Lotus in a melodramatic *Liebestod* constitutes the climax of the novel. Johnstone gives her protagonist a form of emotional rebirth that evades both marriage and maternal love. For Lotus has been on the verge of acknowledging her relationship to Ladybird, who has long sought to meet her mother. It is easy to imagine a denouement in which the heroine is brought back to emotional life by embracing her maternity. Indeed, such an ending would strongly resemble the conclusion of *A Yellow Aster*. But Johnstone's heroine eludes this destiny, and in her final words she denies to Mona that she knows the identity of Ladybird's mother. The only consolation left to Gasparine, grieving with her lesser love, is an eventual artistic triumph: she finally achieves popular acclaim by successfully capturing Lotus's soul in a painting.

A Sunless Heart inevitably strikes a twenty-first-century reader as a strongly lesbian work. Yet it is difficult to know how to understand it in its original historical context. There is evidence that contemporary readers did not see the homosexual dimension of the story. Reviewers failed to single out the relationships between women as unnatural or unusual. The *Bookman*'s reference to the "complex" temperament of the novel—"German sentiment [...] grafted on Irish sensitiveness"—may be a veiled allusion to *Schwärmerei*, the German word used to describe the romantic feelings of one girl for another. The *Athenaeum* reviewer hints at some sexual impropriety, referencing French fiction and noting "unwelcome progress on certain lines." But the English held French fiction responsible for many ills. It is impossible to know where this reader is laying blame—it could easily be on the depiction of Lotus's early sexual abuse and out-of-wedlock child. *Publishers' Circular* goes so far as to call Lotus's effect on Gasparine O'Neill "wholesome." One might on the whole conclude that reviewers found nothing objectionable about the relationships described.

Yet one might also suspect that reviewers simply chose not to see anything that might be objectionable. As Martha Vicinus has observed, "The Victorians were masters of the unspoken and the unsaid, happy to let odd sexual relations flourish as long as no one spoke openly about them" (*Intimate Friends* 54). An example from the reception of George Egerton's *Discords* is instructive. In the story "A Psychological Moment," Egerton dares to name the eroticism that underlies relationships at a girls' pensionnat: the teachers "are favourites and number many 'flames' amongst the crowd of girls filled with sickly sentiment, '*schwärmerei*,' and awakening sexual instinct. They are genuinely in love" (11). This diagnosis attracted the disgusted attention of J.A. Spender, in a section of *The New Fiction* not excerpted in Appendix D: "Here we have a simple and innocent scene, distorted by the pervading sex medium" (87). Spender does not object to the representation of this scene as long as it remains unanalyzed. Allan McLane Hamilton's 1896 essay in Appendix D observes that, until recently, "the mere insinuation that there could be anything improper in the intimate relations of two women would have drawn upon the head of the maker of such a suggestion a degree of censure of the most pronounced and enduring character [...]." Victorians were well trained to see women's relationships in a desexualized way.

Here we encounter the issue that has bedevilled critics seeking to understand women's same-sex relationships in the nineteenth century. Some might see in Mona's dedication to Lotus a culturally sanctioned romantic friendship of the sort described by Carroll Smith-Rosenberg. Or, taking Lillian Faderman's lead, one might see this novel as an example of the greater latitude allowed in women's affectional relationships before World War I—before Freudian psychology put sexuality at the center of the human self, and before sexologists had defined a pathological "lesbianism." Faderman provides examples of intense friendships between women that seemed to exist in ignorance of their implicitly sexual content. It is possible to question whether Johnstone understood Lotus and Mona's relationship to be a sexual one; yet, given the physicality of their interactions, it can seem evasive and even absurd to have doubts on the subject. After all, Mona insists upon spending the night with Lotus before they are nominally to part, "our arms round one another in the way that was always my best rest" (193). When the wounded Mona finds Lotus after the train wreck, the older woman "felt a mouth touch hers, and two wet hands groped over her body" (195). These descriptions seem unambiguously sensual. Terry Castle has effectively exposed the limitations of what she humorously calls "the no-sex-before-1900 school" (93). Just because sexologists had not clearly defined a category of "lesbian," it is not therefore the case that lesbian relationships did not exist or were unimaginable.

The same-sex relationships in *A Sunless Heart* are all the more striking in the context of other New Woman fiction. There the preferred mode of exploring new sexual possibilities for women was heterosexual, as the following list of novels often put in the New Woman category shows: *Dodo, Keynotes, A Superfluous Woman, A*

Yellow Aster, The Story of a Modern Woman, Gallia, The Woman Who Did, A Pliable Marriage, and *Jude the Obscure.* Even Ethel Arnold's *Platonics,* an 1894 novel identified by Phyllis Wachter as "a homorelational narrative" (Arnold xix) represents a much less sexualized female friendship. While the emotional connection between two women does form the backbone of the story, it is the heroine's love for a man that is pointedly eroticized. She may embrace her friend with "a look of [...] benign loving-kindness" (25), but she reserves for her male lover "a kiss which swept away all sense of separateness, and fused their spirits into one" (75). Wachter may be correct in speculating that Arnold "was hesitant to overtly present a fully realized same-sex relationship lest she reveal too much about her own strong attachments to women" (Arnold xvii). *Platonics* is indeed a more self-conscious, controlled artistic performance than *A Sunless Heart*; slight but tasteful, it is the production of an evidently educated and genteel author. Perhaps Arnold would be more attuned than Johnstone to what readers might think of her work. But, as it turns out, Johnstone was able to get away with a good bit more than Arnold tried. At this point we cannot know whether Johnstone's openness was a product of naivety, fearlessness, or an uncontrollable bent for self-expression.

Terry Castle is right to insist that we should no longer allow lesbians to disappear into mere apparitions. Readers today will see the sexuality in the relationships between Gasparine and Lotus, and Mona and Lotus. We can see this novel as part of the real-world tradition of same-sex love that Martha Vicinus has described in *Intimate Friends*: "The adroitness with which these women used and deflected the public gaze upon their more private relations was extraordinary. They managed to be open and closed, to keep a secret and to tell it to anyone who might be listening." It is important to avoid the mistake of historians who have taken "[t]heir success [... as] an excuse to ignore or deny the depth of passion and commitment contained in women's intimate friendships" (230). At the same time, we should continue to recognize the conventional frame that offered plausible deniability to representations of lesbian affections. It is even possible that some Victorian women may have used this frame to avoid facing uncomfortable truths about their own desires. It seems too simple to see the same-sex relationships of *A Sunless Heart* as having potential meaning only as lesbianism in code or only as asexual romantic friendship. We should hold on to both interpretive possibilities when reading this novel. If it were not for the second possibility, after all, if members of this society were not capable of what looks to us like willful blindness, *A Sunless Heart* could not have received the acceptance it enjoyed in 1894. This acceptance reminds us of something that decades of scholarship have not yet quite instilled in the popular imagination: mainstream Victorian culture was not simply the repressive monolith of modernist fantasy. Because of her culture's limited acknowledgment of woman's nature, Johnstone could find a space to tell her story in a way that her audience could accept.

A Sunless Heart is surely worth examining today as a cultural document and as an example of an important literary subgenre. But its originality and narrative momentum also make it an engaging work of fiction. Despite its grandiosity, its sloppiness, its crazed affinity for ellipses and italics, this is some kind of work of art. It is undoubtedly true to its own distinctive sense of human experience. I am reminded of a line from a very different work of the 1890s, Joseph Conrad's *Heart of Darkness*. Marlowe, enunciating his final judgment of Kurtz, declares, "This is the reason why I affirm that Kurtz was a remarkable man. He had something to say. He said it."[1] Edith Johnstone had something of her own to say. She said it. There is always something remarkable in that.

---

1 Joseph Conrad, *Heart of Darkness and Other Tales* (Oxford: Oxford UP, 1998) 241.

Edith Johnstone: A Brief Chronology

1866   (23 November) Born at 24 Princes Street in Belfast, Ireland, to Charles Crockley Johnston and Mary McIver Johnston.

1881   (3 April) Living with father, mother, brother Charles, and sisters Margaret and Flora at 20A Dick Place in Edinburgh (Census of Scotland).

1884   (29 September) Death of brother Charles Herbert Johnstone, age nineteen, of phthisis pulmonalis (tuberculosis) and hemoptysis (expectoration of blood) at Viewfield Lodge, Stirling, Scotland.

1885   (1 August) Charles Crockley Johnston undergoes Scottish Sequestration (bankruptcy proceedings) in Stirling.

1886   Major Charles C. Johnston listed as resident at Viewfield House in the *Stirlingshire (Burgh and County) Directory*.

1886   Major C. Johnston listed as a resident of Ballydugan, Ireland (near the family seat at Ballykilbeg) in the *County Down Guide and Directory*.

1889   (January–April) Attends University Extension Lectures on the English Poets of the Nineteenth Century given by W.S. McCormack, earning a certificate by passing the final examination.

       Publishes a children's book in Blackie's Shilling Series under the pseudonym Miss E. O'Byrne: *Gladys; or, The Sister's Charge*.

1890   Publishes another children's book under the same pseudonym in Blackie's Ninepenny Series: *Daphne: A Story of Self-Conquest*.

1891   (5 April) Living with mother and sister Flora at 26 Frederick Street, Edinburgh; age given as twenty-three and profession listed as "Teacher" (Census of Scotland).

1892   Seeks advice on novel she is writing from the Edinburgh publishing house of William Blackwood & Sons; gives addresses as Carlyle House, Haddington and 19a Duke Street, Edinburgh.

1894   (July) *A Sunless Heart* published anonymously in two volumes by Ward, Lock, & Bowden.
       (September) Second edition of *A Sunless Heart* published.

1895   (April) Cheaper, one-volume edition of *A Sunless Heart* published, now under Johnstone's name.

(by October) Edits *The Canterbury Tales*, volume 14
in W.T. Stead's Masterpiece Library Penny Poets
series.

(23 November) Edith Marion Huberta Johnstone aged
twenty-seven, no profession, marries Walter Ruding,
twenty-five, author, at the parish church of Stoke
Newington, London. Residence given for both is 79
Park Lane, where the head of household in the 1896
Kelly's London Suburban Directory is given as "Mrs.
Johnstone."

(12 December) Walter Ruding, annuitant (receiver of an
annuity), dies of typhoid fever of sixteen days' duration
at the home of his maternal grandmother, 4 Clarendon
Road, Kennington, London. He is buried with his father
in West Norwood Cemetery, London.

Publishes, under her own name with Blackie, *The
Girleen*, a more substantial children's book.

1896 (November) T. Fisher Unwin publishes *The Douce
Family*.

1897 (12 May) Letters of Administration granted to Johnstone
as relict of Walter Ruding. Gross value of his personal
estate is £1542. Johnstone is still residing at 79 Park
Lane, Clissold Park (Stoke Newington), London.

1901 (31 March) Johnstone is not listed as living with her
mother and sister Flora (now a shorthand clerk going by
the name Foley) in Battersea, London (Census of
England).

1902 (1 May) Edith Marion Ruding, aged twenty-nine, widow
of independent means, dies at 2 Tyndale Park, Herne
Bay, Kent of "valvular disease of heart syncope." Her
mother is present at her death.

1915 Foley Johnstone, working on the staff of *The Matron*, a
monthly journal focusing on mature women's fashions,
publishes several stories and poems written by her sister
Edith.

1916 *Thoughts of To-day and Yesterday. Poems and Writings of
Edith and Foley Johnstone* is published from the offices of
The Matron. No copies of this 56-page book seem to
remain in existence.

A Note on the Text

A Sunless Heart was first published anonymously in two volumes by Ward, Lock, and Bowden in July 1894. A second edition followed in September. In April 1895 a cheaper, one-volume edition appeared, with Johnstone's name on the title page. Its front matter also lists a one-volume "Special Colonial Edition" from December 1894 that does not survive in any research library. A comparison of the three available editions yields only a few items of interest. The first and second editions are virtually identical, although the latter does correct a few typographical errors. The third edition corrects a few more errors, but introduces roughly a dozen of its own, along with about fifty variant readings. Most of these variants involve minor matters of punctuation, and most are not clearly improvements over the original.

More interestingly, the third edition omits the first Apology; however, as Johnstone still calls the Apology that opens Book II "a second apologetic explanation" (90), it is possible that the omission of the first was merely an oversight. More obviously deliberate are three changes to the poem "My City of Refuge." Perhaps in reaction to initial reviews, this edition corrects two uses of "thee" as a nominative pronoun and changes the line "Parting my past and me" to "Parting my past from me." On the whole, though, there is no reason to prefer the third edition, and no evidence that Johnstone was responsible for its changes. In preparing the present edition, I have taken the first edition as my copytext, using a very light hand in introducing emendations. Objection to Johnstone's grammar and style was part of the initial reception of this novel, and so I have decided not to regularize her sometimes eccentric punctuation or to correct such solecisms as "had began" for "had begun" (45; corrected in the third edition). However, I have silently corrected about twenty-five obvious mistakes in the deployment of quotation marks, as well as a few other glaring typographical errors in punctuation. I have tried to enforce a distinction between mistakes that a reader might find informative and those that he or she would find merely distracting.

In my footnotes to the text, I have occasionally provided definitions of unusual words or phrases from the *Oxford English Dictionary Online* (<http://http://dictionary.oed.com/>). These definitions are indicated with the parenthetical citation "*OED*." All Biblical quotations are from the King James Version, the translation that Johnstone herself would have known.

A SUNLESS HEART

Behold the sea ! The sun's swift rays unfurl
   Upon her track ;
Yet in her depths, where hides the perfect pearl,
   The night is black.

The sea am I. In billows proud and bold
   My senses sweep ;
And all my songs stream like the sun's full gold
   Across the deep.

Oft-times they throb with love and jest—the creeds
   They fain impart—
While, buried in my silent bosom, bleeds
   A sunless heart.

IN TWO VOLS

VOL. I

LONDON
WARD, LOCK & BOWDEN, LIMITED
WARWICK HOUSE, SALISBURY SQUARE, E.C
NEW YORK AND MELBOURNE
1894

DEDICATION

To CHARLIE, my brother, in oh! most loving memory of a love that was mine. Which I seek eternally.... We sought together ever for an Ideal Land. So painfully we searched! I see the two little figures now, arms linked, trudging the wide, beaten roads, with stone walls at each side—the wide roads, the stone walls, which we hated. Now, in memory, they have become beautiful to me. How? Why?

And we painted the Land—the corn waves there golden, bending beneath the softest, faintest breeze; the sky is blue, the sea laps the rim of hot gold sand with a sound as faint and clear as a little silver bell.

"There," said we, "we shall rest;" for already the strife of life was in us, so that we sought ever and found never.

And when we talked of it once, he said, "But when two have gone together so far, and one, growing tired, falls on sleep, *the other goes on alone*; but after a little, new friends, new hopes, new fears come, even her sorrow has become a friend, *and her dead has no part in them*.

"Then she grows old, older; she passes the age, the knowledge of her dead, and, passing, says, 'Should I meet him he would think me old. And I am old. I am not she whom he left. *I have changed.*' She looks at the young around her. 'He was only so old as they,' she says, 'and he seemed *very* old and wise to me; and they—they are so young, and I see through their young, sweet wisdom, and it is only youth and hope, and innocence and ignorance; it is not serious. It is serious to *them*, but not to me, *now*; that, too, is dead.'"

Then I looked at him, and I saw he spoke of himself and of me in the years to come; and I said, "No love, no; it is not so with love; we love for ever."

And afterwards, when I went to his grave, it was not the six feet of grass I saw, but the Land we dreamed of. And, kneeling there, I dreamt of it, and lived in it again; and I sing to myself the song of

MY CITY OF REFUGE

I sometimes dream of a beautiful land
      That is most fair to see,
Where, bankrupt in love, and hope, and joy
      I might go, and be free;
A land of golden corn, blue flowers,
      And a still sea.

A land where I meet my Dead again,
      Smiling, remembered eyes,
Time, changes, partings are forgot
      Here or in Paradise.
We meet as though no change could be
      By that still sea.

New ties and friends, that cast a veil,
      Parting my past and me,
Drawing the love that I had vowed,
      My Dead, to thee,
Fall off. The past becomes the present verily,
In that still land, among the corn,
      Beside the sea.

Ah! lovely Dead! Ah! eyes that smiled,
      And heart that beat for me!
Ah! yearnings, bitterer than pain or poignant agony,
Reproach me not. Time, and not I, severs my heart from thee.
'Tis God must answer at the bar,
If with each weary passing year
      Thou should'st forgotten be,
Thine eyes grow dim, thy voice grow faint in memory,
Till but a ghost, lovely in pain,
      Clasps hands with me,
Among the corn, upon the shore,
      Beside the sea.

And pleading eyes, once old, now young,
      To what mine are,
Meet mine, sad-questioning: "Dear,
      Thou art so far! so far!
Beyond the years we used to know,

Thou hast learned all they had to show,
    And what of me?
Ever the boy you loved and lost,
    I wait for thee
Among the corn, and the blue flowers,
    By the still sea.

"We were to learn *together*, dear,
    But my eyes fell on sleep.
Ah! thine were dim for many a year
    With tears that thou did'st weep,
So dim that thou for long no life, no love could'st see,
Thus we were like two dead apart, love,—I and thee.

"But afterwards love came, life turned you round and round.
The noises drowned my voice's tender memory-sound.
You grew a woman, learned all life, and thought of me
As something young in your own youth, far past, *that used to be*,
And now among the corn, beside the still, still sea."

"Ah! lovely Dead, it is not so, nor so shall be.
Dear, all the love that I do know is love for thee,
And all life's knowledge I do hold in treasury
Against our meeting in the vast eternity.

"And love will bridge the long, long years that parted us, and all
My tears shall form a prism bright, my sobs shall form a call
To bring again the past in which we planned and hoped to live
Ever together. And, if God is good, He'll find and give,
Out of His universe, the Land we dreamed of, I and thee,
And crown us there, among the corn,
    Beside the sea."

Ah! City of Refuge! Thus I dream of thy waving corn and sea,
And thus when evermore life's stir seems turning ceaselessly;
And thus when evermore I hear life's voices cry,
And when upon my tired breast life's waves beat high,
And I do seem with the great wheel to turn remorselessly,
I seek thy quiet, six feet of grass, belovèd, covering thee.
There are the cornfields, and the flowers, and the still sea;
There—when the voice of God says, "Hush!"—is room for me.

CONTENTS

BOOK I
THE BROTHER AND SISTER

Chapter

BOOK II
LOTUS

APOLOGY

I have given, brief and fragmentary, an impressionist view of two young and tragic lives. Their reality is their only *raison d'être*. I submit them to the mercies of a public, that is often unexpectedly kind.

BOOK I
THE BROTHER AND SISTER

CHAPTER I
GASPAR AND GASPARINE

The first cheap day of the season at the Crystal Palace[1] was attended by the usual rush. Cockneys and strangers were trotting hither and thither, eager to enjoy the entire programme and miss nothing. The restaurants were filled and busy; every one was gaily dressed, moved in a hurry, stared and talked.

In singular contrast to the crowd, a young man and a girl walked about with a timid and uncertain air, which, however, might become aggressive or haughty on provocation. When people filed into the restaurants they went out into the grounds, and finding a quiet seat, rested there, ate some bread-and-butter, and drank in turn from a bottle containing milk.

The young man appeared to be about seventeen years of age, tall and slender, straight when he walked; but one noticed when he stood, he always leaned on something for support, and sometimes he coughed. He was beautiful, with the mournful, dread beauty of one whom death has marked. The startling pallor of his face, the dark, unnatural brilliancy of his eyes—long, blue-black eyes with drooping, filmy fringes that almost met; the bright red of a consuming fever in the lips; the languid stooping as he sat or stood; all were beautiful with a beauty to break the heart that loved him.

There is a time when death comes, clothed in mystery, as it were, creeps into the young eyes, hollows the young cheeks, draws mournful, patient lines round the young mouth, with unspeakable sorrow and yearning, spiritualising the whole expression.

We gaze at the face; it is half spirit already. A pain comes into our hearts. More spirit means more sorrow then? And such sorrow! It is an awful beauty which death gives to the still living eyes. Such a beauty the boy had.

The girl who walked with him was his twin-sister, resembling him, but in an exaggerated way. Where he was slender, she was

---

1   The name given to the distinctive glass and iron building that housed the Great Exhibition of 1851. Its hall was moved from Hyde Park to Sydenham, South London, where it held permanent exhibits and served as a venue for concerts. It was destroyed by fire in 1936.

thin; he luminously white, she ghastly pallid; his cheeks were slightly hollow, her cheek-bones showed, and her delicately square jaw seemed to cut the skin almost; his eyes were dark and questioning, hers black as night, eager, restless, with something wild and painful in their glance. Both were oddly dressed. Glances of amusement or contempt, and occasionally admiration, directed towards Gaspar, followed them as they moved timidly about, enjoying the band and the gaiety. Now and then, with the morbid sensitiveness of the sick and poor, they caught these glances of derision or amusement. They were too delicate to speak of it, but you could see that the smile left their faces, and that they drew a little closer together, and kept to an unfrequented part, until youth kissed the quivering sting, and drew them back among men once more, to be stung once more.

So it is always.

"Gaspar, isn't it lovely to be here? And just imagine hearing quite by chance of it being cheaper to-day!"

"Yes, that was a stroke of good fortune; and to be sure it does us good to have a little amusement occasionally."

All day they wandered about; in the evening, the heat and glare of light seemed to weigh heavily upon the boy; he looked like a spirit of sorrow that smiled; he bent, and coughed sobbingly. The girl looked at him with a hunted expression. The ghost of a foreboding had indeed brought her to bay. Then she bent too, and coughed.

"Gaspar," she said then, "there must be something trying in this air. I feel it in my chest, and it makes me cough."

"Does it, dear Gaspar-girl? Then we must go. Besides, it's getting late. But let us first sit down and hear out this piece of music. Don't you think, Gaspar, music is a good symbol for heaven? How hot and living our thoughts and words are while we listen to the heart of music beating, and always sorrow, sorrow and passion; and when the music has passed, and we try to put down the thoughts and the words, how cold and lifeless they are!"

His eyes yearned as he spoke; he had the heart of a poet, but he would never sing—here. Death stops all that.

Her eyes answered his, but she knew *one* must be strong.

"The music is over, Gaspar. Do let us go—I feel tired."

Both were very silent during the train journey home to a dingy house in St. John's Wood district. Within, the house was even more comfortless than without; the rooms were only half furnished, dirty, and untidy. A small servant of the lower lodging-house type informed them as they entered, "that S' Gaspa 'ad gone hout ov town ova Sunda', an' 'e'd ellowed 'er to 'ave an 'oliday, so she'd be mech 'bliged 'f the'd tike tea 's soon 's possible, as a gentleman was to call fer 'er at seven, mem." Deigning no answer, and without pausing, the two passed to their sitting-room.

"How charming that he's gone," said the girl, "if only he has left some money!"

A search in certain known hiding-places disclosed a small sum, and the two rejoiced over it.

"We can put it in the bank. I have enough for the meantime. It is more than I expected."

The bank—an old tin box—was produced, and its contents again counted over, and the new sum added. They had learned to store up against times of dearth, and often screwed their courage, in weary moments, by counting it and planning how to make it grow. It never grew, however; times of dearth were too frequent for that.

Tea came—a meagre meal. No wonder the brother and sister partook languidly, almost forgetting it in the excitement of discussing the eventful day,—for pleasure-seeking was rare with them. Now, in the security of their own room, they talked, brilliantly rather than cheerfully, and criticised all they had seen. The room in which they sat had one attraction. The walls were hung close with unframed canvasses, most of them remarkable for beauty, originality of treatment, and force of execution. The pictures were Gasparine's, and spoke an artistic power of no mean promise. Gaspar, and her pictures, indeed, made up Gasparine's life. Over them the twins dreamed of a golden future, when Gasparine would be famous and rich, and they could do what they would.

"It will all come right," they told one another, when, with interlocked arms, they faced hard times, "it will all come right when the pictures are known, and sell."

And they did not see the grave that yawned between. Or stop! Did they?

Ah! yes; for when he was in bed, the deadly fear that all his lovely youth fought against believing, the fear that his young life would be cut short and Gasparine be left alone, crept into his heart—crept in with the silence of the room and in and up to his brain. "O God," he prayed then, "not so, not to leave the little one alone, the poor little one—not yet, dear God!"

And she, in her little room, drawing the old blankets round

her, said, "I will not think of it; I dare not think of it. If I believed it, or dwelt upon it, for half an hour I should go mad." And she rose and went to him, and kissed the white, white face, and heard the sweet, hollow voice, "Good-night, Gaspar-girl." "Good-night, Gaspar-boy," and then went back and lay down, resolutely setting herself to count up numbers monotonously, and so lull herself to sleep. Both dreaded the darkness; it was so akin to death. For they each saw the grave; and each dreaded lest the other should see it, and each strove to hide it from the other.

CHAPTER II
SIR GASPAR O'NEILL

Who were they? It is a question we ask about every one when we come into connection with them, and it is as well to know these two.

Not as such neighbours, who troubled to know them at all, knew them, as two shabby, poor, young eccentrics, with a titled, but far from respectable father. Not, either, as they knew themselves, feeling so strongly that most unreasoning and insuppressible of all prides—that of blood; fretting against it because it had brought them only uncertainty and sorrow. In every little adornment or luxury of life, in outward refinement, in any knowledge of the rules of society, they knew themselves to be far behind the class of upper tradespeople among whom they lived; they despised these people, their petty aims, jealousies, ignoble lives, yet often in bitterness were tempted to wish themselves of them.

"They despise us," said Gasparine, "and rightly. These people, at least, have the comfort of homes, money to make life other than an unending struggle for mere bread; friends, mean and self-interested if you like, still what the world knows as friends; and social ties and duties, and at least, if not respect, so much of consideration for one another."

And Gaspar would answer, "If we had these things, Gaspar, we should only fret against them all our lives. No; that class could not satisfy us." And he would sigh.

For their lives had been very sad. Often, looking back, it seemed to Gasparine that she could not remember a day nor an hour, even among the sunny days which she counted happy, when she had not had the haunting of a past sorrow, or the foreboding of one in the future. And always there was that horror, which came and went, and came and went, and dealt with them so evilly at last. It was their father.

Their father was Sir Gaspar O'Neill. About that there could be no doubt. It was one of the oldest baronetcies in Ireland; indeed, it was now so old that there was nothing of it left but the title, and it was often one of the most serious and bitter questions with the brother and sister whether, at their father's death, Gaspar had any right to the title. There had been a time when the O'Neills were great, as far as position and worldly prosperity went. At the time of the Irish Parliament[1] there had been no wealthier or better people. Ballygaspar, in County Donegal, was then the family seat. But the house was doomed, and its fall fatally sure and rapid. Horses, dogs, rout, and riot,[2] were over now. Ballygaspar, mortgaged to twice its value, passed out of the family, and when the present baronet received the title, he received with it, a small farm in the far wilds of Donegal, on which were a few cottages and the last remains of the ruins of an old tower, upon a knoll. With this handsome property he found himself possessed of a yearly income of ninety-five pounds.

However, as I said, the baronet was a gentleman; one, moreover, who knew that no baronet with a proper pride ever dreamt of doing anything but amuse himself. Being Irish, he was a man of resources; being young, clever, handsome, and a baronet, he was in request with certain classes of men and women. He speedily found out his advantages; he did not put his wits to grass. On cards, and in drawing-rooms, the name and the man looked well. He had his little difficulties, but it was not often that he was driven to desperation, and then, if he had a run of ill-luck gambling, and his clothes began to look seedy, he could always retire to his "place" in Donegal, and amuse himself bullying the tenants of the three cottages.

"My place in Donegal" was vague, and sounded satisfactory. As there was no castle nor mansion on the "place," it is doubtful where he housed on these occasions; but we may suppose he billeted himself on each of the cottars in turn. It is certain, at least, that he could not have lived in the tower.

---

1 An Irish Parliament sat from the thirteenth century until it was abolished by the Act of Union in 1801.
2 The wordplay here disparages the activity of fox hunting. In hunting, "routing" is the act of driving a fox out of a hole in which it has hidden; "riot" is "the action, on the part of a hound, of following the scent of some animal other than that which he is intended to hunt" (*OED*). But "rout" and "riot," sometimes used together in a single phrase, are also legal terms for two types of unlawful assembly.

Everybody believed in the "place." The world is small, but it is large enough for that sort of thing, and Sir Gaspar had a finished and artistic way of doing it.

Then occurred one of those strange events, which, belonging to the deeper mysteries of psychology, shock and startle the philosopher, when he meets it in the career of a selfish and vicious man. It makes our reasoning vain; it is inexplicable.

Sir Gaspar was engaged, so report said, to a handsome young woman, belonging to that class which believed in the "place," and were proud of the baronet's card. A lady, moreover, well educated and refined, and with a fortune which would have settled the baronet's difficulties permanently.

Strange! The baronet disappeared one day. Not alone, of course. Some horrid creature from the theatre, or worse, shared his voluntary exile. The world never dreamt of marriage. Marriage would have been still more shocking to its sense of what was right. Yet marriage it was, and love.

For this love is a funny fellow, a droll fellow, quite a wag in his way. And of all his tricks, those he plays on these poor, foolish-wise men of the senses are surely the oddest. A little round, freckled face, red-bronze curls hanging down to a sweet little soft waist one loved to crush, two little white feet, two little white hands— that was all on one side. On the other, five feet seven of good and correct feeding, proper education, excellent manners, irreproachable morals and grammar—and seven hundred a year.

What had the one side to offer compared with the other? Sir Gaspar himself, a year later, could enumerate, more accurately than any one else, all these lost advantages, while the wide mouth belonging to the little freckled face showed all its pretty teeth and laughed. For Sir Gaspar would not have changed it for the fortune twice told. There must have been some grain of good in him, if one could have got at it to water it. The little hands might have done much, but that was not to be, for in three years he, sobbing, folded them white, and cold, over the true, sweet heart. "Darlin'," was the last thing she said to him, her sweet Irish voice faint, "you've been a thrue lover to me. Many's the happy day we've had. Be good to the childher, dear. God guard ye all, agra[1]——"

Gaspar and Gasparine were the only children. They had been drafted off to the "place" as soon after their birth as was conven-

---

1 "My love"; an Irish term of endearment.

ient. The little childish mother had had a "sore cry," as she called it, over this, but hid all her tears, in her deep devotion, from the "boy," and smilingly agreed with him that she could not possibly look after the children, and continue her profession of *danseuse*. As it was this profession which maintained her husband, and as the little *danseuse* had never heard of woman's rights, and felt amply repaid by seeing the handsome, selfish face of Sir Gaspar beaming love and admiration on her as she performed, it never occurred to her to put her heart's yearning for her children on the same platform with his pleasures.

On the "place" Gaspar and Gasparine remained, then, till they were eleven years old. They were not happy. The general opinion as to happy childhood is a fallacy. They had poignant instincts after inexplicable and inexpressible things. Two young, dumb, yearning creatures, they wandered about at six years of age, their arms round one another; and if the wonder in each little heart could have been put into words it would have been, "Why are we here? Why were we born?"

Mammy told them their papa was a "jintleman"; and this vague information was supplemented by hearing the strong language which daddy applied to the "jintleman." This was on market and fair days. They soon found, too, that no visible benefit accrued from having a "pa" that was a "jintleman." They were fed, clothed, treated, and chastised very much like the other children belonging to the three cottages, a numerous brood. When they went into the market town sitting on straw in a cart, they experienced a cruel sense of inferiority to the trim little children of the shop-keepers, who were gaily dressed, and wore pretty shoes. The ladies and gentlemen they saw in carriages were as the gods to them. Mammy told them they would be like that one day, and as they grew older their aspirations tended in this direction. They were great dreamers. Gasparine wove the romances, Gaspar listened. They sat together on the grassy knoll leaning back against the grey wall of the tower, and all that they had seen and envied in the town during their last visit was theirs, and they became great and powerful.

"So then, Gaspar, I should have the big doll in the corner window of Whitesides, and the little narrow shoes with the red ribbons, and I should wear little round glasses at my eyes, not with handles (like daddy's), but like the priest has, and we should live in the Town Hall, and I should——"

"And I, Gasparine, what of me?"

"You should have the horse, the spotted grey one with green

rockers; but we'd have livin' horses too, an' on'y keep the rockin' ones for show and——"

And so on and on for hours at a time. They were mostly alone, for very soon they despised the company of the other children. They wandered about together, seeking some ideal land of beauty; and being always disappointed, they came to the conclusion that the world was a very ugly place, and the only bearable spots in it were the Knoll, and the potato field at the foot, "and the road into town—comin' home."

Sometimes their father came to see them. Sir Gaspar had gone back to his old life in Dublin and Belfast. Three years is not a long time, and the heiress was not yet wedded. No one knew much about those three years in Paris, and fewer about the twins in Donegal; and, as I said, no one had mentioned marriage. Sir Gaspar did not consider it his place to do any explaining. He was received, stiffly at first, but with gradually increasing graciousness, until he was pretty much on his old footing, not so sure certainly, still pretty firm. He determined to make the most of it, but Failure seemed to have marked him for her own. The heiress went off under his nose, and two other heiresses after her. This disappointed his sensitive organisation, and he sank a little, lost heart, forgot to retire once when his clothes were not in a condition to bear the closest inspection, and so fell off from one or two of his best props. Then he drifted into a shifty, shoddy way of living, and by the time he grew to like it he had dropped out of select circles altogether.

Gaspar and Gasparine were about ten years old when the baronet married a second time. A sad marriage this, also; forming, as it did, at once the romance and the tragedy of the honest, right-minded little English governess, who, after a life of hardship and snubbing, suddenly found herself wealthy by the death of an uncle, whose occupation must not be alluded to. Lucy Smith was quite dazzled by the admiration of the noble baronet, who represented to her the dangerous, wicked world she had always been taught to dread, and longed to enter. Then came the marriage, a splendid third-rate affair, then one by one the disillusionments. She found out what the "place" meant, to what world the baronet really belonged, and heard with surprise of the two children. At first she indignantly refused to have anything to do with the latter. This put the baronet in a sore dilemma. The "place" would not hold out any longer; moreover, he had been down there lately, and found the boy and girl a strange young couple. He did not know whether to feel ashamed or proud of them. He was proud of their straight, graceful figures, ashamed of their uncouth manners. He never attempted to caress them, and they shrank from him like sensitive plants.[1] Yet they had a sort of affection for him. They speculated as to the unknown land from which he came, and as to his work there. Gasparine thought it would be glorious if he turned out to be the proud possessor of a toy and sweet shop, and if he was kind and took them there, and allowed them to explore that land of mystery "behind the counter," and play with the toys. Gaspar, on the other hand, favoured the idea of a large grocery business, "as big as three shops," which could offer the superior advantages of sweets, biscuits, ham, etc.; but what he was remained a mystery to them.

About a year after her marriage Lady O'Neill, like a wise little woman, decided to make the best of matters. They were at the time living in London in very comfortable circumstances, and being pressed very hard by Sir Gaspar, Lady O'Neill consented to have the children with her.

For the next five years the two young people lived their lives outwardly in the calm, conventional monotony of a commonplace household. Inwardly, what a volcano smouldered in each young breast! For the first year school, and mixing with other young people, were a torture to them. The new life pressed upon them so heavily that they were dazed and confused.

Ridicule,—there is no ridicule so bitter as that of children towards one another, poured upon them; their speech, dress, ignorance. When released from their different schools they flew to one another and clung together, young, wounded, dumb. Each knew the other wounded, yet neither would speak lest it should make the hurt deeper. Even so young they had began that half-divine deception which their great love prompted. When alone together they were happy, gay, and confident enough, but something in the physical and mental health, strength, and coarseness of other lives seemed to jar upon them. However, they learned quickly, and their cleverness pleased their step-mother, who soon became proud and fond of them, without in the least understanding their strange, wayward natures.

When they were about sixteen Lady O'Neill died very suddenly. There was a tragedy under this. The poor creature's spirit

---

1 A shrub of the mimosa family whose leaves "fold together at the slightest touch" (*OED*); cf. Percy Bysshe Shelley's poem "The Sensitive-Plant" (1820).

had been severely tried by the behaviour of Sir Gaspar, who had begged or swindled from her sums of money, and was a constant drain. By a sudden revelation she now found that her husband had been using her name, and had, by fraudulent means, obtained and squandered almost her whole fortune.

After her death they lived on for a time in the old way, but Gasparine was now housekeeper. Sir Gaspar was almost always from home, and his son and daughter asked nothing better. While she had enough money to attend the School of Art, and he had enough for violin lessons, neither had further desires.

Sir Gaspar's visits were times of great discomfort. The man was sinking. He was drunk almost every night. He railed constantly at his son and daughter. They were vulgar boors, unfit for anything—not worth their salt. Gaspar was an idle hound, Gasparine a slovenly slut. He retailed the ancient glories of his house. Sometimes he became maudlin, and wept for his first wife. At other times he was ambitious and triumphant, and declared he would yet live to see the glory of his family restored.

The two listened to this, and, as soon as they were alone, laughed heartily. They called him "our very dear, very distinguished relative, Sir Gaspar." Refined and temperate themselves, they looked, with the high contempt of youth, upon his vicious habits. But both were glad to acknowledge things might have been much worse had he been always at home. They were well content that he should stay away.

This was perhaps their most hopeful time. As yet, they had felt no bitter pinch. They had a few friends, and might have had more, but they did not wish that. Each began to find in the other's intellect a new source of delight. They became nearer and dearer to one another than ever. People watched them and admired them, always together, and thought them proud. Gaspar, always well dressed at this time, graceful and beautiful, was a young prince in the eyes of many a girl; but Gasparine, with her look of flight, which seemed to say, "Stand off, I am going ahead," kept them back. She wanted no one but her brother, and, unconsciously, her whole look and bearing expressed this.

Money, however, was beginning to be a sore point with them. They had to move from their fine house; which caused a sting to the brother and sister. To get money from their father, from this time, was almost an impossibility, and Gasparine felt her dignity and self-respect bitterly insulted by every rub with discontented tradespeople.

As time went on things grew worse. Gasparine had to invent a hundred lies to extort the smallest sum. Gaspar had to take articles from the house and sell them, knowing they would never be missed. It was sometimes their only way of living. Very often they had no servant, but this they did not mind, when alone. Gasparine kept a cosy kitchen, and every misery only served to draw them closer together.

They read and talked. He played, and sang forth all their young longings; she painted, working hard, and they dreamed of a golden future that would bring success to each, and their dreams always ended with a fair vision, of what, in reality, had not been so fair—the old Irish acres, the cottages, the mound, the potato-field. How sunny they became in memory! Ah! when they were rich they would buy it back, and build a pretty cottage (every room was planned and furnished), a great garden (every walk and bed were arranged), and a pretty model stable (the ponies were named), and all would be more beautiful than words could say; and here they would rest from their work, in holiday time, in their own land.

CHAPTER III
LEON SMITH

An incident, which occurred a few days after the Crystal Palace trip, and which extended over the greater part of a year, must be recorded. Living not far from Sir Gaspar's present mansion was a young artist, a person of some importance in the neighbourhood, not only on account of his young fame, but because he was a handsome, agreeable youth, with a beautiful house, and somewhat ambitious studio. Unlike the typical artist, he was possessed of sufficiently ample private means.

Daily going to and from the School of Art, Gasparine passed his house, and looked at it with longing, envious eyes. The long cottage, with its verandah and creepers; the artistic wilderness of a garden—that was what she wanted for herself and Gaspar. What happiness to sit in the glow of the firelit rooms in winter! What happiness to sit on the scented verandah in summer! To have visitors to her studio—handsome young men (a pleasing, but utterly unmeaning term to her) who would ardently admire the gifted artist, handsome ladies who would hasten to cast themselves at Gaspar's indifferent feet! For Leon Smith, though she knew him by sight, she cared nothing. He moved in a sphere far removed from her.

But one day it chanced, when she was walking with Gaspar,

that they met the artist, who looked at the girl fixedly, and with interest. Then something came over Gasparine, and she felt that a look had changed the world. The air was lighter; the day was brighter; Gaspar was more delightful than ever. What did it mean?

Only this: that day Mr. Leon Smith had visited the School of Art, and had there been much struck with a half-finished canvass. He recognised at once, in the crude immature work, an originality and beauty deeper and stronger than anything he had ever produced himself, successful as he was.

"Whose is this?" he asked; and when he heard the name exclaimed, —

"Not a tall, thin girl? Sir Gaspar O'Neill's daughter?"

"Yes, that is the girl. Tremendously clever. Ought to do something yet. A stand-off, independent girl, though."

Mr. Leon Smith sneered in his blonde moustache. He did not admire stand-off, independent girls, or, indeed, believe in them; they were always readiest to put their heads under some fellow's heel! Besides, he liked to be considered stand-off and independent himself.

"I know the girl," he said. "They live near me. Father an awful old rip. Queer lot altogether."

Then he went away, pondering in his mind how he could, under a thin disguise, adopt the girl's idea, and, with his superior technical skill, make something of it. That was why he looked so closely at Gasparine when he met her. She, all the way home, was silent and dreamy, pondering on this strange new feeling. Strange that she had never before noticed what a handsome young man he was! Her imagination began to dress his commonplace good looks with a score of subtle charms they never possessed.

A week passed, during which Gasparine sought ardently for information concerning Mr. Leon Smith, and during which she made a point of walking, with Gaspar, past the studio two or three times; and if she happened to meet the clever artist who was stealing her ideas, she felt, instead of her former indifference, a strange sorrow, like memories of her childhood. For the transient moment of happiness had vanished. As she read many novels and much poetry, and as she had no women friends to talk to, she was under the delusion that something very extraordinary had befallen her. She tried to reason it away, and as that was not to be done, action was her next resolve. Something she must *do*; to remain passive was impossible.

Sir Gaspar was away at this time. He had had some luck, and

had sent them money. Usually these were their happy seasons. They enjoyed the liberty and peace, but for Gasparine there could be no peace now. She lost interest in her work, pondered and dreamed, and was even a little irritable in her manner with Gaspar. She was treading the old, well-known path, trodden by thousands, thousands of women since time was—treading it, too, with the bewildered feet of a savage, who has had none of the benefits of civilisation. Passion bade her speak, instinct bade her be silent. A new, strange problem stared her in the face. "What is the difference between us?" was the first question; and the second came after much thought: "Why should it be right for a man, and not for a woman?" The weeks passed—so many long, long weeks, but though Gasparine only saw him now and then, sometimes not once in three weeks; it was enough for one whose imagination always played the larger part in her existence.

She regarded him humbly, far-off, as some saint his God, with an eye that trembled lest it should discover any defect, and an imagination quick to cast a glamour over any when discovered.

In the meantime, Mr. Leon Smith had worked at his picture, and it was now almost finished. It stood in his studio, the admiration of his numerous friends, and the envy of not a few of his brother artists. He had conventionalised the original idea, given it a new background and the benefit of his superior finish. It was the very thing for the popular taste. "It's the nicest thing you've done, Smith," his friends said. And so it was—and the nastiest.

Gasparine had named her picture "Love Calls," and it represented the invitation of first love to youthful learning. A young girl stood in a forest glade, holding forth two entreating hands, and smiling pleadingly. In the foreground was a young man, and upon him all the light fell. Irresolution was depicted in his attitude, and in the expression of his face, which was mournfully thoughtful.

Under Mr. Leon Smith's practised and dishonest brush the girlish idea had become a masterly execution. The white-robed girl bending forward, her bare feet showing through the tall sedge grass, was a dream of beauty. The dreamy lake, reflecting light, the strange birds, the glory of sunset clouds—all were very lovely. The young man, too, instead of merely standing irresolutely, as in Gasparine's picture, knelt on one knee, bent, a hand binding his brows—a youthful, melancholy, modern figure.

So far, well. But, in the interest of his work, Mr. Leon Smith had entirely forgotten any one so utterly insignificant as the owner of the idea. He was, therefore, very much surprised when, chancing one day to visit the School, he saw a companion picture on the easel. It showed a great advance in technique from the first, and was the obvious complement of the earlier production. The pleading girl had spread two lovely wings, and, now laughing, was flying upward. The young man was, in his turn, the suppliant, gazing towards her with outstretched arms, upraised eyes, and parted, pleading lips. The life and passion of the picture were wonderful; but the Love's wings were rather wooden, while the trees, and one of the young man's legs, were stiff. "But what an idea! By Jove, what an idea!" Mr. Leon Smith said to himself. "Two companion pictures at the Academy![1] They would take flying—'Love Calls'—'Love Flies.'" He went home, and spent the evening by himself very thoughtfully.

The next day he received something like an electric shock when a lady was announced, and Gasparine O'Neill walked into his studio. Conscious of having performed a shabby trick, his face flushed deeply as he turned towards her. He was not so gay and self-possessed as usual. She mistook this for modesty, admired him the more, and, gathering courage from his apparent timidity, she said,—

"I came about my pictures."

"Dash it!" said Mr. Leon Smith to himself. Then he gathered all the spleen which served him in the place of manliness, and which he had often found of service in brow-beating young women, drew himself up, and said sharply, "Your pictures? I don't understand?"

Gasparine felt a great chill at her heart. The hard, unsympathetic tone was unmistakable. A rebuff, however, had always the outward effect of sharpening her weapons. She laughed. "Of course not," she said, with the lingering remains of Irish brogue enriching the London accent, "I didn't say you did. May I sit down?"

"Cheek, by Jove! Jolly cheek!" soliloquised the artist. With a derisive wave he motioned her to a high, hard chair, and threw himself into an easy lounge. The under-bred action struck the girl like a blow. So, because she *trusted* her dignity to him, he would strike her down to the level of something cheap and unasked. The courage of impulse forsook her; the courage of resolution gathered slowly.

---

1 A prestigious annual exhibition run by the Royal Academy of Arts. The Academy's Council judged which submitted works of art were worthy of being shown.

"I came," she said, her voice alternately too shrill or too muffled, "because ... I want to make way with my painting ..."

There was a pause. He did not help her by a single word. In truth, he was puzzled, and pondering within himself.

"I attend the School of Art," she said disconnectedly. Then suddenly control and memory forsook her, she flushed painfully, and breathed with difficulty. After a miserable pause she went on rapidly, eager to redeem and extenuate conduct which, it seemed to her, he regarded as very vile. "And Mr. Powell told me—that is, I asked him, I mean—knowing you to be a great painter, I asked him if it would be a very exceptional thing if I called and asked you to give me your opinion as to my work."

The small nature began to feel more at ease. But for some doubt that irony might be lurking behind the piercing, brilliant eyes, he would have made some remark. As it was, he thought he would wait to hear a little further.

"I have not had any very regular training," she said, "and of course I am anxious to know that it will repay me before I give my life up to it."

"Ah! just so. I see. What does Mr. Powell think?"

"Oh! he is very encouraging. But you see he told me himself not to put too much weight on his opinion because he is only a teacher, not an artist."

"Yes, yes, just so." ("What the devil *does* she want?" he said to himself.)

An awkward pause.

"I suppose you are very busy?" she said then, timidly.

"Oh yes," with a confident and insolent laugh. The laugh stung Gasparine. It seemed to her to say, "Yes, he was busy; and a busy man had little time to spare for idle talk and young misses' drawings." Her last spark of courage was gone. She rose wearily.

"May I look at your pictures?" she said.

"Certainly." But it was not a gracious permission. "There is something under all this," said Mr. Leon Smith to himself.

There was. There was a terrible heart-break.

However, he rose and walked with her from picture to picture. He wished, if possible, to keep her from one. As she looked critically and admiringly at each, and glanced from them to him, now and again, with a half smile, he softened, began to doubt himself, and spoke to her rather graciously and politely.

In a moment her Irish nature asserted itself. Before they had gone half round the studio they were deep in a lively discussion as to art in general; he amused at the evident earnestness with which she received his chaff; she half pleased, half irritated, and excited, defending herself with sharp sallies. Suddenly she paused, and exclaimed, in her eloquent voice, "Oh! how beautiful. How sad!"

Mr. Leon Smith came to himself with another deep flush. The girl was standing before her own stolen idea, her face now very grave and sorrowful. In a moment she turned to him.

"It is very beautiful," she said earnestly, "but it is very sad for me."

He had only voice to stammer, "Why?"

"It is a death-blow to my belief in my own originality," she said, quite simply. "I hope you will not think me conceited, though I grant that I may sound so to you, but I have been trying and trying for six months past to execute a thought like that, and here I see it worked out far more beautifully than I could ever do. It is sad for me."

The man felt as if he had received a blow. He could only bow, and, like a coward, still dread discovery.

Gasparine stood long and earnestly before the picture. At last she turned to him suddenly.

"Have you a companion picture?" she asked.

It was a dangerous moment. He braced himself to bear it.

"Oh yes," he replied. "It has been finished for nearly a year. Strange to say, I painted the second picture first. It was only afterwards this idea of the two occurred to me."

"May I see it?"

"I should let you see it with pleasure, but, unfortunately, I have not got it here."

"Will you tell me what it is like?"

Again a doubt crept into his heart.

"Oh!" he said, with something of roughness; "isn't it rather hard lines to make a fellow describe his own pictures, especially when they're sentimental?"

Gasparine blushed, with a feeling that her ignorance had caused her to commit some atrocious breach of etiquette, perhaps even of morals. She then giggled hysterically.

"I must go," she said; and, with a great effort, looking him courageously in the eyes added, "If you have time I should be glad to hear your opinion of my work. This is our address."

"It will give me great pleasure to call," he said, with a sudden impulse. "Mr. Powell is an old friend of mine, and I am always delighted to hear of his pupils' success."

Outside in the street an organ was playing a waltz tune. Rare and unbidden tears rushed to the girl's eyes and poured over her face.

"Life is a cruel thing," she whispered.

After a few days, however, she began to argue herself back into her old favourable opinion of her ideal, and tried to persuade herself, remembering his one or two friendly words, that, after all, for a busy and popular artist, he had been very kind indeed. She even boasted of her knowledge of the famous man to a solitary acquaintance at the School of Art. She began to hope and hope that he would come to see her. But as one long week after another passed, hope deferred made her heart very sick and sore; and again the whisper trembled on her quivering lips, "Life is very cruel—crueller even than I knew."

Then one day it happened that she saw him. He was standing on the pavement talking to another man. That he saw her there could be no doubt; he was facing her when she saw him. Then, quite easily and coolly, he turned his back towards her, that she might pass. He meant to have no connection with her; it might turn out uncomfortable for him by-and-by.

When she passed, she felt suddenly as though her feet had become great unmanagable clumsy things; her hands weighed at her sides, her face felt strange and uncomfortable. She felt that she walked crouched and unsteadily. She could not pull herself together. "It is right," she said, bitterly reproaching herself. "You are like the horse in Browning's 'Childe Roland;' 'you must be wicked to deserve such pain.'"[1] It lessened the ache when she jeered at herself.

Yet too much stress must not be laid upon this incident. It was much more Gasparine's imagination than her heart which was engaged in this affair, and soon the delusion was completely shattered.

It chanced one day, when she was up at the School, Mr. Powell came to her and said,—

"Did you get your idea of your two little companion pictures from Mr. Leon Smith, Miss O'Neill?"

"No," replied Gasparine, looking at him attentively; "I never saw his until both of mine were finished, and then I only saw *one* of his."

---

1 In Robert Browning's poem "Childe Roland to the Dark Tower Came," the protagonist, traversing a barren landscape, encounters a blind and haggard horse about which he makes this observation.

"Oh! So! A tremendous success they have been." Then he added with all the world's calm indifference to what does not hurt its precious self, "I rather think he must have taken his ideas from you, then; I know he was here twice, and both times looked at your pictures and admired them."

A sudden revelation rushed over Gasparine, literally overwhelming her in its startling suggestiveness. She went home slowly and thoughtfully.

"Gaspar," she said, "do you know what Mr. Powell says?"

"No, dear."

"He says he thinks that fellow Smith got his idea for his two pictures they are making such a fuss about from my paintings, which he saw at the School."

"Is that possible?"

"I am considering, and I think it is. My opinion is that he must be a cad and a sneak."

"I should say so."

They talked it over.

Next day, walking with her brother, she met the famous artist. She was erect and proud, and, as she passed, she looked him scornfully in the face. It gave him a most disagreeable feeling.

"Just as well I kept out of her way," he said to himself.

But the matter was not ended for her, only begun. A man had insulted and wronged her, and she dreaded like treatment from all men. It made her cowardly. Now, too, she looked questioningly towards all men. She asked herself what good had it done her all those months, fretting, wearing, listless, paralysed? No good; but harm. A year of her young life wasted on a dream. It was not that she had given way to it—she had struggled against it; but even with struggling it had taken a year. And now, after all, she was just where she started. And she asked herself, "Oh! how was it that it took a year to kill what a careless look, in a thoughtless second, bore?"

CHAPTER IV
THE GIRL IN THE PAINTED VILLA

The incident was over, and the year was gone, but the red line of shame would never wear out on the young heart. She never thought of it without her cheeks tingling, her ears singing, and her heart sinking with a sense of degradation.

"If one were rich and protected," she said to herself bitterly, "such a fellow would not dare; but the poor are fair game, it seems." And in a moment of passionate feeling she envied the wealthy Philistines,[1] to whose class he belonged.

Well, now they were quite friendless, quite without companionship of any kind, for soon Gasparine had to stop going to the School of Art—that expense had become too heavy; they were thrown entirely upon one another.

Such amusement as was to be had they got from watching and observing, and by-and-by Gasparine found something and some one to watch.

Their present house stood at the corner of a narrow road which branched off into a wide avenue with villas and gardens in St. John's Wood district. Their small back garden (wilderness, rather) ran, therefore, its little length into the handsome, if limited, grounds of a large, painted villa. When she had nothing better to do, Gasparine sat at the first-floor window, a tiny room they had fitted up as a refuge for themselves, and, while Gaspar lay reading on the sofa, Gasparine watched the gardens, the budding leaves—for it was spring—the fairy palaces of mystery, and pleased herself with imagining how it would be if she and Gaspar were there, rich, strong, and free. The villa itself stood on raised terraces, and was covered with creepers and surrounded by shrubs. Only one side balcony, with a flight of steps from an upper window, was fully open to Gasparine's view.

Studying this, day after day, one rainy week, Gasparine grew to know it off by heart. The bits seen, unseen, imagined; the shrubs, little green banks, parterres, trees; it grew more and more into her heart, and she thought it daily more and more beautiful. She wondered now how she had ever been content to live in the front of the house, and know only the street! Why, with this view before her, she could dream herself in the country, and think of hopeful and pleasant things!

One day two ladies walked round the garden. They were not young nor beautiful. Gasparine was disappointed. But that did not last long. Soon she found the house was only now open after being long closed. Carriage wheels, horses tramping on the gravel, some creepers cut away, and behold! a French window, which every night blazed light, and often, both then and by day, framed some

---

1 A Philistine is "an uneducated or unenlightened person; one perceived to be indifferent or hostile to art or culture, or whose interests and tastes are commonplace or material" (*OED*). Matthew Arnold's *Culture and Anarchy* (1869) extensively examines the phenomenon of Philistinism, which Arnold associates with the middle class.

graceful girlish or womanly form. Now the interest for Gasparine was redoubled. It was seldom indeed that any one came round the garden; its attractions were evidently not great enough for those gay people. One day, however, that too was changed. Gasparine had been working at her open window, and heard distinctly the tramp of a horse's feet. The avenue was hidden from her, but presently she saw, ridden along the narrow terrace, a bay cob,[1] on which sat a little girl, with a brilliant light fuzz of hair. By the side of the cob walked a man, apparently twenty-eight or thirty years of age. It was a beautiful picture to Gasparine—so opulent, so protected those two seemed, pets of society, children of the law. They were good friends too. The girl laughed, shook her fair hair, and stroked the pony's neck. The young man playfully slapped the girl's arm, and pretended to put her over the horse by foot and shoulder. "Ah! brother and sister," thought Gasparine. "How good he is to her!" She watched for them now every day. Soon she found out the young man could not be a brother. He came to the house very often, but close watching showed her he did not remain there. In the house lived three handsome young women and the little girl. The man was paying court to one of the elder ladies. Gasparine wondered which, and by-and-by decided it was the tallest, handsomest, and darkest, for often they stood together at the French window, often they sauntered over a bit of lawn, and once Gasparine was sure she saw the man's arm round the lady's waist—a fashionable, diminutive waist, of course.

Then there came a whole week when Gasparine saw no one. She was ill that week, and there was not much opportunity. One evening, towards its close, she saw, from her window, the little girl walking in the garden alone. She wore a red cloak and hood, and something very striking and peculiar in her attitude caused Gasparine to examine her as closely as possible. As she stood on a terrace at the point nearest to Gasparine's view, she stopped in her saunter, and, with her head turned eagerly, gazed over her shoulder towards the road. The hood had fallen off, and Gasparine saw she was a girl of perhaps thirteen or fourteen, overgrown, for in her low dress Gasparine could see the figure prematurely formed. For beauty she had a striking colouring of eyes and face, fair hair, and a peculiar grace of movement and attitude, unconventional and exceedingly alluring. At her distance

---

1   "A short-legged, stout variety of horse" (*OED*). The short, sturdy cob would be a very appropriate horse for a child.

Gasparine could not see *how* brilliant the colouring was, nor the exquisite little pink ears, indeed, like shells, from which the fair hair was artfully drawn; nor could she see the intense and painful eagerness in the large, expressive eyes—strangely passionate for a child—turned towards the road.

The attitude, however, was so expressive as to impress Gasparine deeply, and the little red-cloaked figure, with head turned, as if listening, haunted her that night.

The next day she saw why; and her fair visions of the opulent pet of society received a cruel blow. She turned from the little back window, hating it with a morbid hatred for what it had shown her, and never observed again.

It was dull next evening, and there was a sort of mist; no lights in the French windows, and Gasparine started when she saw the young man, the lover of the tall, dark lady, walking slowly round a lower path in shelter of a bank of shrubs, entirely screened from the house. He was waiting, or hiding, for twice Gasparine saw him strike a match for a twice-produced cigar, but each time impatiently put them away. Then Gasparine saw the girl, first for a second on the balcony, glancing round, then quickly descending. It was chilly, but neck and arms were quite bare, though she had her red cloak on her arm. She moved swiftly till in shelter of the friendly shrubs, then, with a swallow-like movement of unspeakable grace, she ran to the man's breast.

With a shock, Gasparine recognised whose lover indeed he was, and fell to pondering on the reasons for such secrecy. She turned her head for a moment from the window with a half-pang of jealousy (remembering her own smart) that the joy of love should come so early to that child while she remained alone. Then, drawing a quick breath, she looked from the window again. Something had happened meantime—what, she would never know; but as she gazed, she saw the girl drop on her knees, and seem to grovel, her head lowered, and beating the man off with one hand. He stood looking down upon her; probably he spoke, then touched her with his foot. She sprang to her feet like lightning, with the air of an animal intolerably goaded, but, before she could take a step, he seized her naked arm above the elbow. For a few seconds she struggled violently like one netted, but gradually quieting, until, with a twist of her arm, he forced her to her knees, and there, bending over her, he struck the fair, child-like head, once, twice, and thrice, with brutal and unmanly blows. As he struck the girl seemed to shrink, till she lay on the black path a mere shapeless bundle.

Then the man walked away.

The whole rapid scene had filled Gasparine's soul with revolt and disgust. She breathed hard, and her heart beat fast. She thought she would recognise the girl any time she saw her again, but the man's face she had not been able to see. He was fashionably dressed, and had a red neck, thick, like a bull's; that was all she knew.

She watched the little black bundle a long, long time; it never moved. The patch of red grew black in the dusk, and the white spots that showed the bare shoulder and one little naked arm grew dim. The French windows were suddenly lighted, and Gasparine saw the dark girl and the cowardly scoundrel pass and repass in the light and warmth. But the little bundle never moved. How Gasparine's heart yearned to go out and take the wounded creature to her breast and warm it, or, at least, wrap the white neck and arms from the cold! But she lacked courage.

No. She saw now; not even in such places was there safety or security. All the safety we can hope for, she found, is the safety which our own courage gives us—safety that does not consist in a certain set of circumstances, but in the courage with which we bear and dare. For somehow it was borne into her heart that night, with a certainty not to be gainsaid, that—how she knew not, nor why, but somehow or other—there was foul play, and that she had just seen a child's heart outraged and broken.

CHAPTER V
HOW MURDERS HAPPEN

During the next few years Sir Gaspar's chief occupation seemed to be to hide himself. They changed their abode no less than five times—needless to say, always to a less pretentious dwelling.

For Gasparine it meant nothing; for now there came another matter to occupy heart and brain, with vague foredooming and fear. That little cough of Gaspar's seemed as if it would never go. It was only a little cough, of course, dry and hard, and otherwise Gasparine told herself he was perfectly well. But one night they sat late, laughing and talking, and when they rose at last to part, the fire burst into a bright flame (they had been sitting in its dull red glow), and she saw his face. Was it the red flame made him look so? She lay awake and listened, and heard that cough go on constantly, hour after hour, one painful, exhausting burst after another. Every high-strung nerve in the girl's body tingled. She tossed from side to side, feverish and anguished. It is the only word that describes her state as she lay in the darkness there. "And he never told me," she kept muttering over and over to herself. "Why did he never tell me? How long has this been going on? He does not cough much during the day. Oh! he certainly does not. Brute, that I have been, to sleep on like this!"

She rose and went into the next little room.

"Gaspar," she said, "are you asleep?"

There was no answer. The girl's heart seemed bleeding. "Darling," she whispered to herself, "are you trying to deceive me, that you are peacefully asleep? Oh, my darling!" But aloud she said, bending over him, and speaking complainingly, "Gaspar-boy, waken. I cannot sleep to-night—I am restless."

How quickly he was awake at that!

"Not sleep, Gaspar! What's the matter? Not ill, girlie?"

"Restless and feverish. I'll light your gas, if you don't mind, and wrap myself up, and sit on your bed."

"All right. I'm sorry, pet, you don't feel well."

Gasparine went away for a few minutes to roll herself up in every available article, and return with her arms full of books. She made a nest at the foot of the bed, and settled there, whispering to herself again,—"Now you sha'n't be lonely, dear. I am here, and it always comforts us to be near one another." Then she began her reading, much comforted, and almost happy. Presently the coughing began again.

"Gaspar-boy, you are coughing. I am off to make a mustard-plaster."[1]

"It's a mere nothing. Don't bother."

"Yes, I shall. And I tell you what: I feel seedy, so I shall make a cup of tea, too."

"You'll catch cold, Gaspar-girl, and have no end of bother lighting the fire."

But Gasparine was gone. The house was small, and in the little kitchen she kept up a lively clatter and noise while at work. Instinct told her how grateful such sounds are to the lonely night-watcher. The mustard was soon ready and applied, and the boy felt a sensation of relief delightful to his aching eyes and chest. All this was enhanced when Gasparine appeared, a little later, very gay and talkative, with tea and two hastily re-heated muffins.

---

1   Mustard powder, flour, and a liquid worked into a paste, spread on a cloth, and applied to the skin. This was a common home remedy for a variety of ailments. It worked as a counter-irritant, dilating the blood vessels.

"Quite a feast!" she said. "Isn't it fun? I feel as jolly as a sand-boy[1] now, and I felt as dead as ten ghosts before."

Her cheer was contagious. Gaspar drank the tea, and Gasparine ate the muffins, and a little later the boy fell asleep, looking like an angel, distressed by the thought of earth's sin, through the dreams of Paradise.

He was really sleeping and breathing quietly. And now how quickly the gas was lowered! How noiselessly the books were lifted away!

"Sleep, sweetest heart," she whispered, hungrily. "Rest, darling." And she went back to her own little bed. He could not deceive her, but she could often deceive him.

The blessed daylight, and Gaspar's lovely, loving face, and young, indifferent voice restored the sister's spirits, and dispelled her terrible fears. It was only a little cold, after all, and would wear away in no time.

A little time after this one of Gasparine's few acquaintances spoke to her with frank brutality.

"Is your brother in a consumption,[2] Miss O'Neill? What a terrible cough he has! And how thin he has grown!"

"What do you mean? Gaspar is as strong as possible; he has only a trifling cold. Oh, what *do* you mean?" and she laughed.

But every night after that she heard a voice saying, "Is your brother in consumption?" And when the cough sounded she heard, "What a terrible cough he has!" And when she looked at the hollows in his soft rose cheeks she heard, "How thin he has grown!" Night after night, day after day, he haunted her.

Nor was that her only trouble. Sir Gaspar O'Neill had been growing worse and worse, sinking lower in moral degradation, and with this came a run of ill luck. This always had the worst possible effect upon him. His manner towards his son and daughter became often brutal and threatening. They shrugged their shoulders and were silent, and when he was gone decided that he was certainly an ass. They were in straits themselves, however. They had sold all the available articles which ran no risk of being missed. They had almost no credit. Sir Gaspar gave them nothing; and once or twice, when he staggered drunk into the

---

1   A proverbial expression. Boys who sold sand door to door (to be used for cleaning and covering floors) were apparently notorious for their drinking.

2   "Does your brother have tuberculosis?"

room where Gaspar lay faint and exhausted, Gasparine looked at him with wild, murderous eyes.

"Brute! brute!" she said to herself. "I want the money you have been drinking to buy wine for my boy, and food he would like, not a little cold rice and dry bread, that does not please any one; and he has a little cold just now, my darling, and does not feel inclined to eat." (Alas! he had not been *inclined* to eat for a long time.) "Oh, you brute! You human monster!"

Fortunately Sir Gaspar did not hear these complimentary remarks addressed to himself. Sooner or later, however, he must certainly see the looks of deep hatred with which the girl now never failed to regard him. That was a dangerous day for her when he did.

It was dull autumn weather, close and damp. Gaspar had been ill for some days. It was nothing, of course—a little cold, that was all; it would pass off in a day or two, so he told Gasparine. Just now she was out, and he lay upon the sofa, depressed and sullen, and oppressed with a painful difficulty in breathing. He was watching for her return. She had gone to sell something, and he was anxious about her, for Sir Gaspar was at home, and the boy dreaded some unlucky *rencontre*[1] that would undo them.

The day closed in, dull and murky and dark, before its time. The boy turned restlessly. Presently he heard an unsteady, heavy, lurching step. He closed his eyes, pretending to be asleep. Sir Gaspar entered; he was plainly very drunk. He walked round the room with that pugnacious and aggressive air which characterises a certain stage of the development of this vice. The fire was dull. He kicked it, with an oath. The chairs were awry. He threw them out of his way, with much clatter. Then he looked about for more worlds to conquer. Perhaps the table was impertinent to stand erect upon its legs, but, obviously, kicking would not mend matters. Doubtless the clock had no business to tick, but if it *would* be such an idiot, why, let it. He glared round. Was there nothing he could wreak his vengeance upon? nothing he could hurt? nothing he could wound cruelly, and which would feel it?

The boy lay upon the sofa asleep. He was very pale, and the closed eyelids had that strange expressiveness, as though the soul strove to look through them, and when it did the body would

---

1 French for "rencounter": "A hostile meeting or encounter between two adversaries; a duel; sometimes specifically (after French usage) distinguished from a regular duel by being unpremeditated" (*OED*).

awake. As the baronet gazed upon him a wild irritation against anything so peaceful rose in him, and then the instinct of the devil-beast, to give pain.

"Where's Gasparine?" demanded the noble baronet. There was no answer. He pushed the boy roughly, and demanded again, "Where's Gasparine?"

Gaspar shuddered visibly. To weakness a heavy footstep is pain, and rough contact torture. He turned round and opened his eyes.

"Hulloa, papa! Have you been in long?"

"No," growled the inebriate gentleman, mollified, as he always was, by Gaspar's unfailing but deceptive sweetness. "Where's Gasparine?"

"Why, she's (I wonder you did not meet her, and thank Heaven you did not)—she's—er—at the School of Art."

Gasparine had long left the School of Art for good, but the fiction was still maintained, because, on that plea of fees, strangely enough, they could sometimes get a little money, when they could get it for no other. Nor could they ever manage this without representing that the fees were fees of long standing, which absolutely *must* be paid; for to give ready money for anything was a folly of which the gentlemanly baronet had never yet been guilty. Therefore, the fiction was maintained.

"Whatever does she do at the School of Art? D—d waste of time and money, that's what I call it!"

"It's the only pleasure she has," said Gaspar sullenly.

"The only pleasure she has!" roared the baronet. "And why the devil should she have any pleasure, more than others? What pleasure have *I*, I'd like to know? Keeping and feeding two idle hulks, who do nothing but eat, lounge on a sofa, and go in for pleasure! A nice pass things have come to when I can't speak in my own house, but I'm brought up in this way." He lurched heavily round the little room, working himself into a rage. "I'd like to know what you mean by your impertinence, young sir. Tall as you are, I'd like to teach you that I don't take it from the like of you. D—n me if I'll stand it! What do you mean, you idle cur, lying here all day doing nothing? Ill, are you? Lazy! That's what I call it. A thrashing would take some of the stiffness out of you, and you'll get it one of these days, the sooner the better. What! you'll lie there pretending to sleep, will you? Out of my sight, you young hound, or I'll take the skin——"

He was stopped by Gasparine shrieking "Coward! Bully!" like a maniac, as she dashed into the room. She had entered the house in time to hear the storm, and caught the last words at the room door.

Now she stood between her brother and her father, glaring upon the latter with wild eyes, quivering as only a woman quivers when she sees, not herself, but what she loves best, wounded. She stamped her foot. "Oh, you cursed coward!" she said, glaring in his face.

While his father had been railing Gaspar had lain perfectly still, attempting no sort of speech at all. His frail body had indeed felt some apprehension of cruel degradation where its unoffending weakness should have been sacred, but his proud young soul scorned answer or movement until he saw his sister stand between him and his drunken father. Then, in a moment, unsteady and giddy, he sprang to his feet, for Sir Gaspar, mad with drink, had thrown himself upon the girl, and already his cruel, bloated fingers were on her throat.

"I'll murder you!" he said thickly. And she, with her feeble hands striving to keep him off, cried,—

"Murder me if you like. Do you think I care? It's all that you're fit for, coward that you are, to murder a girl like me!"

"Papa, what are you thinking of? Have you lost your senses, Gaspar-girl?" and the boy struggled, with his arm round the girl's waist, to separate them.

"Gaspar, give way," said the man thickly. "I don't want to touch you—you're a good boy; but this she-devil, I've seen it in her eyes for months, and I mean to murder her."

The boy had managed to free the girl, and was, in his turn, in his father's arms. They held him, but not cruelly.

"Gaspar-girl, go into the kitchen," the brother said.

"I will not!" she panted. "I will not till you come! He may kill me if he likes, the brute! Do you think *I* care?"

The drunkard yelled, and struggled to get at the girl again. With a wrench Gaspar freed himself, and threw the man backward—and one of the chairs which had recently offended and been kicked, broke, in some measure, the baronet's fall.

Gaspar caught his sister round the waist, hurried with her into the kitchen, and locked the door. His heart was full of wild wrath. His sister, his little, precious sister, all he had, his braver, truer, better self, handled like a fish-girl! A curse upon his weakness! If he had been strong, like another, to have snatched her up in his arms, and borne her away from any trouble! It was in his mind to walk away with her out of the house that night. But what then? Where then, with neither money, health, nor friends? What could he do? It was as much as his life was worth to be out in the open air on a day like this, and his life, poor as it was, was her only protection.

He had no idea, however, that she should know all this, and his first words, as he sank into a chair, were words of reproof.

"Gasparine, how could you be such a fool? Don't you know it's never any good trying to convince a drunken man—especially if you go about it in the summary way you did? Oh, Gaspar, what a little ass you made of yourself, and for the sake of a drunken fool! What fancy can you have for becoming a scrap of newspaper intelligence?"

They both laughed, and Gasparine looked rather ashamed.

"He was *such* an ass!" she said, by way of apology; then suddenly and oddly her poor, white face and wild eyes wrinkled up with mischief and amusement,—

"Never mind, sonny, the brute didn't catch me, and I got three shillings more than I expected. But oh! I—I say!" A pause, during which a most lugubrious expression overspread her face. "Oh, sonny, I pitched the things down when I heard him showing off, and they're lying in the passage now. I'll make a sortie for them."

"You shall do nothing of the kind, If you want them I shall go for them; otherwise, we remain here until he goes out."

"But, Gaspar, I had the tea and everything with me, and the kettle is boiling—but *you* sha'n't go. I tell you, let's both go. It won't take a second, and if I hear him I promise to fly."

They opened the door very gently, leaving it wide, and, making a dart round the corner, took possession of the little store of good things. They need not have been alarmed. Sir Gaspar lay where he had fallen—snoring.

As was their way, they made merry over this horror, showering their wit and scorn upon it and its hideousness.

"A united family is a charming thing, and the love of a parent clasps you very close," said Gasparine, as she drew the deal table up to the hearth and arranged the tea-things. "Oh, Gaspar-boy, you wouldn't scold if you knew what an ass I felt. Melodrama really isn't in my line at all."

They laughed.

"I should think they'll have it in the fashionable papers, Gaspar—in the *Morning Post*. How nice it will sound! 'Interesting *fracas* in a nobleman's family. Young and lovely female almost strangled by the ardour of an excitable but well-meaning pa. Gallant rescue by affectionate brother. Consternation among the domestics. Great sensation.' ... Now look at my purchases, boy.

See! tea, jelly, and a cake—I must presently tell you all my adventures, but tea first."

All the evening they laughed and talked, were every now and then tremendously tickled by the memory of some ludicrous incident in Sir Gaspar's uncalled-for behaviour. They were very gay; their eyes and their cheeks blazed gloriously. But if a stranger had been able to look into the room, he must have noticed that the table so carefully spread, with such a gala appearance, was just as it had been laid; nothing had been touched. They had forgotten all about it.

And when she was alone how she wrung her hands and clenched her teeth! All her maiden pride, modesty, dignity, had been degraded and outraged, and the shame was a thousand times worse than the danger. She paced her little room wildly. There was no need of concealment now, no need to laugh. The hysterical excitement was over, and instead she shuddered with a nervous loathing, that was not fear, as she felt the cruel fingers on her breast and throat. Yet even this was not the worst part of her suffering; her helpless rage and fear for her brother's sake were unspeakable.

"You devil!" she said, and stamped her feet. "It was *you* made him struggle for breath all the evening, with that red spot in his cheek, and his poor lips going white and blue every minute; it was *you*, you devil, that you are! Some day I will murder you—oh it will be a happy day! ... I said that life was cruel, cruel! It is hell." She held her brows and stood with staring eyes. "It has happened once," she said, "but it must *never* happen again." She fell to planning how it was to be prevented. It was the first thing that calmed her. She curled herself upon her bed, and sat wakeful and thinking.

About two o'clock she heard a sound in her brother's room. She sprang to her door, opened it, and listened. Then a look of contempt overspread her face. "At the old penitence dodge again," she muttered scornfully. "It's too good a joke to try it on to-night. Miserable brute! Couldn't he let the poor boy sleep quietly?" She shut her door, and went back to her planning. The time was past (for it had been) when she believed in these "penitence fits," as she called them. "What a melancholy satire upon the good storybooks they are!" was her only reflection now.

In Gaspar's room Sir Gaspar stood, leaning on the foot of the old poster bed, a rusty and aged pistol in his hand, his accent strong, as always happened at these times—a miserable object. The devil-beast was out of him, but the maudlin-fiend which had taken possession of him was, on the whole, more contemptible perhaps.

"Gaspar, me boy, do ye forgive me, before I go and blow me wretched brains out? Maybe I'll get some pace thin."

"Doubtful," thought Gaspar; but he lay still and did not speak. He knew he should have to rouse sooner or later; and better later than sooner, he thought.

"Och! och! the miserable time I've had! Never one to speak a kind word to me since me dear mother, who died when I was a mere infant, Gaspar, and put some verses in the front of a Bible she gave me. It was a beautiful morocco-bound Bible, Gaspar, but it was too big for carr'ing about, so, as I had no other use for it, and it was inconvanient, I sould it, Gaspar."

Being an Irish boy, Gaspar could not resist the faintest of faint giggles here, in spite of all his pain.

"Did you get a good price?" he inquired, in muffled tones.

Sir Gaspar drew himself up.

"Price, is it?" he cried. "They chated me, Gaspar, like the thafes the' wur—chated me right and lift. A beautiful morocco-bound family Bible, with Lady O'Neill's own handwriting in the front, as I showed the rascals. And they had the impurtinence to tell me *that* made no difference, and the book would be more *valyable* without it. Och! och! me dear, me noble mother! I have only one rekilection of her, Gaspar, pulling me ear for breaking the cord of the parlour blind. Well, well, well, 'I know I'm farther off from Heaven than whin I wus a boy.'"[1]

Gaspar stifled another convulsive outbreak, and thought Sir Gaspar was probably correct in his quotation. He did not believe in the efficacy of this penitence any more than his sister did, but he knew it had to be gone through, and being masculine he had more patience with his father's failings than she. Yet it was hard for him to realise that, but for a fortunate accident, the whining imbecile before him might have been a murderer. There was a dreary silence in the room, and the boy felt called upon to say something. Sir Gaspar groaned heavily at intervals.

"Put the pistol away, and go to bed, papa. You'll feel better in the morning," the boy said at last. Not that he was the least anxious about the pistol. Sir Gaspar would never commit suicide, that he knew. Besides, the pistol was quite an old friend; it had

---

1 The concluding lines of Thomas Hood's poem "I Remember, I Remember" (1826).

been produced many times during the life of their step-mother, at first greatly to that poor creature's alarm, until very soon they all grew to regard it with philosophic calm—for there were no bullets.

Sir Gaspar looked the pistol up and down attentively. It was really a most harmless-looking article.

"Gaspar," he said, "I'm weary of life."

"I daresay," said the boy drily, "but that old thing won't mend matters much." He felt that this scorn was somewhat dangerous, but he was growing tired.

"Would you mind if I lay here to-night, Gaspar?" the baronet inquired, after another pause for groaning.

"Not at all," said Gaspar. "Would you like the bed?"

"Oh, no, no, no, the floor will do; the floor is quite good enough for me. Anything is good enough for me."

Gaspar groaned inwardly, but saw there was nothing else for it. He got out of bed, fetched a rug and some shawls, with an old great-coat or two, did the best he could, and offered one of his pillows.

Soon Sir Gaspar was stretched among these, sleeping the sleep of the unjust and the wicked; which would sometimes seem to be the soundest.

For Gaspar did not sleep.

Next day the brother and sister spoke to one another.

"Gaspar," the sister said, "it has happened once, and the second time will be easier than the first. I have made up my mind."

"The beggar seemed sorry enough, girl."

"Ah! I suppose so. Same old story, but it has been told once too often, my pet. I have made up my mind."

Thereafter was a weary time of never-failing watch and ward for the girl—of mean, yet tragic struggles; of pence hoarded for advertisements; of long walks in rain, snow, or shine, with rarely the help of a penny 'bus;[1] of applications made at this house and that, often indignantly turned away for incompetency or shabby appearance. Once nearly three weeks passed in angling after the position of nursery governess to the eight children of a confectioner in Kennington, who lived above the shop. All the hopes deferred and heart sickness can never, never be told. Sir Gaspar's

---

1 A horse-drawn public bus whose fare was one penny. Gasparine can only occasionally afford the least expensive form of public transportation.

behaviour, day after day, and the increasing misery of their lives made the girl, in her excitable way, wildly, feverishly anxious to succeed.

Worse than a child—because obliged to take a woman's part—in the ways of the world, brought up dependent and secluded, dangerously clever, seeing she had not the accompanying experience to give her self-confidence, a girl could scarcely have been worse fitted to fight the battle of life than she. She knew, too, that in these days of certificates and cramming, without even testimonials she must be content with something humble. On this point she was sensible. Her drawing and painting certificates, and a strong and kind testimonial from her Art master, were all she had.

The winter wore away, spring came, and still her efforts were wholly unavailing. Sir Gaspar was at home, and behaving so obnoxiously that she and her brother locked themselves in one room most nights. And two or three miserable women, and two or three policemen—opposite poles—hung frequently about the house.

Half the rooms had been dismantled to supply the baronet with ready money to quench his thirst. It was at this time that these two young people knew what it was to have no bread in the house, and no fire. On chilly days Gaspar lay in bed, and Gasparine read to him to pass the time. Once or twice, when, in the night, the girl heard her father's step, she half rose, and her eyes gleamed dangerously as her heart swelled in passionate revolt, and the murder-demon for a moment possessed her. Then, if they were sitting together, the brother would lay his hand upon her arm with some quaint, commonplace remark, and she would laugh, ashamed and cowed, and sit down again.

The summer came before she got her chance, princely as it seemed to her—a situation as English governess in a private school in Scotland, in the town of Stirling, with a salary of £30 pounds a year, to begin work on the first of September. They had all July and August in which to lay plans and make preparations.

Of course they never dreamt of separating. That had not happened to them yet. Gaspar would go and take a lodging, and try for violin pupils; and certainly there was not a doubt but that he would get them.

They became intoxicatingly hopeful, and soon saw themselves rolling in wealth, and famous. And then, too, they had always had an ambition to see Scotland—that land which was not rich, and yet whose children could make such wealth—elsewhere. "As if,"

Gaspar said, "they were clever enough to cheat every one but each other."

In order to make their departure as little like a desertion as possible, they told Sir Gaspar they had both obtained situations in Stirling. Sir Gaspar viewed the matter in ten different lights during the course of that and many succeeding evenings.

"They were an ungrateful couple. A curse upon them!"

"They were low, ill-bred scum. He might have known what they would grow to."

"It was a good riddance."

"His dear, noble children! They were going to leave him and go into the wide, wide world."

"He guessed as much. Rats desert a sinking ship."

"They would find the difference."

And so on, endlessly. It was a new theme. And they, full of hope, half-pitied, half despised him, shrugged their shoulders, and listened while he raved.

As it happened, their departure was fortunate, for Sir Gaspar was unable to keep the house any longer, and was in danger of finding himself sold out shortly. Gasparine, therefore, determined to take possession of everything she could in time, well knowing that her father would give nothing freely, but would allow everything to be stolen from him by her or any one else. So the next time Sir Gaspar was from home she sold all that she dared, and with this store bought for herself and Gaspar such things as she deemed needful, and reserved their expenses, besides writing to Stirling and paying in advance for moderate lodgings. Everything else which she thought might be of use to them she packed and concealed, and, again waiting for an opportune absence on the part of Sir Gaspar—which fortunately fell in the latter part of August—they took flight, leaving behind them P.P.C. cards,[1] and forgetting, in their poor, young, hopeful youth, that between them and their father a grave lay.

---

1   "This is merely a visiting card, whether of a lady or a gentleman, on which the initials P.P.C. (*pour prendre congé*—to take leave) are written in ink in the lower left corner. This is usually left at the door, or sent by mail to acquaintances, when one is leaving for the season, or for good. It never takes the place of a farewell visit when one has received especial courtesy, nor is it in any sense a message of thanks for especial kindness. In either of these instances, a visit should be paid or a note of farewell and thanks written" (Emily Post, *Etiquette* [1922]).

CHAPTER VI
STIRLING

A more helpless couple than the brother and sister could hardly have been found, as they stood together beside their little all in Stirling Station. The station was dirty, the people struck the southerners as rude, and the sing-song, harsh speech disgusted them. The day was wet, and Gaspar shivered and coughed, because a fat woman in the stuffy, third-class carriage would have both windows open. Gasparine was faint with hunger, anxiety, and fatigue, and as she watched one pile of luggage after another disappear, she felt as if some one was dealing her stinging blows. The problem as to how to get their luggage removed was taking all the strength from her. She did not feel equal to addressing one of the bustling officials, and they brushed past her as though she were a trunk.

"I suppose they are busy; they will come presently," she said, evasively.

Gaspar raised his tired eyes.

"Shall I ask one of them?" he said, with a desperate effort.

There was an unacknowledged shrinking in each gentle soul from the rough familiarity their poverty would receive.

"No, no; I will," she said, gaining a desperate courage, as his dark eyes sought hers. "Here comes one." But as she stepped forward, the man, with a half glance, bustled past her, and flushing painfully she shrank back to her brother's side.

Would the world they were going to face be all like this?

As they stood meekly and patiently on one side, waiting till it should please some one to attend to them, Gasparine saw people hurrying to friends or home. The station cleared somewhat. Then a new tide of people entered, ready for a coming train. It was their first view of the citizens of Stirling, and Gasparine watched them eagerly.

At last they succeeded in capturing a porter, and then went in search of the lodgings which, writing from London, they had taken. These were in one of those questionable corner houses, the windows of which look into a good street, while the entry is from a side street of less select character. They had a moment's painful hesitation, as they stood at the stair, and the children playing there gathered round them and whispered; but the worst was really over for the time being.

The landlady was a humble, civil creature, rather impressed by the soft voices and solemn manners of her lodgers, and showed herself so anxious and active about their comfort that they began to think the world was not so bad, and they should have their due in time, no doubt. A little fire burned, and tea was ready. Gaspar flushed with importance when Mrs. Siddle brought him the *Despatch* and the *Stirling Weekly*, informing him she had them in for him. Newspapers they never thought of in their old, aimless lives, but now, being out in the world on their own account, they felt it incumbent on them to be wise in these matters. They read the paper, every word—the bits of intelligence, the news, the fusty politics, the fashionable items, the cuttings, the advertisements. Over the last they lingered long, hoping for a possibility.

When the paper was put aside they sat by the little fire, fighting back some faintness of heart, and talking of Gasparine's probable adventures on the morrow, when she presented herself at the school.

Later, a small, uncertain lamp, with a habit of suddenly going out, was put on the table, and Gasparine set herself to unpack and arrange the few books and trifles which would give their surroundings some feeling of familiarity and friendliness, the meagre wardrobe of each was shaken out and carefully put away, and then Gasparine suggested bed. The brother said good-night with tender wistfulness, and Gasparine, knowing well how little likely he was to sleep, built up the fire, and humming, with the adjoining door kept open, busied herself over many trifles while she made up her sofa-bed. Two small rooms was the limit of their lodging, and Gasparine occupied the room which was their sitting-room by day. When at last all to be done had been done, she took Gaspar's violin tenderly—ah! how tenderly!—from its case into her arms, and with soft caresses, as to a child, and whispered, loving words, sat for a brief time. The little house was very still, and no sound came from the street. The girl moved to the door and looked in at the brother. The eyes were closed, the thick black lashes curving in upon the cheek consumptively; and if he slept she did not know, but the sad expression on the lovely face spoke of suffering even in rest.

"My love!" she murmured; "my own, only love and darling! Now I shall play you your rest-song."

She played, too, and well, though not like her brother. In a little the exquisite strains of one of the loveliest of Schubert's "Müller Lieder" stirred, in spirit-like tones, the air of the little room:—

"Rest well, rest well, close thine eyes,
Good-night, good-night till all eyes wake."[1]

When it was finished she sat with the violin pressed to her breast, and large tears rolling slowly.

"To face the world is hell. To suffer the roughness of these coarse-grained natures is torture. But *for his sake, oh! for his sweet sake*, I will lick the dust from their feet, and to earn money *for him* I will give them my body to spurn.... But I shall hate them, and never think them else than the mud that he and I should walk on had we our right."

It was the exaggerated expression of a sore, proud heart, but it served its purpose of encrusting and hardening the sore.

When the morning came she had need of all her resolution. Gaspar had had a bad night, the fire did not burn, a fine rain drizzled. The good dress, in which Gasparine had hoped to make a favourable impression, could not be worn. The cup of weak tea was left untouched, and, in hopeless depression of spirit, the girl went out to search for the school. Up one street and down another, round Port Street, up Friar's Street, down King Street, round to the Dumbarton Road, warding off, as long as possible, the last, disagreeable expedient of asking the way. Into this she was forced, however, when half an hour had passed, and within an hour found herself at the school gate. It was an ordinary house of rather mean appearance on the terraces, about five minutes' walk from their lodgings. Her spirits sank, if possible, lower still. She rang, and was admitted, wet and untidy, possessed of a vague, night-mareish feeling that she would at once be shown into a schoolroom and told to teach. She was relieved, therefore, when the servant showed her to a little sitting-room and asked her to wait. It was very quiet. The clock and her heart beat time. A faint, musty smell reminded her of houses in London where they had lived, and of their present lodgings. This was hardly her idea of a school. She had seen the advertisement in an English paper, and, understanding that Miss Blurton was English, had felt rather drawn towards her. She wondered now how she would look.

---

1   Both lines are taken from "Des Baches Wiegenlied," #20 in Franz Schubert's 1823 song cycle of Wilhelm Müller's poems *Die schöne Müllerin* (1820). The first line begins the first stanza, while the second begins the final stanza: "Gute Ruh', gute Ruh'!/tu die Augen zu! ... Gute Nacht, gute Nacht!/Bis alles wacht...." The title of the novel's next chapter is also taken from this song.

Miss Blurton entered. The appearance of the teacher was not inviting. Small and stout, with a face once perhaps pretty, now faded; lips thin and mean, and drawn in towards the teeth, with an air that said, "I hold in all I can; even my breath." Yet now and then a faint expression of sweetness was observable about this mouth. Perhaps, after all, it was the world which had pressed the lips inward and made them so pinched and mean, even cruel. The eyes were large and pale blue, the nails bitten to the quick; the manner, nervous and propitiatory, was strangely contradicted by a rarely absent expression of ill-temper in the eyebrows.

Gasparine, whose inexperience had been prepared for any sort of treatment, was relieved by this timidity of manner, forgetting, as generous natures are apt to do, that timidity can be cruel.

"How d'ye do, Miss O'Neill? I'm glad you called. I was anxious to see you before school took up. We don't begin for a week yet, of course."

"I am very well, thank you."

Awkward pause, shifty glances exchanged, thought-flashes within.

"I have a week, a whole week, to be with him and look about."

"Dear me, she *is* stiff! Not like London, either. What boots and gloves!"

"Yes, Miss O'Neill. You see, school begins September 1st. I hope we shall have a pretty good school this year."

"Yes."

"So if you come on the 1st——"

"At what hour, please?"

"At nine; yes, at nine o'clock."

"You could not give me any definite idea of my duties as yet, I suppose?"

"Not yet. Your subjects, you know, are English, French, painting, drawing, music, and violin. But we can arrange all that later. I suppose you are English, Miss O'Neill?"

"No. Irish."

"Oh, Irish!" with a jerk. "I'm English m'self y' know; but I 'ave bin 'ere a long time." Familiarity and confidence now hastened and cut her speech. "My father bought the school, y' know; yes, pa did. We were all very well connected, 'ighly connected, y' know, Miss O'Neill, and we weren't brought up to be teachers. But—people 'ave misfortunes, and ye can't 'elp 'em."

Gasparine felt sympathetic. Miss Blurton spoke quite grammatically except for a peculiar cutting of her words and dropping of her h's, which, however, she did not affix in wrong places. The first stiffness had worn off, and the teacher, who could evidently be voluble on occasion—that is, about herself and her wrongs—waxed communicative. "Yes, pa was most petikler about all our educations. We never thought we'd 'ave to teach. W'y, we kept our kerridge once; we did, indeed."

Gasparine smiled faintly within herself, and murmured, "Yes."

"Well, we'd a very good school for a long time, and after poor dear pa died I 'ad the best school in Stirling. Then the 'Igh School—it's up the Castle 'ill; you'll see it w'en you're sight-seeing I shud think—was enlarged and improved, and our girls went there at first, but people complained of their manners, and the younger ones came back to me. The 'Igh School doesn't do us anything like the harm the College[1] does."

"Oh, there is a College?"

"Why, yes, a Ladies' College, that's the worst of it, just a bit above us, on the terrace—a beautiful building, standing in its own grounds. It was founded and endowed by an English colony. They came down, and took the house, which had belonged to a broken-down gentleman. Professors from Oxford and Cambridge came, and made a great fuss, and got Girton[2] girls and lady M.A.'s, and I don't know what they didn't 'ave; and it's some'ow, I don't know 'ow, in connection with the English Colleges. The teachers and lecturers exchange, and the students, too, I believe. But they're a set quite by themselves, like the military at the Castle; they're too proud to look at us poor private schools, of course, and they take our girls more and more every year. One good thing is that so many of their students come from England and Ireland. But I believe they've hurt even the Glasgow and Edinburgh schools, the College has become so popular."

"It must be nice to teach there," said Gasparine, with an involuntary sigh.

Miss Blurton looked at her sharply.

"Impossible, without the highest certificates, Miss O'Neill," she said shortly. After a pause she went on. "Their lady lecturers are a proud, conceited set, especially one of 'em I 'ear about. A

---

1 A college such as the Ladies' College in this novel offered the equivalent of secondary education, not of university education.

2 Girton College was the first university college founded for women. Established at Cambridge in 1869, it was for many years not recognized as a college by Cambridge University: its students were not eligible for Cambridge degrees. Girton formally became a college of Cambridge University in 1948.

pretty salary *she* must 'ave to drive about in a pony-kerridge, and dress as she does. They say she's most remarkably clever. She goes two months of the year lecturing in England, I know, and to Ireland, too, I think."

"How splendid! How very clever they must all be!" said Gasparine, with a sigh of envy at the thought of such wealth. What might not she and Gaspar do in a case of the kind!

"So they say," said Miss Blurton; "and I never run down any one, or speak positively, y' understand—it's not safe indeed—but if you'll believe me, Miss O'Neill, *I 'ave 'eard people say* that the be'aviour that's allowed to gow on sometimes, and the lectures and all, are quite shocking. Debates and lectures on Socialism and Women's Rights, etc., w'ere the students go in their gowns, and stamp, and rise to give their opinions,—it's really shocking. And they say—*mind*, I only say what I hear, what a friend told me—they *say* this Miss Grace is at the bottom of it. She's the favourite lecturer, and they say the girls are crazy about her."

But Gasparine was not shocked, only intensely interested.

She saw, however, that her interest in the new Ladies' College was not appreciated by Miss Blurton, and, after a few more remarks, and a little shuffling and awkwardness, she retired.

Miss Blurton sought her toady,—a sharp underbred governess of sneakish tendencies. "She looks clever," she said, "but dreadfully stiff and stuck-up. I hope she's not going to try and ride over *me*."

Gasparine, meantime, went away with a vague, dissatisfied feeling of uselessness, and some contempt for the Principal. But just at present, in her relief at the week's reprieve, and the knowledge that the dreaded interview was past, she felt too happy to be really despondent over this all.

During the week of respite Gaspar and Gasparine explored the town, wandered over the Castle in a dream of wonder, and marvelled at the view from the Lady's Rock, went up the Abbey Craig, and out on the tramway-car to the Bridge of Allan.[1] It was

---

1 Stirling Castle, site of a palace for the Scottish royal family, is the foremost landmark of Stirling. Nearby Lady's Rock was supposedly the vantage point from which court ladies watched tournaments in the valley below. Abbey Craig, a knoll to the east of Stirling, played a significant role in the Battle of Stirling Bridge in 1297: from its height William Wallace was able to plan his successful attack on the English crossing the bridge below. Located only a few miles from Stirling, Bridge of Allan was a popular spa town in the Victorian period. Gaspar and Gasparine are making a comprehensive tour of all the most notable local sights.

all very beautiful, but the beauty pained them, with the pain felt in a joyous dream from which one knows, even sleeping, that one must wake. A pain keen, yet intangible and unreal. They felt uprooted and homeless. They sat one day together on the Lady's Rock, from which is to be obtained one of the loveliest views in Scotland. Gaspar was white and panting after the long climb up the Back Walk, and Gasparine realised, with a shudder, that they looked out upon that fair world from amid the tombs. A fair world, indeed! Below, the old Royal Gardens were laid out where the dead kings played once, and the sheep grazed now, hardly troubling their heads about the strangely shaped grassy parterres from which they cropped. Beyond was the King's Park—one stunted tree showed where the forest stood of old. Only the hills were unchanged, the long line of the Touch Hills in their gleaming silver veil, for the day was hot and hazy, and the wide Carse lay golden in the August light. Far down in the Carse was a cottage, a little white nest, seeming to stand in happy isolation, protected by its fields. The eyes of the two were fixed upon it silently for a long time; then Gasparine turned and clasped her brother's hands.

"Gaspar-Boy!"

"Yes, girl."

"That cottage! You see! To be there, dear, together, resting and happy, not needing to face those terrible human beings, who are so rough, and seem to find life so easy."

He only nodded gently, with eyes which the hot sunlight made dreamy.

The first week of teaching was a time of great misery for Gasparine, and Gaspar suffered equally for her. Gasparine was nervous and awkward, Miss Blurton assumed an aggrieved and injured air, quickly imitated by the other two teachers and the pupils.

Gaspar, watching his sister's white face and black eyes, day by day, grew nervous; and at last Gasparine, in spite of all her struggles to hide wounded pride and strung nerves, broke down.

"It's nothin', Gaspar-boy,-me-darlin'." This was the tenderest and rarest of their Irish pet names. "But only, that woman jumped on me to-day, and told me to give the girls half-an-hour's French conversation. I was taken aback, and lost my head, and each time I made a mistake she shouted the right word across from her desk. I grew furiously red, stammered, and was more nervous than ever, and the girls sniggered—the beasts!—and ... she might have given me a word of warning.... I speak French better than she does ... only ... oh, Gaspar, it's fearful! The girls are all ... common ... shop ... cads, you know, and I'm so wretchedly shy."

As she spoke, between little strangled sobs, she was bent, with undying courage, over a pile of ancient lesson-books, by means of which she meant to refresh her memory and prepare herself for her work. As each petty insult rose in her mind her heart swelled. Gaspar bit his lip, and his beautiful eyes glowed.

"Gaspar," he said, "tell me something, honest. Do you think she could do without you?"

"Oh yes. She could—she could get others."

"Curse! ... Well——"

"Darling boy, don't mind, I'm going to stay. I'll work on, and learn. Don't fear; I can bear it."

It was a great bitterness to the high pride of both. Custom came to help bear the burden, and the long weeks rolled on. September, wet and cold, the drenched leaves rotting everywhere. October, chill, chill; Gaspar coughing, and coals very dear. November, with torrents of rain,—a wet, dreary winter, during which Gasparine worked to educate herself, and starve herself in deadly earnest, and Gaspar sat over the small fire, weary and wan. The strife for life was a terrible thing in the two little rooms.

The problem was, "Can two people, occupying the position of lady and gentleman, lodge, board, dress respectably, and keep out of debt on £30 a year?"

And, oh! very nobly the poor, untrained woman-heart answered the problem, "Yes; if one of them has no needs."

An exact calculation of income and expenditure was made. Rent for the two little rooms, £13. For living, a sum of from 3s.6d. to 5s. weekly was allowed, and coal 18s. In this way they managed. They managed, indeed, so well, that when the summer came, there was not only money for the holidays, but something in the bank—that is, the old tin bank. No one can conceive their joy. Further, in May, two violin pupils came to Gaspar, and one for painting to Gasparine.

Upon all this Gasparine had a plan. She unfolded it one evening to her brother. It was a fine June evening, pleasantly near the holidays. The two little rooms were stiflingly hot, and Gasparine and Gaspar sat at the open window, which looked into the front street. This window had been their recreation all winter, and they had watched the people pass and repass, and wondered and conjectured as to whom they might be.

"Gaspar, it is dreadfully hot here. Mrs. Siddle is a decent soul, but, you know, I don't think it is a good situation for pupils."

"No? How is that?"

"Miss Wells, who comes to me for painting, says so."

"Oh! So?"

"Oh yes, and I've a lovely idea! You know we have £7 in the bank besides what will keep us during the holidays, and I see in Viewfield Place a house with two rooms to let, unfurnished."

"That is the road beyond Barnton Place, on the car-line."

"Yes, just there; the back windows look out to the Ochil Hills. It is a lovely view, and the houses are nice; old-fashioned, but respectable."

"You rogue! You have made a whole plot."

"No, no; only a tiny plan. Listen. We can have two of the rooms, unfurnished, for £10 a year. It is a nicer locality, and we can furnish ourselves. We have a good many things; and then——"

"Come, I see your mind is set upon it."

This was their summer occupation. They got the rooms for £9, a shrewd bargain on the part of Gasparine, and, drawing from the "bank," they managed, with their London articles and boxes, to give the rooms a habitable appearance. Before the opening of school they had moved to their new quarters, with Mrs. Siddle's blessing, and feeling now that they could breathe. The rooms were large and convenient, and the possession of a key and uninterrupted privacy were boons the dearer for having been withheld a year. Their little sitting-room was furnished—one had almost said inch by inch—at least, very slowly, because the furniture was all quite new. What an unending pride and excitement it was to both! A chair, a bit of carpet, a what-not, a little rug; these things were studied, day after day, in the dealer's window before the Rubicon was passed, and the article purchased.

One day, three shillings remained over from a chair reduced so much from the original sum. It was the day before the re-opening of school. There was a show of some sort in the King's Park, and Gasparine determined they should go. It was a hot day, and both dressed in all they had of good, enjoyed to the utmost the little crowd, the music of the band, and the flow of life in the place.

On the whole, the second winter was not so bad as the first. For the first year their naturally acute observation had fought with the generally accepted delusion, that the at once reserved and brusque manner of the Scotch, so well expressed by the German as *grob*,[1] meant sincerity and a warm heart beneath. Trusting to the one, and searching ardently for the other, they were gradually disillusioned, and found that abrupt speech is in itself no earnest of sincerity, which belongs indeed to character, not to manner, and is sufficiently rare in all nations to be treasured when found.

"They say the Irish are faithless, and that the English tell you their family history on the top of the 'bus first time you meet; but, after all, it's better than these people here, who seem, by their shut-up air, to say, 'Mines of diamonds lie under this hard exterior,' but when one digs, below are false, coarse stones.... Sir Gaspar, poor devil! was right when he said, 'Good breeding consists in being every one's intimate friend for the time being.' Give me a sunny surface; that, at least, is a good promise, and one gets warmed even if one goes no farther."

In this way Gasparine sometimes spoke to her brother, when the rougher manner of the Scotch, which, to tell the truth, their peculiar circumstances aggravated, grated upon their highly-bred, unprotected, and sensitive natures. For the rest, it was not so bad for Gasparine in school. True, there was a paltry meanness in Miss Blurton's manner which was a source of daily discomfort to the girl; the more so, that she conceived it to be her duty to render every sign of respect to the woman who paid her.

Once or twice, girls with bright eyes made advances to her in the usual school-girl way.

"Miss O'Neill, you know, you're awful nice! Miss Blurton's a nasty pig. I just hate her! She's a real mean one to you! I'm awful sorry for you—we all are."

Gasparine's pride was touched. These brats were *sorry for her*! So that was it! Betty received small encouragement to continue from Miss O'Neill's quiet eyes and cold voice.

"It is not nice of you to say that of Miss Blurton. I'm sure she means to be very kind."

Miss Blurton, meantime, had found out the manifold uses of the governess, and that Gasparine was disdainfully honourable and just; that, however Miss Blurton might sneer, and encourage the others to sneer, Miss O'Neill saw nothing, and yet managed to maintain interest and order in her class.

---

1 "Coarse" or "rough."

All this meant much. Divided between jealousy and satisfaction, she one day asked Gasparine to tea. Flattered and overcome, Gasparine awkwardly refused.

She "never left her brother," she said.

Miss Blurton was very angry.

"Frightfully stiff and stuck-up," she remarked to toady number two. "Y' know I know I'm right. Pa, poor, dear pa, always said I had good instincts, and I *know* that girl has a frightful temper—a hidden volcano, that's what I call her!"

Gasparine went home.

"You know, Gaspar," she said, "I think Miss Blurton is growing quite decent; she asked me to tea. Of course I couldn't go. I had no dress."

"Oh, Gaspar-girl, you must get one, you know, if people are going to begin and invite you around," Gaspar said. "You must have a decent frock!"

With much pains, starvation, and struggle, a "frock" was obtained; but no more "asking about" was forthcoming.

In other respects also the winter rolled more smoothly. They liked their new rooms, and once or twice they went to a cheap concert, or to one of the public entertainments given at the College, and heard Miss Grace give a brilliant paper; and Gasparine whispered to Gaspar that some day, perhaps, *she* would stand there. These outings did Gaspar harm, though they did not know. He usually coughed and was ill next day; but both thought that a small price to pay for the intense enjoyment which the taste of life gave them. Perchance they were right.

The third winter was a sorrowful one. Gaspar was worse, and required medicine. To people living on five shillings a week, at most, two or three shillings for medicine means rather a terrible amount. The savings—gained by occasional sale of Gasparine's pictures, and Gaspar's pupils—went, shilling by shilling. So far, they had managed in dress by altering such things as they had brought from London. Now these things were too shabby to wear any longer. Gasparine sewed, mended, altered—it was no good. Their underclothing was little better than rags; she washed it herself, of course.

It was a time of intense misery and anxiety, and once, when Gasparine bent over her books, weeping, and struggling to conceal the heaving of her breast, he came and knelt at her chair, and took her two hands in his own slender, white fingers, and said, with his beautiful, solemn eyes upon her,—

"Dear, it were better for you I were not here. You would be

better off. Sometimes nature will yield for one and not for two. I feel a brute to sit here useless while you work; a log and a drag I am, nothing more. Oh, my poor little soul! why can I not do more for thee?"

Sometimes, in moments of intense tenderness and feeling, they used the gentle thou and thee of fonder nations. And she, with a piteous quivering all over her face, held his hands tight, striving to control herself to speak.

"Don't say so, darling, don't; it hurts so. Oh, what, what, what should I do without you, my angel, my angel? Ah! God is higher than Nature. When Nature says, 'Let one be there,' God says, 'I have put two. Let love make room.' Gaspar-boy-me-darlin', do you know what you are? You are the soul of my soul; a great, strong soul for my little soul to creep in beside and rest against. Oh, Gaspar! do not say ever again, 'twere better that you were not here; do not say it ever again."

He stroked her hair and said he would not.

"Well, at least," he said, one night, wearily, when they had talked the matter over again, "at least, at worst we can throw ourselves on the charity of the world. Surely they will not murder us. Surely we may live."

"Throw ourselves on the charity of the world?" cried Gasparine. "Oh no! That is the last thing that we may do. Think! Do you know what it means? Oh, when you throw yourself on the charity of the world you get more than you bargain for! It means that the world may throw you a scrap when it remembers you, and claim your gratitude for that; it will watch your clothes, your appearance, your bearing; it will cast its cast-off clothes towards you, nod to you when it suits, and pass when it suits, and all through it will despise you, and care nothing, nothing at all, for all your suffering, and it will expect you to be humble and grateful. Take care! That is the charity of the world. Die first."

"Oh, little sister, you are wise; and I think that I must die, as this charity is so cold."

She looked at him and laughed. But in the night they wept, each apart, long and sore.

The never-absent fears on Gaspar's account now weighed upon Gasparine more than ever.

"If he were only well! Oh, dear God, if he were only well!" she said to herself one dreary January evening, as she wended homeward after preparing one of Miss Blurton's pupils, a duty for which she received an extra pittance, "How small all these troubles would seem then!"

The snow came through her old boots as she walked, and she shivered. She passed the shop windows and looked in. Bright and tempting everything appeared.

"If I could only bring him some little appetising thing! ... I'm sure he could eat. If I might only dare ask in one of the shops and need not pay! ... But I dare not! No, no; it is the last thing my pet would have."

She was standing at a fruiterer's, gazing in at the still-decorated windows, when two people came out—a stylish young lady, and a little girl in furs. It was not ordinary stylishness; there was something, some curve of ankle, turn of wrist, pose of head and shoulders, which made the lady, in movement and attitude, gracious and remarkable. The child, a lovely creature, chattered. The young lady answered,—

"Yes, Ladybird, yes. But do not talk so much," and they passed into the darkness.

"There; that is the girl I should like best to be," said Gasparine to herself. "Miss Grace, M.A., of the College, the cleverest girl in town, Miss Blurton says, and has £300 a year. I suppose she has spent as much money to-night in fruit and sweets for the child as would keep me and Gaspar for a week ... Oh, life! ..."

She went home slowly through the snow. Gaspar sat over the fire; he had prepared tea for her.

"Gaspar," he said, "to-day I feel wretched, and, somehow or other, as if I'd give anything for an egg. It is stupid of me, I know." He broke off to cough.

An egg! He might as well have asked for a golden horse. Gasparine would receive no money for three weeks yet; meantime, there was not a farthing in the house. She had hoped to eke out the month with onions, potatoes, bread, bacon, and tea. It had been done before. An egg! ...

"Oh, Gaspar darlin'! of course you must have an egg," she said cheerfully. "I'll go and buy one at once."

"You have money, then, little one?"

"Why, yes; enough for that."

And the brave heart turned, penniless, into the street again— the brave, breaking heart! She went, slowly and lingeringly, into the light of the shops. She had an idea. She knew a grocer who always kept a barrel of eggs just at his door; his shop was not well lighted, either. Her heart beat to suffocation as she went there, and lingered, and stood....

"Now, *now*. All are busy; the street is empty. Now, *in Christ's name!*" ...

It was done.

At the end of the month she went to the grocer, and, purchasing a few matches, laid threepence extra on the counter and hastened away.

"God," she said, then, "I have paid my debt to *you*. But do not be so hard to me, I pray you; do not be so hard to me and Gaspar. Ah, no, dear God! I have prayed wrong. Be hard to me if you will—I am strong to bear; only, be good to Gaspar, dear God! spare Gaspar, dear, dear God!"

CHAPTER VII
"GUTE RUH"[1]

The winter wore, and Gaspar grew whiter and coughed louder, and had to give up his violin pupils. Their garments would no longer pass unchallenged, and Miss Blurton once gave an injured hint to Gasparine to wear a better dress. Closer and closer they were drawn in their misery and loneliness, and dearer became heart to heart.

January, February, March, April. Then suddenly God and the sun smiled upon them. It seemed that, in a day, Gaspar grew well. His cough stopped; his cheek grew pink, he walked straight, laughed and talked, and seemed hungry. Gasparine's heart bounded with a hope too great to bear. The earth laughed in sympathy, the days were hot, and the green leaves hastened out into the bright sun. Three of Gasparine's pictures, lying all winter in a dealer's window, were bought by a tourist, and an order given for more. A run of violin and painting pupils so filled the day that sometimes, in the tiny room, two students painted under Gasparine's direction, while the violin skreaked under Gaspar's. In a month they both possessed new costumes, sorely needed and highly prized, and, as the fruit of Gasparine's brush, £10 rested in the bank.

Gasparine had wild schemes of taking a third room, and suggested a summer trip.

Yes; for a moment life smiled. The fairest sunset before the night, the burst of glory before the sun sinks.... Suddenly, mysteriously into these hearts, which had hitherto known only sorrow and misery, joy entered. It was a mystery—a miracle. A rose-glow came into the rooms, a hush, a halo—it was an altar....

That the shadow should of itself rise and move from her path,

---

1 "Rest well." See note 1 on page 72 above.

that he should grow so full again of life and life's desires. The people turned in the street as he passed, speaking of his beauty. Young girls raised their eyes to him with wistful admiration. In the greatness of her joy, Gasparine, too, grew beautiful with a beauty of the spirit remarkable and painful. As they sat together in the evenings, his arm round her, her head against his shoulder, they spoke, in continual wonder, of their happiness.

"How cosy we are!"

"Are we not?"

"And the prospect for the summer is so dear!"

"Yes. Now, indeed, we have a little home."

"The whole world seems to have grown kind. Life never was so before. I feel so happy!"

"I suppose that we have both become so strong, content has come."

"It must be so."

Into the brief sunlight of those days their summer had come. Life went on so for some weeks—a mystery incomprehensible but divine; a happiness so enormous, so terrible, after their sufferings, that they seemed to have their eyes ever wide in amazement at it.

In this new tide of happiness and prosperity wine was bought for Gaspar, and Gasparine, too, must drink. They did not know how much they drank, nor how it gave false strength, false life to both. Now, at night, Gasparine, kneeling by his little bed, held the lovely head in her arms, or laid her face near his upon the pillow, and watched, in the starlight and the fireglow, until the fringed eyes closed in languid sleep. What murmured conversations these hours knew! What plans for the new future!—that was never to be.

"Dear, how strange our life seems! We two, alone from birth, belonging to one another; and in the wide, wide world, none other has come near us."

The last of April was a day of midsummer heat. It was a holiday, and Gasparine accomplished an old dream, and drove herself and Gaspar in an aged, rattling vehicle. Where she drove that day she knew not, but she knew that there were budding trees and glancing water, and magical lights between the branches, and thousands of summer whispers in the air. They stopped at a country inn and had dinner and tea, walked through the village, and afterwards drove home in the gathering dark, very tired, very happy, very full of hope.

That night Gaspar died.

They had scarcely reached home when the fatal haemorrhage began.

"I will go for the doctor," Gasparine said, her rent heart suffocating her with its beatings, and her icy limbs trembling almost to the earth. But he reached and feebly took her hand.

"It is no use," he said, pausing between each word to swallow. "Ah, dear! do not leave me for a moment now. I knew it, knew it well, but you were so—so—hopeful.... I could not bear to kill the white thing in your breast. It was fever, the last flame on my cheek, and madness and rage for love of you, that made me eat and laugh and talk. It—is—all—done—now. Go for no doctor, Gaspar, my little one, my friend, my sister. Gaspar, hold my hand through all.... It will be hard.... And listen well. I must speak while I can. I regret nothing, sweetheart, in all our short, sad lives, but that I may not have loved you well enough. It was the only duty that I knew, to love you. I had no strength to work, like other men...."

"Oh, hush, my darling, hush! This is not what you think. You are tired only. Blood came before. Don't—don't——"

But, sunk upon his bed and still clutching her hand, he went on gaspingly, settling, it seemed, the count of his life between himself and God. "And, however we have been, all is well, all. We did in life what we could. Let God judge. I do not fear God's judgment. And you, Gaspar-girl, have no fear. God gives you strength for the last struggle—the strength of my love in your heart, to watch, and say good-bye."

"Oh, if we might go together!"

"If only! What fear then?"

Soon the agony of death was upon him. It distorted the lovely face. The beautiful eyes seemed to spring from their sockets. The limbs, until now so weak, writhed in convulsive strength. Most excruciating of all was that the voice, the eyes, the arms, ever turned towards Gasparine in all distortions, with piercing anguish, beseeching relief.

"Help me, Gasparine. Oh, I *cannot* bear it! If you love me, Gaspar, give me some relief."

And she would answer,—

"Oh, my darling! my darling! What can I do for thee, my own, my only one? If I could bear the sufferings, my little Gaspar, my own wee one, my sweet, sweet boy! It will be over, over very soon. To-morrow we shall say, 'How terrible! It was a bad dream,' and the sun will shine, for it is almost summer now, and you and I will go another lovely day. Think——"

"No, my sweet girl." The solemn tone was exquisitely tender through its agony. "There comes no to-morrow for your boy—no long, sunny day for us two. It is night-time for me now...."

"My boy," she shrieked, "for me it will be always night-time—always dark...."

He shivered and shuddered in the throes that strove to rend soul and body in twain. Then he struggled up, seizing her waist, leaning his chin against her shoulder, and pushing feebly at the bloody saliva which purpled his lips.

"Tell me, does God blame me that we two, having none other in all the world, loved each other only and all? Have I failed in my place, in my work as a man? We were so lonely! I was so weak! Tell me. I will believe what you say, Gaspar-girl, love—Gaspar-girl."

Then she spoke, with the power and the strength of her love, as a woman in her agony will.

"Believe it not, my darling. It is the devil who tempts you in your pain. It was God who bade us love one another—God who left us here, with no one but each other, in the wide world, alone, *alone, alone*! If heaven has no room for a love such as ours, go not thou there, my darling. Wait thou for me in hell. Sure, Gaspar, all we ask is to know each other after death. What does the word Hereafter mean for you, for me, Gaspar? Does it not mean the lasting of our love, or nothing? And even should it be that you must rest until I come; you will not fear, not in the dark, nor in the stillness, for I am thinking of you always, sweet, and with you always in my dreams; and when I come, surely your dear arms will press to me, and fold me, and your eyes seek mine.... Gaspar, Gaspar, Gaspar! what am I saying? How am I talking! You are not—not—not going to—to die!" A sudden, horrid wave of realisation rushed across her, and she shrieked.

He had risen, and, with a fierce, wild, convulsive movement, threw his arms towards her, and shrieked too. She seized him, and, in spite of his struggles, held him close as death itself, and rocked with him as a piece of his own flesh. He strove to wrest himself from her—to throw her from him, and this agony soothed her. His struggles became fainter and fainter, and at last he spoke.

"Gaspar, it is too cruel, *too* cruel!" Tears, wrung from his suffering manhood by the last stress, flowed down the white, dying cheeks. "What *is* God? Had He taken me in my strength I could have borne it! But wasting me from day to day, from year to year, until I have no strength! How cruel! Did He so with the Christ?"

"Darling, I do not know; but Christ was *very* tired." Oh! her woman's courage never failed her. "And when He was as tired as you, my own—and you, tired as you are, may lie on my breast," and she rocked him in her arms, against her bleeding, breaking heart—"they stretched His poor hands out and up. Think, sweetest heart! with nails; and the tired Feet, and the weary, weary Head!"

The lovely, curly head, with its long, dank hair, drooped upon her breast, and the blue eyes swooned.

In the precious seconds of reprieve she crooned over to him his loved and favourite songs:—

> "'You little flowers, all that she gave to me—
> One shall lay you in the grave with me.
> Ach! tears do not make May joy
> Nor make dead love bloom again.
> Spring will come, and flowers will bloom,
> And all the little flowers she gave to me,
> They shall be laid in the grave with me.'"[1]

She sang in German, low and sweet, and he was still.

In a few seconds he stirred, bewildered.

"Have I slept long, Gaspar? I did not want to waste a second. What were we talking of? Ah yes, of Christ. And, oh, Gasparine! how will you live?" The yearning of the future, which the dying so often have, came into his anguished eyes.

The paroxysms came on again, worse and more dread.

The girl never flinched....

In the dawn, with a few piteous words, to ring for ever in her ears, the spirit yielded in the dread struggle.

"Gasparine, I can't bear it. At the beginning I said it was too hard. Think what it is now! I am too weak. I had no strength *then*, and now! ... It is years I have suffered, not hours. Ask God, Gasparine, beg Him, beseech Him.... Sister, *pray*."

She knelt beside him, striving to remember what they used to pray in the church with their step-mother. The Litany was familiar to her. It had once seemed to her a grand, monotonous moan of the world's pain. Now, in a loud voice, she cried it up to God:
"'By Thine agony and bloody sweat, by Thy cross and passion; by Thy precious death and burial; by Thy glorious resurrection and ascension; and by the coming of the Holy Ghost, good Lord,

---

1 Taken from "Trockne Blumen," #18 in the Schubert/Müller song cycle *Die schöne Müllerin*.

deliver us.... We beseech thee to hear us good Lord.... O Lamb of God, grant us Thy peace——"[1]

He interrupted her in fierce agony.

"Be done. Christ does not hear ... and I can bear no more."

No, indeed; the measure was full, for in a moment he sprang up like a strong man.

"Gasparine, I *want* to live, I *must* live for you, and—and—I—I—I—Gasp—ah!—sweet—ah!—sist——"

He was dead.

Round and round the room the girl went, raving.

"God! God! Cursed be God! He has taken the light from the universe. The sun is gone. Alone—alone—alone!" she shrieked. "For ever, and ever, and ever, alone, alone!"

★   ★   ★   ★   ★

He was buried. The hideous noise and movement were over. The light sought him in the empty rooms. He was no more there. Sorrow had made her mad, but through her madness she was wise. For his sake, above all, she knew that their utter poverty must be concealed, that no reproach might touch him. And that first night, in very love of him, she carried the corpse to her own bed, then with untold pain moved his bed to the little sitting-room, draped it, and placed over it her own white muslin dress, his gift and sacrifice, and went for the doctor who had occasionally attended Gaspar.

It was all done now. The people who moved in the rooms—the hideous red-nosed clergyman, who pried into their poor, but most sacred nest; the woman, who wept over the beautiful, dead face, because it was "the loveliest corpse she ever dressed"—they were all gone.

"He will never speak to me again," she said to herself quietly, as one who would convince. "Think, heart, *you will never hear his voice again*, saying 'Gaspar,' or calling. Think! Do you understand? He will never look at you again, or stretch his hand to you."

---

1 These lines come from the Litany or General Supplication in the Church of England's *Book of Common Prayer*. This prayer was appointed to be read after Morning Prayer on Sundays, Wednesdays, and Fridays, and at other set times.

She threw herself on her face, beating the walls and floor with her hands, and shrieked.

★   ★   ★   ★   ★

Meantime, outside life was knocking, with gentle hand, at her door. Two piteous and tender eyes were looking up at the dingy, unlighted windows.

"This is the house! Oh, poor thing! I will call to-morrow," Lotus said.

BOOK II
LOTUS

APOLOGY

Here indulgence is craved, for offering, as seemed to me necessary, though I am aware it is unusual, a second apologetic explanation.

It has been, so far, the province of the novel to deal almost exclusively with lives only in their relation to the passion of love between man and woman, and the complications arising from it, as its depth, truth, fidelity, infidelity, the influence of circumstances, political, economic, social, geographical upon it. But this is only one side of life. There are others. In many lives such love plays but a minor part, or enters not at all. Will no one voice them, or find beauty in them?

To the readers who feel that humanity will right itself the sooner for facing *all* its wrongs, and more particularly to-day, the wrongs which, through many past ages, women have silently borne—I commend Lotus.

Lastly, to all who feel that men and women will come to closer, and higher relationships, when they cease to wear masks each towards the other sex—removed when in the company of their own—to those I have tried to show, in all purity of intent, and belief in the best of humanity, what women may be, and often are, to one another.

CHAPTER I
THE SORROW OF GASPARINE

In the picturesque town of Stirling there had lived, for two or three years, a brother and sister. The brother gave violin lessons when his health permitted; the sister taught in a private school in the town, and, at home, painted. Occasionally she sold her work, which, though weird and unpopular, was strikingly original, and, with more pains, would have been powerful.

Stirling was little interested in these struggling young people. They had come from London, were poor, friendless, Bohemian in dress, and chiefly remarkable for their deep attachment to one another, and the contentment they seemed to find in one another's society.

Who they were none knew. A quiet, humble, yet unapproachable pride kept people aloof.

In the unnatural and brilliant beauty of the young man, as he walked gently round Port Street, his tall figure slightly stooped, it required no specialist to read the swift approach of death. In the languid eyes—long, blue-black eyes, with fringes curving in upon the waxen cheek—in the bright red of the consuming fever in the lips, death spoke.

It must have been the knowledge of the approach of this silent power that gave the sister's eyes a hunted and haunted expression, like a foretaste of the last agony. She was like her brother, but without any of his beauty.

So, one morning, among the violin and painting pupils, there was a little awe, but no surprise, when some one said, "Gaspar O'Neill was out yesterday, and died last night. They say Gasparine O'Neill will go mad."

"How awful! They were so queer! And so awfully fond of one another! Isn't it awful! Just awful!"

One or two romantic young ladies, who had been enamoured of the violinist's beauty, went pale, and became slightly hysterical.

But there was only one mourner: the sister.

In the poor room she knelt beside the bed where the dead lay. The last agony, the last cries were filling her brain and maddening it. Gaspar dead! Gaspar-boy her brother! Her own, the one only thing she had had all her lonely life to love, and who loved her. The companion of her troubles, her comfort, her help, the soul of her! Dead! Gaspar dead! The twin-brother who had, with his frail health, and unearthly beauty and love, made the bounds of her world! ...

For long, long years she had watched, with trembling heart and wildly rebellious soul, the terrible encroachment of a power against which her art, her strength, her hopes, her eternal love, beat unavailingly, however madly.

In her agony, Gasparine now felt like some thing, some element detached from all else in the great universe. She could see only the dark and tender eyes, bear only the piteous voice: "Gaspar-girl, I *want* to live for *you*, my darling! ..."

Days rose before her, days of misery, hunger, strife.... The times in London, of wealth, yet misery, the gradual decline, with the growing drunkenness of the noble baronet, their father. And through the fog and dreariness, ever the smile, the love-glance, the beautiful, tender care of the brother.

Then came their struggles for freedom and separation from that nightmare, Sir Gaspar; their vain, unworldly-wise attempts at independence; and, at last, this settlement in the Scotch town, with its hopes and fears, its little successes, and chill disappointments.

The sunlight of the last day swept over her; not as tender or bright as his haunting smile. That precious day! Their one holiday, when at last hope came to them in the song of birds, the gleam of summer green, drove her frantic. On that one glad day night had fallen; in its red sunset there was a deeper red, flowing from his heart, his dear lips crimsoned, his choking, sobbing breath! ...

Now all was over. He was dead. The word *nevermore* had fallen across her life. Never, nevermore. It was the powerlessness of her great love against that single hideous word that was driving her mad.

★　　★　　★　　★　　★

Days passed. He was buried now. She had followed, in her slender, poor cloak, the miserable one-horse hearse, through the old, steep streets of Stirling, up to the garden of sleep upon the rock beside the Castle, where, among clear, hilly air, surrounded by the carselands, and sheltered by the friendly hill ranges, the dead lie at their ease, and dream of their awaking, in beloved scenes, with those they left mourning.

When it was over, she went along the Back Walk, head bowed, hands clasped, and above the Smith Institute[1] she slipped from the shady, steep path, unto the precipitous, grassy bank, and,

---

1 Now the Stirling Smith Art Gallery and Museum, this important local institution was founded in 1874 as a public art gallery.

sheltered by one of the great boulders which lie there, she crouched, in agony of body and soul, in an abandonment of grief, hope, and love.

"Gaspar-boy! Me own little Gaspar-boy!" she moaned. "What is your Gaspar-girl to do? Oh, what is your poor girl to do?"

When at last she returned to the empty rooms, and realised that she was indeed alone, in wild, impassioned madness of despair she threw up her hands to heaven.

"I curse Thee, God!" she cried. "I curse Thee, oh, I curse Thee! Thou art God in Heaven! Ah! So! In very deed! Yet wilt Thou take from me all I had,—all, all, all! my brother, my love, my friend! ... We were together always in the old days. Thou hast seen fit to part us. See, then, what Thou hast done! ... Thou hast driven me mad! ..."

A pitiless silence reigned. Then she cried again,—

"Oh, stony, unmoved God, strike me dead rather!"

There was silence still.

She threw herself on her face, beating the walls and floor with her hands, and shrieked....

*   *   *   *   *

It was at this moment that Lotus, looking up at the dreary windows, said, wistfully, "Alas! poor soul! ...This is your hour.... No one can help you now—no one. Later, I'll come and try."

CHAPTER II
LOTUS

For a week this wildness lasted, with, each day, a curious lucid interval, lasting from nine o'clock in the morning till two. At about eight she usually stirred from her weary position, shoved back her hair, and groped about for cold water. When she had dashed this on her face, mechanically she brushed her hair, and arranged her dress—she never undressed—with care. By nine o'clock she was in the school, and, save for her extreme pallor and haggard appearance, looking just as usual. The work done, she returned to her rooms, sat down, and seemed to sink, sink, sink. At last, with a cry of unutterable misery, the old tearing, panting, throbbing began.

The room was empty. *That* was the horror of horrors. Even the white, still, unspeaking form was there no more, to be talked to, caressed, recalled. The room was empty.

Sometimes she crawled round and round by the walls, striking them, calling upon them to open.... When it grew dark she sat upon one spot, moaning low like a dog, or moving incessantly and silently. If the moon shone, she sat where she could gaze upon it, and in this way she would remain, staring, and gaping, and suffering, with both hands knitted, and sometimes helplessly wrung. When there was no light but the street lamp, she watched that, and seemed to draw from it poignant and bitter memories.

At the end of a week the rooms presented a picture of desolation beyond description. Dust, dirt, untidiness, added to the close atmosphere, where death had so lately been, gave them something of horror and inhumanity.

The fever in Gasparine was at its height. The week had been wet, and coming home each day, drenched and sick, the girl had shivered, sometimes all night, in her boots and an old waterproof of Gaspar's—now sacred.

This day, when she came home, for some cause, her paroxysms of misery were deeper, more despairing than ever. She cried, in tones of inexpressible torment, "God *is* hard! Oh, indeed, God *is* hard!"

The early dark came, and the street lamp was flickering feebly through the unblinded windows, when a tap at the door threw her into a wildly hysterical state. Who could it be? The landlady never came. The school-girls respected her silent grief—perhaps were indifferent to it. Who, therefore, could this be? The door was locked, and to the repeated tap she made no answer. The tapping continued. Then a delirious thought came.

"*Was it Gaspar returned?*"

There was just that precision and gentleness in the knock; that sound as of an entreaty for welcome, which her fond imagination had always heard in those taps of his, when, returning from a lesson, or a gentle walk, he gave notice to her that he was beside her again.

She sat up, with wild, streaming eyes.

"Do the dead return?" cried her tortured heart.

There came again a tapping.

"*So* he knocked that day we were sulky with one another because he bought me flowers—too dear," cried memory.

Again.

"Who is there?" she called quietly; for in her worst fits she had, with the self-consciousness of morbid melancholy, carefully concealed her pain and wound. There was no answer, but again that gentle and imperious tapping.

Then Gasparine rose, sullenly unlocked the door, and slunk away again into the window recess.

The person who entered did not speak—a girl's figure, in a dark cloak and cap, with curly hair. The cap was laid aside quietly, as a matter of course, and without addressing a word to Gasparine. Then the stranger paused a moment to accustom her eyes to the dark, and involuntarily held her breath for the close and disagreeable smell, while she looked around. Gasparine watched her, lowering, and without speaking. It was not Gaspar—no; but something told her it was a soul, indeed—albeit embodied—that had entered the room. It was a strong soul too. She had a feeling of repulsion and anger.

"I am going to open the window," said the stranger, in a sweet, vibrating voice, "and light a fire." With that she raised the window in her two slender hands, and the street-lamp, as if glad and pitying, cast a stronger beam into the desolate and poor remains of a home which society had placed beyond its bounds.

The stranger passed behind the partition, and sounds of crackling and burning were heard. Gasparine watched with a viciously bit lip. The stranger, the unhallowed one, was at *his* fire, touching the pans that cooked *his* last food—casting them, disgusted, in water. *She was sweeping the room.*

★   ★   ★   ★   ★

A flash of firelight fell at Gasparine's feet through the opening in the partition. A glow was on the ceiling. The stranger flitted in and out, silent and busy. Once she came and touched Gasparine's hair with a gentle, lingering deference, and once the glow of the fire lighted her face, pale, with dark, grey eyes, and brown curls encircling. Something in the eyes, something in the pallor, thrilled Gasparine's forlorn heart with pity, *for it seemed to her that a broken heart was ministering to her own....*

Yes; she knew now who the stranger was, she reflected dimly—Miss Grace, M.A., of the College. She knew her by sight, and had sometimes heard her speak, on those rare occasions, when, with Gaspar, she went to the public College lectures. Why was it that something in the movement and expression of the successful lady-lecturer always sent Gasparine's thoughts back to a scene which had, in London, been branded into her brain? Was there a likeness? No. The girl, or child, in that bitter memory had golden hair and soft blue eyes. This woman's eyes were grey, her hair dark brown.

And yet, in a painful, but vivid phantasmagoria, the old broken scenes flitted across her mind again. The painted villa in St. John's Wood; the artistic garden-wilderness, into which their poor lodgings looked; the French windows; the blaze of light; the men and women that came and went; the balcony, with creepers; the child with her golden hair and red cloak. A mist passed across the garden, and lifted. She saw again the child, with her head turned towards the road, listening.... Then the last scene, on that dull, damp evening, the man waiting, the child's bird-like flight to him, the struggle, the cruel blow ... the motionless bundle on the wet walk, the little naked arm and shoulder ... the lights in the French windows, and the coward, with his thick, red bull-neck laughing and talking indifferently with the handsome women there....

The strange girl worked silently at the room, while this fantastic association passed through Gasparine's sick mind, and was listlessly dismissed.

A moment later it was renewed with sudden vividness, as the stranger, coming through the partition, paused, with a gleam of light across her face, her head turned gazing over her shoulder.

"But the child had golden hair, and such pink cheeks!" thought Gasparine.

Strange that it should so persistently rise from a past of so many years and haunt Gasparine until, beside the slight, girlish form that worked, she could almost see the shadowy child's form, in short evening dress, phantom-tall, with figure prematurely formed, as the low bodice showed; the red cloak like a stain across her arm, then drifting into shadow, and the golden hair drawn artfully back from the tiny, shell-pink ears.... Then the dream vanished, as the gnawing of the agony, diverted for a moment, renewed itself.

Magically the room changed under the strange girl's hands. The dust, the dirt, the closeness vanished. The sweet, wet, spring air came in. The old boxes slipped—deft hands helping them—into places where they looked friendly and at ease. The partition was drawn aside, and Gasparine could see a fire, brisk and clean, a little tin kettle placed thereon, and singing. An easy-chair was at the fire, and in another moment a table was placed beside it.

The sight, the memory of *his* last evening, when the table had been placed just so, and he, smiling and talking, tried to hide even from himself the fact that he was dying—all this was too much for her. With a doglike and most lamentable cry she sank her head upon her knees. Then she felt an arm round her, very lightly and gently, not oppressively, and the soft voice, like a silver, distant sound,—

"Poor soul! How wearisome life is! How hateful the light, the daily routine, the spying eyes! *I know it all*—how empty the rooms are, how every movement, every sound, and every touch, call up haunting memories, that cut and sting with unspeakable anguish; how heartless the harsh, stranger voices sound, speaking of ordinary things, when the world's worst has happened for you."

The arm closed round her more firmly, and a slender hand touched her hair.

"Poor child! poor child! It doesn't do you any good either to know that others have suffered the same. No, no. *I* have suffered, too, poor dear; I hate the people, too. But listen. *Life must be lived.* Life must be lived. You now, poor soul, are friendless, a poor teacher, as I am, too, struck with a great blow. I saw you, the solitary mourner of your dead. *I, too, have a grave.* No, do not mistake me for a sister of charity, or a missionary visitor—I am none of them, but a lonely one like you...."

"Come, poor soul, I am going to put aside your clothes, and you are going to eat something. This hard bread and cold sausage is all you have eaten for a week. That is not wise. First we must eat a little, and then we can talk. Even in sorrow one must eat; it gives balance to the brain."

For a long time she continued to talk on, in this monotonous, gentle strain. Then, so gently and gradually, that the mourner was hardly aware, with hands angel-tender, she moved the coarse water-proof cloak, and, kneeling, unlaced the wet boots. Shadows of deep pity and disgust crossed the strange young face as she saw the threadbare clothing of the elder woman, but she did not rest until she had placed Gasparine in bed, and forced her, gently, irresistibly, to take the soup she had prepared.

Still talking low and continuously—for the dazed mourner never spoke—she folded the poor clothes, leaving everything ready for the morning.

The extreme poverty of the rooms, combined with an unerring refinement, except for the dust and dirt which had lately gathered, struck her. "Ah, God!" she whispered to herself. "Some of us are born into the wrong world, I think."

"Dear, you will sleep to-night. To-morrow I shall come again. You know me, don't you? I am Lotus Grace of the College. I know you are not angry that I came. To-morrow I shall tell you more. Now lie quite still, and close your eyes, and I shall stay here till you sleep...."

It was late when the fevered, brilliant eyes closed, and the stranger, with a little quiver at the corners of her patient mouth, laid the thin hand under the bed-clothes, and, with a last look round, went softly away.

For the first time in a fortnight Gasparine slept without moans and cries.

CHAPTER III
THE COTTAGE INMATES

After leaving Gasparine, the strange girl turned across the town. She moved with the rapidity of a shadow, which a bird casts as it flies—swift, unerring, as if some winged thing from above directed her. Head bent a little, in thought, she went up Queen's Street, through the Wynd, apparently unaware of the curious glances and remarks of the rowdy population of that district, and out by the High School unto the Castle Walk. Descending by the English Church to Clarendon Place, she cut across Victoria Square, and the King's Park, and out into the Polmaise Road.

Up the dark road, soft with recent rain, she strode, with the steady air of one who has a good distance ahead.

About two miles from the town, close to a pine plantation, and on the right of the road, a cottage stood—a pretty nest, with large gardens. Passing the iron gate, and entering the gaily-lighted and welcoming hall, the girl paused, for a child's voice was heard singing.

"Madam," called the girl, standing at the foot of the staircase, and speaking to some one in a room to the right, "why is that child allowed to remain awake so long?"

"The brat is a witch, I think," called a pretty voice, querulously. "No one could work with her to-night. What kept you so late, Lo?"

"A lecture," answered the girl, and was about to go upstairs, when again a shrill burst of song proclaimed a small and wakeful presence. Lo turned and entered a room on the left, an airy bedroom, with a large, white bed and a tiny crib. In the latter sat the troublesome baby, a dear, solemn, precocious-looking creature, who peered, between yellow elf-locks, at the threatening and insulted intruder, and paused in her shrill, Shakespearean madrigal, with a badly pronounced word on her lips.

"Ladybird, do you know how late it is?"

The elf vouchsafed a nod.

"And don't you think it's naughty to sing loud about 'Full

fathom five thy father lies,'[1] annoying Mrs. Grace? Lie down quietly, and go to sleep."

"I can't sleep," said the elf solemnly.

"Then you must be quiet, without singing."

"I don't want to sing," said the elf. "It bursts out of me itself."

"Well, Mrs. Grace will come and whip you."

"She's been twice. I don't care."

Lo went over, laid the child down, covered her, and said,—

"You are to be quiet. I forbid you to sing."

The creature turned on the pillow silently; but the little, rueful face, and a tear, claimed sympathy for her weariness. At another time, perhaps, it would have been unnoticed, but to-day Lo felt her own pain anew.

She bent and lifted the child.

"Hush, then," she whispered. "Don't let Mrs. Grace hear you, and you can come upstairs with me."

The baby entered into the spirit of this secret, rubbed her last tear on Lo's nose, and whispered loudly into her ear, as she was borne upstairs,—

"We bettah be vury cay-ah-ful not ter let Mrs. Grace heah, eh? She kent ketch me upstairs, eh?"

"No. But you mustn't sing."

"Oh no. It doesn't burst any more, just at present."

Lotus hastened with her burden upstairs.

The inmates of the cottage formed a strange household, much criticised by certain of their townspeople. A handsome, middle-aged lady, of rather dashing appearance; a young lady of eccentric style, and incomprehensible, unapproachable character; and a little girl of bird-like presence and sound.

About three years before, Miss Lotus Grace, M.A., had been appointed to a lectureship in the Ladies' College, a preparatory school for the University education of women, lately founded. It was an experiment on the most advanced educational methods, and in connection with all the Universities and highest schools in the three kingdoms and abroad. For a short time, Miss Grace, remarkably youthful for her position, lodged alone, and succeeded in making herself obnoxious to many people, necessary to the College, and adored by a few.

---

1 William Shakespeare, *The Tempest*, Act I, Scene 2; sung by Ariel to Ferdinand, who believes (falsely) that his father has drowned in a ship-wreck. The final scene of the play reunites father and son.

Then Mrs. Grace appeared, the cottage was taken, and a strong impression went about that Mrs. Grace was wealthy, and must be devoted to her niece to come and make a home for her in Stirling. It was also decided that they were both very proud; probably because Professor Raymond, President of the College Board, who lived in Oxford, and came to examine the College occasionally, was a great friend of theirs, and always dined with them. It was undecided whether or not they came from Oxford or were related to Professor Raymond. It was *quite* certain they were too reticent and "uppish" to be really irreproachable.

Indifferent to all these impressions, Miss Lotus Grace tilled her soil arduously. Nervous and uncertain of her work at first, and concealing all her feelings and fears under a sullen, gentle impassiveness, she was soon considered one of the most promising lady-lecturers, and occasionally was sent to give lectures in neighbouring towns, for the benefit of the College. People declared that the brown curls which fell to her shoulders were an absurd affectation;[1] but to her students her curls, cap, and gown, were perfection, and her mysterious smile held them like a spell. Perhaps it was true, as people said, that she bewitched the girls.

A short time after the arrival of Mrs. Grace there appeared for several weeks in the local papers advertisements for "child to adopt," "child-boarder," "home for child." Now it was a child wanted a home, now it was a home wanted a child. Then the advertisements ceased, and Ladybird made her appearance.

"What an absurd thing to do, Miss Grace!" a fellow-teacher remarked to Lotus.

"Yes, isn't it? Not the sort of thing you'd be guilty of," was Lo's answer, with her ineffable half-smile, and the matter stopped perforce.

For within the College Miss Grace had the name of being the cleverest young woman, and the greatest devil. The teachers generally were 'ware of her. The story went that to a poor young teacher, she had, for a year, been exceedingly kind. Discovering, at the end of that time, that her *protégée* had acted a traitor's part, and amused the younger students by imitating her peculiar accent, turns of speech, walk, and small mannerisms, giving them out as affectations, and falsely colouring many little acts, Miss Grace smiled her mystic smile, and was heard to remark, casually,—

---

1 With the exception of a brief period in the 1870s, the custom in the Victorian age was for adult women to wear their hair up. Lotus wears her hair in an unconventional (and childlike) fashion.

"I don't think that girl will do in the College."

Then—how it happened, none knew; Miss Grace was never heard to say a word against the girl—but, step by step, bit by bit, Miss Bell lost favour. The girls turned against her first, and at the end of a term she was advised to send in her resignation.

One girl in the College held and flourished the secret.

"I know all about it," cried Ethel. "Miss Bell had to go because Miss Grace had made up her mind to it."

These words were brought to Miss Grace.

"The absurd child!" said Lo, with an indulgent smile, arranging her College gown, and picking up her lecture roll. "What a compliment to me! I wish I could boast so much power with truth."

Yet, strange to say, the misguided Ethel who had made the remark was miserable for a month. In class and out of class she was wretched. The teachers slighted her, she was snubbed, the opinion diffused itself through the College that she was impertinent, and her most innocent remarks were met with a reprimand.

"The only person," she remarked, sobbing, to a friend, "who is decent to me is Miss Grace. Miss Grace is the only person I care for. Why have all the others grown so beastly?"

"I don't know, Ethel. But do you really like Miss Grace? You know when Mona Lefcadio snubbed you to-day, and Miss Grace snubbed her for it, she had such a *funny* smile on her face; it was like—shall I tell you?"

"Yes. What?"

"You won't repeat?"

"No, of course not."

"It was exactly like the smile of a gentle devil. I mean, you know, a devil who has got to be gentle."

"I don't think so at all. She is always decent to me. But I do *hate* that Mona Lefcadio. Anyway, I am one of the six who have to go to Germany next month, so I can put up till then. There's that Mona—ugh! Pretty, indeed! I can't see it. I hate her!"

In the College there was one girl, a creature of flame and water, genius and strung nerves; a mad, lovable thing; a West Indian heiress, who owned a pitch lake in Trinidad. The secret was a secret easy to unravel. The West Indian, a girl of extraordinary force, ruled the College, and adored Lotus.

Walking through town one day with her adorer attendant, Lotus saw a sad sight. A one-horse hearse of the oldest fashion (for we love to die as well as live fashionably), and behind, the only mourner, a girl in an old black mantle.

"Now, who happens to be so keen for a drive this cold day?" said the West Indian, lightly.

And Lo said, in answering, sardonic tones,—

"We all become eager to drive so once in our lives, and no one begrudges us our chariot, howsoever splendid it may be."

But at the same time her eyes were on the lonely mourner, with, in them, anguish and pity.

"It strikes me," she said, "the corpse is walking behind. Who *is* the creature?"

"I know," said Mona. "She is one of Miss Blurton's teachers."

"And who is Miss Blurton?"

"She has a private school in town; a poor mean rat, she is."

"And this is her governess?"

"Yes. And I know some girls there; they say Miss Blurton treats Miss O'Neill like a dog, and pays her hardly anything, and says the meanest things of her behind her back! And——"

"I thought you despised petty gossip?"

"So I do, my own precious little Curly, so I do. But doesn't she look a poor rag?"

Lotus followed the mourner with her eyes. "Despised ... rejected ... of sorrows."[1] The words sang through her ears.

"Who is the corpse?" she asked.

"Oh, I can tell you that, too," Mona said. "Can you believe it? That ghoul had a brother. Oh, pet, you can't *think* what a beauty! Such a figure! Such eyes! We were all in love with him. Jessie Low had violin lessons from him, and sometimes he came to the evening lectures. My goodness! He listened and smiled, and looked like an angel, and that scarecrow held his hand all the time, like a mummified Juliet in second-hand clothes. Have you never observed him? Blind Curly! Well, *he* was always *beautifully* dressed. The stupid fellow gets consumption—he lies in there."

Suddenly, Lotus, with a swift, fierce motion detached the girl's arm.

"Go home!" she said imperatively. "Go home, you heartless creature!"

Mona opened her lovely mouth, and gaped.

"What? What is it?" she gasped. "Oh, my sweet, what?"

---

1 Cf. Isaiah 53:3: "He is despised and rejected of men; a man of sorrows, and acquainted with grief: and we hid as it were our faces from him; he was despised, and we esteemed him not." While this passage comes from a book of the Hebrew Scriptures, Christians have traditionally seen the "man of sorrows" as a prefiguration of Jesus.

"Leave me," said the other. "Your heartlessness disgusts me."

"Why, Lo, it was you yourself!"

Lotus stopped her fiercely,—

"*I!* You dare to question what *I* say and do? I! I! That is another affair. But who gave *you*, in your health and beauty, the right to sneer at death?"

"Oh, forgive me, Lo!"

"Do you not see? An awfully bruised and broken heart goes there."

"Lotus, I meant nothing. I know she hasn't a friend in the world."

"What!"

"Not one in the world. She and her brother lived on £30 a year."

"What!"

"It's true. 'Least, they say so. But you needn't be so mad at me."

The friend vanished; the teacher appeared.

"Go home; and please remember yourself to-morrow in College."

"Lo, please, please! ..."

"Good-bye."

Mona remained staring, too angry and hurt to move. Lotus hastened after the hearse. Up in the high cemetery on the Castle Hill, in a lonely little corner, she saw the coffin lowered into the grave. She saw the mourner, stony and unmoved, hasten away, as one hastens from a plague spot. Lo followed her. The girl got out on the Castle Walk—the beautiful Back Walk, which winds, sloping, at the top of a wooded bank, round the Castle of Stirling. Finding a sheltered spot, the mourner slipped from the path down on to the bank. Lo bent over and watched her. She was gathered, a shapeless bundle, between a boulder and a tree.

Strange! The sentiment which you possess towards me to-day, I may possess towards you to-morrow. The position you occupy to-day I may occupy to-morrow. The hero of to-day is the victim of to-morrow!

Once, with a yearning heart, Gasparine had watched a shapeless bundle of humanity, longing to give comfort, but lacking courage.

The woman who watched Gasparine now did not lack courage.

She paced quietly up and down, keeping guard, as it were. Nor did she cease to stalk the mourner until she saw her safe to her rooms in Viewfield Place.

"Do you know anything of Miss Blurton, who has a private school in town?" Lotus asked, next morning, of one of her fellow-teachers.

"I know she knows nothing of teaching."

"Do you know a Miss O'Neill with her?"

"Yes, yes; a lank creature, like a walking almshouse unsupported." The College was modern and advanced, and adopted a satirical attitude.

"Well?"

"Why you ought to know her, too, Miss Grace. She tried to get Miss Bell's place here last year. Don't you remember? Of course she hadn't a chance. The President would never dream of taking a governess of Miss Blurton's—half-educated lot, as they all are!"

"Ah!"

"Why did you want to know?"

"For no reason that you need worry over," was the coolly insolent answer, and Miss Grace departed, leaving the teacher muttering furiously.

"She is alone ... friendless and poor ... and her heart is breaking," said Lo, to herself. "In a few days her first fury of grief will be over. Let me see? I shall have finished Lady's summer frocks, Mrs. Grace's lace skirt, and Mona's sketches. That fits in well.... At the end of next week I shall go to see her."

Ladybird's dresses were interesting; to have them very dainty meant time. And these, with College and other duties, so occupied the lady M.A., that only at times she felt and remembered faintly that she had a pain to face.

CHAPTER IV
THE CREOLE

Mona, all this time in disgrace, called one evening at the cottage.

Lotus was upstairs in her study; Mrs. Grace sat in the drawing-room; Ladybird nursed her baby on the steps. Mona scowled at the child, of whom she was jealous, and Mrs. Grace, jealous too, scowled at Mona.

"Where is Miss Grace, Lady?"

Ladybird frowned.

"Can't you tell me, you spoilt cabbage?"

Ladybird nodded.

"Is she upstairs?"

Lady bent contemptuously over her doll. She did not love the

Creole's cavalier treatment, and was at no pains to conceal her resentment.

Just then Lo's whistle sounded, and waiting no further direction, Mona passed the child, and entered the hall. It was square, large for the size of the house, and light and roomy. The whole house spoke a dominant, artist mind. No crowding, only the necessary articles of furniture, and those in the simplest taste, caused the apartments to appear larger than they were. Artistic draping, soft colouring, perfect order and cleanliness, made a little palace of the cottage.

Lo's study, where Mona now went, was a large attic with French windows opening on a balcony.

"I took this house, use this room," she said to a friend once, "because all my life was lived in one hour, on a balcony, long ago. I lived there, and I died there. And now, fulfilling the necessary years of my physical life, I feel better, never well, with my balcony."

A huge writing-table, of manifold uses, with all sorts of wings, shelves, and drawers, occupied one side of the room. A wide sofa, some chairs, piled with books and papers, and a bookcase, completed the furniture. The floor was stained brown; the wide, low hearth a deep red. The walls were quaintly painted, with some skill, by Lotus herself, with all sorts of fairy scenes and glades, mountains, forests, rivers, little villages, people. This room was Ladybird's fairyland. Here, when she was particularly good, Lo took her, and told her stories, wonderfully illustrated by the walls. From the French windows and balcony a wide view over the town and plain, to the far, purple hills, added a last charm to a room of charms—a room, indeed, of magic and spells. For here it was that the student sat, and seemed to draw to herself, at will, whom she would. What her charm was none knew. Perhaps it lay in the fact that, until drawn within its resistless, relentless wheel, no one believed in it, no one thought such a thing could be.

When Mona entered, Lotus sat at her table. On a basket at her side was a pile of cambric and lace and soft-coloured ribbon— Ladybird's finery. But the student was not sewing.

Bent, with cheeks on hands, she gazed sideways from her window. Mystic, fathomless eyes, what did they see?

"Miss Grace," said Mona softly; and, coming forward, she laid an offering of whitest lilies at her shrine.

"What is it?" asked the other coldly.

Mona sat down, abashed, angry, tumultuous.

There was silence. Lo gazed from the window as if unaware of any presence. Mona fumed.

"I don't know why you treat me like this. I don't know what I've done," she whined angrily. "You won't tell me. You won't speak. It's—it's—a whole week now ... and you treat me like a dog all the time.... In College all day I——"

Lo began whistling opera airs dreamily.

Once begun, Mona raved on, yet in language curiously guarded and reserved; even while raving she seemed apprehensive.

Lo continued to whistle, or hum.

Then the passionate West Indian broke into sobs.

"It isn't kind of you. You know how I watch for you. You know I'm miserable when you're not kind to me. You do it on purpose." She suddenly lost all control. "It's true what they say of you, that you've got no heart. They all say so, and it's true."

For the first time, Lo turned and looked at her. The sad, reproachful, silent eyes pierced the young girl. She stopped, appalled. She felt where her passion had carried her—into the under-bred, *on dit*[1] style of accusation which Lo detested. She sobbed, and became violently hysterical.

Lo turned, and was again humming as she gazed from the window.

"Miss Grace, forgive me! As if *I* care *what* they say! I didn't mean to say those horrid things; I'm a pig—a beast. Forgive me. Oh, dear, sad Lo, my darling, let me call you Lo again. I've been afraid to all this week. I cried every night. Oh, Lo, don't make me wretched! You know I've no one—no one I love but you."

She hurried across the room and knelt at the girl's knee.

"You know how lonely, how unhappy I am, Lotus; there is no one understands me but you. Don't cast me off, Lo, don't!"

The lovely face was drenched in tears, which the trembling hand wiped piteously away.

Then Lo turned, and, as if only now becoming aware of her presence, she spoke gently.

"My child, you need not add your little sting to everybody else's—and yet, why not, if it relieve you? Sting on. 'Let every man please himself';[2] that is an excellent motto."

"You don't think so."

---

1 French for "it is said"; here, "gossipy."

2 In Chapter 1 of *Liberty, Equality, Fraternity* (1873), James Fitzjames Stephen sums up John Stuart Mill's moral system in *On Liberty*: "Let every man please himself without hurting his neighbour." Stephen is critical of Mill.

"Yes, but I do. My own motto is, 'Because I choose.' It is, I find, my best, unfailing reason for everything."

"Lotus, that isn't true. I know you better."

"Very well; it doesn't really matter. And you said I was cruel."

She turned her grey-black, piercing eyes upon the melting brown ones of the Creole.

"Let me see. You are, at present, at the ecstatic, school-girl age of eighteen, and I—I don't know how old I am; but when I was eighteen, I was very, very, very old."

The eyes melted into the darkest, tenderest violet. Her voice had sunk to a whisper. The earnestness of her face was indescribable; she was looking at the past, as a spirit, without emotions, might look back on its earth-life. For the pity in her eyes was not self-pity.

"Cruel? Well, perhaps; perhaps qualities are grafted on to us, or a seed sown in us that thereafter shows and acts through us without our knowledge, even in our own despite."

She seemed to muse. Mona strained towards her like a chained dog, and laid her still wet cheek upon the other's hand.

"Lo, sweet-sweet, do not look or speak like that. You who are so young—the youngest teacher in the College, and you do not look so old as I! Everybody says it."

"To return," continued Lo drily, voice and eyes changing. "At present you yearn for sentiment, emotion, passion. I am your lay-figure. In a few years you will find man is the right and legal object of these hysterics—you would have found it out long ago, but your beauty has made you proud and scornful. It will come, however, rest content."

There was a long silence. Mona seemed to reflect and puzzle over something. Then she said,—

"You mean to say, that in a little while I shall give to men that admiration and love I give to you now?"

"Yes."

The beautiful Creole smiled magically.

"No, Lo; I shall never love any one as I love you—never; man nor woman. No man will teach me life as you will. We shall always be together—in life and death. I know it."

Her great eyes grew languorous, mesmeric.

"I see it; therefore, I know. In life and death; in death, indeed, for I have seen us die together often."

For the first time a smile came into Lo's eyes, and Mona drank it in. Lo bent and kissed her.

"No more hysterics, my little girl. No wonder you frighten the canny Scotch! Fortunately I know what importance to attach to all this. Well, you came with some news. Tell it."

"Of course I have some news. Do you think I should have dared to come without some excuse?"

And now, feeling herself restored to favour, the tall creature, laughing, took her beloved in her arms.

"Oh, Lo, what a terrible creature you are! When you are good, I wonder how I can ever be afraid of you, but when you are angry (and you know, Lo, I have never yet been able to find out what I do that makes you angry), then how miserable I am! The girls, the teachers, the lectures, are all separate miseries. When you sweep past me in the halls, and the girls laugh to see me turn white, I suffocate with pain and anger. Why do you make me suffer so?"

"*What* did you say your news was?"

"Ah, yes; it's about that—that lady, you know."

Mona did not, indeed, know how she had offended, but she knew the offence had come in talking of Miss O'Neill, and now she spoke warily of the whole matter.

"What lady?"

"Miss O'Neill; Miss Blurton's teacher."

"Oh!"

"Can you believe it? Miss Blurton would have dismissed her if she had not gone to school the day after the funeral! And you know she's in most awful distress. Some one saw their rooms—the clergyman, I think—and he said they were worse than some in the Wynd. And she lives on a penny loaf and a little tea, and wears almost nothing under her dress."

"This is probably all nonsense. Gossip usually is."

"Yes, perhaps. It sounds horrible."

"Well, you must go now."

When Mona was gone, Lo sat on thinking.

"So *they say* I have no heart! No heart! ... Yes, why was I angry with Mona? General disgust at human nature, I suppose. Let me see. After all—why, bother! ... No, that must be stopped. I cannot tolerate these thorns in my path. Pin-pricks on whole flesh are trifles, but pin-pricks on a wound!" Then a look of pain settled on her face. "I must go and see this mourner. It means courage to intrude, even with help, at such a time ... and my system is non-interference ... and touching sorrow opens the old sores.... Nevertheless——"

Moving Mona's white lilies carelessly aside, she saw, beneath, a parcel. Opening it, she found a white silk sash, finely embroidered in gold and silver—an artistic treasure she had often admired. On a slip of paper was written,—

"MY LOTUS,—Measure my love. I send the child I hate the sash I most value, to please you.— MONA."

"Ladybird!" called Lotus.

The little feet pattered quickly upstairs.

"Here is a sash for you from Mona. Don't you love her any better now?"

"No. May I do what I like with the sash?"

"Yes."

"Then I shall take it to Sonny Thomas, and he will put it in his hutch, and the rabbits will tear it."

"I should like you to wear it over one of these pretty white frocks I make you."

But Ladybird shook her head, and moved towards the door.

"Love does not move her. Let us try vanity," said Lotus, to herself. "Ladybird, you will look very handsome in that sash on Sundays, walking out of church before Sonny Thomas' very eyes."

The infant paused.

"Shall I?"

"Yes."

"Then I shall keep it." And she dropped it and retired.

"Vanity, pride, jealousy, revenge—a promising character, truly," said Lo, bending to pick up the sash. "Well"—into her eyes came a strange expression—"it is no wonder!"

CHAPTER V
THEREAFTER

Gasparine wakened, the morning after Lotus' visit, with a strange feeling, as if the sacredness of her grief had been invaded.

Added to her grief was now a horrible nervous depression. She wept and screamed no more. The wildness was gone, but misery, deep, heart-piercing misery, spoke in every line of her white face and trembling frame. The courage of semi-unconsciousness, which her wildness had given her, was gone. To-day she only wanted to sink away, and be, and know nothing, for evermore. She went to school and taught, how she never knew. The words came from her parched lips, and her pupils, neither loving nor respecting her, were moved to pity. Even Miss Blurton, that wily little cockney, thought "the volcano"—for so she designated Gasparine, in confidence, to her under governess and toady, "A volcano, my dear, for all her quietness, you take my word for it"—sunk enough for pity. Her loud offer of a little wine seemed to Gasparine the last insult she could bear.

"No thank you," the girl murmured, with a piteous smile, which hid floods of the poor broken heart's tears.

"You look tired, Miss O'Neill. Rest when you get home; be sure and rest. There are the exercises you take with you; they won't take you long—but be sure and rest. And you *shud* take a glass of port wine to dinner and supper, you *shud* really, to keep up your strength. Now you're sure you won't 'ave a glass? I have it in the house, you know; 'ere in the house."

Then Gasparine went home. How awful it was! What an eternity! The clean-swept rooms, how much barer they seemed! The dust and dirt were more in sympathy with her mind. She sank by a chair, and put her head in her hands.

So Lotus found her at six o'clock, when, quietly, as before, she entered the room, laid aside her dark brown velvet cloak and cap, and came and sat on the edge of Gasparine's chair, and drew the miserable head into her lap.

"Poor soul! Poor soul!" she said. "Oh, my poor child, it is all so hideous, is it not? The swept rooms seem so empty. The dust was better; it spoke of death—and all this energy speaks of life. My poor, poor dear, I know it *all*, all so well."

She paused, and drew the thin shoulders up against her knees, and passed her tender hand over and over the untidy hair.

A long time passed silently. Once Lo, who waited for a sign, felt the body press hers, she spoke softly,—

"It will come better, dear. And there is one thing: you are very lonely, how empty! How sore! But you *have* a friend.... I'm not going to be biblical, unless you are a saint already, and not in need of biblical phrases, they're no good, and when you *are* a saint, they're mere luxury. No; I mean that I want to have you for a friend, for my friend. In a little while you will understand what I mean. We shall visit each other, and talk of our dresses, and all we mean to buy ... and take tea with one another, and have walks."

Gasparine gave a moaning sound, and stirred.

"I know, I know," Lo said. "It reminds you—no matter. Try and follow me as I speak. You know the Elm Avenue, and the King's Park where the people walk? It is lovely there. Imagine us, when we are very friendly, going there to walk some day. We might take my little boarder, a small girl, dreadfully precocious and pert, but good on the whole. Are you fond of children? She will skip in front of us with her doll. I shall have your arm—for we shall be great friends; and, by-and-by, we go up Polmaise Road, where my cottage is, and have tea, and——"

Then there broke from the mourner a cry of torture, so keen and terrible, that Lo drove the nails into her palms, to prevent the shudder, which passed through her body, from communicating itself to the figure leaning against her.

"Oh, but *he is dead*! *Dead!* Do you not know? Do you not understand? Think! *In the ground!* Oh, he would have been so glad, so glad of a friend! So glad and grateful that any one should be kind to me! And now that it should come, and *too late*, too late! He is dead, my poor, poor bird and darling, dead and cold! Oh God, God, *cruel*, unjust, accursed God!"

"She has found her voice," said Lo, to herself. "The worst is over."

It was so. With sobs and cries Gasparine's sorrow found speech, and the sense of hurt and cruel injustice by an Unseen Power faded somewhat.

With comfort wise and gracious, Lo soothed and dressed this open wound—now with a few tactful words, now with a little hopeful gleam, now with a gentle commonplace, faintly promising a smile.

"I know how you loved him, poor dear, and I know how beautiful and good he was, and how lovable. One quite a stranger to him told me so, and said that you were like him."

The flattery was balm through all her pain.

"Like him! They thought she was like him! That god! That angel!"

"And do not be afraid that he forgets you, or does not know. Ah, no, poor dear! The grave is narrow and deep, and the grass above is green, but love will pierce the darkness, oh, fear not! And he, lying there, still, so still! Undreaming, thinks of you; and your love fills the stillness, and darkness, with light and fragrance."

Her voice grew dreamy. (To herself she was saying, "What nonsense I am talking.")

"I have flowers in my little garden. You shall pluck the best. You shall lay them above him; he will feel them there, and their perfume will go down to him like your love on his breast."

Drowsily the words died away, and the last, caught sobs were faint in Gasparine's throat. When Lo spoke again, it was in a cheerful, awaking tone.

"Listen to me, dear. I have a plan. But first, will you tell me your name, if I may ask it?"

"Gasparine—and *his* was Gaspar."

"Gaspar! It is a lovely name. Well, then, Gasparine, does it matter to you if I make tea? I have been working this morning from nine o'clock, with only five minutes' rest. A teacher I am fond of was ill, and I took her place. I am very tired." She raised herself. "If you would help me, Gasparine, it would not take so long."

The voice was so soft and love-like, that Gasparine could not resist. She rose, and in a few minutes the kettle boiled, and the tea was ready.

"Now you must hear my plan, Gasparine. I want you to come and stay with me for a few days. It must be gloomy here just yet. Come. I have a little white room, so fresh. It gets all the west sun, and such a view! It is next my study."

Gasparine shook her head. She was, indeed, quite overcome, flattered, overwhelmed, self-reproachful. That this strange, fascinating, dream-like presence, whom she dimly remembered and recognised, should seek her out, visit her, *invite her*, was a marvel to a life that had known none of society's common courtesies. But that it should come so late, *there* was the sting, that *he* should not know, should not share ... to desert his rooms.... She shook her head.

But Lo was stronger, and that evening she turned the key in Gasparine's door, and in her own hand carried the bag, with the one or two required articles.

It was a wonderful journey, that two miles' walk up the hill to the cottage. Lo steadfastly carried the bag, and a faint murmur of humour overcame Gasparine when she contrasted the ragged bag, a relic of the O'Neills, with the rich velvet mantle of her new friend. The sound was instantly stifled in pain—*he* was not there to laugh too.

The walk was a silent one. Gasparine felt, with dreamy intensity, the softness of the air, the wafting of the leaves, the aroma from the grass, and the friendly lights from the cottage windows. In the square and brightly lighted hall she experienced a curious sensation, as if the past were rushing over her with torrent-like force. A fair child stood in the light, in a peculiar, listening attitude. The fair hair, the remarkable colouring of skin and eyes, seemed in some way to pierce Gasparine's memory. Then her new friend said to the little girl,—

"Ladybird, why have you not gone to bed?"

The child started, and bounded towards Lotus, then drew up sharp, and stared.

"Tell me, Lady, why was it?"

"I could not help it," said the child. "The dog howled, and I heard you crying."

A ghastly look came over Lo's face, but she spoke quite gently to the child.

"I was not crying, Ladybird."

"I heard you," said the child, gathering her little fair brows with a look of suffering. "And the dog howled so. Somebody will be ill," she added, convincingly.

Silently Lo bent and lifted Ladybird, and, still with the bag, and smiling faintly to Gasparine, went up the stairs. With the same intensity of realisation Gasparine felt that her new friend had grown very weary, and that there was, in her attitude, something which expressed an awful burden borne with patience and courage.

The little white room next Lo's study was indeed a nest. Gasparine had not been in such a room since her step-mother's lifetime, and for whiteness, and freshness, and comfort, no spot she ever knew could compare with it. The brightness of the fire, the whiteness of the bed, the cosiness of the morning breakfast-tray! She began to realise what is meant by rest.

Here she moaned out her sorrow and her loss, cared for, she knew not, perhaps never realised, how tenderly. She was too sick and life-weary to know why she never felt teased, why, just when the loneliness became unbearable Lotus appeared to talk for a few minutes brightly, or the child came up with flowers or fruit, or Mrs. Grace, with her work, to chat or propose a stroll in the garden. She never knew how the fine mind of Lotus consoled her without words, remaining invisible.

In a few days Gasparine's great pleasure was to sit at her window, gaze on the dreamy view, yearn over the past, and write letters to Gaspar. Strange letters! Strange, agonising effort of the living to reach the dead! Then she would pause, and put her hand before her eyes, and out of the darkness call that face.... And, answering the magic of her love, would come, dim-clear, the shining eyes and sweet smile of the dead.

"Oh, the dear face that bent to me, when I only asked leave to worship! Oh, lovely love and time! What shall I do to bring you back, here to my eyes as in my heart? The days cannot be so cruel as to divide your memory from me. Oh, that love that was mine, that crown that was mine!—My crown, that death has turned to thorns! ..."

At other times she loved to imagine a miracle by which he was restored to her. She pictured it to herself with all its details, and saw herself show him the letters she had written, and tell him of the agony she had suffered, and then sink upon his breast in rapture.... To have that, was there any scorn or suffering she would not have borne!

That poignant stage, too, passed, and, in softened moods of many tears, she told her sorrow anew, in gentle verses and little songs, too sacred for judgment; the reality of the words being their greatest strength with her.

On one of these days Ladybird came to see her, bringing her doll, to show its new shoes.

"Lotus made them," stated the child, as who should say, "God created the world; it was a trifle for *Him*, of course."

Then she settled herself in an arm-chair, and looked, with a child's remorseless scrutiny, in Gasparine's face.

"You've bin cryin' *again*," she said reprovingly, with knitted brows. "Would that man *like* you to cry so much?"

"What man, baby?"

"I'm not baby, I'm *Lady*; it's short for Ladybird." She looked put out. The mistake bothered her. Then she recovered herself, and said, "P're'ps you didn' ketch my name? I mean the man they put in the ground so's you couldn' kiss him any more. I heard Lo tellin' Mis' Grace 'bout it, en' she said I mustn't sing 'Willie's drowned in Yarrow,'[1] these few days.... I'd *prefer* to sing it."

Gasparine looked at the odd little creature with a feeling that was almost fear. The thing was so wise and old and heartless, in spite of her dangling locks of gold, flower's face, and wee blue shoes.

"How old are you, Lady?" she asked.

Ladybird looked at her sharply, to discover whether this question was asked out of idle curiosity or genuine interest. Satisfied, she returned, "I'm six," and added, "I'm small for my age," with the air of one disclaiming an honour.

"You may sing the song if you like, Lady."

"Oh no," said the creature, with gathered brows; "not when Lo told me not to."

---

1   "Rare Willie Drowned in Yarrow, or, the Water o Gamrie," a traditional Scots ballad that is a woman's lament for her dead lover.

"You are a good girl to obey Lo."

"Yes. And, besides, I'd as lief sing 'The Jew's Daughter.'[1] You know it?

> "'The rain rins doun, the Mirrilan' toun,
> Sae does it rin doun the Spa,
> Sa do the lads o' Mirrilan' toun
> When they play at the ba',
>   *   *   *   *   *
> An' oot an' cam' the Jew's daughter.'"

The little voice was deliciously shrill. Gasparine was enjoying it when Lady stopped abruptly, struck by additional reasons.

"An' then Lo will give me the green paroquet I want; and, besides, if I didn't obey Lo, Mis' Grace would beat me, you see."

Mrs. Grace seemed, indeed, to be a somewhat strict disciplinarian; but then it was necessary with so indulgent a person as Lotus in the house. And certainly with Gasparine the aunt of Miss Grace was courteous and kind.

"It is kind of Miss Grace to have me," Gasparine said, one day, as she sat with the elder lady under the verandah. She said the words mechanically, not really realising, in her deep sorrow, that the world required any courtesy from her. She was even vaguely surprised at the warmth of Mrs. Grace's acceptance of the words.

"Lotus lives to make others happy; she is the best and noblest girl that breathes, I think."

"You love her dearly?"

"She is the light of my eyes."

"The little girl is fond of her too?"

"Oh!" in an indescribable tone; "that boarder-brat! Her latest fad, for whom she will never receive a penny! Small wonder the imp loves her! She spoils the child, and it has no gratitude. Lotus sows always on barren ground, and reaps what she has not sown—reaps the sorrow of the sowing of others."[2]

---

1 This is another Scots ballad. The title character kills a knight who is trying to recover the ball that he has accidentally kicked into the window of her castle. It is also known as "Sir Hugh."

2 Mrs. Grace's remark combines elements of two of Jesus' parables: the parable of the talents (Matthew 25:26) and the parable of the sower (Matthew 13:1–9; Mark 4:1–9; Luke 8:4–8).

"She shall not for me, I hope," Gasparine thought; for something stern and sorrowful in the aunt's handsome face struck her.

The conversation was not continued, for just then the shrieks of Lady caused them to look towards the gate. Lo entered at a trot, to which she was urged by the blue heels of Lady, driven into her slender sides, that damsel being mounted on her back.

"Faster," cried the little slave-driver. "Faster, donkey, faster!"

All laughed—even stern Mrs. Grace. It was Gasparine's first laugh for many weeks.

When Lady went off, the aunt said,—

"You are spoiling the child, Lotus."

A look that was almost terror came into the girl's deep eyes.

"Surely not, Madam, dear," she said, gently. "One must be easy with all childhood. Childhood is such a pliable age. Any hardness will at once impress itself upon it. Do you not think so, Gasparine?"

"I know so very little of children. Ladybird is very amusing to me."

"Here comes Mona," said Lo, turning towards the gate. "Let us ask her."

The beautiful Creole entered. She nodded contemptuously to Gasparine, who secretly admired her, and felt unreasoning pride only to come within speaking distance of such fashion, beauty, and grace.

"We are talking of childhood, Mona," said Lotus, skilfully, yet carelessly avoiding the kiss Mona desired to give. "Should one be indulgent or strict with children?"

"I don't know anything of *children*," said Mona, sullenly, "but if you allude to the brat Lady I should advise bread and water, and daily whippings."

Lotus shot a look at the Creole, but said nothing.

"I certainly think Lotus spoils the brat," said Mrs. Grace, but with a conciliatory smile.

"What do *you* think, Gasparine?" Miss Grace asked, turning to her guest with an odd quiver of the eyelid.

"I think it's too bad that every one should call her a brat," said Gasparine, with instinctive resentment of Mona's contempt.

"She *is* a brat—a nobody's child," growled the West Indian, with a sullen set of her teeth.

Lotus left them for a minute. When she returned, Ladybird was in her arms. She carried the child into the centre of the group.

"Now, Ladybird," she said.

Ladybird pointed imperiously towards the garden gate.

"Go home, Mona," she said, with curious vindictiveness for a child. "Go home, now, at once. We don't want you, Lotus nor I. Go away."

Mona turned her stung face and quivering lip to Lotus.

"Lotus, do you mean it?"

Lo nodded; so slightly, Gasparine scarcely saw. Mona turned and silently disappeared.

Then Lotus kissed the child and put it down.

"Good-night, Madam," she said briefly.

Though it was only five o'clock, they saw no more of her that night. But Gasparine found Mrs. Grace sitting in the drawing-room alone, weeping grievously, and heard Lady crying and complaining loudly,—

"Mis' Grace w'ipped me, an' I mean to tell Lo. I hate her, I do!"

END OF VOLUME I

CHAPTER VI
LO'S TEACHERS

Meantime Lotus drove Gasparine to school every morning, going herself to the College. Gasparine did her teaching as usual, and Ladybird and Miss Grace called for her at two o'clock.

The all-unusual care was delightful. Every time the little dog-cart stopped, Miss Blurton screwed her pale blue eyes, and snapped with her thin lips. She was in truth bursting with curiosity to know how Miss O'Neill came to be staying with the haughtiest of that haughty College set, Miss Grace. But Gasparine's habit of silence left her no opportunity for gossip.

The first time that Gasparine roused voluntarily to anything like outside interest, was on hearing one of Gaspar's songs ascend from the cottage garden to her little room. She opened the window and listened. A tremulous soprano was singing one of Schubert's mournful "Müller Lieder." It was Gaspar's favourite, "Withered Flowers."

With what an anguish his violin used to cry the pain of the heart-broken lover!

> "All ye little flowers that she gave to me,
> One shall lay you in the grave with me.
> Ach! Tears do not make May-joy
> Nor make dead love bloom again.
> And spring will come, and flowers will bloom,
> And all the little flowers she gave to me,
> They shall be laid in the grave with me."[1]

Again the old agony swept over Gasparine.

"Thy song, my own! Oh! When the old love dies of the cold, of the cold, sweet love," she moaned, "I have only to hear your songs, and, kindled once more, as at a white fire, it burns and I see you again; again the hands, and eyes, and voice.... Oh! my love, my dear love!"

She looked out of the window, and saw Lotus and the tall figure of Mona cross the lawn. The Creole, with her willowy form and fashionable dress, was a picture to give pleasure to eyes however critical; her arm encircled Lo, and the tall head was bent

---

1 This is "Trockne Blumen," as in Book I, Chapter 6, but with the first line more accurately translated.

over the curly one. Gasparine turned away, bowing her head in anguish. She remembered how she had crooned the song to her darling in his death agony. Nevertheless, from now the song had another association for her.

Life began to call to the bereaved one. The bright little room, the dainty and nourishing food, the soothing and exciting magnetism of the house, roused, in spite of herself, an interest in Gasparine. She began to watch the people and question. Who? What?

She found out soon that visitors were frequent, and further observation told her that they were disciples, for the same people came again and again. As she grew better, she spent her evenings in the drawing-room with Mrs. Grace and Ladybird; for Lotus was usually in her study, and often Gasparine, going up to her room, heard voices ringing the changes from merriment to tears. Mona was a daily visitor. By-and-by, gently invited by Lotus, Gasparine went and sat in the study too. And there she saw the people coming and going. Girl-students, young lady-lecturers, rather rarely a man, often children. To meet so many people, observe their manners, and hear them talk, was at once a great excitement and a grateful distraction to Gasparine.

One evening, after dinner, going upstairs, Mona joined them.

"Do you expect any one to-night, Lo?" she asked.

"Yes; Gray Grayson."

"That hideous one! Why will you throw your time away upon him?"

"Why, the poor fellow has lately been converted, as he calls it; he is at boiling-water point. His people at home laugh at him. He wants sympathy,—some one to listen to him."

"And his sister meantime says, in the College, that you want to marry him," cried Mona furiously.

Lo gave a faint, faint smile, and looked dreamily across her balcony. Mona sat devouring her with her eyes, yet speaking in an angry, scolding voice.

"Converted! Rubbish! Who believes in all that nowadays? He——"

She paused, but not abashed, as the youth entered. A tall young man, some books in his hand, and Lady on his shoulder. Gasparine turned indifferently from his pleasant, rather sensual face; nothing less than her brother's beauty pleased her yet. Mona, in very ill humour, bounced away.

Lady followed.

"You know, Lo, I brought those two sermons you thought you'd like to hear."

Lo gave a tiny sigh, and took up some sewing. Gasparine looked listlessly out of the window.

"They are tremendously convincing, Lo! I cannot understand how any one can read them and remain blind."

"It *is* curious how obstinate people can be."

"And, you see, when we can believe in this doctrine of spirits.... why ghosts are explained. And it is so reasonable, and——"

"Yes; let me hear."

The young man settled himself and read. With an earnest and serious air he laid down his doctrine of ghosts. Lo worked meanwhile, with now and then a movement of the lips, and a far-off smile in the eyes. Gasparine listened with impatience.

"Imagine!" she said to herself. "The man makes mistakes in pronunciation even. And what nonsense he reads! ... How amused Gaspar would be! Ah! *He is dead!*"

"Is it not tremendously convincing, Lotus?" Gray Grayson asked.

"I'm sure there is a great deal of truth in it, Gray. It does not appeal to me, of course, with quite the same force as it does to you. Perhaps I have not the same grasp of faith as you.... I believe I have a very selfish nature."

"Oh, I believe there are heaps of people quite as selfish as you," said Gray Grayson generously, though he felt it hard to forgive her for what was so plain and obvious. "But I confess I cannot understand any clear intellect remaining unconvinced after hearing a sermon like that."

Lotus only smiled.

Gasparine became fully awake, and, without pausing to think, indignantly remarked that "she thought the sermon was nonsense." Then, conscious of her great step into social life, she blushed crimson. The young man gave her a look of polite dislike.

When he was gone, Gasparine said,—

"Miss Grace, how have you patience to listen to all that nonsense?"

Lotus drew a sigh.

"One *grows* patient. It is kind to give him a safety-valve. He is a good young fellow, and those religious views, absurd to you and me, may save him at a dangerous stage of his life. His is a nature requiring restraints, and it is good to see him seek them. He deserves encouragement."

Then Gasparine went wondering away.

The next day, greatly to Gasparine's surprise, when she came out of school at two o'clock she found Lotus standing with the dog-cart at Miss Blurton's gate.

"Gasparine," she said, "Professor Raymond has come to examine the College to-day, and will dine with us. I can't go out now, so will you, dear, drive yourself out, and give this letter to 'Madam'?" Madam was Lo's pet name for Mrs. Grace.

With a delightful sense of responsibility, Gasparine took the reins and the letter. The new charm, of being connected with other people's lives, and of use to them, began to make itself felt.

Great excitement reigned in the cottage on production of the letter. Ladybird went about shrilling, "Rayez is coming! Payez is tuming! Coming, tuming, juming!" Mrs. Grace at once drove into town, with a grave, housewifely face.

Late in the afternoon, Gasparine, who had been sitting on the balcony, heard triumphant shrieks of merriment from Ladybird, and, looking to the road, saw the mite in a gentleman's tall hat, and, a second later, a man of unusual height appeared in Lady's sun-bonnet.

At dinner, Gasparine was introduced to Mr. Raymond. She watched. Mr. Raymond was a magnificent man. His age might be guessed at anything between forty-five and fifty. Not a thread of grey was in his thick, tawny hair. In the intense sapphire of his tender eyes one seemed to see his childhood and his boyhood still, and in his ringing laugh when he romped with Lady. The face was clean-shaven and bronzed, the expression joyous, stimulating, commanding. If there had been sorrow, the carved lips held it subdued. Faith, and love of life, and human joy, shone from the eyes. Tall, broad-shouldered, moving gracefully, fashionably dressed, this professor was a revelation to Gasparine, whose keen eyes and ears were all on the alert. "If he has a fault at all," she decided, on first impression, "it is that he is too much the 'young lady's' hero, after his first youth. And perhaps he squares his shoulders too often, and throws back his head."

He was *grand*, all the same. Beside him, Lotus, who impressed most people as being tall or commanding, seemed shrunk to a child. The brilliant talk between her and her guest dazzled Gasparine, and it seemed to her that the man watched Lo as one searches a mystery. Constantly he seemed to turn to her with a question in his eyes.

And Lo was changed. The gentle, weary, listless air was gone. A white spirit, burning and fervent, listened and spoke. Gasparine forgot herself listening. The revelation of a wide, new life going on all around her, which she had never realised, entranced her. Politics, questions of the day, socialism, women, education, literature, and, last, and most earnestly, religion; the conflict of newer forms of the old faiths with science.

It was late when at last there came a little sigh of silence. Ladybird lay asleep in Mr. Raymond's arms. He rose, as if to lay her on a sofa, and said, smiling,—

"Come, do not tell *me* you are a pessimist. Why, I look to you as one of those who will help unravel our problems, and make the upward path an easier one for this little lass and her generation."

Lo smiled gently, and shook her head.

"Ah! I shall convince you one day," he said, forgetting his purpose with Ladybird, and dropping on one knee lightly, with the sleeping child still against his breast, by Lo's chair. "You say my faith is only an emotion fostered, and stronger or weaker according to temperament. But what will you say, friend, if I tell the case of a man, who, in the easy, commonplace circumstances of life, suddenly wakened one night to the conviction that he was not his own, that his life, his intellect, his health, everything he had, indeed, were his only in trust, to be accounted for; that he was, indeed——"

He paused.

"Bought with a price,"[1] quoted Lotus, with raised eyebrows, and supplying the words she knew he sought, with a scorn too gentle and refined to be taken amiss.

"Yes, 'bought with a price'; not in sentimental emotionalism, but in real, serious earnest. Well, this came home to the man, and from that moment, in the commonplace of every-day life, he felt that his belief was a real, living thing. In the depths of a trouble that deprived him of friends, threw him into sordid circumstances, among ignoble aims, he felt it was the one reality for him. How of that?"

"Such a man would naturally cling to an ideal," said Lo gently.

"Nay, then, listen. He stood one night alone on London Bridge, after two days' starvation, no farthing, or prospect of bread or bed; yet he never doubted Christ's love."

He paused, clasped one arm round the little child, and, raising the other hand, he seemed to preach at a long line of young white women, who listened but did not heed. To Gasparine it seemed that his voice rolled over the bowed, brown head, away into space.

---

1 In 1 Corinthians 7:23, Paul stresses that Christians belong to Christ: "Ye are bought with a price; be not ye the servants of men."

"Oh, Lotus, do you not believe in the salvation He wrought for us here?—for you, for me, for this dear little one we both love?"

A deadly pallor passed over Lo's face. Slowly she raised her head.

"You have not finished your young man," she said. "I am anxious to hear the end."

"Yes, yes. Hear then. When his love proved false; when by a step he could have made himself rich, respected, loved, and taken his revenge,—he folded his hands for love of Christ." He paused, and bent his lips to the child's fair hair, for tears were in his eyes. "What say you of him, Lotus?"

"I should say his nature was noble and emotional, and that adversity proved it," she said, very softly; for something told her he spoke of himself.

"Ay, but," said the man, looking up, the wet flash in his tender sapphire eyes, "when all these things have righted themselves, and life has become pleasant and fair, what do you say when you hear that, to the man still, the joy in life is the joy in Christ?"

"I should say," she said slowly, "that his training had been strongly religious—either Puseyite or Evangelistic[1] (they usually achieve the same ends, with a difference, *when* they succeed); that his nature was sweet, healthy, and tenacious, with the Saxon tenacity at its strongest, which *never* alters, and only death can cut."

He bit his lip, slightly blushing for the truth of what she said. He might have answered, but she suddenly sat upright, and spoke as Gasparine had never heard her speak before, throwing out her hands.

"Read me the case that I give you, in my turn," she said. "What is it, when a woman, a child, kneels in agony, night after night, praying, 'O Jesus, help me!'—only that, moaned out, hour after hour, like the cries of an animal? What is it when the woman, passing through the waters of Mara,[2] scorned, scouted,

---

1 These words identify two very different forms of religious enthusiasm within the nineteenth-century Church of England. Puseyites (those who sympathized with the clergyman and scholar Edward Pusey) were "High Church" Anglicans who sought to bring the Church's religious practice closer to the model of Roman Catholicism. Evangelicals, who tended to be "Low Church" in their devaluation of ritual elements and their focus on the unique authority of Scripture, emphasized justification by faith and deemphasized the power of the institutional church.

2 Exodus 15:23–25. In their exodus from Egypt, the people of Israel encounter the bitter waters of Marah, which become sweet when Moses follows God's instructions and throws a tree in them.

desolate, prays incessantly, 'Christ, help me! Only a little comfort; only a little help; only to know it is for Thy sake, and I can bear it'? What is it, when the woman, with brain matured now, sits listening, listening—oh God, *how* she listens for the whisper of the Spirit, that will make her life bearable—only bearable, no more! What can you answer me now?"

He sprang up, so eagerly, almost hopefully, that Ladybird nearly fell, and, waking with a start, buried her nose in his neck, and clung there, too happy to be cross.

"I say, dear, dear friend, that, if the woman will but wait and listen, she shall hear the Spirit's voice at last."

He bent and touched her hand.

"I do not know the woman, but I think she has grown weary," she said, with sudden coldness.

There was a silence; then he kissed the child, laid it on the sofa, and bowing, went off.

Lotus turned and spoke to Gasparine, with a tired smile.

"There he goes—a great heart. Some day he will take into its shelter a girl and make her, ah! I cannot tell you how happy, with his love. Well, well, I seem to be a good subject for sermons. My friends are all anxious to convert me. I must, indeed, be very wicked."

The next evening came half-a-dozen young satellites from the College; splendidly dressed young peacocks, who glared superciliously at Gasparine—"that Miss Blurton's teacher."

Lotus was the soul of them. She teased them, flirted with them, admired or criticised their dresses, amused, entertained, or fed them, and, when they were gone, sat down to a pile of work with her weary, mournful air.

A questioning wonder came into Gasparine's heart. Who or what was this being of manifold aspects? She watched Lotus now with a closeness that allowed not a look or tone to escape. She knew the very sound of the light step. She speculated on each fresh dress, and the eccentricity of the brown curls, and made shy attempts to be agreeable—a duty which had not occurred to her before. As she came more and more out of the sorrow-mist of her bereavement, she realised her position, and the debt she owed to Lo. But now she felt she owed the debt to a new person. Her comforter, whom she had known, by sight and reputation, Miss Grace—M.A., lady-lecturer at the College, was one person; "Lo," who sang and laughed, talked, worked untiringly, dreamed silently, ran, sat, ordered, listened—all with that strangest air of mournfulness—was another.

Gasparine rose, shook herself, and sought Miss Grace.

"I do not know how to thank you. All you have done for me I do not know how to express. Let me love you. I have had, in this white cottage, such a taste of peace, after strife."

Lotus looked up with strange, mystic eyes, and took the other's hands.

"The house is humanity's. You will be stronger if you will stay another week. Yes, Gasparine, let us be friends. Not that you are a very friendly girl, you born aristocrat"—there came a winning smile—"but soon, I think, you will be friendly to *me* at least. Then, when *all that* is further past, and you can bear to talk of it, you will tell me——"

"Ah, yes! And I may come to see you?"

"*I* shall certainly want to see *you*."

Then Gasparine returned to the rooms, from which she had been absent six weeks, as one goes back to a forgotten life, and there found strange things had happened. The second room was completely furnished. In a wardrobe hung some new black dresses, a coat, and hats; a chest of drawers held a plain but excellent trousseau. *Now* she knew why Lo sewed so incessantly late of nights. Then a second thought came, and she wept over it all bitterly. It was too late for *him* to know of it, and be glad; for he was dead.

CHAPTER VII
BORN OLD

Then the weeks took up their old roll; for when Gaspar died, time stood still for Gasparine—the teaching life, more lonely now— terribly lonely it would have been but for that white cottage, a beacon towards which Gasparine's steps were drawn each day by some mysterious force. To hear the name of Lotus mentioned, however casually, even by a schoolgirl, made her heart bound.

Once Miss Blurton spoke to her.

"You are better, Miss O'Neill. I'm so glad to see you look so much better. You've had a nice long visit to Miss Grace; I hope you enjoyed it?"

"I was very happy."

"They say she is very entertaining. I did not know you were friends."

"I do not know that we are; only I love her," said Gasparine, in the serene voice that nettled Miss Blurton.

"Well, I don't know, of course, but people *say* she's a terrible character—a Women's Rights woman, a socialist, and, worst of all, an atheist. I don't know, of course, an' I never say ill of any one, *never*. Only they say so, you see."

"Yes, I see."

"Mind, *I* don't say it, but people *say* she's an atheist; and that's not a good character for any one."

"Well, I don't know," Gasparine retorted, with the many sweet memories crowding upon her, "but if she be an atheist, may God send more like her!" And, with this furious and paradoxical retort, the teacher passed into the class-room, leaving Miss Blurton more than ever convinced that "that Miss O'Neill was a volcano."

There was always a welcome at the cottage, and the white face of Lo to smile. To Gasparine it soon became the most beautiful face, save one, that she had ever seen. The changes on it; the fleeting, strange smiles; the depth of sadness; the self-mockery in the eyes. Like a barren and mournful landscape, from which the traveller turns with aversion, seeing no beauty in it, but which, to the poetic soul dwelling on its borders, is full of a mystery and beauty, waste and wild. For there was in the face an expression which can only be described by the word *marred*—something painful and inexplicable.

One June evening Gasparine walked up to the cottage for some promised flowers for the dear grave. The day had been hot, and now the air was heavy with perfume, and in the garden of the cottage the breath of dying roses was oppressive.

Up in her study Lo sat, brows bent and bound. For the first time, she failed to rise and smile at Gasparine's approach.

"I came for the flowers, Miss Grace; and I wanted a little talk with you so badly."

Then Lo turned, and Gasparine saw in the eyes, and whole face, an expression of agony, intense and terrible.

"Go, Gasparine," she said. "But, oh! when you gather flowers and place them on the grave, do not forget that the dead have *rest*. And think of the graves in the hearts of the living, where there is no rest—none."

She half raised herself, and seeming to regret that she should not be as gracious and welcoming as usual, she struggled to her feet, one hand holding the white cloth which bound her head, and stumbled to the balcony.

"Look, Gasparine!" she said. "The sun and shadow on the Ochils—how beautiful it is! And the warm mist round the Abbey Craig, and here, the Castle ... and in that corner—do you see?— where the cemetery lies there the dead are—*at rest*. Talk! No.

Leave me to-day. Do not expect me to talk. It is one of the old moods come again. My life is passing, passing, and I cannot say that I have lived a day. Everywhere I see but pain. Pain, and the suggestion of pain."

"I shall go," said Gasparine. "I only tease you. May I come to-morrow?"

"Come?" Lo moved restlessly. "Yes, come. Why not?"

Gasparine went away. It pained her to think of the sorrowful face she had left—becoming so dear to her now. What was the trouble that darkened the deep eyes?

When the next day came she trembled for the time when she might go and say, "*You* are in sorrow *now*, let *me* comfort *you*." But when she went in the afternoon to Lo's study no words would come.

The student swung herself on her chair, in cap and gown, with a look of reckless, graceless scorn. It was an air Gasparine had never seen before.

"Forgive me, Gasparine, for yesterday. I was stupid. I must have been tired—over-worked."

"No; you were in trouble. You had some grief."

"Grief! Yes, a strange one!"

"Tell me. Let me comfort you."

"Alas! No. For me there is no comfort."

"Is there *any* grief that has no comfort?"

"Yes; one."

Gasparine sat down and looked involuntarily around. Surely if there was any place where grief should not come, it was there! The wide, sweet-aired room; broad windows, thrown up on a clematis-covered balcony, where the passionate, purple flowers hung, in fulness of their joyous flower-life.

"It seemed to me," said Gasparine gently, "that *my* sorrow was not bearable; and yet—your kindness made it *bearable*, at least."

"Yes, yes. I know the old cry of the world—'All ye that pass by … see … if there be any sorrow like unto my sorrow.'[1] But I—I do not stand in the market-place to cry, Gasparine, because I know what I know. God Himself could not make my sorrow bearable."

"Surely, then, it is an evil more strange than one has ever heard?"

"Yes, it is, indeed, a strange one. It is, Gasparine, that I was born old."

---

1 Lamentations 1:12

"Born old?"

"Yes; it is the last and worst curse that can befall mankind."

The mixture of intense earnestness and deep cynicism gave Gasparine a shock, like one touching a fair-seeming fruit, and finding it bitter in the mouth. There came a long silence. Lo took up a cigarette and smoked, still swinging her chair on one leg, as she sat sideways, all the light from the window in her large eyes.

One hand rested on the back of her chair; the other elbow was supported by her writing-table. The whole attitude pressed itself into Gasparine's heart. The small face brightened, quivered, and at last, throwing aside the cigarette, and steadying herself, she seized the back of her chair with both hands.

"Think! Born old! Corrupt, artificial, with death in every gentle action! How horrible!"

With each word the voice and face changed as she went on, monotonous and low, cutting, sardonic, mournful.

"There is pity given to the passionate, the sensual;—'Oh, it is young blood.' Praise to the cool, the temperate;—'Ah! steady fellows!' The wild Bohemian—one excuses him. The poet! Who does not pardon the poet-passion, which sees all things through a glamour? But, ah, God! What of us? Who understands, dreams of pitying *us*—the artificially born, the babes born with worn-out blood in their veins—the tired children of tired parents. I tell you we are born with abnormal cravings, not natural appetites and desires. We look upon the mere sensual animal as something comparatively innocent. At first we do not understand ourselves ... this is the terrible part ... unutterably tragic. We question vaguely. We reflect—dimly and inarticulately of course, 'We are young. The young act thus and thus. For instance, they desire pleasure, admiration, to attract, to fall in love.' We taste the fruit of pleasure. Strange! Even that first bite was tasteless! Then we begin to think *consciously*, 'Why is this? Is it that the excitement was not enough? That we did not bite deep enough?' Yes, perhaps so. We try to assure ourselves; we try a greater excitement. The result is the same. Then we acknowledge, degree or kind, it matters not. *We have not the capacity to enjoy.* For some reason, it is dead in us. Horrible! And we are so young! To be dead so soon! Are all like this? We look to see. We seek, and soon find the answer. No; the simplest pleasures suffice for some. But what will inspire *us* with pleasure? We try it all. No. The pleasures of a great town cannot amuse us. The quiet of the country cannot strengthen. It is not that we scorn these things—the dead have no scorn; only it is all so clear to us. The life of the actor before the footlights, painted, and playing at passion, is no more unreal to us than the bourgeois taking his Sunday holiday—and playing at passion too. One strain runs through all, the weariful *'Cui bono.'*[1] We are young, but we cannot be intoxicated; our blood is old and cold. 'At least,' we moan, 'there is rapture in love.' We taste it, and know it is as the rest. We are not vindictive; we only say, 'Yes, it may be sweet for others, surely; but not for us. To them the joy; while we, dead, pass, in our pain and bewilderment, through the living world, marvelling at the emotions, the strifes, the interest over worthless and trivial matters.' We see it is the life put into these things which makes them of value. To us they are worthless, because we, being dead, have no vital spark to infuse into them. Then, alas! We know that for us life must be acting, good or bad. Mine has been good."

"It has, indeed," thought Gasparine, as she tried to keep up with the other's rapidly uttered thoughts.

There was a pause; then Lo continued in another tone, cool and indifferent,—

"We are not without our peculiar virtues. As a rule, we are gentle and not jealous; we cannot be—the true value of things is too well known to us. What we have—and those who do not know us often mistake it for jealousy—is a craving, often intense, to try and deceive ourselves into the belief that we *do* possess the capacity for enjoyment. This causes us often to partake of, and seek feverishly, every pleasure. When it is forbidden pleasure and in despair we seek it, the world cries, 'Ah! Passion of life! Jealousy of life!' Little knowing how gladly we would answer 'Guilty' to that charge if we might. But, within us, we know that our hearts are dead; we cannot. Also, we are incapable of that vigorous form of social bullying known as 'Pushing.' That is a manifestation of energy, in the 'Pusher,' which we do not understand. Place us on a pinnacle, and bow round us, and we will smile upon you gently. Lie down and put your head under our feet, and we will walk over you indifferently. But that species of conquest which the 'Pusher' achieves is an enigma to us. We admire his results. We look with contempt and wonder at the means he employs. Therefore we,— although we often possess genius of a mournful and dead sort— remain as a rule, in the background of the world; for the world rarely bows without the help of the whip."

---

1 Latin, "popularly but erroneously taken in English to mean 'To what use or good purpose?'" (*OED*).

Again there was a pause. It seemed that Lo was only half conscious of a listening presence, for her glowing eyes looked into space, and seemed to see things there. They darkened, saddened, an anguish came into them. Her voice became low and bittersweet.

"From childhood we know what it is to *feel* despair, but there is a crowning woe which is not laid upon our brows until experience has made us ripe for it. Then cold hands come and bind on us that last woe, conscious despair. You have grown to that."

Her face changed. A fearful passion came into it. Hitherto she had sat in her student fashion, her gaze bent on the far hills. Now she turned, and her blazing eyes held Gasparine with a painful fascination.

"Do you know what it means? *This:* that you know, you feel, *you* in your soul, that though all the wealth of the world was poured upon you, you have no power to enjoy it. Though you were a king; though you had beauty that brought every eye thirsting to you; though your brain could hold every thought, and your eloquence bow every heart; though your hand could paint as no man painted yet, and your voice sing like God's angels; it would all be nothing to you. Though you had love, that great sunlight of the world, it could not warm you. You place yourself in every conceivable position; you give yourself lover, child, home, heroism; it is all no good. You throw down your hands. You do not wish to be other than you are; it would only alter the circumstances and the work, not the dead heart within you. This is what is meant by *conscious despair*. Pray that you may suffer every woe but that. That is what we suffer, we that are born old."

Again she paused. A cold sense of desolation overcame Gasparine, and, almost unconsciously, her tears fell.

"When we have fully recognised our inheritance," Lo went on, "there are two ways for us."

She twisted round to the table. On it was a tray and liqueur set of cut crystal. With growing horror, Gasparine saw her pour some liqueur into a glass, and hold it up.

"This," said Lotus, "gives oblivion. Your heart is dead? This will burn it alive. You have no ambitions, no hopes? This will give them to you. When you are born dead, this is life." She raised the glass and looked at it critically. "Those who can find comfort in this," she said then, coldly, "are not the worst; *at least*, the passion for life is not dead in them. When this tempts you, when this raises in you a momentary glow, and your lips are eager to drink——"

A flash of light shot in on Gasparine. A passionate question rose to her tongue. "This girl? Her own father? Oh, impossible! Horrible!"

"But beyond this stage," continued Lo, in a dead, cold voice, "there is a worse. Yes, in spite of preachers, it is worse. When even *this* cannot deceive you, cannot give you a counterfeit life, you do not drink it because"—she quietly set the glass on the tray—"putting a liquid down your throat does not seem to you an intensely interesting occupation."

Gasparine could bear no more; her heart seemed to burst with pain. The life that had seemed to her so beautiful, the heart that had seemed to her so whole, a dead thing like this!—Hideously, callously dead to life's beating pulse!

"Do not, ah! Do not tell me that is true!" she cried passionately. "You wrong yourself. You are not what you would have me believe—artificial and corrupt from core to rind. You live honourably and temperately; you are generous and loving to your friends, and they love you. I—I——"

A peculiar smile passed over Lo's face.

"Of course," she said, with a sneer Gasparine would not see, "I did not imply that we were born without brains. On the contrary, all our life seems to be centred there. We see the necessity of performing our part in life; we do so reasonably and well. What seems our generosity is a sense of fitness. What seems our justice is reason. What seems our love and affection—that, too, is our perception of what is fit. Our patience is our weariness. We rarely hesitate or are puzzled. What need? All things are *so* small! And we never cry over spilt milk; that is for babes. One thing only our aged hearts and shattered nerves cannot suffer to see, and *that* is personal cruelty."

"But your interest in your work, the sentiments you express, the advice you give—all I have seen and heard myself."

Gasparine spoke in gasps, fighting against this horrid chill.

"Because *I* am born old, because *I* see the world's gifts, nature's gifts, as useless to *me*, does that blind me to the *general* value, the *general* duty? I said I acted; I said I acted well; I did not say I acted in the interests of vice."

"No; ah, no! I did not mean that—I did not, indeed. But I feel sure you wrong yourself. You have had, perhaps, some sorrow, some trouble, that has taken away your hopes *for a time*."

Lo gave a short, sardonic laugh.

"No, I am not that interesting sort of young lady," she said. "The young lady with *a past* is falling into it, I'm glad to say, with many other handsome shams."

There was silence. Lo seemed again to fall into a sort of dream. Gasparine drew back, and watched the pale face and brilliant eyes. What was there in the eyes that thrilled her heart? In the piteous, worn face that caused her breast to yearn over it? Did they hide a woe deeper than any she had ever dreamed of? Did they speak of some terrible strife? Did that tenderly formed breast indeed cover a heart—murdered?

With a movement of irrepressible passion, she threw herself at Lo's feet.

"Oh, Lo, Lo, now I understand that look in your face, stranger than any face I ever saw! Now, oh! Let me love you, let me call you Lo. I have no one to love. The world is empty for me. You saved me. Let me give you all my love; it will bring you back to youth; it will be so strong; it will make your dead heart live again."

The eyes which turned to her spoke indescribable tenderness and pity in their pained depths.

"Call me Lo? Surely, dear. But I! I! Do the dead ever live again, Gasparine?"

"Do not speak so. What has given you this terrible sense of isolation among so many living and loving people!"

"Because, in my soul, I am alone, utterly, utterly!"

"But, Lo, why? Why should you feel *so* lonely, dear?"

"I will tell you. Because I have never yet found any one stronger than myself; so I must needs feel alone. In life I have had to do everything for myself; it is such weariness. It seems like a vision of heaven, the ideal of a nature stronger, higher than mine, which yet would love and pity *me*."

"Will nothing heal you, Lo?" Gasparine sadly asked.

Lotus paused, caught her breath, then answered, measuredly,—

"Yes; when some one takes me, and wraps me in a boundless and perfect love that does not question—oh! never questions, but covers me up ... and breathes upon me ... till—till my dead heart——"

A spasm crossed her face. For the first time, she hid her proud, brave eyes.

Then Gasparine took the slender, sinewy brown hands in her own.

"If perfect love, unquestioning, will heal you, Lo, you shall be healed. Lo, kiss me, now that I see you with open eyes, as you kissed me, thankless, when my eyes were blind with grief."

Lo bent and kissed her; a long, sweet kiss.

Then Gasparine went away, pledged. For what? A perfect love? What is a perfect love? Service and utter self-abnegation? Nay; there is more.

CHAPTER VIII
LIFE'S LOVELESSNESS

That night Gasparine could not rest; her lonely rooms were filled with the shadow of a presence. The strange, mournful being! The young, dead heart! Her own beat and thrilled with fresh strength and love. Her head was full of plans. A strange, sorrowful—gladness possessed her.

"A perfect, unquestioning love I will give her, and save her. And to think *she*, who was my ideal, and seemed to be happy, and blessed in the mere fact of existence, should suffer!"

It seemed to her so long till next evening, when she could go and see her friend.

But the time came.... Then she went. Ladybird was in the garden. The little face was pale, the eyes red with weeping. Gasparine lifted the child in her arms.

"Have you been crying, dearie?"

"Yes."

"What was it? Tell old Gasparine!"

"I wanted Lo to let me call her 'ma-ma.' Sonny Thomas has a mammy, and is rude to me about it. And Lo—Lo"—here the poor mite burst out sobbing and choking with painful violence—"Lo put me from her room ... and said if I ever said it again I must go quite away; and Mis' Grace heard me crying, and came an' w'ipped me, good an' sore."

"Poor dearie! Never mind, don't cry."

"I'm not going to cry any more," said the child, strangling the last sob viciously, and speaking with remarkable self-control. "I love Lotus, but I hate Mis' Grace and Mona. I'm going to ask Sonny Thomas to kill them dead, one day."

"That would be very naughty, and grieve Lo."

"I don't care. She kisses Mona more than she kisses me. I bit Mona yesterday. It made a big red mark and made me laugh. Let me go."

Gasparine put the child down, and went into the cottage.

She meant to go straight upstairs to the study as usual, but the bedroom door, on the left, was open, and the sound of voices made her pause, and look into the room. Lo lay on the bed, her eyes almost closed. The long, white arms of Mona clasped her, with indescribable expression in the clasp. The Creole was in evening dress, and her long silk and lace skirts were trailing on the floor.

"Lo, one word! only one!" she pleaded. "If I have annoyed you, I am very sorry. If you would tell me what I have done, or what I can do! Oh, Lo, they were all dancing, and I slipped away, and walked here alone, in my slippers. I could not keep away. The night is an eternity of despair if we part in anger. One word, Lo— only one!"

Lotus raised her head, and slightly moved.

"Go," she said.

It was the one word.

Mona sank, sobbing, beside the bed.

"Oh, you are cruel—cruel! To love you is as bitter as it is sweet. When people love you, you treat them like slaves, and some people you can't be good enough to. Do you know what Gray Grayson says of you now? 'You are decent and clever, but too queer for his taste.' *That*, after your patience with him!"

Silence. Then sobs. Then, "Lo, Lo, forgive me!"

But Lo had given the one word.

Gasparine still stood hesitating when Mona came through the doorway. In a flash, her face changed, and, with a sudden rush of passion, she seized Gasparine's wrist.

"I believe it is *you*," she said. "Well, I warn you."

Her voice was cut with sobs. Thwarting, to her imperious and passionate nature, was unbearable—something must receive her displeasure. The two faced each other—Gasparine thin and spiritualised away to an uninteresting shadow as far as the outward eye could be pleased, the other a beauty of the most brilliant West Indian type, lithe form, mature and rounded, eyes of dreams, and mouth to kiss.

"I do not know what you mean, Miss Lefcadio."

"I can tell you what I mean easily enough. Lo is my friend. I love her better than my own life. She has been everything to me. She has taught me everything. She has shown me the something in life without which life is worthless. I am not going over it all."

"May I ask what this has to do with me?"

"This. Lo taught me all that. She is all I have—all I want. If you go between her and me ... do you hear? She is mine. She was always mine in the College. A girl tried to take her from me once. *That girl's gone.* No one shall ever part us. She shall be mine until we die together ... as I have seen. No one will *want* to part us then."

There was almost a hunger for death in her words, which were painful, and sounded like one voicing a prophecy, not speech of his own.

"This is all very fine," Gasparine said coldly. "She is yours. And so you stab her with every cruel thing you can say?"

"Yes," said Mona, at once losing her dreaminess, and speaking with her usual frankness and hauteur; "because I get mad with love and rage. But afterwards I could kill myself that I am so cruel. My precious little tired Curly! Why, I love her anger better than any one else's sweetness. *When it's over* I *glory* in her scorn."

She gazed back longingly to the room; then, biting her full, red lip, she went away.

Gasparine went out to the verandah for a moment, to ponder and recover herself. She watched the tall, swinging figure out of the gate.

"What a wild, passionate creature!" she said, "and yet, how deeply she loves Lotus. Oh, strange, strange Lotus, to rouse such love in others, and never feel the warmth yourself!"

She re-entered the house, and knocked at Lo's door.

"Come in."

The words were a mere moan.

Gasparine went over to the bed hastily. Lo's face gave her a shock. It had the ghastly and drawn look of one who is suffering mortally, and yet about the mouth there was an expression so cruel and imperious that Gasparine was at once repelled and attracted by it.

"Lotus, you are in pain?"

"No."

"Tell me, what is it?"

"Ah! It is you, Gasparine. I thought it was Mona returned. Do you know that girl has taken to teasing me lately—I can't think why? If it continue I shall have to punish her in earnest. This fretting on shattered nerves is like trying to tune broken harp strings; it is unbearable."

"But she loves you, Lotus; and surely you love her?"

"Oh, you are going to begin again. You, too! Loved? I? Listen. I never loved any one in my life. I never, I hope, shall."

Silence; pained, and chill.

"Yes, yes; you said what was the matter? Why, only the hideousness of life, and the worse hideousness of death—all, all hideous to me; but, worst of all, the lovelessness, the lovelessness of life!"

"The lovelessness of life to you, Lo, whom every one loves? Who might love so many?"

Suddenly Lotus sat up. A mirthless smile broke over her white face.

"Loves me, Gasparine? Pray do tell me. Who loves me?"

"All those people I have seen here, particularly your schoolfellows and teachers."

"Listen, then," said Lo impressively. "You say my girls love me. Yes. Why do they all come here, and *love* me? Is it love? You want to say, I know, that they give me love, and that I give them contempt? Is it not rather this? I do not admire them; I see them as they are, contemptibly selfish animals. Do I ever deceive myself that it is for love of me they come? No, no; they know that when they come to me, however bored I am, I put my work aside, and help and listen. I win them by much toil and patience. I do not, by my mere presence, command love, as Mona, who wins by existing ... I by toil, that I may live. Have you any idea how thoroughly people dislike and fear me until I compel them to do otherwise? I do not take my geese for swans, but while I give them what they want it's little they care—geese are not high-toned animals, you know. And then that foolish girl says I deceive people. I do not. I do not need to. They deceive themselves."

She leaned forward on her arm, her eyes again dreamy, talking.

"It is a great point that you do not expect anything from them; they do not even wish that you should love them as you could; *they do not comprehend such depth.* If you showed it to them they would only be bewildered. Be gentle to them when with them. Do not even say to them, 'I have sorrow you cannot reach. I suffer pain you do not know.' The world is amused at deep grief, or bored. Is deep grief sacred?

"Well; you said these people loved me. Listen. A young fellow came to me night after night. I thought what was kind to do for him—callously, as if he were a plant or a rabbit—oh yes, I own it; still, the best I knew. It helped, the trouble grew better. Then there came along a girl, a harmless creature, and laughed, not very ill-naturedly, at me, and he ... laughed too. That is their love exactly—so deep, no deeper.

"And then that girl to-night! Did she move me? That poor little effort at self-control, the quivering lip, and hot eyelid! Why, no, it was for herself she suffered ... and what have I to do with all that? If that doctrine of re-incarnation be true, I must before have been a man of many loves, and the women somehow recognise the old lover."

She laughed sardonically.

"Come! that is what you would call a poetic idea, is it not? Think of the women, held by the awful bonds of sex, seeing the spirit of the old love gazing at them through the eyes of a woman who cannot love them back! ... Did I say life was hideous, and loveless? On the other hand, there is death ... to die, to give up *all*—all that freedom, those days to go where I would, those dreamy days in the dying countries we have, Ireland, Poland ... in homely old Germany, in gay France—all that with some dear companion ... all talks and little merriment, all plans about shopping, dress, fun ... such as one has—all those little confidences—during walks, on sunlight days."

After a silence she seemed to awake.

"Gasparine, I've been wandering, after my foolish fashion ... over the old, old track of hopeless hopes and fearless fears. It's done. You came to talk; let's talk."

Gasparine did not speak for a minute or two. When she did there was something of scorn almost in her earnest voice.

"Yes, I came to talk, Lotus—but I cannot rest till you tell me something. Do you mean that you have no love, and no wish to love any one?"

"Wish? I have no wishes. I find it wiser."

"You do not love Mona ... yet take all her love?"

"It is not so much that I do not love Mona as that I do not believe in her love for me. She believes what she says—oh! I don't mean that ... but it would be incredible.... On the other hand, no, I love neither her nor you, Gasparine."

"Leave me meantime," said Gasparine coldly, though the blood came to her cheek at the cruel frankness. "You do not love the little girl Lady, who adores you, nor Mrs. Grace, who maintains you in luxury here, and lives to serve you." An indescribable smile crossed Lo's face, mocking, mournful. "Your apparent love for them was all acting?"

"Acting?" wearily. "Yes. I am grateful to them for their kindness. What more can I be? Ah! Gasparine, why deceive yourself? There is *no* love here in this world. There are for us moments of passion, of inspiration, of nearness. There are lives bound together by interest, association, custom. But love! Love! I have yet to find love that will do and dare all, and cling to the loved one out of love.... No, I do not believe in love."

It seemed to Gasparine that ashes had been laid on her heart. Was her joy, that she had hugged to her aching heart, to be so short-lived a thing as this? Only last night her feet had seemed to have wings to them to bear her to her lonely lodgings, where she had sat for hours, looking into the empty grate, and pondering on this strange, new honour. How real it had seemed! How she had planned to keep it all her own! And now!

"Lotus," she said hoarsely, "I couldn't bear it.... Tell me—I am almost afraid to ask—do you mean that, though I gave you a love perfect and unquestioning, you would not love me? ... Do you tell me yourself that I should be lavishing my love on a stone? You said a great, unquestioning love...."

Lo raised herself, smiling the old winning smile.

"Is this your great *unquestioning* love, my little Gasparine? That on the first day, finding me sick and joyless, begins to probe and question? Ah! I knew what I said."

"Lo, Lo, forgive me, forgive me! It was the sudden pain. Blind that I am. You are right, you are right.... Oh! my new joy, Lotus!"

Then into the student's eyes came a look of brooding love; she bent forward, and held out her hands.

"Gasparine."

It needed no other word for Gasparine. The look in the eyes and the tone of the voice were all she wanted. She sprang forward and took the dark head to her breast.

"My poor darling! I thought my heart was broken. I could not bear to think you withered and dead like that. You don't know how happy I was! ... All last night I never slept. I was not tired.... In the morning I never felt so gay, so well. I heard a bird sing outside my window—it is so long since the birds sang for me! ... and, oh! how glad I felt! All day at work I kept saying to myself, 'This evening. It is not too long. I can wait.' Why could I wait? Because to think of you even was such a great joy, to remember things you said, to say them over to myself aloud or in a whisper.... Lo, do not cheat me. Let me believe you all you seem, lovely and patient, and to be won by much love."

Lo did not speak at all. The smile of her drawn lips said plainly, "How easily we believe what we want to believe!"

"I have never had a friend, Lo, never. You have had many. You do not know what life means, when you are like me, hungry for love, and quite, quite alone. Think what it is to have a friend to love—something to fill one's life. It is tremendous to me. I can hardly believe it. I come only gradually to realise it."

Still Lo never spoke. She turned her head away from Gasparine upon the pillow with a strange expression. Long afterwards, the words she had spoken came to the other's mind.

"I do not deceive people. What need? They deceive themselves."

So Gasparine, too, was within the charmed circle; unknowing!

CHAPTER IX
GASPARINE'S CREATION

The time went for a year. Otherwise things bettered for Gasparine. She found out what was meant by the amelioration of circumstances which experience and age bring. She knew her work,
was confident and unbending. Her painting pupils, though an
uncertain source of income, were a certain source of local fame.
When she heard herself spoken of as "Miss O'Neill, the artist,"
she felt a new zest in life. Lotus came and took painting lessons,
and obtained several pupils for her. But Mona, glooming jeal-
ously under her beautiful brows, would not notice the struggling
artist.

Owing to the severe economy of her life—rather more than
less severe since Gaspar's death—her bank-book came to be quite
a valuable possession. Her early dreams of fame and glory took a
sober tint. She found that life for her meant *work*; and as, in the
old days, it had meant Gaspar and her pictures, now it meant, in
all the earnestness of her earnest soul, work—and Lotus.

The strange being became always dearer and more distant.
Day after day, week after week, new phases, aspects of character,
appeared, to charm, pique, soothe, or tempt. But always Gasparine found herself as far off as ever.

After a long struggle against it she was forced to acknowledge
that Lo received her worship with no other feeling than a gentle
scorn, which yet trusted her completely.

Each day found her, when school was over, trudging up the
hill to the White Cottage. Now Ladybird would bound to meet
her with a shout, at which some one would come from the verandah, or the garden—Mrs. Grace, with her stately welcome, or Lo,
with a smile in her deep eyes.

Lo's help in all her little affairs, and ready sympathy in every
trivial trouble, made the mountains turn into mole-hills; and the
stings, which can only wound loneliness, became a laugh.

"Are you happier now, dear Gasparine?" Lo often asked, as
they gathered flowers for the grave on the Castle Hill.

"Yes, dear; happier, better for knowledge and love of you. Ah!
Lotus, if you knew all the difference it makes! ...When I am tired,
when I am stupid, when the girls irritate me, when life seems

dull, when I remember how poor and plain I am—when the streets seem dreary, the shops dingy, the people selfish and uninteresting ... you come along and all the street lights up ... suddenly a flash of you passes through me, and life is worth living again ... and I would not change, or be other than I am, for all the world, if being so, I had to lose you."

"That is good. I am glad, for your sake."

"And you, Lotus, are you no happier?"

There came never an answer to that question but the sweet, sad smile.

And at last—for so are we fashioned—that something of the calm of death that, in her strangest moments, never left Lotus, and against which the warm and living love of Gasparine had fretted for so long, came to be—or perhaps it always had unconsciously been—the chiefest charm and fascination. Calm when her mobile face told of torturing suffering; calm while she spoke words of intense, often cruel bitterness to some poor, weeping worshipper; calm when she turned from Lady's outstretched hands, and wild jealous sobs, as the unfortunate little wretch was being dragged, protesting, from her presence.

Would this dominant, relentless calm never break? Yes; once. And after that Gasparine prayed nightly, most earnestly, that it never might again.

It was one autumn evening. There had been wild rain that day. Mona and Gasparine were both spending the night at the cottage. As they sat round the fire in the drawing-room, Lady on Lo's knees, chatting, Mona fell, first to describing storms in the West Indies, and then, by untraceable transition, to speaking of the Southern States, where some of her people belonged—of the blacks, and the remnant of the feeling of old slave days and cringing fear. Then, suddenly, without seeming to realise the horror of the tale, the girl began relating a story of woman-flogging, heard from her old nurse. A revolting story, too common to Mona to strike her civilised senses, blunted by nearness to the common attitude of indifference towards the inferior races.

"And in the morning, the poor girl—a pretty creature, just fifteen, a gentleman's daughter, they said, was induced by her husband to consent.... He had not been able to save her; he was afraid of the same punishment ... so——"

She stopped, for Lady, with a shriek, had stretched up her hand.

"Lo, Lo," cried the child, "do you hear the dog howling? Take me away, oh! take me——"

But Lo cast her violently aside, and rose, twisting her hands round her wrists with the action of one washing. She gasped out a few awful broken words, and, with a look of terrible appeal from one to the other, staggered about with outstretched hands, searching for the door. When found, she opened it uncertainly. Before it closed behind her they heard a smothered groan.

"You should not relate those horrors, Mona," Mrs. Grace said calmly. "You know how overworked and sensitive Lo is at present."

Mona pouted and was sullenly silent, not even raising her head when Lady, in vindication of herself and Lo, slapped her repeatedly. To Gasparine's surprise, this naughtiness was not reproved by Mrs. Grace, who took the little girl away with her to see about tea, as a means of soothing.

Late that night, Lotus came into Gasparine's room.

"I came to say good-night, Gasparine," she said gently, "because I could not see you when you knocked at my study door. I—I was busy."

She was calm again, but about her eyes there was still that awful look, as if between her and the light a vision of horror hung eternally; and still, in the curious fashion, she twisted and twisted her hands round her wrists with the "washing-action." Gasparine had never seen her do it before.

"Gasparine," she said huskily, "did you ever think of the deadly sin, the unpardonable sin—the sin against the Holy Ghost—against the Spirit of Life, that will never be forgiven?[1] I am not speaking of religion, but of life—of the sin eternally unpardonable against life?"

"No, Lo."

"It is that of which Mona spoke. Listen. *The ruining of a soul through untold, inexpressible torture of body, through shame, fear, horror,* that *degrades the soul;* that *makes uprightness impossible, as no self-committed sin, no willingly committed sin ever can.* Yes, that is it."

She spoke with frightful energy in this strange, husky voice.

"Who *pities* the Christ? He went to the cross because He *willed* to do so! If I go to the scaffold to-morrow I ask no pity. It's the driving of a helpless, shrinking miserable; the crushing of thought or right of judgment in a mind; the injustice of brute force; *the degradation of a helpless soul, through fear. That's* the damnable sin and crime."

---

1 Cf. Matthew 12:31–32, Mark 3:28–29, and Luke 12:10. All identify blasphemy against the Holy Spirit as the one unforgivable sin.

"I think I do not quite clearly understand, Lo?"

Lotus roused, and passed her hand across her eyes.

"No, no, of course not—of course not. God forbid that I should speak more plainly. Few, I do pray, know the meaning of that fearful snaring and crushing of the will in its own despite, till it is dragged low enough *to consent....* But I must not stay to talk—I came to say good-night. Gasparine, sometimes you pray?"

"Sometimes, sweetheart, of old; often now, for you."

"Pray, then, to-night. Not for me—no, no, but this: 'For all who are desolate and oppressed'; for all, mind—all; that will do. For *all*; not for me."

Thereafter, the calm was as unbroken as before.

One other tussle took place between Mona and Gasparine, in which the latter could not help feeling that the victory was hers, in spite of all Mona's superior advantages of position, beauty, and glib speech.

It happened that both, wending towards the cottage, met at the junction of the Newhouse and Cambusbarron roads. It was an early autumn evening, cooling after a sultry day, whose sultriness still lingered in the pine trees, and hovered among the grass, while above, clouds, moving, showed the clearness of a sky that promised stars.

Mona wore a dress of pale rose and cream lace, lifted from the road and her small French shoes by a gold, Norwegian catch. Light locks of her glorious hair broke free from her big hat, and the warmth and panting animation of her lovely face bespoke the eagerness with which she hastened to her darling.

She scowled, the soft, pleased curve leaving her lips, as Gasparine crossed her path. Then, with frank displeasure, she said,—

"Good-evening. I suppose you are going to see Lo?"

"Yes."

"You go very often?"

"Yes."

"How do you know she can be bothered with you?"

"I don't know."

"H'm, I shouldn't like to be so."

Gasparine did not answer, and in silence they walked on together. Then Mona said,—

"You know Lo is very busy?"

"Yes."

"Even *I* can scarcely see her; and she *never* refuses *me*."

"That is nice for you."

"I don't quite see that it is your business."

"I agree with you."

"Miss O'Neill, you think perhaps you will get to be Lo's best friend?"

"I have no opinion to give."

A grunt of contempt came from Mona. In silence they reached the cottage gate. There Mona paused, the latch in her hand. She looked Gasparine up and down; it was an unmistakable look, full of contempt and disgust. With her noble and haughty head thrown back, and only her heavy eyelids moving, she seemed to take in the plain, black frock, collar and cuffs, and the thin, sad face, and strained, brushed hair. Gasparine felt stung, but did not wince.

"I hope," Mona said, then, in a tone of virtuous severity, "you won't bother Lotus as much as you do. I know she is overworked, and it took her nearly all night to correct those examination papers for you."

The blood burned in Gasparine's face. The examination papers were a sore point with her. It stung her that Mona should know. She answered with dignity, however.

"I am sorry if Lotus had to complain to you about them."

Mona looked uncomfortable.

"I didn't say so," she said testily. "You snap so!"

"The examination papers were quite beyond me," continued Gasparine firmly, "but if I refused them it meant losing my bread-and-butter. Lotus told me always to bring them to her."

Mona looked more and more uncomfortable.

"You needn't take it so seriously," she said.

"Not at all; but I must apologise to Lotus."

Then, suddenly, all the hauteur left Mona's face; it was full of terror, and passion, and humility.

"Oh, Miss O'Neill, don't! I didn't mean! Lo never said a word. I found her at the papers one night, and we had a great storm, and she forbade me to speak a word to any one; and now, if she found I had, she—she—oh! Miss O'Neill, you won't speak, will you? Lo would ignore me, and that drives me quite mad."

"I sha'n't speak," said Gasparine, her generous nature always ready to accede when appealed to.

Just then Lady called from the balcony, and they entered the garden together.

As a result of this conversation, however, Gasparine one day said to Lotus,—

"Why do you do so much work for other people when you don't believe it's any good?"

Lo smiled.

"My dear, when you *can* do a thing, and are asked to do it, that seems to me the best reason. The mistake lies in trying to do the things you can't do, and are not asked to do."

"But what you are doing now, for instance?" and Gasparine pointed to the pile of papers where Lo was at work, making up her accounts, as secretary and treasurer for the flood which had devastated the neighbouring villages, and reduced the poor to destitution. "Why do you work so hard at *that*? *You* don't believe it is going to do any good."

"That is true. I am working as hard as I can, but hopelessly."

"Hopelessly?"

"Yes; that's the worst of it—quite hopelessly. Only because I must—because I'm not a brute. You ask what good it will do? Very little. The unsaved die; the saved die, too—later."

"But that you do it shows you are not a brute, does it not? And if you recognise a lower, surely you must also recognise a higher nature?"

The smile that turned to Gasparine was worth a year of her life.

"My unrecognised Genius" (for so Lo now often called her), "it might be so. But,"—the glory left the eyes—"the god might be hopeless."

"A hopeless god? Oh, Lotus! A god who has done good, who lives to make others happy! Such a god hopeless? Who has heard of such a thing?"

"Words, my child, you use only words! What is doing good? What is happiness? To certain sounds we attach certain significances of certain sensations. How do you know that that has anything—anything at all—to do with the great eternities? ... And if we are the poor creations of gods, why is it foolish to believe that in us they have created the remnants of their old god's passions, hopes, and fears? A hopeless mortal: why, then, not a hopeless god? A suffering mortal; why not a suffering god? At least, it would be no disgrace to them." The strange dream-look of pain crossed her face, then, suddenly brightening, and laughing, she said, "What nonsense we talk when we are tempted for a moment to ponder on the meaning of life. Come, my Genius, I see through your little argument. You think I work too much for *you*. There, pass me over those papers in your hand. Miss Blurton, the valiant, must be outwitted. I have no idea she shall triumph. Hand them me."

*   *   *   *   *

Gasparine sat by her window that night and wrote:—

THE LOTUS

"Dear, I sat by the old window last night, and heard a voice singing. A dying voice; a voice that had sung and now passionately cried against the stillness that was coming to it. Beautiful voice! Through whose melodious lament I saw, in my vision, the life of a soul. I saw the beautiful, passionate soul struggling to grow, to expand, in an alien soil. It could not grow. The close air weighed upon it. Once a hot sun poured down, it struggled, with rapturous, perfumed motions of its white leaves, until its heart lay bare. But the petals dropped under the scorching rays. A poisonous wind chilled and shrivelled the quivering, uncovered heart. Then there crept around the soul-flower crawling things; and some fed on its heart, and others cankered its leaves, till it was lovely no more. Still it lived, cankered, withered, eaten—for its life was in its perfume, strong, irresistible, the magnetism of a passionate soul. And by-and-by the loathesome things dropped away from it in scorn, but the bird of sweetest song, the butterfly of fairest wing, gathered near, within the circle of the perfume's charm, and sang above the flower, and rested by it, and lived in its strength. Beloved, it was thy life I saw—thy beautiful, fair soul, crushed, compressed; and I, poor bird, sang near you, and lived, joyous, too thoughtless and glad in *thy* strength to know how weak and worn thou wert."

When it was written, she read it over, and pondered upon it, and then spoke.

"If I can paint it! If I can only paint what will express all that! Ah! what a face of mystery! ... I shall not ask for fame; I shall have the glory of it in my heart.... I shall not have lived in vain.... No Leon Smith will take *this* idea from me."

Her face hardened as she remembered Leon Smith. The man who had stolen and traded upon her girlish ideas at the School of Art had never been forgiven by her.

CHAPTER X
THE RAIN'S INFLUENCE

The next summer Lo and Mona were abroad together. It was lonely for Gasparine, who, however, spent it in hard work. Again and again she attempted to paint *the Face*, again and again failed of her ideal.

For a few days she found a violent partisan in Lady, until that fair damsel went off to Wemyss Bay for her holidays, with Mrs. Grace.

"I hate when Lo goes without me," the small one said; "'speshly if she goes with thet eggly ole Mona."

"But you like Lo to have a good holiday, don't you, dearie?"

"She could have a beaut'ful holiday with me; an' I'd show her where to dig cockles."

"I'm very lonely, too, Lady, since Lo went away."

"Are you? But you're big, you see. Big people don't mind; 'least, Mis' Grace ses so. Don' b'lieve 'er quite."

The end of August saw the Cottage household returned, and Gasparine again joyously visiting. Her love had grown in the lonely summer days, and now, as, bit by bit, she fancied she came into comprehension of this strange nature, she read and re-read those words which she had written to guide her in painting *the Face*.

"It is much, but it is not enough," she said. "However, the rest will come."

And this expectant mood grew upon her into a certainty that hardly left room for surprise, when, on that wild August day, the mad rain wrung the words from Lotus.

It was very wet. Gasparine had finished with school unusually early, because the last week of August, when Miss Blurton took up, was generally an easy one. She had gone direct to the cottage, and, finding that Mrs. Grace and Lady were in Edinburgh, she went up to Lo's study to await the student's return.

She had brought with her some examination papers belonging to the new session, and now bent over them with knitted brows. Outside, the wild rain lashed the panes, and shrouded the town and the far hills, giving an indescribable, mist-like green to fields and trees around. Within, the fire crackled on the wide hearth, and, sitting there, Gasparine contrasted the warmth and comfort of the room with the wildness without. On the wall opposite to her, with the flame from the wood fire, and the grey of the rain-light striving upon it, was a large picture of Ladybird. Gasparine fell again to pondering what in the exquisite colouring, and strangely brilliant expression appealed to her like a memory of something unforgettable. Where before had she seen gold hair drawn from a nobly intellectual brow, giving to view the little shell-ears, and curves of the neck, at once piteous and imperious?

She looked and looked, pondering.

Lotus had given her a commission to paint the child, and she was therefore doubly interested in studying the small, defiant face.

Presently the click of the gate sounded, and, on the stair, the quick step. She rose hastily, and, as Lo entered, went towards her, amazed at the strange, wild look, and pale lips.

"Are you not well, dear Lo?"

"Well? Yes, I think so."

"Oh, Lo! what is it then?"

With her white teeth showing on her lips, Lo shrank away.

"The rain!" she gasped; "the fearful rain!"

"Yes, it's terrible. But—why, Lo!—something has happened to you. You have had a fright!"

"Yes ... it was ... the rain; it is so fearful. It slashed and struck me ... till my breath went, and my very heart turned cold. I tried to think of you ... and this warmth and firelight ... but it was like one dying looking back to life.... Oh, the rain! ... the rain! ... the cold, cruel, dismal rain!"

Gasparine was busy removing the wet boots, cloak, and cap. Lotus talked restlessly.

"I wonder Mrs. Grace has not written or wired. You know she and the child are in Edinburgh for Lady's winter outfit ... but she certainly should have written. One must not be careless about a boarder, ... it is not right or fair."

She moved about the room, arranging books and papers, tossing over work—dainty work—for Ladybird, on which she had been busy.

By-and-by she seemed to throw aside this mood, and adopt one unusually cheerful. She rang for lager, lighted a cigarette, and, whistling and chirping about the room, directed Gasparine in her corrections of those examination papers which Miss Blurton, unable to manage herself, had handed over to her governess.

Suddenly, again, the rain seemed to strike her. She stood and watched the branches of a lime tree waving in the wind, and blackening, each minute, against the darkening sky. She turned, and spoke to Gasparine.

"Have you ever thought, while watching the trees tossed in the wind and rain, of the analogy between the anguish of their motions and the hearts that you know? I, as I watch them, see them sway altogether as the world is swayed, by an irresistible force. When they toss wildly, I see so many wringing arms, thrown up in the strife to be free, cast down in the despair of defeat...."

She watched the branches of the lime tree dreamily. Gasparine watched too. For a while there was silence; then Lo spoke again. It seemed the necessity to speak was on her.

"Gasparine, long, long ago, I remember when I was taught, 'God is love.' It was my nurse; a good, religious woman. She tried to teach me what she called 'a happy child's faith.' She would say to me, when I shrunk from the dark, and shuddered, 'Do not fear, darling, it is *God's dark*!' Everything was God's, and God was my Father. Then I grew older, and I saw God's earth was— ah, Gasparine! The cries I have heard, are they God's? The tears I have seen; the wringing hands; the empty breasts. Are they God's?"

There was no answer to her question. Another long silence came.

Gasparine had no word to say. She waited for Lo, who spoke at last.

"We may suffer much; but remember, *the suffering for wrong may come at one stage of development, and realisation of wrong at another.* I began to realise my wrong, first, *when peace came.*"

"Your *wrong*, Lo?"

"Well, why not? Will you deny me that?"

"Lo, of course not," Gasparine said, in her serious way. "But how often have you said you had no wrong, no past; that there is no past for any one? Past, present, and future are one ... you said."

"Said! Said!" returned the other impatiently. "Do we not always try to say the thing we do not believe, and believe the thing we do not say?"

"So, after all, you had a wrong, Lo?"

Lo spoke as if she had not heard.

"I went with some of the girls to gather forget-me-nots. They grew thick in a field among nettles. While gathering them one is stung. Nor have they any fragrance, the forget-me-nots.... It was pretty to see the girls gather; their souls were in the work. As for me, girls and flowers were alike, both pretty to look at, endlessly suggestive of sentiment, and equally unable to sympathise, or heal me. *There I realised my wrong.* My heart cried and cried, and broke in the soft, evening air, among the little blue flowers, and the affectionate girls—cried and broke alone."

"Cried and broke alone? Over what, Lo?"

"Over a fair-haired child, that lived once."

"And who?——" questioned Gasparine, roused by the tone.

"Who, after growing from childhood to womanhood in dumb, mute, suffering torture, realised what had happened to her, and what might be happening now to thousands of others."

"Lotus, what do you mean?"

"A broken heart; that's all."

"Oh Lo! My little Lo! ... *Your* heart broken!"

"Well, well. What then?" irritably. "Why pity me? What need? I am no better than others. That my heart should break is, surely, no great thing. There are so many breaking hearts!"

"Yes, but, Lo, why did you try to hide what was in your eyes—and on your lips?"

Lo strode across the room, put one foot on a chair, her elbow on her knee, chin in hand, and looked at Gasparine.

"Well, my friend," she said, in the cynical, self-mocking tone, that always cut Gasparine like a knife, "when you see a woman standing, outside the herd, with an injured air, you may bet your bank account—and that won't be deadly for you, dear—that the herd has trampled on her some time or other.... A wise woman does not boast of it."

"Lo, you would stop if you knew how horrible it sounds to me to hear you speak so. I think of you always as something as white——"

"I know, I know," hurriedly, contemptuously. "Don't let's have a repetition of old metaphors.... Snow isn't in it. Go on."

"As white," said Gasparine steadily, "as snow—when it fell, trampled perhaps by busy, thoughtless, careless feet ... but white, to my eyes, Lo, always."

The great tears stood in her eyes.

"Ah! Then you had better know.... Why should I hide it, after that? I see you are the sort of girl will worship me the more for it.... Then, listen ..."

Lo, too, seemed moved.

Still, Gasparine saw the next words came with a frightful effort, for the white face changed from pallid white to pallid green. At last, contemptuously, the words came.

"One hears so often of wrongs—so often of that ... great wrong."

Suddenly she bent towards Gasparine. She spoke rapidly and low, her breath came quick, her eyes were terrible.

"A man once ..."

Over Gasparine's face came a look of indescribable horror. Sometimes, as she listened, she gave a cry.

★　　★　　★　　★　　★

"There, do not weep; it is over. I was only a little child, Gasparine—a poor, trembling child, the most helpless creature under the sun.... No, I never believed there was any God after that—no! ..."

*   *   *   *   *

"I was twelve years of age.... That was at the beginning. The servitude lasted four years.... He afterwards married my sister. My three sisters had always treated me badly. My mother and theirs was a guilty woman.... Their father was a wealthy stockbroker.... Mine—it was thrown in my face—an old and disreputable peer."

In swift, disconnected jerks the words came. Gasparine strained forward and listened, catching the broken thoughts and events, and trying to string them as she heard.

*   *   *   *   *

"Years, years, years! ... long, long years—one, two, three, four.... He was the partner of my mother's husband. All bowed to him in the house, I, the lowest ... I, the lowest.... He knew about me—that I was sheltered and named for my sisters' sakes ... my mother dying at my birth.... He knew—he—he—knew—it—would—not—matter. He—knew—they—would—not—care."

In the last sentence she made a curious pause between each word, so that they dropped, with their full force, like cold and heavy stones into listening water.

"Four years of slavery, torture, secrecy, and mortal terror.... Then, a month before my sister's marriage, they discovered...." She began to speak with frightful rapidity. "Gasparine, as I speak now, though years have passed, my heart turns cold as death when I remember what I listened to, pretending to sleep, as they came into my room ... that I, their butt and scorn, should have robbed my eldest sister! Note well, *they did not blame the man....* That night I escaped.... Trembling with ignorance and helplessness, with only the one mad thought, to escape them, I went to him. It was late at night, and wet and dark ... and he ... he was furious with me.... He said I was an idiot not to warn him.... I! I! who knew nothing! He would teach me, he said, to get him into trouble. It was not my first lesson, but, oh! ..."

Suddenly she burst into a laugh so horrid that a thrill of terror beat in Gasparine's heart.

"Gasparine!" she cried, laughing. "Just imagine! Look at me! Oh, do! Lady-lecturer, so slim! So cared for! See my two hands! Gentle woman's hands. I know nothing of shame or degradation, do I? There is no mark on the wrists to show where they were tied up!"

She stopped with a jerk, put her closed hands together above her head, staggered, and laughed again.

At the movement, sound, and look, Gasparine fell on her knees, crying aloud.

The sound calmed Lotus' weird merriment. In an instant she was herself.

"Hush!" she said peremptorily. "I forgot! We can bear more than we can bear to hear of...." Then again, with sudden wildness, incoherently, "Besides, my hair was gold.... I hate gold hair—brown, and dark, and close round one's face, that hides one somewhat from the eyes that always seem to glare, and peer, and read the brand on one's brow." She clenched her hands above her head with a frightful, guttural "Ach!" then went on. "Yes. Then one can forget the other face, with the gold hair drawn back, and nothing to veil it ... nothing to veil it.... And, God help me! you see I was so young, I had been so cruelly tortured—and the years were so long."

She was silent for a little, struggling for composure, then, sinking beside a chair, she began in a wailing voice.

"And it rained, and rained, and rained. Through all I heard the rain beat on the window.... And when the woman came to take me I felt the rain.... Oh, the rain, the cruel rain! ... I hate the rain! ...

"Yes, that woman was to take me home—back to them. He knew what he did—he knew that he could make *his* peace.... *He knew to what he sent me*—I was his sacrifice to their wrath! ..." No cries, no outburst of curses, could have given the frightful impression of these bald words. "Oh, Gasparine! in the quiet of the nights now, I hear my own voice, stifled, crying, promising impossibilities wildly, beseeching, imploring him for mercy—that he would not send me back ... till it is faint, and then I hear again the swift, voiceless breath, whistling, and cutting my chest in the anguish and stress with which it was drawn.... Well, I escaped—no matter how...."

Gasparine looked at the face, then turned in agony from the unspoken horror written there.

"I went to an old servant—she had been my maid, and was dismissed by my sister for stealing. Yes, and more than that I do not know. She was a pretty, fiery, black-eyed girl. She kept me for six months, and never reproached me, though she was sometimes rough, and struck me silent when I was fretful, until she found that morphine quieted me, and then she gave me dose after dose, until my senses almost left me."

The pallor of Gasparine's face, and the dry swallowing, touched Lotus.

"Don't mind," she said. "It is over, and I have learnt to bear. Listen, and learn what a woman can bear, with not a soul to understand her suffering, not a hand to touch her wound with knowledge. *The abomination of desolation!* I have known it," she said. "Yes, in those times I learnt that in all deeds of heroism, love, courage, reform, it is given us, by some eternal law, to have companionship. But the *deaths* of existence, physical, mental, moral—these we must die alone. In death is no companionship. Loneliness, the horror of it! The absolute loneliness of the soul! Solitude is beautiful, the withdrawing of the soul apart, but loneliness is a horror! That horror I have suffered; that death I have died. And horror does not strengthen the mind. Courage and endurance, yes, by right of their moral worth, but horror, the crushing of the soul by the remorselessness of an evil we have not ourselves power over! that weakens the soul! Well for me it came when I was too young to realise its fullest power and degradation. That piteous passivity of youth is, many a time, the saving of a soul. I could not bear it now....

"For a week before my time a dog howled outside my window horribly, and I used to fancy it waited to take me to hell for my wickedness....

"And when I saw the strange live thing beside me in the bed— a poor, seven-months baby—I hated it, how I hated it! And longed to kill it ... but something kept me back.... I wanted to beat it to death with my hands, but no; for I said, 'It never hurt me, but if I killed it it would hurt me; its dead face would haunt me.' Can you imagine a look of reproach on a dead baby's face? And so I would not; and sometimes when she looks at me now, poor dove, I fancy I see a questioning look on her little face.... And you know she cannot bear a dog to howl."

Gasparine started, then held herself still. A swift and blinding panorama passed before her. She saw the little fair child standing in the hall, and seeming to listen mysteriously. She saw the young girl in the garden ... the brilliant colour, the golden hair, the listening attitude. And then she saw a little bundle, a red cloak, a bare white arm.

"Oh, mystery of life!" she whispered to herself, remembering what she was then, and the many gates of experience which had unfolded to her since. But she would not interrupt the girl ... her own little red-cloaked dream-girl of long ago.... She listened now more eagerly than ever.

"Then there was another craving in my heart; for when one is a mother one becomes desperate. I said, 'Nothing matters. But I will go and kill the other woman, my sister. What is life to me? What is the child to me? Perhaps the gnawing in my breast would stop if I might go and kill the woman....'

"I thought it all over, in the first week of the child's life, in the moments of intense and awful consciousness, sharp and old, which the morphine gave me, between two o'clock and the dawn.... And the same thing fought for the woman as fought for the child.... Something in my heart that said, 'You know what it is to suffer. Will others' suffering ease *your* pain? Look around. Everywhere are men groaning, and bowed to the earth. They, too, perhaps for their sin to you. Will you fill your hands with ashes to lay upon them?'

"Then, with the passing weeks, questions rose in my heart. 'I will not murder,' I said, 'but I will go and see if the great sin she has committed has marked her face, so that men wonder what it is?' And so, one night, in Rosalie's absence, I went, with the child. Oh, that journey! the glare, the dust, the hansom bells, the tramp of horses' feet, the omnibuses, the wailing of the poor, rabbit-like baby! But I was there at last ... faint and trembling, clinging to the railings. I saw *their home*. It was lighted up. Some festivities were in progress, and I saw my sister pass in the light ... and he, the father of the child I held, stepped, for a moment, into the balcony.

"*Then* I wanted to kill them both, and the child too, for on their faces was no sign of the sin they had sinned.... She was painted, and, with her jet hair and brown eyes, looked an adorable woman; showing in her low laces, the curved whiteness of the softness that covered her woman's heart. The treachery of her appearance drove me mad.... Of *him* I did not think so much. Only the thick red neck, of which, in my best moments, I had always been afraid, roused in me again something of the old terror....

"I looked, and looked, and looked ... and turned away...."

She paused.

Across her colourless cheek went a strange streak of red. Gasparine watched it die away, too choked to speak.

"Day by day the struggling remnants of my youth strove to heal and go forward, in step with the great march of life. No; impossible! I shrank from all humanity with unspeakable dread.

I wished only, never to know right or wrong again, only to be wrapped in some warmth that would kill the chill, some kindness that would give me again a place, a level among those who worked and went not knowing depths like mine.... But in my soul revolt was growing, and the calm of my murdered heart was giving me strength.... The child was three months old, and I seventeen, when my intellect roused, and asserted its supremacy. I found, one day, among Rosalie's belongings—how they got there heaven knows!—an old Latin grammar, and a book of Euclid. Never shall I forget the intense intellectual awakening of that moment! I threw the baby down, and took the books with a flood of old memories over me.... I had been clever as a child, something of a prodigy, indeed, in mathematics and the classics ... but my little triumphs were joyless, for no one cared;—indeed, it was a source of anger with my sisters.

"Now I resolved. I was seized with a great, vague ambition, in which I should be tremendously clever, make a fortune, become world-famous, and avenge myself. The reality has been less gilded, but better on the whole. My first step was to throw away the morphine, my next to beseech Rosalie to help me to a situation. The child was put to nurse, and I became servant in a lodging-house.

"My mistress drank; she was a widow, a lady by birth, once the beauty of her county, now seized by the remorseless passion of drink. She earned a precarious living by keeping lodgers.

"When drunk, she forgot to pay me; otherwise, she was kind.... Then arrived a time when she would not pay me, and Rosalie, destitute, came to upbraid me. Something entered to me that night, and I found what *a will* can do. I took her brandy-bottle in my hand, and told her my story, asking for my wages regularly....

"Gasparine, look in my eyes; there are no drops of water, but there are tears and tears.... If I could weep for any of that past I would weep here. My death was her life. As she folded me in her arms, the Voice cried to her, 'Awake, thou that sleepest, and arise from the dead....'[1]

"That woman is Mrs. Grace, and *now* she does not drink. Unfortunately, she cannot become fond of the child.

"'Let us blot out those years,' she said. 'You shall become again a child.' And so it came out."

All these words fell with inconceivable rapidity.

---

1 Ephesians 5:14.

"A friend, indeed, a lover, of her early days was Professor of History at Oxford. He still befriended her, and—for you know that undying charm she has about her?—loved her. She told him something, a fictitious, but sufficiently pressing story, about me, and he offered to see me through the University until I took my degree of M.A.

"In my school-girl's sailor frock I, at seventeen, passed for any age between thirteen and fifteen. At thirteen I was a woman; at seventeen I had the thin air of a little girl who grows out of her frocks.... Three years later I was the University prodigy, when I took my degree.

"At twenty—my real age—I got this post. I was not in reality fit for it, but Professor Raymond worked untiringly to get it for me. The salary was exceptionally high for one thing, the work not heavy, except in considering my age; and the advantage for Mrs. Grace and me to get away to an unknown country! These reasons all weighed with him. Of all his loving help I can speak no thanks, but I can, and do, feel him a king among men, knowing he did it all in tender pity for a woman who once terribly betrayed and scorned him, learning, too late, his worth.

"That is all the story. Ladybird is my daughter. Her hair is gold, like mine was. To hide such likeness as is between us, mine is dyed, and worn like this. Her age, and my supposed age, keep me perfectly safe.... Yes, that is all! ..."

There was a long, long silence. Gasparine's horror was so great that she remained still and tearless, yet with keen pain. When next Lo spoke it was in a voice of such softness and sweetness that involuntarily Gasparine's eyes were drawn to her. A piteous sight—the pallid face, the brows bound with restless, long fingers, the eyes looking at the dream of which she spoke.

"I had a dream one night—one night when my heart was very full of its misery. I thought I heard God call me and say, 'Come into the sunlight, oh! my little child!' ... (No one had ever called me 'little child' before. When I was scarcely more than a baby people seemed to think me old, but, you see, to the great God I was only a little child. There was such *rest* in the thought!) 'Come into the sunlight, oh! my little child! My hands hold your face while I search your soul ... and the sunlight is my hands, and the light is my eyes.... Come into the sunlight and be strong.' But I would not go until"—there came a choking pause—"until God called all who were weary and sorrowful, and born old like me— till He called them also 'little children,' and bade them come into the sunlight; and we all went together."

Gasparine's heart was wrung. The expression of strife and agony on the loved face was terrible to see. Lotus, with the awful memories crowding upon her, fell into one of her dreamy states.

"Rosalie died," she said. "Poor Rosalie! Often she tried to persuade me to let her take me to the Halls[1] and get me a sweetheart. 'Gracious, missy!' she would say; 'don't you worry! Come an' be 'appy.' ... I don't know what kept me back, certainly not a sense of virtue—at least, as far as I knew—for the world was all to me a hideous charnel-house,[2] without love, justice, or mercy. And the only things I feared were the dark and a blow.... (Have you never noticed how hideous it is to me to have to go into the dark, and how I hate to sleep alone?) ... Rosalie died in a Home. She hated it, was full of nervous horror at the cleanness and whiteness of the rooms, and in trembling terror for the gentle Sisters.... Just imagine! That poor woman.... We have not yet fathomed the power of association. I wonder what religionists, socialists, salvationists, make of that? No need to tell us the devils will not get into heaven.... The poor devils! They only ask to be left in peace in hell! When an angel comes, and, for some reason or other, hauls them up for a little into the clean, bare place, they grow terribly nervous and awkward! The gentle sisters oppressed poor Rosalie. She longed to get back to hell. She thought that she was going to get better, but she died, suddenly, one night. I was glad when I heard she had had no time to suffer or to know."

She paused, and pressed her temples with her fingers, as if holding back the rush of thoughts.

"A sinful woman? Yes. Yet when she died I felt my heart empty as for the loss of a sister."

The yearning pressed on Gasparine's heart like a physical weight. She longed to go and kneel at Lo's feet, and say some word of comfort; but Lo seemed to awake, and, with a slight, imperious motion, stopped her.

"There! Let be!" she said addressing herself, impatiently, and rising, walked once or twice about the room, then threw herself

---

1 This may be a reference to the Music Halls, popular features of the London entertainment scene that offered a variety of musical and dramatic spectacles. For an overview, see F. Anstey, "London Music Halls," *Harper's New Monthly Magazine* 82 (January 1891):190–202. There was a seamy side to even the most upscale music halls: Anstey notes that in the first rank of music halls, prostitutes openly solicited potential clients.

2 "A house for dead bodies; a house or vault in which the bones of the dead are piled up" (*OED*).

into a chair, legs crossed, arms folded, her head sunk on her chest.

"Well, all this charming experience does not go for nothing," she said, in cheerfully sardonic tones. "I have learnt many things partially, and one thing thoroughly. *Never take the world into your confidence.* You must never let the world know the *real* reasons and motives for your actions. The world is a bad master, but a good slave. Then I found one must either tread or be trodden upon. I do not mean that one need tread brutally, or without relative regard to the capacity of that, or whom, whereon or on whom you tread; but a choice you must make. Study the foibles and follies of your kind, flatter them, and you gain power; but exactly in degree as you throw yourself away for them, staking your soul and life for the benefit of their highest good, so exactly will they use and abuse you. Then I found out, too, the power of indirect influence. Direct influence is nothing. The strong man who floors another in a physical, mental, or moral contest, is nowhere. The world is ruled otherwise. The disciples had no awe of the Christ, but the apostles who heard the disciples had! An opinion, an announcement only becomes powerful when it has passed through several minds; the stream at its source has potential energy, but at its mouth it has power....

"But the last thing I was taught, the truth I fought longest against, most slowly acknowledged as a truth, was *that the power of love was dead in me....* How I tried to love! How I tried to rouse some passionate emotion in my heart towards those who were gentle to me! Ah! love, love is better, though in vain, than the emptiness that unlove knows. What did I say to you once long ago?—'There is no love.' Let me say now, in gentler mood, the power to love or believe in love is dead in me. I said a great, perfect, unquestioning love would heal me. I knew what I said— I spoke of the impossible! You see the agony was too great ... that wicked and unnatural outrage dried up with damning fire each natural and womanly impulse, turning my child-heart to stone, my mother instincts to gall. Yet when I found I could not love, I found, too, that I could act love irresistibly, and, in return, give patience and gentleness. To all them, 'distant in humanity,'[1] to whom my dead hands stretch yearningly, I am, indeed, like one

---

1   This phrase comes from John Keats, "Isabella, or, the Pot of Basil." At this point in the poem the murdered Lorenzo appears in a dream to his love Isabella to tell her of his fate.

dead. It would seem the very smell of death is on me, so the people draw back.... They are very young and innocent of heart, or very old and wise of head, who love me, save through compulsion, and it is I who feel it most in every gay and lively scene, the awful curse upon me—'Between them and me a great gulf fixed.'[1]

"Some one has said that no one can be truly dishonoured solely by the action of another. That is wrong. Too, too often the blow that humiliates the body also degrades the soul.... I feel my soul profaned.... I ..."

There was another long silence. Gasparine broke it first.

"In a little I shall know better how to speak to you, Lo. But first let me say just what strikes me most. You are *not*, in dress or general manner, like one weighed by a terrible past, and whose hopes are done. Lotus, what is there now to prevent you living life as others, and happy? It was terrible, but it is all over. You—you——"

"The highest law we know prevents it," Lo said solemnly; "the law of nature. One can outrage the law of nature mentally as well as physically. That is what has been done to me. And do not say that it is past; *nothing is ever really past.*"

"Lo, may I ask one question?"

"Why, surely; as many as you will." The mournful voice became sarcastic in an instant. "My narrative has been sketchy, I don't doubt; but I shall be happy to fill in all details, as you require."

Not noticing the bitter tone, Gasparine said, gently,—

"Did you love the man, Lo?"

A dangerous gleam crossed the girl's face. Gasparine saw her question had been a mistake. Yet, with marvellous control, Lotus answered, in a fairly steady voice,—

"No; but at first he flattered, and was very kind to me. That was rare, for I was the butt of my sisters' spite, and my mother's husband, keeping me for his credit's sake, loathed me. He never lost an opportunity to strike or affront me wantonly. I was a sad, passionate, clinging, child. The cloud that hung over me I attributed, at first, to some wickedness within myself. I had a nervous, slavish feeling instilled into me. A threatening look made me

---

1 Cf. Luke 16:26, from the parable of Dives and Lazarus. Abraham in heaven tells the rich man in hell that the beggar Lazarus (now in Abraham's bosom) cannot alleviate his agony because of the gulf fixed between them.

cower, the lower that my piteous child's pride endeavoured to conceal it. *He* knew this well, and soon taught me to cringe for his occasional kindnesses.... No, I did not love him, but I was proud of his attention, half proud even of his brutalities.... My eyes were wide open to all his faults, yet I did not dare to question why *his* weaknesses should pass unchallenged, while mine were so severely dealt with.... "

The courage with which she spoke these fearful truths against herself was more terrible to Gasparine than any lie she could have uttered. Again the look of dream-anguish crossed her face.

"Born a victim, already, what chance was there for me? ... No chance, no chance! Oh, me! And yet often, oh, often, visions of higher things so torture me that it seems sometimes as if the lost soul of my mother had entered me at birth—when, most unhappy woman! she died—to torture me with her wild longings.... And this dead soul in me seems to say, 'Oh, give us a chance! Give women a chance! Heavily, heavily a woman is punished when wrong befalls, either through her fault, her weakness, or her, perchance, unwise, but justifiable effort towards freedom.'"

The silence that came now was long. It was late; the rain had stopped; the summer dusk dimmed all outside. Lo roused and stretched her arms above her head, then threw them out as if to throw the agony away. Then she opened the windows, and a thrush across the road gave a final note of adieu. Lo stepped into the balcony, and, seeming forgetful of the recent wild rains, knelt, laying her weary, fevered cheek on the wet, sweet clematis leaves; and, from within, Gasparine heard her whispered moan,—

"Will nothing cool the burning? Will nothing cool the burning?"

The rain dripped from the leaves among her hair.

In a little she returned to the room. She had swept every trace of raging storm from her face; she was again, as always, gentle, smiling, piteous.

"Gasparine," she said coldly, "I never told any one so much except Mrs. Grace, and *then* it was not so hard. Why did I tell you? Talk of indirect influence. It was the rain forced me to speak to-day. I fought against it, but the past was on my breast with every raindrop—*for it rained just so that night*. Nevertheless, I trust you very completely.... But do not consider it a compliment. If I loved you, *could* love you, these are things I would hide."

The remark, cruel and uncalled for though it was, only made Gasparine's heart burst into brighter, fuller flame.

"Lotus!" she said, in a voice full and rich; "oh! my Lotus-flower! Have they cast you out from among the good women, you queen of women, queen though in exile? Only the truest woman-nature could have borne as you have borne. You are as pure as a snowdrop to me, Lotus. Dearly-loved one, I asked for your love—I said that I would heal you till you gave me love—but now I ask your love no longer. Even had you love to give, I am not worthy. To think you are my little red-cloaked girl! Oh! why did fate keep us apart so long? Don't you know how, in the old stories, the prince in exile has always with him a fool who is faithful?"

"And so you would be my fool—my little fool?"

"Yes; let me be your fool—your fool, who asks only to follow and serve you, whose faithfulness you cannot doubt; for when was the fool ever faithless in the old tales?"

"But I think I cannot let you be my fool. I must give you that compliment. I am surrounded by fools. You, my Genius, are wise."

"Let it be so; I will take the compliment. In the old tales was not the fool always wise?"

CHAPTER XI
LADYBIRD DISCUSSES THE ADVANTAGES OF PARENTAGE WITH HER LOVER

It was a lovely day after the wild rain. Ladybird sat on the steps, nursing her baby. Bright sunlight came down and drew the perfumed breath from the late flowers, and the insects hummed approval as they went about their business. Ladybird's hair glittered like a glory, and every now and then her clear voice broke the air—snatches of old ballads, the plaintive infant voice, with its strange, forlorn notes.

"Hush! hush! baby. Now don't cry.

"'Oh! thy *muver* has gone from her cares to rest;
She hath taken the babe on her quiet breast.'[1]

"I am your mother, baby; I have gone to rest. I take you here on my *boosing*. Do not cry."

The white awnings of the balcony moved, and Lo appeared above. Ladybird had burst out singing anew:—

---

1 From Felicia Hemans, "The Adopted Child." In these lines, an adoptive mother tells a young boy who wants to return to his birth family that he would not be able to find his birth mother at her former home (presumably because she has died).

"'All a green willow, willow,
All a green willow is my garland.
Alas! by what love may I make ye to know
The unkindness for kindness that to me doth grow,
That one who most kind love on me should bestow
Most unkind unkindness she to me doth show,
For all a green willow is my garland.'"[1]

"Strange baby! Where did you learn Rosalie's song; and why do you pierce me by singing so often the truth about yourself?" Lo said to herself; and aloud she called, "Go away, Lady; you disturb me. There is Sonny Thomas coming up the road; go and meet him."

The child rose carefully with the doll, and moved across the trim little lawn to the gate. The sunlight caught the elegant curves of her little person, the shining, hatless head, the lace frock, the browned calves of her slender legs.

"How do you do, Sonny Thomas?"

"I am very well, Lady," said the little lover, hurrying up and showing himself the same height as Ladybird, and three times as broad. "I called to know if you could play with me to-day, and the tall lady sent me away. She's not a bit nice, not like Miss Grace. So I said, 'May I sit on the steps till she comes; it's so far to go to Snowden Place?' And she said, 'No.' So I waited about till I saw you feed the pigeons, and I called, but you didn't hear, so I went to mother. You see that's the difference. You haven't any mother. I shouldn't like that. When you are my wife you must have a mother."

"Why?"

"My mother says everybody *ought* to have a mother."

"Why?"

"Because everybody has."

"Have I, then?" with a glimmer of hope.

"No."

"Why?"

"'Cause you're an adopted child."

"What's an adopted child?"

"Some one without a mother."

"Well?"

---

1 Adapted slightly from John Heywood, "The Ballad of the Green
Willow." The green willow garland traditionally signifies abandonment
by a lover.

"It's bad."

"Why?"

"Mother ses so."

"I *wish* I had a mother."

"Yes; an' then you'd be like me."

"Couldn't your mother do?"

"Oh no."

"Why?"

"Because she lives in a different house, and takes care of *me*."

"What does she do?"

"She makes my clo'es."

"You said your trouse's were bought in a shop, Sonny Thomas."

"Yes; these ones with the pockets were. I didn't tell no story. But my nightdresses, an' shirts, an' old clo'es, she sews, on a machine; an' she puts me to bed, an' gives me sweets, an' ses 'God bless you!' every night."

"But she whips you sometimes?"

"Never!" declared the youth, lying valiantly in defence of the general soundness of his argument.

"But one day, when you cried, you said you hated her?"

"I didn't; and I meant Jane."

They were quite silent. Then Sonny Thomas said, with some bitterness, because Ladybird had had him on the hip rather severely twice,—

"Mother ses you're not quite respectable, an' when I'm bigger I'm not to go with you."

"I don't want you to; and I am."

"No you're not, indeed!"

"But I am."

"How are you?"

"Because I am; but *you're* not, Sonny Thomas."

"*I* am; *I* have a mother."

"No," with provoking certainty, "you're not, I know."

"*How* do you know?"

"'Cause Lo calls your mother 'The Fat Philistine.'"

"You're a bad girl. I'll tell mother that."

"So shall I."

"You have no mother."

"Yes, I have."

"Oh! you tell stories."

"So do you; for you *did* say you hated her, and you *were* whipped, and it was *not* Jane."

Then both wept for anger.

Later, Ladybird sought Lotus. It was evening. Slanting shadows lay across the little lawn, and a large lime tree made a bower of shade. Here Lo sat, a book on her lap.

"Does everybody have a mother, Lo?" Ladybird asked.

Lo looked up.

"A very deep question, my infant."

"Oh!"

"Yes; most people have."

"Sonny Thomas ses I have none."

"You have no mother like his, certainly."

"I don't want a mother like his; but I should like one. May I not have one?"

"Ah! I do not know.... Look here, Ladybird, look at me, straight in my eyes.... Yes, just so, and listen while I speak. I think you are an abominably ugly little girl; your dress is ugly, your face, and eyes, and hair are ugly, very ugly. I'm glad you don't belong to me. I expect it's because you're so naughty and ugly you've got no mother. There!"

Ladybird dropped, crushed, upon the grass, and wept in a childish agony of passionate grief and wounded pride.

Lo watched with a face that grew paler and paler; then she bent and drew the crushed lace bundle to her breast.

"Hush, hush! Beauty, darling!" she whispered wildly. "You are not ugly; you are beautiful; you are my darling. Hush, beloved! You have a mother, Lady; perhaps she will come to you, one day."

That evening, Ladybird, still burning with the sentiment of quest, made a last effort to provide herself with that benefit of which the world and Sonny Thomas seemed anxious to deprive her. She betook herself to the cottage kitchen, a model apartment like the rest of the house, and settled herself to have a chat with the cook-housekeeper, a more than middle-aged, pock-marked, and far from attractive, single lady.

"Cooky, is it *very* bad not to have a mother?"

"Well, it's bad enough, my lamb, but it's worse to have no friends."

"H—m."

Pause.

"Sonny Thomas is an extremely nasty boy, Cooky."

"Dearie me! What's the vagabin' bin up to now?"

"Oh! so very rude to me!"

Pause.

"You never were a mother yourself, I suppose, Cooky?" cautiously.

"No, thank the Lord, I never was," retorted Cooky, with an aggrieved air, all the same.

This did not sound encouraging for Lady's proposal. She attempted an amendment.

"I don't mean exactly a mother—I mean a sort of a one, you know; not one with a papa for your child, like Mrs. Thomas, but just any sort of a one, you know, Cooky."

But this pleased Cooky even less, and Lady, opening her large eyes, considered the matter.

"Well, you *had* a mother?"

"*Had* a mother? Bless your heart, yes."

"H'm. I suppose," suggestively. "*You* couldn't be *my* mother, just for a change, you know, Cooky?"

There was a silence. Then Ladybird was surprised to see, when she looked at Cooky, that the unlovely eyes were full of tears.

CHAPTER XII
GASPARINE'S YEAR WONDERFUL

There was no autumn that year. The winter came down sudden and fierce. In September the passionate storm-spirit seemed to brood in the air, threatening a wild fruitfulness. The floods again rose wildly, and for days the far hills were wreathed in shrouds of rain. The wind tore the still green and clinging leaves from the trees, tossed the scanty fruit away, and made a mockery of the harvest. Yet, of all years, that was the year—Year Wonderful, as she called it—of deepest love, and joy, and service, for Gasparine. She used to go to the tossed and drenched grave, and tell the boy beneath of the broken heart for whom she toiled now, with incomprehensible passion and fervour. To heal the dear, broken heart, to bring rest into the lovely, tired eyes, to give youth to the old-young brain.

In her after life Gasparine knew what it was to possess such moderate domestic happiness as most of us, in time, learn to be content with. She knew what it was to possess a dear little husband—a head shorter than herself—with a true little heart in a narrow little chest. She knew what it was to have little children—weird creatures, only one of whom resembled Gaspar, and that one died. Yet that year in the white cottage was the golden year of her life; deep marked, never to be forgotten. For after that she grew old. It was right; a year in our youth means much.

It seemed that Lo, after the confession forced from her, as she said, by the power of association acting upon shattered nerves, ignored her past. She was as if she had none, or it had been a trivial past, easily forgotten. She was more than usually brilliant, enchanting, gentle, and her companionship, conversation, thoughts, and words, became the light for Gasparine.

Without any force, it naturally fell out that Gasparine gave up her rooms, and occupied the little white room next Lo's study. Then only it was that she found out by what untiring work the income was earned which maintained the cottage.

Gladly Gasparine threw her poor pittance into the general fund, imitating, as well as she could, the lovely patience of her dear one. She worked at her paintings and studies, was sweeter, as she saw Lo was, with her pupils, and found, to her surprise, how thoroughly, even if selfishly, they appreciated gentleness and help.

Strange to say, Mrs. Grace took to her kindly; and Ladybird, finding her a willing slave, became attached. A delightful feeling of homefulness and friendfulness filled Gasparine's heart. Little by little, through the winter, she found what she could do. First the bills, taxes, tiresome correspondence, which Lo never had time to do well. By-and-by, the entire household business came into her hands. She wrote letters, saw people; and the more she worked the more her amazement grew.

"Lo," she said, one day, after having struggled for two hours over a lawyer's letter, "how in wonder, with all your work, did you find time to make good your claim to the bank at the foot of the garden?"

"I was cheated twice," said Lo briefly. "That sharpens the wits. Don't forget the interest on that bill of mine the Jews[1] have. The 28th is the date."

"But, Lo, excuse me, the interest is so deadly."

"So was the need. You must pay for convenience and pride; it is better than prospecting one's friends."

"If only one could do it in a less extravagant way!"

"Extravagant!" said Lo. "Let me see, what is extravagance? Extravagance is giving away in money, energy, or time, what your own power of reception is not large enough to receive in its new

---

1 Historically excluded from most professions in English life, Jews had been associated with moneylending since the Middle Ages.

form. Make your money reach as far as possible. In your smaller economy do not forget the wider economy of the world. Circle, give out, draw in, but not to the same mouths and sources. Hoarding is not only vicious, it is stupid. Yes, yes, I know it is often morally excusable."

At this, Gasparine, with her clear common-sense in business matters, would only smile, and inwardly sigh; for she saw the money given freely as water which she knew had been earned on nights when the bright, dark eyes were held wide open by the horror of the past, and the pen went ceaselessly to still the pain. And she said to herself, "This is one of the cases, sweet, where it is morally excusable to hoard." And she bent her energies that way.

Nor was it all peace in the cottage. Between Ladybird and Mrs. Grace a constant war waged. The child was a remarkable creature, babbling French and German picked up from Lo and the French and German lecturers, who made much of her. Undoubtedly, Mrs. Grace was very severe; but Lady resented vigorously. Once Gasparine went to Lo.

"Lo, do forgive me for seeming like a tell-tale. I like Mrs. Grace so much, but she is really unkind to Lady; she punished her twice to-day on pretext of the merest trifles. In reality she was jealous and angry because Lady slapped you this morning, and you only petted her."

Lo put her hand to her head, puzzled. How well Gasparine now knew and loved the action of the slender fingers!

"I know, I know," Lo said. "I don't find fault with you, my Genius—not at all. Only, here is the difficulty: We must all live together—surely better in peace than at war. *There is so much war!* I know Madam is jealous of the child. I know I could forbid her to touch Lady—she knows it, too, and she would obey. But then, think! All those repressed blows, those forbidden strokes, how they would water the seed of hatred that is in her heart—water and ripen it against the child's later years. Whereas, allowed free scope now, it may die. 'Resist not evil'[1] is stronger than you think. We have not fathomed its power yet, and are too timid to dare. Lady's is not the nature to suffer bonds when she is strong enough to cast them off; and I hope much from the child's clev-

---

1 See the words of Jesus in Matthew 5:39: "But I say unto you, That ye resist not evil: but whosoever shall smite thee on thy right cheek, turn to him the other also."

erness and fascination, and from Mrs. Grace's womanly qualities—for she has many, and good, poor dear! She has her faults.
Yes, why not! But think! Just imagine what she is and does, and
how she keeps house! And then compare her old life. Her little
vanities! Why I would do more, if that were needed, to give her all
the trifles with which she now amuses herself—hats, bonnets;
whatever they cost they are cheap, compared with brandy-bottles.
And then, Gasparine, can I forget a sailor frock once bought for
me by the sale of one or two precious girlish jewels that had
escaped the insatiable hands of thirst?"

"Dear Lotus!"

"And as for the child—each blow she gets hurts me twice; but
I bear, and for her courage I do not fear. Ah! is she not beautiful
and clever? Oh, Gasparine! That free, wild soul has nothing in it
of my mother or of me; that sweet, pure face has nothing in it of
his brutal passion.... My own creation!—my wonderful baby! ...
Gasparine, sometimes I think if I should live, it may be that the
years will kill even the death of my soul. And I will live for her,
and through her for all women, and all the wisdom of my sorrows
and my sufferings I'll consecrate to make her great and pure and
true ... the woman who knows to save all women.... Pshaw! what
folly I am speaking! What a fool I am occasionally! There is
Madam calling. I must go."

In swift allusions like these, after the fashion of her old moods
of dreamy talking, Gasparine understood how close she had
come into the confidence and trust of Lotus.

As for Gasparine's installation in the cottage, it was all
arranged between her and Mrs. Grace, who acted as go-between;
and Lo, hardly realising any change, to begin with, from the daily
visits, took it as a matter of course when she did, divining how
the girl's happiness lay in giving her work and time to this dear
cause.

"You do not mind, dear Lo?" Gasparine said, once. "It is my
salvation."

"A cheap salvation and convenient for me," said Lo, sarcasti-
cally, but with a smile.

Christmas that year was good. Light, crisp snow and hard
frost. The cottage party often drove out to Airthrey, where the
horse-shoe pond was thrown open to visitors and skaters, by the
generous owner. There Ladybird, on a pair of small skates, went
up and down the lake like a fairy of the North Pole.

Then it was that Gasparine learnt the daily and unbearable
stings which Lo's motherhood received.

Every one stared at the little child. The house-party from the Castle paused to comment,—

"The fairy! The sweet thing! The little Eskimo!" And then the inevitable question, "Who is she? Who is she?"

Gasparine left the child in charge of Professor Raymond, who was there, and skated over to Lo. The lady-lecturer on the bank was a well-known figure.

"What a gay scene, is it not? You are enjoying it, Gaspar?"

"Yes; I love skating. Lady and I are learning outside edge."

"So I see." Lo's eyes sought the child.

"We are the observed of all observers.[1] Lo, Lo, forgive me, but I don't know how you can do it!"

"Do what?"

"If Ladybird was mine"—Gasparine sat down beside Lo on the trunk of a tree, and spoke in a lowered voice—"I could not bear it. To hear the people ask continually who she is, to see her beauty is a spell to them all, and to have to call her 'boarder' and 'nameless.' I couldn't do it. I should feel too proud and fond of her for that. Why," cried Gasparine, with sudden vehemence, "I'd take her there in my arms and say, 'She's mine; my own baby. The rest is no one's business.'"

Lotus looked at her with cynical and cold reproof.

"I understand," she said. "You reproach me. Yes! I should own the child, and give her a life of nameless and unbearable shame.... Look around, my enthusiastic, unrecognised Genius, and take this scene in well. You see, at the first, only the gay figures moving on the white—all innocent, all gay. Look closer, and see the invisible lines dividing them. There is the county set, the set from Stirling Castle, the College set—a proud set, of whom I am one—the Glasgow visitors to Bridge of Allan, recognisable by their intolerable twang, and then the rag-tag, the nobodies. Still, they are honest—do you see?—all honest, so they may skate together in one place. Let me be honest with them. What happens? Not one of them, from Lady Esther, who at this moment is kissing the child, to that vulgar-souled Fat Philistine, Mrs. Thomas, but would draw aside from me and from her as if my suffering damned them, and her sweet smile soiled.... The men! Yes. When the *honest* women were gone, the noble, manly men would troop around, and then ... I might resign my position in the College,

---

1   William Shakespeare, *Hamlet*, III.i. Ophelia uses this phrase to describe Hamlet as a model of noble behavior before he succumbs to (apparent) madness.

and, leaving the quiet and the security of home comforts, which strongly influence Mrs. Grace, return to the old, uncertain, hand-to-month grasping, the lodging-house, the beer-jugs, the brandy bottle.... Thank you, Gasparine. I will rather stifle, if I may, my ardent motherly instincts," she sneered, "and try how far my name for cleverness and unimpeachable honour will launch my little foundling on her way." She softened and spoke more gently. "My Genius, I do not mean to be hard, but I speak from knowledge of the great, silly world that I have fathomed. Humour it, the huge Natural! .... Leave us, I and my Lady—we know best, I assure you."

Gasparine was abashed, but not convinced.

"Gasparine," Lo continued, "do you see the Professor has taken the child to speak to the house-party? How do I know my father is not among them? or my sister?—or, or *him*? Shall I give them that triumph, do you think? Bah! Whether we will or no, the world forces us to frauds and shams. I, my aunt, my boarder, what are we but frauds? How else may we be honest?"

During this winter, Mona Lefcadio was away. She was with her parents abroad, and in spring was to return to London to be introduced to society.

Letters came for her daily, and to Gasparine, who, as secretary, opened and read them, they were a revelation. They filled her with jealous pain. They were beautiful letters, speaking the worship of a young, pure, opening soul for a larger nature, which it had idealised.

Once a sense of eavesdropping came over Gasparine, and she spoke to Lo.

"Lotus, are you anxious any of your letters should be kept private?"

"Yes; those marked so."

"Mona's letters are not marked private."

"I did not know."

"Shall I read them?"

"As you like. Mona has never led me to believe that privacy or secrecy were any part of her pleasure. Read or leave, as you like."

As she spoke she smiled strangely.

Within herself Gasparine pondered.

"My salvation was in her; but hers, where is it? Not in Mona; I can see that. Yet for each of us there is a salvation, if we could find it. Where is hers? I wonder where? ..."

While the winter went she sought and strove to know; and once or twice it seemed to her that she caught a gleam of it.

CHAPTER XIII

LO'S SALVATION DRAWS NIGH

"Yes," said Gasparine to herself, "it is there."

For during this winter Professor Raymond came oftener than before; came earlier and stayed later. Once or twice he even lost his train. He was a grand creature. Gasparine was hopelessly in love with him; so was Ladybird, who informed all whom it might concern that, in the fulness of time, it was probable she might see fit to honour him with the priceless gift of her hand.

He was, in truth, worthy of the love showered upon him. He gave the impression of a lion's strength and a king's nobility. His gentleness was tender and caressing. Towards Lotus he was always very gentle. At first Gasparine knew that these visits bored and disturbed Lotus, though she always entertained him as best lay in her power. But it meant expense and worry, for Raymond was a muscular Christian, who kept the body in excellent condition, yet fought humanly and whole-heartedly for the old faith and religion. Modern scepticism and pessimism had hardly touched him. To be sure, his health was superb, and his circumstances prosperous.

A change came, however, and soon Gasparine knew how welcome that sudden telegram was. It made a joyful bustle through the whole house. Lady skipped, and sang her weird madrigals, unreproved. Gasparine got her violin ready—Lo and Raymond loved her playing. Mrs. Grace alone wore a face of tragic expression. Yet, with bitten lip, and restless fingers, she made things perfect in the pretty rooms.

The strong and alluring presence of the man gave them, more and more, a feeling of pleasaunce and befriendment. He brought a breath from the great world. He gave the right balance to local sores when discussed. With a word he made the misty things clear, even to Lo; not only because he was a man, but because he was a man with a heart and brain unusually brilliant and warm.

Over the two Gasparine pondered long of evenings, as they all sat in the lighted drawing-room, with curtains drawn, Lady, sleepy and cross, declining to be pleased with anything, and denying that she felt the least tired or could possibly go to bed, in spite of Mrs. Grace's peremptory glances.

Gasparine, over her work, watched Lo as she talked. The sprite-like creature, how she flashed, and her voice seemed to sing at these times! And now Gasparine saw a strange transformation take place in her. A transformation that had in it something awful—like life returning to the dead. For through the worn and pallid face seemed to come again that look of passion, that tender blueness of the eyes, that alluring grace of movement which had so driven the memory of the red-cloaked child into Gasparine's soul. And now, too, she seemed to fathom that shrinking motion of Lo's with which she withdrew from any attempt at a caress, even from the friendly touch of Raymond. The fear of humanity lingered in her still.

But, with him, Gasparine thought that now he had unravelled the mystery of Lo's eyes and wound it round his heart. It gave her a keener pain than Mona's letters could to notice how he lingered, seemed loth to go, and often hastened back, giving some small excuse, to say good-night again. Then an evening came when Gasparine saw him, with a swift, irrepressible action, bend and touch, fondly, pitifully, the bent, brown head.

"Good-night, until we meet, my own Lotus," he said.

"Good-night, dear Raymond," Lo said gently.

It seemed his words did not strike her as having any special meaning.

Not so Gasparine.

"Her salvation is there," the watcher said, with a cruel pang of jealousy at her heart, "if she but raise her eyes to see."

Was Lo, then, blind?

That night she stood in her study long after the others were asleep and all the house was still. Outside a chill, sleety rain struck the window every now and then, driven by a gusty wind that brought with it a moan from the pine plantation. Her head was bound in a linen cloth, and from its white folds her pallid, anguished face gazed up to the night sky for help. Her hands were clasped, and thrown straight out.

"One death, then, is not enough," she said. "*One!* Oh God! How *many* deaths have I died? I did not know that in me there was this life to live, and, therefore, this death to die.... It is not love I feel—no, nor passion. It is not to have the position of chosen one, before all the world, in the pride of bridal, and the honour of wife. What are the outward signs to me? ... Let me be true here to myself ... I, humbled, humbled beyond raising, in my person; I, unworthy as I know myself to be, in soul, heart, mind; I, I, receive from him ... tenderness, respect, perhaps ... can it be? ... *love.* And I, in return, *worship him.* I did not know that so much was left in me ... but now I feel, I know, that from him I might receive *salvation.* Ay, salvation.... What a thought! Salvation to one damned—life to one dead! ... If I might, nameless, unknown, leave my old dead heart buried here,—might drop off my old life like this dress, might rise and leave each one I've known, and follow him, barefoot even, as only his servant, only to work very hard, and be very tired for his sake; only to hide it from him, only to sleep on a mat at his door, only to know that *he needed me*—needed my worship, needed my service.... This, this is salvation: *that one shall give service, and one shall need it, and both make payment by love.*"

And her salvation drew nigh indeed. For, with the next week, Raymond came again, and when Gasparine slipped away with the child after dinner, and Mrs. Grace went to see about coffee, he rose and took Lo's hand.

"Lotus," he said, "I feel to-night like looking back to the time when I first met you. You don't mind, do you?"

Of her past before he met her he only knew that it had been sad. "An unhappy childhood—abroad," was his impression.

When he spoke, she shuddered still-ly, released her hand, and in a moment said, quietly,—

"No; I do not mind."

Between these two, in spite of years of kindly, generous help on the one hand, and sad, futile gratitude on the other; in spite of a mental nearness, and a great familiarity of speech; there was a gulf, which he strove, often, impatiently to bridge.

He put her gently into an arm-chair, and, seating himself with his hand on the chair arm, bent his brilliant eyes upon her.

"Mrs. Grace wrote me," he said, recalling, "that she was anxious to see me. We had been friends since childhood, and," with a spasm, "lovers later; but," laughing hardly, "I was the only one who loved, and, therefore, suffered. That hasn't to do with my present story. Listen, dear. I went, and found her greatly distressed about you, the child of her friend, dead abroad, now suddenly thrown upon her hands. She was always a generous woman. And you! I can see you now, in that house in Bloomsbury—a shy little girl in a navy blue sailor frock, thick brown curls round a little white face, eyes that never lifted, except when one was not looking.... Such an odd little soul! ... but, oh! what piercingly brilliant eyes for a child; for I saw them without looking."

He paused. Lotus corrected inwardly,—"Seventeen ... victim of outrage ... a mother."

"How your remarks on life amazed me! How certain I was that I had discovered a genius! Do you know, all that first conversation between you and me is as clear in my mind to-day as in the day it was uttered! Clear, but not real; do you understand, Lo?"

"Oh, I understand."

"I said to you, 'So, my little girl, you want to study, and be M.A., and get a name?' 'Yes,' you said earnestly; 'I want a name—a name of my own, that I may be proud of, to give to another, perhaps.' To give to another! Imagine a child saying that! I said to you, 'But to take a degree, my little maid, means hard work with many books.' 'Do not, for heaven's sake, "little maid" me,' you said contemptuously; and added, in a moment, penitently and softly, 'Yes, but the books teach, and are silent, and do not reproach. I am not afraid.'"

Lo smiled wanly at the accuracy of his memory. Her mind went back through the years, too—the terrible years, when his face, like the faces of all other men, was strange and cruel; and now it had grown friendly and kind.

"So I took you to the College and commended you," he went on.... "You poor child! How miserable you were! ...Yet you amazed professors and students as you had amazed me. They used to say you would not speak. They called you the 'Pent-up-Promising-Prodigy,' and pointed your short frock out among the tall, flirting ladies."

("While I, in thought, was with my white baby," commented Lo, in her soul, "bidding it wait till I had wherewithal for it and me.")

"And once or twice," continued the man fondly, "they were proud of you; and when your successes were noticed, people asked you how you came to know so much so young? Your pert answer became a bye-word in the College, 'We are all eternal.'"

At the memory she smiled her strange, alluring smile. He watched her, and his eyes grew passionate and large.

"And, Lo, when at odd times I saw you, I used to say to myself, 'What sorrow one sees in a child's face sometimes!' And, ever since, your dear face, growing from child to woman, has been a mystery to me. The searching question of your eyes has been the question of my life; but at last, at last, it has, I think, unravelled itself to me.... Dear Lotus"—he rose, still with his hand on hers. His face grew pale with a great emotion. "Lo, my own Lotus! ..."

She started and looked at him, half-thrilling, and yet with an expectant horror in her eyes. There was a pause, heavy with life. At that moment, the two souls rushed towards each other and stood still.

Gasparine entered the room.

It was over.

The souls looking from those lovely, passionate eyes paused, stilled, and sank once more to thought and watching. The supreme moment of vision had come and passed.

Mrs. Grace came with coffee, and, later, Raymond went away.

"My salvation is come," Lo said to herself. "He will write. This anguish of dead life will pass from me, and I shall live, and be *as others are! As others are!* What blessedness there is for me in the sound! ... He will write or come.... The magnanimity of his character is the crown that he shall wear for me. Oh! to have been a queen—the fairest of virgin queens! To have knelt at his feet, to have taken the crown from my head to lay before him.... To put my hands between his knees, to bid him accept my worship or let me die! ... *Worship!* It is better than love—to give everything and ask nothing, and to feel rich in giving."

The gratitude of her dead heart was a terrible thing.... That one should draw her back into the bosom of humanity, calling her "love" and "sister"! She, who had known all humiliation of body, soul, and mind! ... The Impossible had become the Possible! She would go in step with the time! Oh! the mystery of it!

It was February, but the long night she spent at the open windows of her study, neither feeling nor heeding the chill air. The years of her life passed before her in procession, and, strange to say, in the passing they became majestic and benignant, enriching her with the strength of their suffering. She saw a little girl, a brilliant creature—even more brilliant than Ladybird—in cream satin and costly laces; they set off her sister's dark beauty—driving in the park.

Again she saw the little girl home from her Parisian boarding-school, riding with her sister's lover. It looked so romantic and interesting.

She saw the soul of the child tortured, amazed, questioning ... the wild terrors, the nightmare dreams, the impotent pleadings ... the wild, grey swamp of London ... the long years of stillness and death; and now, *now* life was to come to her. It was unutterable, unbelievable, indescribable. In the fulness of her amazement, she knelt and whispered to the dead clematis roots,—

"After all, I could almost believe in a good God!"

It was well that she said almost.

For the days passed, and Raymond neither came nor wrote, and in a silence, appalling and chilling to each member of the family in a different way, the winter rolled.

"How strange that Lionel does not come or write!" said Mrs. Grace, learning nothing from the still, sweet smile of Lo.

"Ain't Payey-Rayey comin' any more?" queried Ladybird. "He promised me a singing dolly next time, he did."

"He is busy, wasp; he asked me to get you the singing doll—you shall have it next week. We will go to Edinburgh together and buy it."

And, as she spoke, Lo smiled. Only to Gasparine's questioning eyes she said, in her brave, vibrating voice,—

"I do not know, Gasparine. There may have been a mistake."

CHAPTER XIV
MONA ARRANGES HER FUTURE

Summer had come—a glorious contrast to the wild rains of the last. Every morning the sun came into Gasparine's little white room betimes, and she sprang up with a glorious sense of life before her for the day. The routine of her twelve happy hours began with a plunge into her bath, and then a race downstairs in her dressing-gown to take Ladybird from the white-and-gold crib she occupied next Lo's bed. Then they had a fine romp while the small damsel was bathed and dressed. It pleased her to be well satisfied with her nurse, and soon, with firmness, Gasparine had her better in hand than either Mrs. Grace or Lo could boast. It was a lovely life. Happiness and health made Gasparine look years younger, and so bright as to be almost pretty.

The summer session at the College asked but one lecture a week from Lotus, and Gasparine, after working herself into an indispensable position at Miss Blurton's, enjoyed her holidays with all the satisfaction of one who knows that the new session will begin with a "rise." So they had long, sunny mornings in the garden, on the lawn, or shopping in the little town, now so friendly to Gasparine, as they went from shop to shop or lingered with Lady in the Arcade to look at the toys. Or sometimes they went golfing in the park with the College Golf Club, or took glorious drives by the foot of the Ochils. Often, in the evening, they took dreamy walks in the park while Ladybird rode the pony round the old race-course.

Sometimes, in these walks, Gasparine and Lotus paused at that part of the course near the Castle, overlooking the carse, and giving a misty view of Bridge of Allan nestling in its trees beneath the hills, and the red-gold peaks of the grand Grampian range.

"Is it not beautiful, Lotus?"

"Yes; beautiful, Gasparine."

"Are you happy, Lotus? *I* am so happy. It is as if living in the same house with you opened the gates of life.... I mean it, Lo.... My life has become a joy to me, a thing I never dreamed could be.... Only once, a few brief months of his life, we both wakened to know that the time was passing, and we must love each other ... I have told you of it all ..."

"Yes, dear Genius."

They were sitting on a seat where often the brother and sister had sat. Lady was riding round the course.

"It is so strange to remember," said Gasparine. "Once we sat here, he and I, and saw you pass. You walked quickly. Lady was younger then. I said to him, 'That is Miss Grace, of the College.' He said, 'She is clever.' 'She reminds me of some one,' I said. Was it not strange?"

All her sorrow had, ere this, been uttered to Lotus, and many dream-like scenes recalled and pondered over.

So the sweet days went, and preparations were being made for a month at the seaside. Gasparine and Lady were beside themselves with jollity, packing was going on vigorously, when an interruption came.

One evening, as they all sat on the verandah, drinking tea, and talking, the gate swung open, and Mona Lefcadio entered.

She was a glorious vision in her cool, faint blue *crêpon*[1] and coffee-coloured gauzes of delicate embroidery. Her little shoes, her elegant gloves, and rainbow sunshade, all bespoke her affinity to the great world of fashion. She had grown lovelier, more womanly, during her absence, and various artificial aids to beauty did not pass Gasparine's eyes, although they only made the girl more and more a type of the world to which she belonged and from which she came to claim Lotus for her own. With a cry, she made a little rush at Lo, and took her in her arms; then, seeming not even to see the others, she drew her to the door.

"My birdling! My wildling!" she said, with wild joy. "My precious, precious one! Lotus, *my* Lotus, if you, dear, knew what is in my heart as I have my arms around you once again! Oh! I shall not let you go, my beautiful one!"

They stood together in Lo's study now, and Mona, with pas-

---

1 "A stuff resembling crape, but of firmer substance, made of fine worsted, silk, or a combination of the two" (*OED*; usually spelled "crépon").

sionate fondness, stroked the brown hair and thin cheek. Lo released herself and stood apart, a cynical, contemptuous smile on her lips. Her usually beautiful eyes were inflamed and weak from some specially heavy night work, and from the same cause her dress was somewhat more neglected than was her rule. Opposite to her stood the lovely woman in her fresh and fashionable costume. The absurdity of Mona's eulogies struck no one so keenly as the recipient.

"Stop, stop!" she said lightly. "You were always fond of strong language, Mona, and——"

"Strong language!" cried Mona. "Oh, Lo! when I can't find words to tell you how beautiful you are in my eyes! How I have thought of you, Lo, night after night! But there, you only sneer. How terrible life is, that when one gives one's heart away in worship one receives a sneer." A mournful look filled the beautiful eyes. "Lotus, I have so much to say—so much that cannot wait. The winter has been a strange one, full of experiences ... and always the ache of your absence ... and you would not come to see me when I returned to London ... though I had everything ready for you, and three such dear men, who think of things just as you do, ready to worship you. Ah! what a blow it was! How I cried! You did not care to see me....

"I told you about the first man. I sent you his letters. My father was furious, and behaved like a bully to me, and my mother whined. It was charming. The brute was father's age, and rich—as if *I* had not money enough! But the next man is harder. It is about him I have come. He *is* a man—yes, in everything. We were splendid friends at first. He talked so like you, and everything went well until he proposed, and made a scene. Father is not furious, but mad—off his head—and even mother perks up a little, and tries to tell me my duty. My duty! And then they raved about your bad teaching, and advanced ideas. And there I had them, for *his* ideas are just like yours—and so I told them. And, Lo, I've come because I think they're going to write to you, and try to get you on their side. But you won't go? Will you, Lo? Marriage! I am not fit for marriage. I am not ready—I, who know what marriage means. Leave me, I will not be. After all, why should I talk nonsense when I know the real reason so well? Do not laugh at me, Lo—you did not laugh at me once. Oh, Lo! I love you, I live for you. Ah! the dreams I have! No, don't interrupt me, my sweet. Here we sit together, we two. What a smell there is in the air of summer, and life, and love, and you! I have not felt the air speak like that since we parted.... Hush! Oh, don't speak, darling! I know you want to say that everybody dreams, and that a year makes all the difference. But don't. Wait. So much boils in my head that I *must* say. Look at the hills; hear the sounds coming from the garden; see the mist over the town! Lo, Lo, Lo, how they chime to me! Well! How I dream! Not a year now, and *I* am free, my will, my wealth my own. Thank heaven, father can't interfere there. Oh! then I shall come and take my darling out of this weariful life. Lo, what shall we *not* see? I have such endless plans! That decent Gasparine O'Neill—goodness! I was once jealous of her! The idea!—is to stay here with Mrs. Grace, and that vindictive little brat, Lady. Fancy that child finding time to make a face at me as I came into the house! We will leave them money enough, and you and I will travel. We shall go to all the great towns of Europe, and taste their pleasures and intoxicating life. There can be no tiring with you. Each day will be a new life to me ... and all over the world we shall go, even to my golden West Indian Islands ... and I shall see how well my darling grows, and how happy.... This bothering old life, with the drudge of work, will be gone ... and no one will serve you, and care for you as I shall, and I——"

The sweet woman burst into tears, the tender heart was so full of its noble, idealising love.

Lo watched her coldly until the passionate eyes were raised, with the tears gone.

"Lotus, you would not cast away my love? It is my life I plead for."

"No, dear child; it is a passionate desire into which your imagination has crowded your life. It will pass."

"Lotus, you will not agree with them; you will not help them to chain me and break my heart?"

Lotus laughed cruelly.

"I might be glad to have you chained, out of my way," she said.

But Mona did not seem desperately afraid. She held Lo in her arms and kissed her, laughing.

"No, no; I know you better, you bad Curly."

Thereafter Mona was in a state of the highest good humour. They went downstairs and out to talk to the others. Mona fawned upon them for forgiveness in her graceful, subtle way, that blinded no one; nor was it intended to. She took them in turn, described London toilettes to Madam, the Art Exhibitions to Gasparine, and tried to induce Lady to play with her. In the last attempt, indeed, she seemed to be serious. In all her excitement, she had remembered the child—it was a tribute she always paid to Lotus to be sure—and had brought her a tiny bracelet, with a heart attached, a baby ring of pearls, and other trifles. Lady, the vainest of mortals, shrieked and chatted incessantly over them, consenting to sit on Mona's knee while she called upon everybody to admire her small finger and wrist. Later, Gasparine and Madam went into the house, Lotus was bent over some papers at a distance, and Mona attempted to charm the child into submission, or gain her for an ally. Elsewhere, she was noted for her charm with children.

"Lady," she said softly, "do you like what I gave you?"

"Yes."

"Are you going to be a sweet girl, and love me now?"

Lady looked at her sharply.

"Come, you are quite old, and you ought to be nice with me. You're not a baby any longer, you know."

"I'm quite polite," said Lady resentfully.

"Yes, just now; but always. And you should love me."

"Why?"

"Because I love Lo."

"You don't love me?"

"Yes, I do."

Lady looked at her—puzzled, unbelieving.

"Come, Lady, promise to love me, and give me a lovy-kiss, like you give Lo and Miss O'Neill."

"I *don't* give Lo and Miss O'Neill the same kind o' kisses," said Lady wrathfully. "Lo's kisses are all for her. I keep 'em here," touching her lips. "They're gold-kisses. Nobody else gets 'em. Gaspar on'y gets small silver."

"And I?"

"Tin," was the prompt, and remorselessly frank answer.

"Have you no other kind?"

"Yes," mysteriously. "They've never been kissed yet, but they're, oh! such beauties!"

She smacked her lips.

"What sort are they?"

Whether it was a creation of the moment, suggested by the ring and what Mona had told her about it, will remain for ever Lady's own secret. She answered, sweetly,—

"Pearl-kisses, made of angels' tears."

"And for whom are they?"

The child was sitting on Mona's knee. She turned now, and with both her hands pushing the Creole from her, she looked into the brown, beautiful eyes with an intentness that gave Mona a sudden start.

"They're for my mother," she said softly.

The piteous hope was never abandoned.

Mona's eyes filled.

"Lady, will you not give me a gold-kiss like you give Lo—just one?"

"No," said Lady curtly.

"Will you love me, then?"

Again came the deep look that struck a painful chord of fascination, recognition, and dislike, in Mona's heart.

"I will love you as much as you love me," was the cold, diplomatic answer.

Mona put the child down and looked across at Lotus, still bent over the papers. Then she covered her eyes with her hand.

"My God!" she said. "The child has caught Lo's trick of looking, and speaks with just the same measured, heartless, unanswerable frankness."

Late in the evening, up in Lo's study, Mona relieved her wounded pride—for the child had wounded her—by relating the conversation of Lady, and pretending to make light of it.

Lo listened attentively, but made no remark.

"Poor little nameless brat!" said Mona. "What a strong desire she has to possess a mother! Well, well, her mother must have been a bad lot indeed. A child a mother might be proud of, too. But there, she has better than a mother, she has you, my angel! Oh! how I grudge you to her! How jealous I am of your care of her! The little heartless imp!"

Lo looked towards the hills, and seemed to ponder. When she spoke, it was on another matter.

"You told me the name of the first man, Mona, but not of the second. Who is he?"

"Oh, that affair! Yes, yes, to be sure! I forgot. Why, he knows you. That's how we were such good friends at first. He used to come to the College often, and never noticed me there then, he was so full of you ... and no wonder! He's the President of the Board. His name is Raymond. Professor Raymond of Oxford, you know."

★   ★   ★   ★   ★

It was the loveliest of summer nights. Ladybird, in her little cot, felt restless. She was sure she heard a cock crowing, and she was extremely anxious to know what rooster was so dissipated at that hour. She sat up, then rose, and went to the door-window, unlocked it, and put her bare feet out on the grass with a delicious sense of coolness. She listened. "Where *is* that Cocky-Leeky?" she pondered; and then, not daring to sing, though much inclined, she began telling herself the story of Cocky-Leeky and Henny-Penny, sitting on the wooden steps of the window. The summer night-wind came wooing round the little creature as she sat in her white gown, the huge frills round neck and sleeves giving her the appearance of a small phantom clown past joking.

She did not hear the door open, and when Lo came and stood behind her she was babbling to herself.

"Is my baby not in bed?" asked Lo, in the faint voice of one who is calm from exhaustion.

The child turned without alarm, and explained, certain of sympathy and understanding, "I was hot here," tossing back her curls, "and *here*," touching a less romantic region, "and I wanted coolness."

Lo wrapped a shawl round the child, and sat down on the steps with her in her arms.

"Now, if you will be very quiet," Lo said, "so as not to disturb Mona, who sleeps next door, or Gaspar, who has such ears, or Madam, who hardly sleeps at all"—Lady chuckled at this, appreciating the accuracy of the statements—"we two will stay here, and talk to the grass, and the sky, and the wind; and they will tell us wonderful things."

"Yes, yes; and don't forget Cocky-Leeky."

"No; but first, before I begin, give me a gold-kiss, the very biggest you have, and put your arms tight round my neck. I have a pain, too, and that helps."

They spent the night there. The stars paled, and a magic dawn-land spread before them. Far off, Lo could see Bannockburn,[1] indistinct, green, and dream-fair in the breaking light, and giving, now, no sign of the human passion of blood that had raged there long ago. Lady roused with the birds, and softly spoke.

"Where's over there?"

"East, my baby."

"It's nice."

"Yes."

---

1 Just south of Stirling, Bannockburn is the site of Robert the Bruce's decisive victory over the English in 1314, which firmly established Scottish independence.

"And what is that?" pointing to a line of glory on the horizon, the promise of a fair day.

"The dawn, my child."

"It's nice, too."

"Yes. It brings the day, and the sunlight, and the birds singing."

Lady nestled into the warmth of the tender, tired heart, and looked up drowsily into the deep eyes above her.

"The night's good, too," she murmured. "Then one sleeps ... sleepies ... sleepies ... 'cep', o' course, that res'less rooster 'at crowed," and she turned and slept again, while the first sunbeam broke across the lawn, and lighted Lo's pale face.

Still they remained, feeling through them the peace and stillness of that hour—frail outcasts from humanity, instinctively creeping as close to the one Mother as they could get.

CHAPTER XV
LO'S SALVATION PASSES BY

The next day, Mona returned to her friends, comforted and soothed. Lo had given her some advice, a little vague, and had promised that she would not interfere. All that day Lo was just as usual—busy, but bright and natural, so that even Gasparine's keen, loving eyes could discover nothing.

There was a children's party for Ladybird that evening, and the merriest of the play-makers was Lo, whom all the children adored.

A few days later, without any air of truancy, Professor Raymond arrived, handsome, happy, and caressing.

On some small pretext, Lo left the room, and sent Lady for Gasparine.

"Gasparine," she said, "I want you to take Lady and Madam out of our way for this evening. I have sent for Raymond; I have a number of things to explain to him."

Gasparine wondered, but obeyed. She proposed to Mrs. Grace and Lady to go and see her old landlady; and Mrs. Grace, who loved to peer and gossip in a simple way, contrasting with her former life, readily agreed. Lady, very lively and chatty, fetched her silk hat, and all three set out.

Within, Lotus sat listening to Mr. Raymond's profuse apologies and brilliant talk.

To-day it sounded to her strangely shallow, painted, and unreal. He had not spoken long before she put up her hand.

"Stop!" she said. "I have something to say first. I cannot listen to your talk of your gay and manly doings till I have said what is on my heart to say."

There came a silence that felt long, and then she raised to him her face. Such a face! To its whiteness his blindness could be no longer blind. In the eyes was that expression of mystery, and the sad mouth held secrets of how to smile, though bleeding inwardly—of how to speak, saying nothing.

He roused, and wakened from the dream he had lived in, and remembered the old life and its hopes.

"When you came to see me in the winter," she said, speaking in a dead, passionless voice, "when you seemed to give your time and thought, both valuable, to me in this quiet place, and when you seemed to feel companionship in me, I ... I began to have a strange heart-stirring, as if a great weight moved, strove, and might at last roll from my breast. You have known me since I was a child—a miserable child.... Yes, I had lived a very wretched life.... I shall not speak of it. I would be brief and say all quickly, and have all quickly done.... It happened when you bent and touched my hair, and kissed my hand, and spoke ... ah! ... I felt— those words, those actions of yours seemed to me full of protection and love.... I thought, 'I am going to pass away from the old nightmare life, and *be as others are.*' I dreamed my dream for a time. Then came my pupil, Mona Lefcadio, and told me you are her lover.... Lionel Raymond"—she raised her hand, and the calm, deep reproach of her voice, which changed now, was powerfully impressive—"of what stuff are you men made—the best of you? *Was I not worthy of trust? You might have told me.* But I, that you may know that I am braver than yourself, say all this to you, trusting you."

While she spoke he watched her, his large, beautiful eyes growing more and more pained.

"Lotus," he said, when she had ended, "I have sinned. But unknowing how deep my sin was." A pause. "But you shall have all truth, for you deserve it. You are brave to bear. Courage gives courage. Let me be brave to speak."

She bowed her head.

"When I came, in the winter, it was for you. You had long been a mystery to me, and I, in my turn, had long sought an ideal. In boyhood, Mrs. Grace, a woman older than I, almost ten years, was my ideal. Lotus, she was a beautiful woman, the pride of our county. She drew from me a love passionate and strong, and though she deceived me cruelly, broke my early hopes, and even ill repaid my later help, I never forsook her. Bear witness for me, Lotus," his voice pled humbly.

Again she bowed her head.

"I do bear witness, heartily," she said earnestly.

"Lotus, I am not a man of capricious taste, but I am uncertain and diffident in my affections. I half feared you, in spite of the many years between us. I feared you as a man fears a woman who possesses some strength he cannot fathom. Your unmoved calm, for one so young, the depth of your despairing convictions, in contrast with your noble endeavours in every good cause, and that something wofully innocent and timid, like the look of a young, hurt child, which so often I saw in your small, white face—all attracted and repelled me, making me feel sometimes young and weak beside you, and sometimes centuries too old, and always far, coldly, immeasurably far. But last winter I thought the distance lessened, and, from my long doubts, I fancied you were indeed the ideal I sought, the bride for me—a woman free from every weakness, who lived for the future of our race. But—and for this my sin is not so great—though I was so near to love of you, I never dreamed that you loved me, or saw in your eyes any love towards me. You seemed to me like one who gave out every good and gentle feeling save *love*. You chilled me. And yet so terribly you drew me with your piteous eyes that I said I would dare all, and try if there was love in you for me."

Lo moaned to herself, "My curse upon me! Ah!"

"The last night I was with you that was all in my heart to tell you, and to beg your patience for my love. Some one interrupted us, and I went away. Lo—I speak truth—it was a day later I met Mona Lefcadio. Her beauty dazzled me, and I did not write to you as I meant. When a week had passed, my past life had become, in the vivid, passionate life her beauty gave me, so much a dream that it seemed to me there was no need to write at all. Her beauty, her charm, her mind—so like yours, but softer, lovelier, younger, with the passion you lacked—all appealing to man with beautiful dependence. All this blinded me. I was no longer young, yet it was like the passion of my first youth come back to me. I knew myself. This was no transcendental craving. *This* was love—human, passionate, near, and strong.... You do not blame me?"

"No."

"I forgot you, Lo, completely. She spoke of you a great deal, I know, because my memory now tells me that she did so, and that I answered. But it seemed to me she spoke of a person I knew but vaguely—to whom I owed no obligations. But that she is in the country now, your letter would hardly have brought me here yet. I forgot everything but her."

There was a silence. The man had spoken reluctantly, with pain and humiliation. The woman listened with brave calm, as if he spoke of some one else.

"Lo," he said, "what now?"

"There is nothing more to say, my friend. You love her; you can make her happy; she is necessary to you."

"I shall win her if I can."

"Win her. If I can help you, I will help you."

"I knew you would. I felt always almost an awe of your generosity. But for you, Lo—what for you?"

"Go, now.... That will be best,—best, ... soonest ended for me.... And, if you will, remember me at times." A pause, and then, "You will not see me again," she said dreamily; "and I, again, shall never see you.... But wait, let me look a moment on your face. There is good there, happiness, and love, for another life beside your own, but not the salvation I had hoped for me.... A salvation for each of us, you said once.... Yes; to one it comes in a cross, to another in a crown.... The crown saves as well as the cross, but woe when our salvation is in a cross, and for a moment we are tempted to believe it may be a crown.... Let me take my cross again ... let me lay aside that crown I thought to wear ... so ... good-bye."

She had come near to him, and, as one preparing to gaze on a bright light, she swayed her head sideways once or twice, with one arm and shoulder raised, and half shielded her eyes; but as she said good-bye she turned them full upon him, and he saw her look of yearning agony.

"You thought I could not love," she whispered. "Ah! Lionel, I—am—only—a—woman...."

She bent forward, and with hand and lips touched his coat at his breast.

A swift, wild thrill passed through him. Something in his spirit cried out, "Lotus, come to me."

But she had glided, like a shadow, from the room.

*　　*　　*　　*　　*

In her study she knelt and looked over the balcony railing to the hills.

"So Mona has wrecked me," she said. "But for her, he would

have taken me ... and, once his, he would have loved and cared for me ... and, soon, the more for all my woe. Do I not know him? He would have loved the child—Madam—all.... It is past. I am awake. What to do now? I said I would help him. I will help him. Will he, perhaps, in the future, find which love would have been best? And of whom his ideal, Mona, is only an echo? Or is he, like all other men, in love with the *woman*, not the soul? ...

"There! Let me make an end. Can I begin life again? Bury a last hope, and live smiling on? Horrible! The thing is done. Let me arrange."

CHAPTER XVI
MOTHER AND CHILD

All that night she sat and wrote, and in the morning she looked like one who perforce has spent the night in a tomb.

"After all, life is sweet; it is the best good we know," was her verdict in the morning.

She was quiet and dreamy all day, but in the evening, seeing Ladybird playing under the lime, she went towards her.

She thought of that evening, so far away, when the little child had asked her if she might have a mother; and never since had the poor little one ceased to hint at this desire, though dreading to speak out again. It came back to Lotus! How long ago it seemed, and oh! how peaceful!

Now she called Ladybird. Something in her solemn face and air seemed to strike the child, and her little face grew grave.

"Lady, come here to me."

She placed the child upon her knee, and wondered to feel the little limbs against hers.

"Lady, I am going away; perhaps for a long, long time, perhaps for only a little while. But I want you to promise me faithfully to remember what I say to you. You know how well you can remember things when you like. I want you to remember this better than anything else."

"Yes, I promise; I shall not forget."

"Listen, then. You have always wanted a mother, have you not?"

"Yes."

"Perhaps your mother is going to come to you, but I do not know."

"Then I *have* a mother? I?"

"Yes."

"*Well!* I shall let Sonny Thomas know *that*. He did so boast about his! ... Oh! he's a dreadful false boy. He's half an hour late for school every day, an' he *ses* it's because the 'knots' in his porridge are so difficult to eat; but his mother——"

"I don't want you to think of Sonny Thomas; I want you to listen to me."

"Yes, yes. Tell me about my mother! I'm mos' anxious to hear."

"She was very sad; she often longed to be with you, to take you in her arms and say, 'My little baby,' but the world kept her far away; and now, perhaps, she may come to you.... But if she may not, she would have you to remember this, Ladybird, when you grow old, and old, to be a big lady. Remember that your mother was a girl, very unhappy—more unhappy, Ladybird, than you can know; and she bore it all ... until, at last, when she could bear no more ... she ... died.... And remember that she was young, Lady, and that for a long time she bore it, and tried, until in her breast something broke, and she knew she could work no more—it was her heart."

The child listened with terrible intentness.

"Lady, do you know what 'desolate' means—a desolate place?"

"Yes," answered the child mournfully; "it means the end, the end of everything, the very end of a place, where the dog howls always."

Lo started at the childish definition; it was weirdly accurate of her feeling.

"Then, Lady, remember this. Your mother had to live in the desolate place at the end of everything; and it broke her heart."

Lady did not speak.

"You must watch for three days. When the sun goes through the lime, and it is teatime, you must watch through the end window down the road. The sunlight will shine; you will watch. The third day, if you see a lady coming up the road, go to meet her; it is your mother. She will love you very well, and take care of you for always after that."

Still the child did not speak.

"And if, when you run to meet this lady, it seems to you that you know her, still you will love her, for you will remember that she is your mother; and whoever the lady is, you must not be disappointed ... for your mother will not come like an angel clad in white, oh! little Ladybird."

The small, practical madam curled her lip.

"I don't want a white angel. I want a mother, in a dress." With her large eyes she scanned Lo's face. "I should like her to have a dress like you," she added, with that wisdom of children that cuts and thrills.

"If she comes she will wear a dress like mine."

"Shall *you* be there?"

"I do not know. If your mother comes, I think I shall be there:"

"And I shall know it is the lady who is with you who is my mother?"

"The lady who comes up the road—yes."

Ladybird drew her brows mysteriously.

"Lo," she said, then, in a whisper of awe, "when my mother comes will the dog stop howling?"

"What dog, dear?"

"It always howls, you know, 'speshly at nights, when I'm 'sleep. Last night it howled dreadful. Then some one is always ill or crying.... I shall tell my mother she must stop the dog directly. She will be able to, won't she, if she is my mother?"

"I think so. But also you must pray to God to tell the dog to stop because your mother wishes it; if you pray that always, then the dog will stop."

"Oh, then, I'll pray to-night."

"But if your mother does not come?"

"Not come? Oh, she surely will!"

"I hope so; but if the road is empty, and if your mother does not appear, then you will know you had a mother—a sad, sad mother—but that she could not go to her child; and then remember what I have told you of her when you are a woman yourself."

"When I am a woman, I will never forget."

Then Lo, with the memory of the other night upon her, spoke softly.

"And before I go away, Lady, will you give me one of the pearl-kisses you keep for your mother, so that I may have one of them to give her from you, if I meet her?"

But Ladybird had a soul as steadfast as that of the woman who held her. She shook her little head.

"No; oh no!" she said seriously. "I must give her the kiss myself—I, wif my own mouf." And she touched her red lips with the little finger on which was Mona's pearl ring.

With a painful feeling, as of one unshrived, Lo wrapped her arms round the frail creature, and kissed her and kissed her. Her little child—neglected, hated, unowned! A passion of remorse overcame her. Why could she not love?

Her time had almost come; and now she went to Gasparine.

"Gasparine," she began, "I am going away—for a time."

"To lecture, Lotus? In summer?"

"No, dear Genius, not to lecture." And the seductive smile for a moment passed across her face.

"Lotus, you do not look well. Are you really going away?"

"Yes, Gasparine, I am going away. I am called away. I may come back in three days, I may not come till—long—till," a gasp, "that soft, brown hair of yours is grey."

"Lo!"

"Hush! I have arranged most things for you. Take care of them," she pointed through the window to the lime where Mrs. Grace sat with the child, "till I come."

Then, with a movement of exquisite humility and grace, she went and knelt at the feet of her slave.

"Ah, Gasparine! you have tried so hard to heal me! And I thank you, dear. You have done much—this stillness, this service, this sunlight. But I think it will not heal me. I fear me the wound was a fatal wound...."

She raised her white and solemn face as she knelt.

"I go in search of something else ... and yet I do not know. I may come, perhaps, in three days, and *if I do, it is because I think that you can heal me.*"

She bowed her head for a moment, almost as if in prayer, then said,—

"Gasparine, there is a white rose in the garden; take it, and lay it on the grave you love for me.... There is another thing—the little stone you wanted. I got your sketch of it, and ordered it. You can go and see if the wording is what you like.... It would have been sooner, but I have been poor lately.... Do not cry or speak.... Go, and take Mrs. Grace and the child up to the ford ... where we went our first walk—longer than long ago, it feels.... I must get my train in twenty minutes, and they must not see me go.... Good-bye. Live well.... I commend thee all to God ... until we meet again."

CHAPTER XVII
AT LAST

During the night she went southward; a dream-journey of unreality and torturing thought. The pause at London disturbed her brain a little, but by noon she had reached the tranquil and lovely southern village where Mona Lefcadio was recruiting[1] after a London June and July. It was a dreamy place of woods and vales, and, on this sultry first of August, still as a painted picture.

Mona, in white, stood at the station, wild with joy.

"My bird! My flower!" she whispered, rapturously. "Why, Lo, to think you came! And I! I can't speak, I'm so glad. Your wire put me so wild with joy. You will stay? I have the dog-cart here. We have three miles to drive, lovely——"

"Yes; it is pretty here, and a lovely day."

"Yes; and to see you in that stuffy gown, my birdling! My own little Curly! Never mind; we can soon put that right."

"No; wait. I have come to talk. Is the village three miles off?"

"No; our place is. The village is close here."

"Let us go there, to the inn."

"To be sure. You want a rest, sweet darling. Let us go there, and have luncheon."

"Listen, Mona. Send your dog-cart away. Let us have this day together. I have come a long way to see you ... and in the evening I must go back."

"*This evening!* Lo, my pet! Oh, Curly, what nonsense you talk!"

"Hush! It is decided. No disputing, please."

The old habit of obedience was still strong in Mona; she clenched fists and teeth, but remained silent.

The dog-cart was sent away, with orders to return that evening. They went to the inn, a quaint place with a sanded floor, and the smell of past generations in the parlour. They had luncheon there, and then Mona, gloriously, deliriously happy, took Lo to walk in the narrow lanes among the summer fields. It was, indeed, lovely. The song of birds came from the copse, the hum of insects in the hot, still air. Above, the intense blue; beneath, the cool green.

Lo was in one of her most enchanting moods; she told Mona all about the College, old and new friends, plans, and gossip— told her of new books, her thoughts and dreams of late, and, in her soft voice, told over verses of beautiful poetry, all the marvellous things that singers have said of hot, sunny days such as this.

Mona was in raptures.

"Oh, it is a foretaste of my dream!" she cried.

Then Lotus softly took her hand, and, looking at her, said,—

---

1   "To increase or restore the vigour or health of (a person or animal); to refresh, re-invigorate (one's spirits, etc.)" (*OED*).

"You must waken now."

Mona started.

"Mona, little girl, listen to me," Lo said.

They were sitting together on a bank, russet with wild strawberry leaves, which Mona was making into little bouquets. She dropped them.

"I have been thinking over the matter of Mr. Raymond. When did you see him last?"

"In London, more than two weeks ago." The joyous holiday look left Mona's face, and she spoke in a timid tone that would have been sullen if it had dared. Then pleadingly she bent, and laid her cheek upon the other's shoulder. "Ah, Lo! let me be happy. Let me be true when I so would. Surely there are enough untrue people in the world?"

"It is not that; but I must tell you the man is worthy to be the lord of even a better heart than yours, Mona."

"He may be; I shall be the first to wish him joy," said Mona.

A sort of exultation came into Lo's face; but she subdued it and said,—

"Consider seriously what I say, Mona. I want you to answer me the truth, from your heart. *If you had never seen me; or if I were about to pass entirely from your life. If I had never loved you; or if my love were about to become utterly utterly dead, could you be this man's wife? Could you give him duty, and, later, when his love had won it, love?*"

Mona's eyes were wide, and her face white with a vague fear.

"These are impossibilities, dear Lo."

"Consider them. Could you?"

"I do not know. It would take me months to think."

"No, my child, only minutes. Think, could you?"

A pause. The strawberry leaves were torn.

"I do not know. I suppose—yes, I think I could."

"Then, Mona, hear me. It is so. First, I never loved you; next, even that regard I gave you is about to pass. I am going away so utterly that I shall be as one dead. You need not ask. You need not question. *Only* before I go, I ask one thing—that you should marry that man. I know what I say. It is of your happiness I think. He is worthy. He will make more than I could ever make of you."

The sweet face blanched, and the limbs shivered, yet, controlling herself, Mona spoke.

"You have often treated me harshly, have often subdued me to the most degrading submission of my tastes and will by threatening the withdrawal of your favour. Yet, it seems to me, you go too far. I am a woman now, remember."

"You need not pose or pout, my child," said the chill voice. "I have said what I have said. I do not love you, and I am going away. Make what you will of that."

The great tears rolled down Mona's cheeks. There was a silence; then, steadying her quivering lip, she said,—

"Lo, will you let me speak of the time when you first came to the College, and drew me to love you?"

"Speak."

"You must remember how they all hated you—the other lecturers—because you were younger and cleverer than they; the girls taking their tone from the others. I hated you, too. I thought you hideous, severe, cruel, sarcastic. But you did not seem to notice. Then I watched you. You worked, but how quietly! And I saw you could make the women redden, and wince, and weep, yet never raise your voice. I saw you suspend three students whom no one had dared to suspend before.... Ah! I remember it all! Then we began to love your teaching in spite of ourselves, and longed to speak to you because you never seemed to see us. I watched the movements of your hands, the way you walked, your dress and manner.... By-and-by, I treasured every word of yours, and began to realise what you said.... And still your eyes drew me and drew me like a spell, until I trembled whenever you entered the hall. I saw others had the same feeling, and I felt passionately angry and jealous.... Then, one day—I call it the birthday of my soul, Lo—I saw you walking alone on the Back Walk at Stirling, and something came over me, and I went after you, and threw my arms round you, and said,—

"'I love you; oh, I love you! Do you love me?'

"You did not answer, Lo; you only looked and smiled; but, oh! in your eyes I saw so many things ... thoughts and struggles ... a deadly sweetness; oh, I cannot say! ... But from that moment I wakened to life, and began questioning all things that I saw and knew of life around me. The world was new ... I could not understand. But, from that moment, I was your slave.... My chains were not made of roses, Lo, you know; but I hugged them, all the same."

"Yes," said Lo; "you have spoken the truth. And why did I draw you and others? I found my hard-won chance of honourable livelihood, which meant not *my* life only, but the lives of helpless ones depending on me, being overthrown, and my situation becoming unbearable through the antagonism of you and others. I flattered your vanity, piqued your curiosity, and compelled your love.... But shall I value such love? ... Hardly, I think."

"Don't say that, Lo; ah, don't! I have had my punishment long ago, for my blindness at first. Don't say you formed my character for years, trained me to high and noble thoughts, and took all the best love I had, shall ever have, to give, to tell me that now! Lo, I have given you all my love; I have no more to give. You did it.... What answer can you make, and what defence?"

"None; none!"

"And you can tell me that you never loved me?"

There was silence. Then Lotus turned and looked into the lovely, agonised face, one of the old, deep looks.

"Do not speak to me of the past, Mona. I want to leave it."

"Yes, yes."

"Ah, Mona! my little Mona, my little school-girl—listen. If I deceived you, only forgive me. Your vexed girl's feeling will pass, too soon.... Only, dear, be sure I know what is best for you, and me, and—and—the other one. You are beautiful, lusty, and strong. The passion of life, and its pleasures, is in you. I go from you. Do that for me——"

"So, Lo, you would have me untrue to all I would be true to?"

"Yes; to all dreams to which you imagine you would be true."

"Are *you* a dream, beloved?"

"I shall be, soon."

"Lo!"

"If the past be a dream, I shall soon be a bit of the past."

"The end is coming, then," said Mona dreamily. I dreamed of it lately.... But, how soon!"

"Yes, my child, the end is coming. Face it bravely. The end of fantastic dreams, and insecure existence. You will go into the world of ordinary sensations, and your health will soon accustom you to it. Romance passes. Be—oh, my child, think well of what I say—*be as others are.*"

Then Mona turned, and, with plaintive and dreamy softness, said,—

"Dearest, let us cease to talk of it to-day. Do you feel the air, how rich it is? How full of life? Do you hear the birds sing? Oh, God! to live a little longer, and be happy!"

A cry broke from her, instantly stifled.

"Let us walk in the sunlight, in the clover-scented air, and thank God for life.... It may end for both of us we know not how soon.... And let us go to the old inn, and sleep there together for to-night, our arms round one another in the way that was always my best rest."

"I will go, Mona. If you are content, it shall be farewell."

"I am content now with all that comes."

"You see the reason of what I say?"

"Yes."

"You know that a life with such a man is better than a life of vain regrets?"

"Yes."

"You are content never to see me more?"

"As you are, yes."

In the hours of silence which followed, Lotus thought often within herself of Mona's many desperate vows.

"It is well," she thought; "but easier than I thought. And yet I might have known.... And yet, it's easier than I thought...."

In the morning they stood together on the platform.

"Good-bye, Lotus. All that you ask me to do, I do. Only, when you get into the carriage, turn your head away. Do not look out; I could not bear it. Promise me that last thing."

"I promise."

But to herself Lo said,—

"Well, strange! I never asked her love; she always scorned my doubts of her everlasting faithfulness; yet—she was easier to persuade than I had thought," and there was an added anguish in her face.

When the train started, she was in a painful dream.

"Nevertheless," she said, "let me begin again. Why seek elsewhere for what I can never find? I shall go back and train the child, and let Gasparine heal me, and work in silent, hopeless, cheerful patience, until the grave is dug, and fitted out, and ready.... How the child will dance to see me, and poor Gasparine, and Madam!"

A faint expression, almost of pleasure, crossed her face.

When one faces the inevitable it always becomes more bearable.

★　　★　　★　　★　　★

It was in the long tunnel that the two trains rushed madly into one another, like enraged and sentient monsters. Groans of agony, piercing yells, death-cries, and the agony and darkness of eternal death filled the tunnel. No light, no salvation, no help!

Lotus was thrown out between two parts of a window and door which had been crushed into her, and in the awful darkness and agony a vague dream of the cottage lawn and Gasparine, Ladybird, and others, passed torturingly before her eyes. Of

Mona she did not think, until, in the darkness, she felt a mouth touch hers, and two wet hands groped over her body.

"Lo! my little Lo!"

"Mona," she moaned faintly, "is it you?"

"Yes, surely. Did you think, beloved, that I was so easily driven away? Ah, no, love, no! I meant to follow you, ... have I not dreamt of this for years? ... Ah! I must groan ... both my legs are crushed and one arm.... I dragged myself to you on one side.... I can see quite clearly, though it's dark, Lo, so I knew just where you lay.... I was in the next carriage.... There is glass in my face, and ..."

Silence, darkness....

"Beloved, can you feel my arms? Now let me lay my head there, in the old place.... Ah! the glass does not hurt *now*, nor the burning rack...."

The long, bruised arms were round Lo, and the voice of Mona came so clear, and soft, and slow, it seemed to break the darkness gently, and float away upon it.

"I dreamed, last night, beloved, that somehow we slept through this wild and passionate time, and wakened, *so calm, so cold, so like other people*, with just so much of passion left in us, to love the earth, and enjoy the sunshine ... and in our hearts no more doubt, or heartburnings, or uncertainties, but such a *rest*! ... oh, God! ... such ... a ... rest! ... We looked back to this time, and said to one another, 'Do you remember?' and half shuddered, and wondered very greatly, and laughed to think how real life was to us now."

There were sounds of agony in Lo's throat.

"The old wounds!" she moaned. "The old wounds! ... He strikes again ... it burns ... ah! ... Mona, will you sleep?"

"Yes, sweet, surely, as I have always said, we two together ... the long, long sleep."

Still there came no light, no help, and were the dead or the living round them they knew not.

After a long, long time Mona regained a weak, semi-consciousness, and put her bleeding hands beneath the dear face, and drew it close to hers.

"Lo?"

"Yes, sweet."

"How dark it is."

"Yes."

"Will it ever grow light again?"

"Yes, I think so, when morning comes."

"You think the morning will come?"

"Yes; and sunlight."

"Why?"

"Because you did not leave me. Now I have faith in love."

"I have no longer any pain, Lo. Ah! kind death that drew us close!"

"My own sweet girl! ... he said ... how long ago! ... 'If the woman will but listen, she shall hear the Spirit's voice at last' ... and now I hear it; it is love."

"Lo, I feel so sleepy."

"My pet, nestle closer; it grows so cold."

"Lo, do you remember the little girl, Ladybird?"

"Yes."

"She always disliked me so, poor bird! ... I wonder who she is really! ... I wonder who her mother is! ... I wonder! You do not know, Lo, do you?"

"Ah, yes! the little girl Ladybird? Her mother? No, I do not know...."

Within five minutes of each other they died.

★ ★ ★ ★ ★

These two were never found. Who buried them, who claimed them, friends never knew.

Ladybird watched vainly down the road ... and Gasparine, day after day, with the little fair child at her side, watched too, hoping against hope, for one who would never return.

★ ★ ★ ★ ★

Was life, then, done for Gasparine? Nay. There were two who passed her window daily, and who were, to her, haughty and magnificent beings, whom she looked upon with half-contemptuous admiration, telling herself how they would regard her. She did not dream that the beautiful blue eyes of one held for her a future, in the golden fruition of which this poignant and anguished present would become but a dim, sick memory of the past.

For when the later days of new love came, once she said,—

"It is only a memory now—the past, when that beautiful life was part of mine. The sunlight that bathed the dear head and lighted up the eyes is round me in dreams at times, but I cannot waken the old joy or pain that once, it seemed, would never leave me at the thought: *it is only a memory.*"

For so do we ever go onward, whether we would or no. We cannot say, "I will remain here with my dead, my past dreams, my old love ... let the world go on." It is this very past which throws us forward. We meet and knit together for a time; then comes calamity or death, in one form or other, and parts us with an impetus that throws us, it may be, against another life or love. As it was in weeping over her dead that Gasparine found Lo, so, in watching for that lost darling, she found a new love.

★ ★ ★ ★ ★

One other note. In time, when the amelioration of age and experience had toned Gasparine's once bright dreams and ambitions into a pleasant neutral tint of satisfaction and achievement; when the world began to give her credit for a busy, inoffensive life; when many things had happened; when Mrs. Grace had become a deeply religious and ritualistic woman, whose one passion was for the beautiful and wayward Ladybird, the marvel of the College; when, in short, a calm comprehension of existence had made existence easy for Gasparine; the baronet, Sir Gaspar O'Neill, arrived, a white-haired gentleman, and claimed his daughter. How he had fallen on his feet it would be hard to say. The fact remained. He was acting as secretary to a fashionable Club, and, having plenty to eat and drink, nothing to do—for he had three under-clerks—a good salary, and courteous treatment, he liked his position.

He wanted his daughter to keep house for him. It was in this position that Gasparine found her little husband—the smallest and ugliest of the three clerks who did Sir Gaspar's work—and built up for herself yet another future.

Belonging to this future were the little husband, whom she treated scornfully enough, and children, whom she loved. But she brought to it two treasures from the past, dearer to her, she knew, yet hardly dared own, than any love or possession of present or future.

One was a grave.

And one was a picture, which she exhibited in 18—on the line,[1] and which brought to the gaunt woman of nearly forty a

1 "Said of a picture in an exhibition which is hung so that its centre is about on a level with the eye" (*OED*). A position on the line was highly desirable and was reserved for works of particular merit. Not every work could be so easily seen: Victorian galleries covered their walls with art-works in a manner that would by modern standards seem cramped.

tardy fame. Crowds stood round to gaze at the mystic face, with its expression of crucifixion and patience, which at first seemed to meet them only from a cloud of light, where rainbow flowers were faintly shadowed. Only after looking longer one saw in the shadows of the cloud, and round the dark head, phantoms of things, like the suggestions of horrors; an infant, in a shroud, the grey-blue hem drifting into the purple of a mass of violets; a cross on a dim hill, and blood-red leaves near; a swamp, across which spectral birds flew; dim roads, far hills, and weary wastes, powerfully suggested, though hardly outlined, expressions rather than forms, in the distances of the exquisite perspective of the picture. It was, said the critics, the most powerful presentation of thought-life, of the subjective, that had ever yet been given, in form or colour; for in the eyes of the strange face one seemed to see all that the cloud could tell.

Numberless offers came to the artist from all parts. But she would not sell her treasure. It brought the lost back to her longing, aching eyes. It was called "The Lotus-Flower."

THE END

Appendix A: Contemporary Reviews

1. *Glasgow Herald*, 19 July 1894: 9

For a long time people have been asking for a novel which should find its chief interest elsewhere than in "the way of a man with a maid." The anonymous author of "A Sunless Heart" has at last produced such a work, and it is at the same time one of distinct though amorphous power. The theme of the story is, first, the love of a girl for her twin-brother, and then, after his death, the love of the same girl for another woman. There is decided novelty in the idea, and still more in the way in which it is carried out. The author, who is very unmistakably a woman, has a curiously vigorous way of impressing her meaning upon the reader. Sometimes it verges upon hysterics and sometimes upon bad grammar, but it is always forcible, and generally succeeds in conveying a distinct meaning more sharply than a less mannered and more even style might do. [...] What is really new and striking in this book is the way in which it depicts the relations between the three women in whom the interest of the second half centres—Miss Grace, Gasparine, and Mona Lefcadio, the West Indian heiress, "a creature of flame and water, genius and strung nerves." Few writers seem to know so thoroughly what one woman may be to another, or to have explained it so completely. In these days of "woman-novels" the story of this "Sunless Heart" ought to find many readers and much appreciation. It has some of the faults of immaturity, but at the same time a distinct note of power and originality. Whoever the author is, she need not be ashamed to put her name on the title-page of the next book of this kind which she gives us to read.

2. *Scotsman*, 23 July 1894: 3

There is nothing on the title page to indicate who is the writer of *A Sunless Heart*; but the dedicatory pages, which contain a poem of lamentation by the living over the dead, and which is, as regards sentiment and construction, of considerable merit, would indicate that the story is by a lady, who has lost a brother to whom she had been dearly attached. [...] After the death scene at Stirling, the narrative becomes more complicated, but continues always clear and interesting. But why, it may be asked, does the writer deprive us of two interesting personages by such a thing as death in a collision on the railway, and that, too, in a tunnel, where the two trains rush "madly into one another like enraged and sentient monsters?" There are frequent indications that the novel is the work of the 'prentice hand. But the hand is one of considerable strength and promise.

3. *Pall Mall Gazette*, 25 July 1894: 4

Much sickly admiration and a marvellous overloading of endearing epithets also mar the pages of an anonymous tale in two volumes entitled "A Sunless Heart." The curious fact about this novel is that although it is thus disfigured, although it is depressing in the highest degree and heavily weighted with a purpose, it yet remains fairly interesting. True, it is impossible to guess at the exact nature of the message it is intended to convey to humanity, and this may account for much. Anyhow, the fact remains that it *is* interesting, and this excites curiosity as to its authorship. A plausible theory is that Olive Schreiner, having been hypnotized by Thomas Hardy, dreamt the story and then commissioned somebody else to write it down. This would explain a bewildering mixture of Tessishness and Lyndallism[1] with something of an inferior quality. [...] At one or two points the reader confidently expects that the frozen heart of Lotus will thaw, but tragedy is kept up relentlessly to the end.

4. *Daily Telegraph*, 3 August 1894: 6

In [...] "A Sunless Heart," an anonymous author apologetically professes to have given "an impressionist view of two young and tragic lives"; adding "their reality is their only *raison d'être*." The writer presumably meant that the reality of the persons described is the only *raison d'être* of the book; and we must frankly declare that we are unable to recognise its sufficiency. That such miserable beings as Gaspar and Gasparine O'Neill should actually have existed is surely not an adequate excuse for inflicting upon the novel-reading public the most obdurately dismal and painful story which has appeared in print within our remembrance. As it is, for some time past fictional literature has been far too darkly

---

1 The reference is to the heroines of Hardy's *Tess of the d'Urbervilles* (1891) and Schreiner's *The Story of an African Farm* (1883).

shadowed by the deep gloom of pessimism, and novelists have done their utmost to dry up whatever springs of cheerfulness may have lain latent in the breasts of their readers. The author of "A Sunless Heart," however, has outdone his harrowing contemporaries in their grim speciality [...]. From its first page to its last there is not a single flash of geniality or sparkle of pleasantry in "A Sunless Heart." It might have been written by Timon of Athens,[1] so exclusively does it deal with the "seamy side" of male and female character, and its author might appropriately have inscribed upon its title-page the misanthropical device, "Man delights not me, nor woman neither."[2] Here and there, however, it reveals unmistakable literary power and intense sympathy with the sufferings and sorrows that flesh is heir to.[3]

5. James Ashcroft Noble, *Academy*, 4 August 1894: 83

Unless *A Sunless Heart* fails altogether to catch the attention of the great body of the reading public—and such failure is, I think, hardly possible—it will inspire exceptional interest, and be made the theme of excited discussion; for, whatever it may be, it is certainly not an ordinary book. To some readers it may appear attractively powerful and beautiful; to others it may seem repellently painful and morbid; but no one is likely to dismiss it as simply mediocre and insignificant. Of the three verdicts which are always possible, it may be said that *A Sunless Heart* presents a strong case for "good," a very plausible case for "bad," and for "indifferent" no case at all. As a narrative structure or organism, the book must be given over to the tormentors. The story of the brother and sister Gaspar and Gasparine, with its prevailing beauty and pathos, and its one grimly powerful chapter, "How Murders Happen," comes to a close with the death of Gaspar; and the transference of the interest to the one person who provides the book with a name and a *raison d'être* breaks the story in two, and deprives it of constructive unity. But then, as it happens,

---

1   Timon: "The name of a noted misanthrope of Athens, the hero of Shakespeare's play of the same name; hence, one like Timon, a misanthrope" (*OED*).

2   William Shakespeare, *Hamlet* II, ii. Spoken by Hamlet to Rosencrantz and Guildenstern.

3   Yet another display of erudition. This is evocative of *Hamlet* III, i—"The heart-ache and the thousand natural shocks/That flesh is heir to" (from Hamlet's "To be or not to be" soliloquy).

A Sunless Heart is not a novel in which constructive unity is not [sic] of the first importance. It is a work in which invention is quite subsidiary to imagination: it is not primarily a story of incident or even of character, but a study of naked emotion. For example, it can hardly be said that Lotus, one of the most impressively sombre creations in recent fiction, is in the strict sense of the word a character, any more than it can be said that Gaspar and Gasparine and Mona are characters. The reader will probably fail to realise what she *is*, but he will certainly realise what she *feels*, and most intimately and poignantly of all will he realise what she *suffers*. The title of the book is aptly chosen, inasmuch as the author deals not with an entire personality, but simply with a heart—a tortured heart in which the full possibilities of suffering are attained and exhausted. There would have been something morbid in the choice of such a theme had it been deliberately chosen; but *A Sunless Heart* owes its impressiveness and power very largely to the fact that it strikes one as being an instinctive book—a book which has behind it the irresistible compulsion of temperament and experience. [...] From what has been said it will be inferred that *A Sunless Heart* is not a book for the crowd; but those to whom it appeals at all will find that its appeal is a curiously strong one.

6. *Athenaeum*, 4 August 1894: 153

This is not the place to treat of literary tendencies in general, or much might be said of the material chosen by the anonymous author of a book called "A Sunless Heart." Those who have for the last twenty years compared our own fiction with French [fiction] know the peculiarities and growing influence of the latter. Such readers will see what there is to see, and judge accordingly. For the rest the book is too inartistic in form, too crudely and badly executed, to be really important except as an instance of unwelcome progress on certain lines. It does not, however, need an expert to see that it is grossly second rate in manner, and that though it has disagreeable tricks of expression, these are not its worst faults. Reality is said in the preface to be its reason for existing. Whether based on real or imaginary circumstances, the book is nauseating when not ridiculous, and lurid where it is not altogether against taste and judgment. One or two pages show a glimmering of force and purpose, and they are not the least diseased and morbid in character.

7. *Stirling Journal and Advertiser*, 10 August 1894: 2

[Makes reference to "The Novel of the Modern Woman" in *Review of Reviews*.] The notice itself is flattering, but more flattering is the place accorded to the authoress alongside of such famous names as those given above. It is true that few of us can follow Mr. Stead in some of his recent vagaries, yet when all abatements are duly made, we cannot deny his ability to estimate literary power. [...] We do not deny that there may be crudenesses of style, there may be improbabilities in the details of the plot, but the sense of power is so pervading, that, speaking for ourselves, the critical faculty is in abeyance. [...] The picture of [Gasparine's] inconsolable grief is very powerful. Some of our readers may remember a poem called "A Dead Hope" sent in to Professor McCormack when he conducted the University Extension Lectures. The passage in the novel looks like a prose description of the circumstances of the poem. [...] We commend it to our readers with all confidence that they will enjoy it.

8. *Spectator*, 25 August 1894: 248

The author of *A Sunless Heart* is certainly a woman, and probably a young woman. It is clear that she lacks literary experience, which, however, may be acquired; and on the evidence provided by this book, we should say that she also lacks the feeling for literary form, which perhaps cannot be acquired, or which at any rate can be acquired but partially. The book is shapeless in outline and often crude in workmanship; it is more or less painful from first to last; and it is probable that many readers will find certain portions of it not merely painful, but repellent. It is nevertheless, in its uncomfortable way, an exceptionally strong book; and the newspaper critics who have compared it to *The Story of an African Farm*, would not have been guilty of any great ineptitude had they been careful to distinguish between the purely emotional appeal which is the only appeal made by *A Sunless Heart*, and the combination of intellectual with emotional interest which gives so much more of specific gravity to Miss Schreiner's gloomy romance. [...] The author may have thought that she was making an addition to the numerous feminine impeachments of the cruelty and tyranny of man; but such an impeachment is only effective when the instance chosen is really typical,—when we can at once recognise the fidelity of the representation to the observed facts of life, as we certainly do not recognise it in the terrible story of Lotus. Lotus herself is hardly a character; she is more like one of Shelley's personified abstractions; she represents the writer's attempt at an embodiment of wronged and suffering womanhood. [...] Still, when one has noted everything in the book that calls for animadversion—its strain, its morbidness, its feverishness, its lack of proportion—one has to admit that it has genuine imagination and power, and that in the opening story of the brother and sister there are passages of fine pathos and beauty. With all its faults the book is not to be ignored [...].

9. *Bookman*, 6 (September 1894): 184

There is some good material in this particularly undisciplined book. Fastidious readers, impatient of the hysterical spirit of the first chapter or two, and irritated by the absurd italics like those of an old-fashioned lady's letter, should be told that though the novel never ceases to be hysterical, and the italics, or at least the moods they signify, continue till the end, the story increases rather than diminishes in interest. It is all at a very high-strung pitch, and not one of the characters is fit to be trusted to live comfortably in a rough and prosaic world. The love of the brother and sister whose story forms the first part of the book is narrated at a kind of white heat, and the love of the women in the second part is described with no less intensity. It is a queer, formless, and absurd book, but likeable and readable. If the authoress could control her feelings she might write something much better, for every now and again she shows humour and vivacity. The temperament the book expresses is a little complex. We guess that German sentiment has been grafted on Irish sensitiveness. The mixture is never a very happy one; it tends often to gush.

10. *Publishers' Circular*, 15 September 1894: 272

Undoubtedly clever, but terribly sad, is this anonymous story. It depicts some intensely tragic scenes from modern life with such remarkable power and vividness as to gain for it a place among the more notable novels of the present day. Although no author's name appears upon the title-page, the work is unquestionably written by a woman. It deals, indeed, almost exclusively with the sorrows and terrors of bereaved and betrayed women. [...] In the second part we are introduced to Lotus Grace, M.A., a very young lady lecturer of a remarkable disposition. Gasparine, when in the midst of almost madness and sorrow after her brother's death, is visited by Lotus, who, with a terribly tragic history, appears to find her mission in doing loving, friendly acts for others, and gaining their strong affections, though herself incapable of feeling any love whatever for them. She saves Gasparine from a state bordering upon madness, and wins her back to take a wholesome, and even happy interest in life. Gasparine grows to love the mysterious friend, and eventually to share her home. Lotus is a remarkably talented woman, who, so far as the prying world is concerned, has succeeded in letting her dead past bury its dead, but who has the memory of it ever present to her own mind, destroying her faith in all people, and her capacity for really caring for anyone. [...] Lotus is a character who is drawn with considerable power—is, indeed, a very clever psychological study. The story of her life is painful in the extreme; indeed, terrible sadness is, as we have said, the dominant characteristic of the tragic romance told in these two volumes. Original in its conception, clever in its workmanship, and of sustained interest, "A Sunless Heart" is a work which should be read by all who can appreciate fiction which is yet something more than mere entertaining romance. It is undoubtedly one of the most remarkable of recent novels.

11. "A Remarkable Book," *The Lady*, 8 November 1894: 606

[*The Lady*, chiefly concerned with fashion and high society, is a surprising venue for this rhapsodic review. Earlier that year the magazine had, more predictably, attacked the New Woman's "Feminine Fiction" for its dangerous unwomanliness (26 July 1894: 99).]

The impress of genius is stamped indelibly upon its every page, nay, is discernible in its every sentence. In concentration of tragic power it far transcends all the fiction that has been written for very many years. It is like no other novel we have ever read, and its originality is, mayhap, its most painfully interesting attribute. There will be those who will declare that "A Sunless Heart" ought never to have been written; but even these will confess [...] that it deals in a masterly and incisive manner with an anomaly of the moral code of modern Society which is responsible for—ah! how many?—lost souls. "Why, why should the man go unpunished?" is the question—now sobbed out wailingly, again thundered out fiercely—which goes ringing through "A Sunless Heart," and which is agitating the noblest-minded moralists of the times. Seldom has the injustice of the man-made laws been so effectively assailed as they are in the bitterly trenchant passages of this book. [...] The writer plumbs the profundities of broken-hearted sin, suffering, and sorrow, sounds every note in the gamut of woe [...]. As a word-painter this author is a very magician. In a few burning phrases we find conjured up such vividly realistic scenes of squalid misery, maddening despair, and soul-searing villainy as the best among our modern masters of prose would find it difficult to depict in as many chapters. A few strokes of this potent pen, and heigh, presto! the reader finds himself a weeping spectator of one of the most impressive death-bed scenes ever limned, a spell-bound listener to one of the most tragical stories of brutal wrong and martyr-like sacrifice ever wrung from suffering mortal, or the shuddering witness of one of the most horror-striking catastrophes ever conceived by man's or woman's imagination. In ten passionate lines there is conveyed in "A Sunless Heart" as much of intense human interest as would suffice to fill the average three-volume novel to overflowing. The writer of this strangely powerful book is a woman. With that modesty which characterises all real greatness, she has withheld her name from the title-page of "A Sunless Heart." But the name of so forceful a writer as Miss Edith Johnstone [...] has not long remained "a shade." [...]. Miss Johnstone has already been enrolled, tacitly, at all events, among the "immortals" of English fiction [...]. Our object [here] has mainly been to call attention to the facts that a remarkable book has been born into the literary world, that it is the creature of a woman's wondrous imagination, and that it is replete with intense interest for those who honestly seek to solve one of the most complex of the social problems which vex the spirits of latter-day reformers.

Appendix B: Controversies over Modern Fiction

1. From W.L. Courtney, "Books of the Day," *Daily Telegraph*, 30 March 1894: 6

[Courtney (1850–1928) was the literary editor of this middle-brow London paper, writing a weekly "Books of the Day" column about contemporary English letters. He was one of the first critics to identify (and criticize) a group of novels about advanced women that have come to be known as "New Woman novels."]

We live, in fact, under the domination of the female psychologist, the female novelist, the female student of types of humanity. What are the most successful novels of the present day? Without a doubt Mrs. Caffyn's "Yellow Aster," Madame Sarah Grand's "Heavenly Twins," and the anonymous "Superfluous Woman." No higher tribute could be paid to "Iota's"[1] extraordinarily popular story than the fact that on one and the same day appeared a review in which she was highly praised and one in which she was savagely condemned. [...]

At the same time, the feminine style in character-drawing, which seems to have taken possession of the whole artistic field nowadays, is a tyranny under which some of us are inclined to fret and groan. With the exception of a few historical studies and romances, the vast majority of contemporary novels are written by women, and they seem to have impressed upon the art of fiction a peculiar stamp. I am quite aware that generalisations are perilous in these matters, and we all know some honourable instances to the contrary. But it seems to me that we owe to the feminine type of intelligence not only that peculiar love of morbid specimens of humanity which is so significant a feature of modern romance, but also a discussion of moral problems which is neither quite sane nor quite philosophical. [...] The great thing is to dissect a human soul, and if the soul be thoroughly perverse, cross-grained, and stricken with some dire cancer of sorrow and uncleanness, so much apparently the better. [...]

The worst of it is that our moral judgments become distorted

---

1 "Iota" was Kathleen Mannington Caffyn's pseudonym.

by this ill-starred perversity. We get interested in neuropathic[1] criminals, and thence the step is easy to the belief that crime is only disease, and that therefore it is not just to punish it; because in these cases the agent is not a responsible creature. The logic of this feeble "humanitarianism" is as weak and nerveless as its moral fibre. [...] It is too readily forgotten by those who ask us to sympathise with interesting neurotic subjects that the sole chance for human society in its future development is to encourage the sane, the rational, and the normal, and weed out all those noxious growths which impair the health of the body politic.

2. From W.L. Courtney, "Books of the Day," *Daily Telegraph*, 6 April 1894: 6

"The eternal feminine!" On all sides the conquering element is pressing itself upon our attention, and winning victories, in the literary, artistic, poetic, and dramatic spheres. [... Courtney names a number of recently published books, including Mrs. Humphry Ward's *Marcella* and Havelock Ellis's *Man and Woman*.] And we have not got to the end of our record yet. A new novel, describing a woman of the "Yellow Aster" and "Superfluous Woman" type, is announced by Messrs. Ward, Lock, and Bowden, written by an Irishwoman and destined probably to receive the significant title "A Sunless Heart." [...]It is idle, therefore, to attempt to escape from this contemporary burden of femininity. But there is no reason why we should greet our conquerors with excessive fervour. [Courtney goes on to question the aesthetic value of women's poetry and fiction.] Of course the ordinary novel, which is a transcript of life, and demands only a rapid perception of phases of human character and existence, is well within the range of feminine ability. Girls can easily write novelettes, just as they can give extremely glib and vivacious accounts of their experiences, with a strongly-coloured emotional background to add piquancy and distinction to their facts. Nature herself has assigned them loquacity and lucidity. [...]

3. From W.T. Stead, "The Novel of the Modern Woman," *Review of Reviews*, 10 (July 1894): 64–74

[Stead (1849–1912) was the founder and editor of this monthly periodical, as well as a noted journalistic crusader. On this occa-

---

1 "Suffering from or susceptible to mental or nervous disorder" (*OED*).

sion he devotes his regular "Book of the Month" column to ten novels by women, including Olive Schreiner's *The Story of an African Farm*, Sarah Grand's *The Heavenly Twins*, George Egerton's *Keynotes*, Iota's *A Yellow Aster*, and Ella Hepworth Dixon's *The Story of a Modern Woman*. He places *A Sunless Heart* in this company.]

The Novel of the Modern Woman is one of the most notable and significant features of the fiction of the day. The Modern Woman novel is not merely a novel written by a woman, or a novel written about women, but it is a novel written by a woman about women from the standpoint of Woman. Many women have written novels about their own sex, but they have hitherto considered women either from the general standpoint of society or from the man's standpoint, which comes, in the long run, to pretty much the same thing. For in fiction there has not been, until comparatively recently, any such thing as a distinctively woman's standpoint. [...] Woman at last has found Woman interesting to herself, and she has studied her, painted her, and analysed her as if she had an independent existence, and even, strange to say, a soul of her own. [...]

The first note of the novel of the Modern Woman is the recognition of the fundamental fact that in society as at present constituted woman has the worst of it. [...] Woman at the end of the nineteenth century demands, just as man demanded at the close of the eighteenth, the opening of the career to all who have talents, without distinction of caste or sect or sex. [...]

But this in no wise involves or implies any forgetting of her sex, of her destiny, and of her duty as the mother of the race. So far from this being the case, it will be seen that in almost every case the novels of the modern woman are pre-occupied with questions of sex, questions of marriage, questions of maternity. To be a mother is and always will be the chief responsibility, the crowning glory of woman. So far from ignoring this, the novel of the modern woman dismays Mrs. Grundy[1] by taking marriage seriously. [...] If woman is to suffer and to be sacrificed to the new generation which she must nurse at her breast, she must know and understand all that marriage involves, all that maternity demands. [...]

---

1   "An imaginary personage [...] who is proverbially referred to as a personification of the tyranny of social opinion in matters of conventional propriety" (*OED*).

The last book on my list is so different from all the others that I had more than once some doubt whether it ought to be included under the heading of the novels of the Modern Woman. But its intrinsic merits, its originality, and its pathos, its distinctively woman's outlook into life, and the singular glow and genius of its author forbids its omission. In "A Sunless Heart" we have the first work of a woman who has suffered, and who has trodden out the wine of life in the wine-press of misery and despair. It is a woman's novel treating woman as an object of interest apart from her relations to lovers, and the difference is made all the more remarkable because it deals with the love of a sister for a brother, and the love of women for each other.

[...] The character of Lotus is the gem of the book. Gasparine, the luckless Gaspar, and the others are but as setting to the figure of the young-old teacher whom everybody feared and everybody loved, and nobody understood. Lotus is a distinct creation—vivid, life-like and original—a welcome relief from the horde of commonplace mediocrities with which most novels are cumbered. You do not wonder that women loved her. You only fail to understand how it was that men did not. [...]

[...] I leave the readers to find out for themselves how the story ends, merely assuring them that the author is far too much a woman of her generation to avert the tragedy which broods in every chapter, and which culminates and bursts fatally in the last.

"A Sunless Heart" is a woman's book—a young woman's book—it has been brewed in bitterness, and the atmosphere over it is sorrow and pain, and a grim sense of bitter destiny.

In reply to my question as to what she wanted to prove, the authoress wrote:—

What I wanted to do in "A Sunless Heart" was to show people the awful and hideous crime, the worst, the unpardonable one of *taking advantage of weakness*. It is all one to me, whether it is taking advantage of man's weakness or woman's weakness—the crime is the same. And the crime is unending; the effects can never be eradicated. The nature that is subjected against its will and without its knowledge—I mean without the a[c]quiescence of its reason and soul—will bear the impress of the slave upon it while it lives. Therefore I want fair play and justice; not to make women ape the man, but to let women know and choose. Another thing I wanted to show—the absolute rottenness of our social distinctions and conventions, and the eternal wisdom of the sayings, "Judge not that ye be not judged," and "Let him that is without sin among you cast the first stone."[1]

[...] Woman having discovered, apparently very much to her own astonishment, that she has really a soul after all, and that all the rhapsodies of the poets but faintly suggest the essential divinity of the element of sex, is not going to go back to her old position. Through whatever stormy seas and across no matter what burning desert marked by the skeletons and haunted by the ghosts of those who have fallen by the way, she will press on; fleeing from the monogamic prostitution of loveless marriage and the hideous outrage of enforced maternity [...]. All social conventions, all religious teachings, and all moral conceptions will have to be reconsidered and readjusted in harmony with this new central factor in the problem, and woe be to us if we leave that reconstructive task to the fretful fingers of impatient ignorance or the hot hand of impulsive passion.

4. From "The Philistine" [J.A. Spender], *The New Fiction (A Protest against Sex-Mania) and Other Papers* (London: "Westminster Gazette" Office, 1895), 104–08

[This book contains articles that were originally printed in March 1895 in the *Westminster Gazette*. Spender (1862–1942) criticizes a variety of male and female writers under such rubrics as "the defiant man" and "the revolting woman." In his "Recapitulation," excerpted below, he summarizes his objections to advanced fiction, which he sees as predominant in his day. This piece and the next by Stutfield demonstrate the wide-ranging nature of attacks on modern fiction in the mid-1890s.]

For the situation, as it appears to "The Philistine," is briefly this. A claim is being put forward that no novels are to be considered as "true to life," as "art," as really *"written,"* to use the last slang phrase, or as worthy of serious consideration, except those which explore a particular relation between man and woman in its irregular or morbid manifestations; which see everything in the world as a mood of sex; which, as we Philistines should say, abound in coarse details and assume that current morality is a thing for the *bourgeois* and unenlightened. [...]

---

1 Both sayings are Biblical: Matthew 7:1 and John 8:7 (slightly altered).

I. *Is it Art?*—A Philistine has always a wholesome suspicion when he is told that a thing which is repugnant to ordinary taste is "Art." He knows the extraordinary capacity of the artistic temperament for persuading itself that the morbid or abnormal is high art. [...] In the present case it is urged that art has nothing to do with morality. There is a certain limited meaning which may attach to this expression, but the meaning which it seems generally to convey to the people who use it is that art has a preference for the immoral. [...]

II. *Is it Life?*—Upon this question I have tried to give the reader some material for forming his own conclusions. The "defiant man's" view of life seems to me to differ hardly at all from that of precocious schoolboys who imagine that they know all about this wicked world [...]

I do not wish to be more dogmatic about the "revolting woman's conception of life," but it is open to similar objections. It represents life as one monotonous problem of sex, from which there is neither escape or diversion. Every situation is pervaded with sex, the world itself is penetrated with "erotic mysticism." The exponents of this view of life are "surgeons who lay bare the hidden places," or "pathological hunters in the *terra incognita* of the human soul." They interpret human action by "psycho-physiological keys"[1]—which is a grand and nonsensical way of saying that they peck at and probe and analyse the sexual nature. It is surely sufficient to say that life does not present itself thus to any normal human being. The most sensual man or woman has a hundred places of escape from the question of sex. [...] To a Philistine, then, the new fiction is not life, but a morbid abstraction from it. And since it excludes most ordinary motives and enormously exaggerates one, its knowledge of human nature is very imperfect, and its boasted psychology often very absurd. [...]

III. *Is it Modern?*—The claim for the new fiction that it is in any sense "modern" or "advanced" is one that puzzles a Philistine exceedingly. Its theory of life is, apparently, that everyone has a sacred duty to yield to their impulses, whatever inconveniences and upheavals may result to other people in consequence. They must obey the "ruling passions" and defy all laws, rules, conventions, or supposed moralities which dictate any other course. This is called "being true to themselves"—the "triumphant doctrine of

---

1 The preceding four quotations come from George Egerton's preface to her translation of Ola Hansson's *Young Ofeg's Ditties* (1895). Spender has criticized this preface earlier in his work (101–02).

the ego." Holding this view, they naturally "wear their sexes on their sleeves,"[1] become proud of their passions, and talk about them incessantly, without reserve or shame. Now this, I should have thought, instead of indicating an advance toward "modernity" and civilisation, was rather like a relapse into savagery.

5. From Hugh E.M. Stutfield, "Tommyrotics," *Blackwood's Edinburgh Magazine*, 157 (June 1895): 833–45

[Stutfield (1858–1929) was one of the most apoplectic reviewers of the modern literary scene. This article was published at the height of popular frenzy over Oscar Wilde's arrest, trials, and conviction for "gross indecency" under the Criminal Law Amendment of 1885.]

[I]n spite of these faults and certain others of tone and temper, [Max Nordau's *Degeneration*[2]] remains a memorable protest against the foulness and hysteria which deface modern literature, and the waywardness and maudlin sensibility which impair the intellectual "movement" of the latter half of the century.

[...] [O]ur pale English imitations of Continental decadentism are almost as objectionable as their originals. They are less highly seasoned, no doubt, because the authors (or their publishers) have still some fear of Mrs. Grundy before their eyes, while it is easy to see that they would say a great deal more than they do if they only dared. On the other hand, they display less talent, and they lack the saving merit of originality. Both their style and their matter are borrowed—so much so that our late apostle of aestheticism is said to have earned the admiration of a brother *précieux* because he had "the courage of other people's opinions."[3] Decadentism is an exotic growth unsuited to British soil, and it may be hoped that it will never take permanent root here. Still, the popularity of debased and morbid literature, especially among women, is not an agreeable or healthy feature. It may be that it is only a passing fancy, a cloud on our social horizon that will soon blow over; but

1 From John Davidson, "Proem to 'The Wonderful Mission of Earl Lavender,'" *Yellow Book* 4 (January 1895): 284–85.

2 Nordau's book, which had just been translated into English, attacked modern European artistic expression as degenerate.

3 The painter James Abbott McNeill Whistler observed of Oscar Wilde that he "has the courage of the opinions ... of others!" (See Frank Harris, *Oscar Wilde: His Life and Confessions*, 2 vols. [New York: Self-published, 1916] I:79.)

the enormous sale of hysterical and disgusting books is a sign of the times which ought not to be ignored.

Continental influence upon our literature is more apparent now than for many years past. The predilection for the foul and repulsive, the puling emotionalism, and the sickly sensuousness of the French decadents, are also the leading characteristics of the nascent English schools. The former [...] are the direct intellectual progenitors of our aesthetes [...]. Recent events, which shall be nameless, must surely have opened the eyes even of those who have hitherto been blind to the true inwardness of modern aesthetic Hellenism, and perhaps the less said on this subject now the better.

A somewhat similar, and scarcely less unlovely, offspring of hysteria and foreign "degenerate" influence is the neurotic and repulsive fiction which so justly incensed the "Philistine" in the *Westminster Gazette*. Its hysterical origin shows itself chiefly in its morbid spirit of analysis. Judging from their works, the authors must be vivified notes of interrogation. Their characters are so dreadfully introspective. When they are not talking of psychology, they are discussing physiology. They search for new thrills and sensations, and they possess a maddening faculty of dissecting and probing their "primary impulses"—especially the sexual ones. [...]

It is noticeable that most of these profound psychological creations belong to that sex in which, according to Mrs. Sarah Grand, "the true spirit of God dwells," and which, we are assured by another authority, "constitutes the angelic portion of humanity." "To be a woman is to be mad," says the notorious Mrs. Ebbsmith.[1] Possibly, but the woman of the new Ibsenite neuropathic school[2] is not only mad herself, but she does her best to drive those around her crazed also. [...]

The physiological excursions of our writers of neuropathic fiction are usually confined to one field—that of sex. Their chief delight seems to be in making their characters discuss matters which would not have been tolerated in the novels of a decade or

---

1 *The Notorious Mrs. Ebbsmith* (1895) is a play by Arthur Wing Pinero with a New Woman heroine.

2 Like the Norwegian playwright Henrik Ibsen (1828-1906), Pinero wrote several plays that were concerned with contemporary social issues. But Stutfield may, like some other critics, be hurling the epithet "Ibsenite" without a great deal of precision. William Archer, one of Ibsen's translators and greatest supporters, notes the use of the term as part of a popular conservative strategy to vilify Ibsen and all those who admired him. ("The Mausoleum of Ibsen," *Fortnightly Review* 60 [July 1893]: 77-91.)

so ago. Emancipated woman in particular loves to show her independence by dealing freely with the relations of the sexes. [...]

The pathological novel is beyond question a symptom of the mental disease from which civilised mankind is suffering. [...] As far as our decadent lady novelists are concerned, we may console ourselves with the reflection that there is one failing which they certainly do not share with their foreign originals—over-refinement of style. Whatever else may be said of them, they are, as a rule, robustly ungrammatical.

[Stutfield goes on to attack a number of figures often considered notably modern, including the following: Ibsen; novelist and science writer Grant Allen (1848–99); poet and essayist Richard Le Gallienne (1866–1947). Stutfield also attacks contemporary critics.] [...]

I sometimes wish that Dr. Nordau would extend his method of investigation to some of our latter-day revolutionaries, founders of Utopias, and builders of socialistic castles in the air. It might furnish us with some interesting reading. The connection between revolutionary principles in ethics and politics is obvious. The aesthetic sensualist and the communist are, in a sense, nearly related. Both have a common hatred of and contempt for whatever is established or held sacred by the majority, and both have a common parentage in exaggerated emotionalism. [...]

Hysteria, whether in politics or art, has the same inevitable effect of sapping manliness and making people flabby. To the aesthete and decadent, who worship inaction, all strenuousness is naturally repugnant. The sturdy Radical of former years, whose ideal was independence and a disdain of Governmental petting, is being superseded by the political "degenerate," who preaches the doctrine that all men are equal, when experience proves precisely the opposite, and dislikes the notion of the best man winning in the struggle to live. [...]

But let the Philistine take heart of grace. He is not alone in his fight for common-sense and common decency. That large number of really cultivated people whose instincts are still sound and healthy, who disbelieve in "moral autonomy," but cling to the old ideals of discipline and duty, of manliness and self-reliance in men, and womanliness in women; who sicken at Ibsenism and the problem play, at the putrid eroticism of a literature that is at once hysterical and foul; who, despising the apes and mountebanks of the new culture, refuse to believe that to be "modern" and up-to-date is to have attained to the acme of enlightenment,—all these will be on his side.

6. From "The Innings of the Philistines," *Review of Reviews*, 11 (June 1895): 538–39

[It would be a mistake to see British opinion as uniform, even in mid-1895. Here Stead's journal, which covered the highlights of the periodical press each month, has some satirical remarks to make about Stutfield and Harry Quilter, another like-minded writer that month.]

The catastrophe that has overwhelmed Oscar Wilde has let loose the flood-gates of scornful criticism. It is quite extraordinary to discover how virtuous so many people have become the moment vice is locked up. It is edifying indeed to read some of the articles in the current periodicals, but we can only regret that their appearance should have been delayed until the chief offender had been safely laid away in Pentonville.[1] It is neither a manly nor a noble practice to exult over the bodies of the slain. Mr. H.E.M. Stutfield, however, and Mr. Harry Quilter, appear to think otherwise, and we have two very lively articles as the result. [...]

[After summarizing Stutfield's application of Nordau to English letters, the writer continues.] It is "Stutfield," therefore, "to the rescue!" and we should have more hope in him as a leader of the crusade if he had shown that he possessed the preliminary qualification of an ability to discriminate between things that differ, instead of confounding with an indiscriminating anathema every one of whose literary style or journalistic methods he disapproves [...].

---

1 For the first few weeks of his sentence, Wilde was incarcerated in Pentonville Prison in London.

Appendix C: The Expansion of Women's Roles

1. From [William] Withers Moore, "The Higher Education of Women," *British Medical Journal*, 14 August 1886: 295–99

[Moore (d. 1894) was president of the British Medical Association. This piece, the "President's Address" at the BMA's annual meeting, reveals contemporary anxieties about the effects on maternity of women's education.]

This, then, is our question. Is it for the good of the human race, considered as progressive, that women should be trained and admitted to compete with men in the ways and walks of life, from which, heretofore (as unsuited to their sex), they have been excluded by feeling and usage, and largely, indeed, by actual legislation? [...] Will it be well, then, that our women should be equipped and encouraged to enter into the battle of life shoulder to shoulder and on equal terms with men? [...]

The old chivalrous ideal, certainly, was a very different one. It was, that sweat of the brow and sweat of the brain should be mainly masculine—that man should go forth to adventure and achievement, "to his work and to his labour until the evening,"[1] while woman should wait at home and welcome him back again, and lend her ear to his tale of doing or of suffering, and reward him with her gentle sympathy and loving appreciation. [... The thought of men of old] was, not that woman should have her fair chance with man in the battle of life, but that she should be shielded and sheltered from that rude battle, if possible, altogether; that man should fight it for her. But, if we are to "change all that," then those who enter into the conflict where cuffs are going—man or woman—must be content to be cuffed, and to cuff back again; and the age of chivalry and chivalrous courtesy (so far as woman is concerned), with all which that courtesy did to make life noble and beautiful, must indeed be held finally to have passed away.

[...] I think that it is *not* for the good of the human race, considered as progressive, that women should be freed from the restraints which law and custom have imposed upon them, and should receive an education intended to prepare them for the exercise of brain-power in competition with man. And I think

---

1 Psalm 104:23.

thus, because I am persuaded that neither the preliminary training for such competitive work, nor the subsequent practice of it in the actual strife and struggle for existence, can fail to have upon women the effect of more or less (and rather more than less) indisposing them towards, and incapacitating them for, their own proper function [...]. For bettering the breed of men, we need and claim to have the best *mothers of men*. This "higher education" will hinder those who would have been the best mothers from being mothers at all, or, if it does not hinder them, more or less it will spoil them. And no training will enable themselves to do what their sons might have done. Bacon's mother ("choice lady," says the biographer, and "exquisitely skilled," as she was) could not have produced the *Novum Organum*, but she—perhaps she alone—could and did produce Bacon.[1] [...]

When, therefore, we consider that the mother cannot be thus healthily and well conditioned if her powers have been persistently strained and over-taxed by competitive efforts and struggles against strength superior to her own, and consider, also, that the strength of man is thus superior, we see already the ruinous unwisdom of encouraging the competition of woman with man, in the severe brain-work of those "higher" studies which make such vast demands upon the vital powers. [...]

In short, education is very expensive, physiologically as well as pecuniarily, and growing girls are not physiologically rich enough to bear the expense of being trained for motherhood, and also that of being trained for competition with men in the severer exercises of the intellect. [...]

Mr. Herbert Spencer, in his *Principles of Biology*,[2] after noticing that too much bodily labour probably renders women less prolific, proceeds as follows: "That absolute or relative infertility is generally produced in women by mental labour carried to excess, is more clearly shown. [...] This diminution of reproductive power [among upper-class girls] is not shown only by the greater frequency of absolute sterility, nor is it shown only in the earlier cessation of child-bearing; but it is also shown in the very frequent inability of such women to suckle their infants. In its full sense, the reproductive power means the power to bear a well

1 Francis Bacon (1561–1626) was a politician and philosopher. *Novum Organum* is his most important philosophical work.
2 Spencer (1820–1903) was an important philosopher of science, society, and psychology. He is considered the founder of Social Darwinism. *Principles of Biology* (2 vols., 1864, 1867) is part of his multivolume attempt to use evolution as the basis for a new Synthetic Philosophy.

developed infant, and to supply that infant with the natural food for the natural period. Most of the flat-chested girls who survive their high-pressure education are unable to do this. Were their fertility measured by the number of children they could rear without artificial aid, they would prove relatively very infertile." [...]

Sir Benjamin Brodie[1] says: "The mind, in the case of girls of the affluent classes, is educated at the expense of the physical structure, they spending more time in actual study than their brothers." The same eminent practitioner once said to a sister of my own who was consulting him (what, perhaps, he might have hesitated to put into writing), "When I see a girl under twelve with a book in her hand, I always feel an inclination to throw it at her head." [...]

It used to be said that Parliament could do anything but turn a man into a woman. But, in these days, there seems to be danger, both in and out of Parliament, that the attempt may be made to turn women into men.

Let us recall to recollection, therefore, some of the natural difficulties in the way of that transformation. The power of the human brain varies with its weight and size. But the brain of woman is 10 per cent. lighter than that of man [...]. Giving 10 per cent. as the excess of weight in the male cerebellum, in the two hemispheres, [...] man has the advantage by 12 per cent. Nor is this difference accounted for by difference of stature, which, between the two sexes, is, on the average, not more than 8 per cent. [...]

But time admonishes me to make an end. My argument may be summed up very simply. Excessive work, especially in youth, is ruinous to health, both of mind and body; excessive brain-work more surely so than any other. From the eagerness of woman's nature, competitive brain-work among gifted girls can hardly but be excessive, especially if the competition be against the superior brain-weight and brain-strength of man. The resulting ruin can be averted—if it be averted at all—only by drawing so largely upon the woman's whole capital stock of vital force and energy, as to leave a remainder quite inadequate for maternity. [...]

In the prophet's words, "She will not have strength to bring forth;"[2] her reproductive system will more or less have been atro-

---

1 Presumably Sir Benjamin Collins Brodie (1783–1862), physiologist and surgeon.
2 2 Kings 19:3 and Isaiah 37:3.

phied; she will have lost her womanhood's proper power. With the power, she will have largely lost also the inclination; of "Love's sweet want," as Shell[e]y calls it,[1] she will know little, for, in Dr. [Matthews] Duncan's[2] more matter-of-fact language, she will have lost "sensuality of a proper commendable kind." Unsexed it might be wrong to call her, but she will be more or less sexless. And the human race will have lost those who should have been her sons. Bacon, for want of a mother, will not be born. She who should have been his mother will perhaps be a very distinguished collegian. That one truism says it all—women are made and meant to be not men, but mothers of men.

A noble mother, a noble wife—are not these the designations in which we find the highest ideal of noble womanhood? Woman was formed to be man's helpmeet, not his rival; heart, not head; sustainer, not leader. Many times, indeed, woman's fate has set her in the foremost place; in some of those times, no doubt, such place has been well and grandly filled by her. Yet even then, our admiration is not untinged with compassion. Even in this year of approaching or commencing jubilee, is it not so with us when we think of that Crown, Royal and Imperial, which, splendid as it is, has so long been left "a lonely splendour"?[3] "Victoria Regina et Imperatrix"[4]— bravely, proudly, gloriously is the burden borne; but would she, who knows its weight, wish a like weight to be laid upon any daughter?

2. From Lucy M. Hall, "Higher Education of Women and the Family," *Popular Science Monthly*, 30 (1887): 612–18

[Hall (d. 1907), later Hall-Brown, is listed here as "Associate Professor of Physiology and Hygiene and Physician to Vassar College." Vassar was a women's college until 1969.]

The address of Dr. Withers Moore, President of the British Medical Association, delivered before a general meeting of that body, August 10, 1886, has attracted very wide attention. The

1 Percy Bysshe Shelley, "The Sensitive-Plant" (1820).
2 James Matthews Duncan (1826–90) was an obstetric physician who was an expert in fertility.
3 From Alfred Tennyson's dedication of *Idylls of the King* to Queen Victoria's late husband Prince Albert. (The dedication was first published in 1862.) The line refers to Victoria's widowed state.
4 Latin: "Victoria, Queen and Empress."

importance of the subject with which the paper deals can not be overestimated. [...]

Surely no one would be more ready than I to accept the conclusions of Dr. Moore and his supporters could I but be convinced that they have been drawn from reliable data, and presented in an unprejudiced manner. [...]

There is something almost ludicrous in the spectacle of a physician, educated and professedly observing, passing over without a word all the death-dealing follies which are making invalids of tens of thousands of women all about him, while he lifts his voice in dismal croaking over the awful prospect which looms before his jaundiced vision, of a time when more women shall be educated. Forgetting all else, he might have spared one thought for that doomed multitude, shut off forever from honorable motherhood, gone to dire destruction, because untrained in anything which would insure to them a self-respecting independence.

Just what is meant by the term "being trained for motherhood," or why this training should be designated as "one of the two great channels of expenditure of physiological force," I find myself unable to understand. But it may safely be asserted that *any* training which exhausts without more than correspondingly strengthening a part, no matter where applied or for what purpose, should straightway be condemned. The "competition" and the "terrible strain" theories seem to me to have but little foundation. In my university life I saw nothing to confirm them. The work was pleasant and inspiring, and I am sure I can safely say that for the most part we enjoyed it. We did not trouble ourselves about the relative weight of our brains, and, as in the district school or the high-school, so here, it mattered little whether it was Jane or John who stood best; and it was quite as likely to be Jane as John.

As I recall the animated faces, the healthy bloom, and high spirits of the young women, I fail to find any ground for the assumption that their work was in any sense done at the expense of their vitality. On the contrary, I know that in many cases there was decided improvement in health from the beginning to the end of the course.

All this much-talked-of "physiological expenditure" is a myth. The intellect is quickened and strengthened by proper use, not at the expense of any other organ, but in and of itself. It is with this as with the muscles: strength comes with use. The fault has lain, not in the training of one set of organs, but in the neglect of others. The balance of health has thus been lost, and all parts have suffered in unison. To correct this, to establish a harmonious development of mind and body, is what true higher education aims to accomplish; and in doing this it is striking at the very root of woman's disabilities.

Seeing daily, as I do, young women in college in far better health than young women in society, or living in pampered idleness at home; seeing them healthier as seniors than they were as freshmen; knowing that my records tell me that they average a smaller number of excuses because of illness than do those of the men's colleges with which I am able to compare data, and knowing from statistical evidence that woman college graduates enjoy a sum total of twenty per cent better health than the average woman, how can I conclude otherwise than that college-work, *per se*, is not injurious to health [...]?

Where is there a physician who does not know of countless numbers of women among the wealthier classes who are beset by all manner of ailments, for no other reason than because they have nothing to do, or rather because they have brought nothing into their lives which called forth the strong motive forces of their natures? The petty, selfish considerations which have dominated them have been too shallow to float them out into the broader channels, and they have become poor, stranded wrecks, with no interests but their aches and pains, no comfort but in the doctor's daily visit. The contemplation of these wasted lives, powers for good gone to rust and decay for lack of use, should make the angels weep. God forgive the man or woman who would wish to keep alive the baleful thrall of old prejudices and customs which work such irremediable evil to the human race! [...]

Men and women must ever be one in every interest which affects the public good. It is difficult to see how even individual welfare can be made distinct. Women with low ideals, selfish, and untrained; women with feeble, undeveloped physiques, as well as women whose high moral and intellectual worth is enhanced by bodily perfections, all have an influence that puts its stamp upon the household of which each forms a part. And to "train a girl for motherhood" can be done in no better way than by building her from day to day upon the noblest plan which the grand and growing facilities of our time have made possible to us.

3. From Karl Pearson, "Woman and Labour," *Fortnightly Review*, ns 55 (1894): 561–77

[In the course of discussing women's work, Pearson (1857–1936), a socialist eugenicist with some feminist sympathies, seeks to reconcile women's maternity with their right to self-determination.]

[...] We do not for a moment underrate the social importance of giving to women with special aptitude and power the freedom of entering any career where their capacity can be of service to society, but this is only an offshoot of the greater problem of woman's emancipation. That problem is summed up in the words: How can woman follow her sexual and maternal instincts?—how can she do freely what she alone can do for society, and yet have full power to control her own special activities, and develop her own individual life; in short, feel herself a free citizen of a free state? The answer to this problem does not lie in "equality of opportunity"; it lies in special protection, in the socialisation of the State. The advanced woman of the near future will be as thorough a socialist as she is now an out-and-out individualist.

A woman of the upper middle classes can take a great part to-day in social and political life, but it is only by hiring others to rear the children whom she cannot hire others to bear for her. The woman doctor or schoolmistress in whom the maternal instinct is strong must be at a disadvantage as compared with their unmarried sisters. This disadvantage can only be compensated by obviously superior ability or by increased exertion. [...] It is only in the case of exceptional and picked women that the intellectual worry and ceaseless anxiety of modern professional life, the physical and nervous strain of its many demands, will not be detrimental to the growth of the young life. The mentally restful, the moderately active, but not overstrained physical life, which is so essential to many women during pregnancy, is not compatible with the wear and tear of the modern competitive system. Descending in the scale to the handworker, the same remarks apply with even more force. The race must degenerate if greater and greater stress be brought to force woman during the years of child-bearing into active and unlimited competition with man. Either a direct premium is placed upon childlessness, upon a crushing out of the maternal instincts on which the stability of society essentially depends, or woman has a double work to do in the world, and she can only do it at the cost of the future generation. Are we then thrust back on the old solution? Is woman's sole field to be the home, and her chief activity maternity? Must she be content for the future with that dependence on the *individual* man which has been her fate in the past? Some may content themselves with fondly imagining this to be the only solution, if they resolutely shut their eyes to every sign of the times, if they try to believe that the great awakening among women of the last twenty-five years has been limited to a small class, and if they content themselves with the idle dogma that the status of woman is an eternal necessity of her nature and not a factor varying with each phase of civilisation.

If, on the other hand, we open our eyes to facts we must recognise that society is steadily and surely becoming socialistic, that womankind from high to low is gradually perceiving its solidarity, and that women are organising in such a way that they will in the near future become a great power in the state; if, in addition, we note that in all history great changes in the status of woman and in the status of labour have been correlative and often contemporaneous; if, shortly, we throw aside our prejudices and seek merely to understand what is taking place—then assuredly we must admit that the old is passing irrevocably away, and that the woman of the future will have aspirations and, what is more, a power in the state to realise them, which was hardly even dreamt of by her warmest champions a decade ago. [...]

To reconcile maternal activity with the new possibilities of self-development open to women is *par excellence* the woman's problem of the future. It is not one which can be solved by "equality of opportunity," but solely by the recognition of maternity as an essentially social activity, by the institution of some form of national insurance for motherhood [...] and by the correlated restriction and regulation of woman's labour. We may be far distant at present from any such solution, but the growing feeling of solidarity among womankind, the gradual but steady organization of women to give expression to their needs, and the training which even party organizations are giving to women in political methods, can in our opinion only culminate in precisely the same way as the similar movement has done in the case of labour, namely in the cry for special protection and special provision for the essential conditions of efficient activity.

4. From D.S.M. [Dugald Sutherland MacColl], "Women Artists," *Saturday Review*, 87 (1899): 138–39

[MacColl (1859–1948) was art critic for the *Saturday Review* and later keeper of the Tate Gallery and curator of the Wallace Collection. This piece demonstrates that art was also a contested field in debates about women's proper place.]

The year of the forty-fourth exhibition of Women Artists is not too early a date for some general reflections on the results of the efforts made by women to gain a name and a living for themselves by the practice of the arts of design. Here is nearly half a century's record of an activity which in the last twenty years has been feverish. Those who have watched with sympathy the fight women have made to secure bread-winning careers, or the right of entrance to intellectual occupations, and the success that has crowned these efforts in various directions, have been unwilling, however free from illusions as to the upshot, to pronounce judgment before the experiment in this line had been fairly tried. The experiment has been tried, girls in vast numbers have studied art under the same conditions as men, [...] and practically nothing has come of it. In other fields there is a different story to tell. Women have made good their footing in all the subordinate ranks of the teaching and medical professions, and in these professions the work of subordinate ranks is valuable and necessary. They have also proved themselves capable in clerkships, and even the direction of business. [...] But the arts of music and design have not from the beginning of time till now a single woman of the first rank, or even of very high rank, to name. In these fields women have been little more than parasites; only some rare exceptions have given to their imitative work anything of individual charm. [...]

The disappointing nature of the prospect is very much disguised for women and those about them by the fact that, exactly in measure as a woman lacks the originating inventive power of design, she makes an admirable art-student, eager, industrious, docile. The first steps are delightful. To get away from an ungrateful social routine at home into the amusing society of a band of students, with the prospect of the businesslike setting up in a studio later on, is in itself tempting. Add the halo that hangs about the word "art," rapid progress in the early stages of rendering the appearance of models, the emulations and admirations of the art school, and it is easy to understand its seduction. Above all, the instincts of the woman prompt her to mould her efforts upon the teacher's ideas with a devotee's ardor; where the boy of character keeps something of obstinate suspicion under direction, the girl is plastic to a hint. Hence an astonishing progress in the school of a quite deceptive kind, a burst of precocious imitative production upheld by example and precept, and when both are withdrawn, nothing more. The imitation weakens or hardens, or the pupil tumbles about among new influences on emerging from the first. [...]

5. From Florence Fenwick-Miller, "The Ladies' Column," *Illustrated London News*, 21 December 1889: 795

[Fenwick-Miller (1854–1935) was trained as a physician, but devoted most of her life to journalism. Later she became involved in the movement for women's suffrage. Her comments here reveal the disadvantages under which female art students suffered in the late nineteenth century.]

I regret to hear that the unworthy attempt to exclude women students from the Royal Academy art schools is about to be renewed. As most people know, admission to those schools is gained by competitive examination; and the result is that the number of women in the classes is exactly the same as that of the men. The life school—i.e. drawing from the nude model—an essential part of an artist's education, is still closed, and always has been denied, to women. There is a constant, quiet agitation maintained by the lady students to secure admission there also; nor are they fairly treated so long as such a course, which every artist admits is necessary for drawing figure subjects correctly, is denied to one sex and provided for the other. But whenever the agitation for a "female life class" appears likely to succeed, it is met by a counter demand for the exclusion of women from the Academy Schools altogether. As they succeed equally with men in passing the necessary preliminary test, their opponents are reduced to declaring that test valueless. They say that the women who pass the test so well do not distinguish themselves afterwards. "There has been no woman artist who would have been elected an R.A. in the last quarter of a century," they aver. The fact that Rosa Bonheur's pictures bring higher prices than those of any other living painter may perhaps be ruled out of the argument, as she is not an Englishwoman. But Miss Thompson's vigorous battle pieces, Mrs. Allingham's and Miss Montalba's landscapes, Mrs. Jopling's portraits, Mrs. Henrietta Rae's nude figures, Mrs. Alice Havers' "subject" pictures, Miss Mutrie's and Miss Youngman's flower pieces, and many others that might be mentioned, make such wholesale depreciation of living women artists quite absurd.[1]

---

1 Rosa Bonheur (1822–99), painter and sculptor; Elizabeth Thompson Butler (1846–1933), military painter; Helen Allingham (1848–1926), watercolor painter; Henrietta Montalba (1856–93), sculptor; Louise Jopling (1843–1933), portrait painter; Henrietta Rae (1856–1928), painter; Alice Havers (1850–90), painter known for her depictions of rural life; Annie Mutrie (1826–93), still-life painter; Annie Mary Youngman (1859/60–1919), painter.

Appendix D: Sexuality

1. From W.T. Stead, "The Maiden Tribute of Modern Babylon," *Pall Mall Gazette*, 7 July 1885: 1–6

[Stead reported the results of his investigation into child prostitution in a series of articles that ran from 6 July to 13 July 1885. The Criminal Law Amendment, which raised the age of consent to sixteen, was concurrently under consideration in Parliament. It would ultimately pass, along with its notorious Labouchere Amendment, which criminalized acts of "gross indecency" between "male persons." Stead's series caused a sensation, with the City Solicitor seizing copies of the 8 July *PMG* in response to charges of obscenity. Stead himself would be jailed for abduction because he had "bought" a 13-year-old for £5 to demonstrate the ease with which girls could be procured for immoral purposes. This excerpt reveals Stead's immediate political purpose (raising the age of consent), as well as his broader commitment to dispelling ignorance.]

I described yesterday a scene which took place last Derby day, in a well known house, within a quarter of a mile of Oxford-circus. It is by no means one of the worst instances of the crimes that are constantly perpetrated in London, or even in that very house. The victims of these rapes, for such they are to all intents and purposes, are almost always very young children between thirteen and fifteen. The reason for that is very simple. The law at present almost specially marks out such children as the fair game of dissolute men. The moment a child is thirteen she is a woman in the eye of the law, with absolute right to dispose of her person to any one who by force or fraud can bully or cajole her into parting with her virtue. It is the one thing in the whole world which, if once lost, can never be recovered, it is the most precious thing a woman ever has, but while the law forbids her absolutely to dispose of any other valuables until she is sixteen, it insists upon investing her with unfettered freedom to sell her person at thirteen. The law, indeed, seems specially framed in order to enable dissolute men to outrage these legal women of thirteen with impunity. For to quote again from "Stephen's Digest,"[1] a rape in

---

1   *A Digest of the Criminal Law*, by James Fitzjames Stephen (first published in 1877).

fact is not a rape in law if consent is obtained by fraud from a woman or a girl who was totally ignorant of the nature of the act to which she assented. Now it is a fact which I have repeatedly verified that girls of thirteen, fourteen, and even fifteen, who profess themselves perfectly willing to be seduced, are absolutely and totally ignorant of the nature of the act to which they assent. I do not mean merely its remoter consequences and the extent to which their consent will prejudice the whole of their future life, but even the mere physical nature of the act to which they are legally competent to consent is unknown to them. [...]

The ignorance of these girls is almost incredible. It is one of the greatest scandals of Protestant training that parents are allowed to keep their children in total ignorance of the simplest truths of physiology, without even a rudimentary conception of the nature of sexual morality. Catholic children are much better trained; and whatever may be the case in other countries, the chastity of Catholic girls is much greater than that of Protestants in the same social strata. Owing to the soul and body destroying taciturnity of Protestant mothers, girls often arrive at the age of legal womanhood in total ignorance, and are turned loose to contend with all the wiles of the procuress and the temptations of the seducer without the most elementary acquaintance with the laws of their own existence. *Experientia docet*; [1] but in this case the first experience is too often that of violation. [...] Even more than the scandalous state of the law, the culpable refusal of mothers to explain to their daughters the realities and the dangers of their existence contributes to fill the brothels of London.

2. From Allan McLane Hamilton, "The Civil Responsibility of Sexual Perverts," *American Journal of Insanity*, 52 (1896): 503–11

[Hamilton (1848–1919) was an American physician.]

Until within a comparatively recent period the mere insinuation that there could be anything improper in the intimate relations of two women would have drawn upon the head of the maker of such a suggestion a degree of censure of the most pronounced and enduring character, but since the publication of the cele-

---

1 Latin: "Experience teaches."

brated *Mdlle. de Maupin*, which was written by Théophile Gautier about thirty years ago,[1] and other romances from the pens of French and German writers, the eyes of observing persons have been opened to the fact that, as the result of a perverted sexual appetite, the relations of individuals may undergo an extraordinary change, so that one person may entertain for another all the ordinary feelings that he or she should feel for the opposite sex. It is difficult, unless one has been brought in contact with such individuals, to believe that close and absorbing intimacies can exist of a purely platonic nature, and while the writer does not for a moment dispute the existence of an all-absorbing friendship which may arise from a similarity of tastes or the congenial enjoyment of many things, or from loneliness, or the desire for society of a particular kind, he realizes, as have others, that a great many of these too close attachments mean a transposition of sexual feeling, which leads to moral degradation, as well as impairment of individual rights, when a stronger will dominates a weaker. [...]

That a large number of individuals exist who, from birth, are in nearly every way different from what we are led to expect from their external conformation, is a fact not half realized, and while it is true that some of these subjects of the contrary sexual instinct present a physical departure from the ordinary standard, approaching that of the other sex, there is no arbitrary rule to guide us; but there, nevertheless, exists a dominant mental defect which sometimes is so marked as to absolutely control the individual's relations with his fellows. The circumstances under which dangerous intimacies occur vary greatly, and we are called upon to consider an active and passive agent, the former being usually a neurotic or degenerate, who is a sexual pervert, and whose life is pretty well given up to the gratification of his or her unnatural appetites.

Of the sexual female examples that have come under my notice the offender was usually of a masculine type, or if she presented none of the "characteristics" of the male, was a subject of pelvic disorders, with scanty menstruation, and was more or less hysterical or insane. The views of such a person were erratic, "advanced," and extreme, and she nearly always lacked the ordinary modesty and retirement of her sex. The passive agent was,

---

1 This French novel of 1835 deals with a woman who disguises herself as a man.

as a rule, decidedly feminine, with little power of resistance, usually sentimental or unnecessarily prudish. Sometimes the subjects have been married women, with uncongenial husbands, and they nearly always had no desire for children, resenting the normal advance of the male. Again the unnatural attachment was casual, and in no way premeditated, the two women, for economical or other reasons, living together.

The mere infraction of moral laws, which such an alliance implies, is by no means the only evil that confronts us, for it can be readily understood that the weak victim can be made the tool of the designing companion, and extortion may be the end. Of course where the victim is under age, a variety of legal remedies present themselves, but if the woman be more than twenty-one the matter becomes more difficult, and we are then called upon to decide the question of responsibility, and to determine whether she is insane or not, and should be deprived of her civil rights. The difficulties that lie in the way of controlling the diversion of property may be very great while superficial appearances are apparently perfectly proper. [...]

The attitude of the law so far is very harsh regarding the punishment of offenders of this kind when detected, when they happen to be distinctly responsible, and it rarely recognizes any extenuating circumstances, and while possibly this restriction is the best for society, there is no doubt but that in cases where a congenital taint exists, some degree of protection should be afforded the possessors of developed mental weakness who are apt to be the prey of designing persons of their own sex.

When contracts or wills are made by one woman under the influence of another, something more should be conceded as an invalidating factor than the existence of a pertinent and dominating delusion, for there is no stronger dominating influence than a continued appeal to the passions, and especially the sexual feelings; and the apparently harmless intimacy of two women may, if misunderstood, lead to the perpetration of great wrongs and diversion of property. As the matter of proof is so difficult, and the rights of women are so zealously, if not unwisely, guarded by sentimental judges, [...] the matter of determining the degree and depth of the intimacy is often hedged by seemingly insurmountable difficulties, which are increased by the indignation aroused by the merest insinuation that women, in certain ways, can know each other too well.

In my mind a relationship which is carried to such a point that all other ties are neglected, and that personal association

approaches that of man and wife, is enough to enable the physician to diagnose a state of affairs that greatly militates against the
proper exercise of free disposing or contracting power; and I hold
that under such circumstances not only may the aid of habeas
corpus[1] be implored for the purpose of effecting a separation, but
that in aggravated instances the physician should, in manner
specified, bring the matter before the attention of a committing
judge.

3. From Havelock Ellis, *Sexual Inversion*, 2d ed., vol. 2 of *Studies in the Psychology of Sex* (Philadelphia: F.A. Davis, 1901), 121–22, 131–33

[Ellis (1859–1939) was a pioneer in the study of human sexuality. The first edition of this book (1897) had dealt with female
homosexuality to some extent, but the second edition expands its
treatment of the subject. This is the first edition to include an
appendix on "The School-Friendships of Girls," which provides
many accounts of intense relationships between women that supplement Ellis's general treatment of the topic below. Ellis, whose
own wife was a lesbian, is remarkable in the period for his relatively unjudgmental treatment of homosexuality. The excerpt
below omits Ellis's footnotes, which are of only minor interest.]

Yet we know comparatively little of sexual inversion in woman; of
the total number of recorded cases of this abnormality, now very
considerable, only a small proportion are in women, and the chief
monographs on the subject devote but little space to women.

I think there are several reasons for this. Notwithstanding the
severity with which homosexuality in women has been visited in
a few cases, for the most part men seem to have been indifferent
toward it; when it has been made a crime or a cause for divorce
in men, it has usually been considered as no offense at all in
women. Another reason is that it is less easy to detect in women;
we are accustomed to a much greater familiarity and intimacy
between women than between men, and we are less apt to
suspect the existence of any abnormal passion. And allied with
this cause we have also to bear in mind the extreme ignorance
and the extreme reticence of women regarding any abnormal or

---

1   An order from a court that a person be brought before a judge for a
    specified purpose.

even normal manifestation of their sexual life. A woman may feel a high degree of sexual attraction for another woman without realizing that her affection is sexual, and when she does realize it she is nearly always very unwilling to reveal the nature of her intimate experience, even with the adoption of precautions, and although the fact may be present to her that, by helping to reveal the nature of her abnormality, she may be helping to lighten the burden of it on other women. Among the numerous confessions voluntarily sent to Krafft-Ebing[1] there is not one by a woman. There is, I think, one other reason why sexual inversion is less obvious in a woman. We have some reason to believe that, while a slight degree of homosexuality is commoner in women than in men, and is favored by the conditions under which women live, well-marked and fully-developed cases of inversion are rarer in women than in men. [...]

The ardent attachments which girls in schools and colleges form to each other and to their teachers constitute a subject which is of considerable psychological interest and of no little practical importance. These girlish devotions, on the borderland between friendship and sexual passion, are found in all countries where girls are segregated for educational purposes, and their symptoms are, on the whole, singularly uniform, though they vary in intensity and character to some extent, from time to time and from place to place, sometimes assuming an epidemic form. They have been most carefully studied in Italy [...]. But exactly the same phenomena are everywhere found in English girls' schools, even of the most modern type, and in some of the large American women's colleges they have sometimes become so acute as to cause much anxiety.

These passionate friendships, of a more or less unconsciously sexual character, are also common, even outside and beyond school-life. It frequently happens that a period during which a young woman falls in love at a distance with some young man of her acquaintance alternates with periods of intimate attachment to a friend of her own sex. No congenital inversion is usually involved. It generally happens, in the end, either that relationship with a man brings the normal impulse into permanent play or the steadying of the emotions in the stress of practical life leads to a

---

1 The German psychiatrist Richard von Krafft-Ebing (1840–1902). His *Psychopathia Sexualis* (1886), one of the earliest studies of "abnormal" sexuality, was an important influence on Ellis.

knowledge of the real nature of such feelings and a consequent distaste for them. In some cases, on the other hand, such relationships, especially when formed after school-life, are fairly permanent. [...] The actual specific sexual phenomena generated in such cases vary very greatly. The emotion may be latent or unconscious; it may be all on one side; it is often more or less recognized and shared. Such cases are on the borderland of true sexual inversion, but they cannot be included within its region. Sex in these relationships is scarcely the essential and fundamental element; it is more or less subordinate and parasitic. There is often a semblance of a sex-relationship from the marked divergence of the friends in physical and psychic qualities, and the nervous development of one or both the friends is often slightly abnormal. We have to regard such relationships as hypertrophied friendships, the hypertrophy[1] being due to unemployed sexual instinct.

---

1 "Enlargement of a part or organ of an animal or plant, produced by excessive nutrition; excessive growth or development" (*OED*).

Appendix E: Conceptions of the West Indies

1. From James Anthony Froude, *The English in the West Indies, or the Bow of Ulysses* (London: Longmans, Green, and Co., 1888), 66–74

[Froude (1818–94) was an historian and Thomas Carlyle's first biographer. In this description of his visit to Trinidad, which the British had acquired in 1797, he reveals his sense of its geographical and racial otherness.]

To walk is difficult in a damp steamy temperature hotter during daylight than the hottest forcing house in Kew.[1] I was warned not to exert myself and to take cocktail freely. In the evening I might venture out with the bats and take a drive if I wished in the twilight. Languidly charming as it all was, I could not help asking myself of what use such a possession could be either to England or to the English nation. We could not colonise it, could not cultivate it, could not draw a revenue from it. If it prospered commercially the prosperity would be of French and Spaniards, mulattoes and blacks, but scarcely, if at all, of my own countrymen. For here too, as elsewhere, they were growing fewer daily, and those who remained were looking forward to the day when they could be released. If it were not for the honour of the thing, as the Irishman said after being carried in a sedan chair which had no bottom, we might have spared ourselves so unnecessary a conquest.

Beautiful, however, it was beyond dispute. Before sunset a carriage took us round the savannah. Tropical human beings like tropical birds are fond of fine colours, especially black human beings, and the park was as brilliant as Kensington Gardens on a Sunday. At nightfall the scene became yet more wonderful; air, grass, and trees being alight with fireflies each as brilliant as an English glowworm. The palm tree at our own gate stood like a ghostly sentinel clear against the starry sky, a single long dead frond hanging from below the coronet of leaves and clashing against the stem as it was blown to and fro by the night wind, while long-winged bats swept and whistled over our heads. [...]

[Froude responds to men who invite him to a rally in favour of a constitution for Trinidad, which was then a Crown colony.] I

---

1 One of the glasshouses at the Royal Botanic Gardens in Kew that would be kept hot to promote the growth of exotic plants.

could but reply [...], that I was greatly obliged by the compliment, but that I knew too little of their affairs to make my presence of any value to them. As they were doing so well, I did not see myself why they wanted an alteration. Political changes were generally little more than turns of a kaleidoscope; you got a new pattern, but it was made of the same pieces, and things went on much as before. If they wanted political liberty I did not doubt that they would get it if they were loud and persistent enough. Only they must understand that at home we were now a democracy. Any constitution which was granted them would be on the widest basis. The blacks and coolies outnumbered the Europeans by four to one, and perhaps when they had what they asked for they might be less pleased than they expected. [...]

Trinidad has one wonder in it, a lake of bitumen some ninety acres in extent, which all travellers are expected to visit, and which few residents care to visit. A black lake is not so beautiful as an ordinary lake. I had no doubt that it existed, for the testimony was unimpeachable. Indeed I was shown an actual specimen of the crystallised pitch itself. I could believe without seeing and without undertaking a tedious journey. I rather sympathised with a noble lord who came to Port of Spain in his yacht, and like myself had the lake impressed upon him. As a middle course between going thither and appearing to slight his friends' recommendations, he said that he would send his steward. [...]

Out of a total population of 170,000, there are 25,000 whites and mulattoes, 10,000 coolies, the rest negroes. The English part of the Europeans shows no tendency to increase. The English come as birds of passage, and depart when they have made their fortunes. The French and Spaniards may hold on to Trinidad as a home. Our people do not make homes there, and must be looked on as a transient element.

2. From J[ohn] J[acob] Thomas, *Froudacity: West Indian Fables by James Anthony Froude* (London: T. Fisher Unwin, 1889), 74–79, 154–56

[Thomas (1840–89) was himself a native of Trinidad. His book, as its title suggests, attacks Froude's work broadly. Thomas sees Froude's treatment of Trinidad as exemplary of his ignorance and racism.]

Mr. Froude is not likely to impress the world (of the West Indies, at any rate) with the transparently silly, if not intentionally malicious, ravings which he has indulged in on the subject of Trinidad and its politics. [...]

At any rate, whatever political fate Mr. Froude may desire for the Colonies in general, and for Trinidad in particular, it is nevertheless unquestionable that he and the scheme that he may have for our future governance, in this year of grace 1888, have both come into view entirely out of season. The spirit of the times has rendered impossible any further toleration of the arrogance which is based on historical self-glorification. The gentlemen of Trinidad, who are struggling for political enfranchisement, are not likely to heed, except as a matter for indignant contempt, the obtrusion by our author of his opinion that "they had best let well alone." On his own showing, the persons appointed to supreme authority in the Colonies are, more usually than not, entirely unfit for holding any responsible position whatever over their fellows. [...] Mr. Froude's deftly-worded sarcasms about "degrading tyranny," "the dignity of manhood," &c., are powerless to alter the facts. Crown Colony Government—denying, as it does to even the wisest and most interested in a community cursed with it all participation in the conduct of their own affairs, while investing irresponsible and uninterested "birds of passage" (as our author aptly describes them) with the right of making ducks and drakes of the resources wrung from the inhabitants— *is* a degrading tyranny, which the sneers of Mr. Froude cannot make otherwise. The dignity of manhood, on the other hand, we are forced to admit, runs scanty chance of recognition by any being, however masculine his name, who could perpetrate such a literary and moral scandal as "The Bow of Ulysses." Yet the dignity of manhood stands venerable there, and whilst the world lasts shall gain for its possessors the right of record on the roll of those whom the worthy of the world delight to honour. [...]

It behoves us to repeat (for our detractor is a persistent repeater) that the cardinal dodge by which Mr. Froude and his few adherents expect to succeed in obtaining the reversal of the progress of the coloured population is by misrepresenting the elements, and their real attitude towards one another, of the sections composing the British West Indian communities. Everybody knows full well that Englishmen, Scotchmen, and Irishmen (who are not officials), as well as Germans, Spaniards, Italians, Portuguese, and other nationalities, work in unbroken harmony and, more or less, prosper in these Islands. These are no cherishers of any vain hankering after a state of things in which men felt not the infamy of living not only on the unpaid labour, but at the expense of the sufferings, the blood, and even the life of their fellow-men. [...] These reputable specimens of manhood have created homes dear to them in these favoured climes; and they, at any rate, being on the very best terms with all sections of the community in which their lot is cast, have a common cause as fellow-sufferers under the *régime* of Mr. Froude's official "birds of passage." The agitation in Trinidad tells its own tale. There is not a single black man—though there should have been many— among the leaders of the movement for Reform. Nevertheless the honourable and truthful author of "The English in the West Indies," in order to invent a plausible pretext for his sinister labours of love on behalf of the poor pro-slavery survivals, and despite his knowledge that sturdy Britons are at the head of the agitation, coolly tells the world that it is a struggle to secure "negro domination."

3. From T. Lothrop Stoddard, *The French Revolution in San Domingo* (Boston: Houghton Mifflin, 1914), 26–29

[Stoddard (1883–1950) was an American best known as the eugenicist author of *The Rising Tide of Color against White World-Supremacy* (1920). While describing the culture of Haiti (then called San Domingo) at the turn of the nineteenth century, this section reveals popular notions about Creoles. The full bibliographical entries for Stoddard's references (given in parentheses) can be found in a section at the end of this volume's Select Bibliography.]

The Creole whites differed in many respects from those of European birth. [...] Both in mind and body the Creoles showed the influence of their tropical environment. Physically they were tall and slender, well-featured though pale, and with a proud non-chalance of bearing (Moreau I:12; Vaissière 301–02; Hilliard II:45; Mills 13). In character they were generous, warm-hearted, and brave, with a lively intelligence and an ardent imagination; at the same time they were reckless, frivolous, passionate, and often cruel, while their indolence usually hindered the development of their talents (Moreau I:12, 16–17; Vaissière 306; Wimpffen 65).

The two main causes of the Creole's special nature were climate and slavery. It was the burning climate of San Domingo which gave him his mercurial temperament,—his intense crises of reckless passion or feverish energy, followed by reactions into languorous apathy (Vaissière 302–03; Hilliard II:31). But even more important was the influence of African slavery. He certainly owed most of his bad qualities to this evil institution, which seems to have degraded the master even more than the slave. Vaissière comments upon this very well. "Lost as they were among their immense herds of slaves, the colonists suffered two fatal consequences: by contact with these primitive beings, they necessarily absorbed much of these people's nature, defects, and vices; from a life spent almost wholly among inferiors, their own characters naturally degenerated" (Vaissière, 303).

This fatal influence weighed upon the Creole from the very moment of his birth. A royal officer laments those Creole children "corrupted in the cradle by the negresses' milk and vices" (Vaissière 305). And everything contributed to stimulate the Créole child's wilfulness and vanity. That slave nurse, who dared give him no direct command (Vaissière 306); those slave play-mates, "condemned to flatter his lightest whim" (Moreau I:13); those parents, proverbial for over-fond indulgence (Moreau I:12–13);—all these combined to make of him a pampered little tyrant, unable to endure the slightest opposition (Moreau I:13; Vaissière 305–06). Most writers on San Domingo quote the classic story of the Creole child who, told there was no egg, demanded two (Moreau I:12; Vaissière 306–07). Add a precocious knowledge, gained by constant observation of the indecencies and cruelties of plantation life (Vaissière 303–06; Wimpffen 268), and the conduct of the future man when exposed to the temptations of unrestrained authority is easy to foresee (Moreau I:15–16; Vaissière 305–06). [...]

In the Creole women, the type characteristics came out most strongly. Piquantly beautiful, their languorous grace charmed all observers. Their love was passionate in the extreme, their jealous hate often terrible in its consequences (Moreau I:17–21; Vaissière 308–19; Hilliard II:31–32). An American woman, who saw them in the days of their adversity, is favorably impressed. "The Creole ladies," writes Miss Hassal in 1802, "have an air of voluptuous languor, which renders them extremely interesting. Their eyes, their teeth, and their hair are remarkably beautiful, and they have acquired from the habit of commanding their slaves an air of dignity which adds to their charms. Almost too indolent to pronounce their words, they speak with a drawling accent which is very agreeable. But since they have been roused by the pressure of misfortune, many have displayed talents and found resources in the energy of their own minds, which it would have been supposed impossible for them to possess" (Hassal 19–20).

Even more than her brothers, the Creole girl suffered from the blight of slavery and the lack of education. Too often, she lived in the most complete indolence; passing her days, like an Eastern odalisque, amid the chatter and singing of her slave girls (Vaissière 313–18; Moreau I:20–21).

Select Bibliography

Works by Edith Johnstone

Cinq-Mars [Edith Johnstone]. "My Dead Hope." "University Extension Lectures." *Stirling Journal and Advertiser* 15 March 1889: 4.

Johnstone, Edith. *The Douce Family*. London: T. Fisher Unwin, [1896].

——. *The Girleen*. 1895. London: Blackie, 1896.

——. *A Sunless Heart*. 2 vols. London: Ward, Lock, & Bowden, 1894.

Johnstone, Edith, ed. *The Canterbury Tales*. By Geoffrey Chaucer. The Masterpiece Library. The Penny Poets 14. London: "Review of Reviews" Office, [1895].

Johnstone, Edith, and Foley Johnstone. *Thoughts of To-day and Yesterday: Poems and Writings of Edith and Foley Johnstone*. London: J.B. Andrews [office of *The Matron*], 1916.

O'Byrne, E. [Edith Johnstone]. *Daphne: A Story of Self-Conquest*. London: Blackie, [1890].

——. *Gladys; or, The Sister's Charge*. London: Blackie, [1889].

Sources for Johnstone's Life

Atalanta. "Ladies' Column." *Stirling Journal and Advertiser* 17 August 1894: 3.

Brehony, Kevin J. "The Kindergarten in England, 1851–1918." *Kindergartens and Cultures: The Global Diffusion of an Idea*. Ed. Roberta Wollons. New Haven: Yale UP, 2000. 59–86.

Bury, Patrick. *The College of Corpus Christi*. Cambridge: For the College, 1952.

G., A.G. Letter. *Stirling Journal and Advertiser* 26 April 1889: 2.

Johnstone, Edith. Letter to William Blackwood. 1892. Ms. 4589, ff. 32–33. William Blackwood and Sons Papers. National Library of Scotland. Edinburgh.

McClelland, Aiken. *William Johnston of Ballykilbeg*. Lurgan: Ulster Society, 1990.

Rev. of *Thoughts of To-day and Yesterday*. *Times Literary Supplement* 16 March 1916: 131.

Ruding, Walt. *An Evil Motherhood: An Impressionist Novel*. 1895. London: Mathews, 1896.

Samuels Lasner, Mark. *A Selective Checklist of the Published Work of Aubrey Beardsley*. Boston: Boss, 1995.

"Scotch Sequestration." *Times* 25 July 1885: 14.

"Truth about the Militia, The." *Punch* 11 October 1884: 177.

"University Extension Lectures." *Stirling Journal and Advertiser* 15 March 1889: 4.

——. *Stirling Journal and Advertiser* 12 April 1889: 3.

"University Extension Scheme." *Stirling Journal and Advertiser* 27 January 1888: 6.

"Ward, Lock & Bowden's Announcements." *Athenaeum* 30 June 1894: 849.

Waugh, Arthur. "London Letter." *The Critic* 11 August 1894: 94–95.

Whyte, Frederic. *The Life of W.T. Stead*. 2 vols. 1925. New York: Garland, 1971.

Young, Matthew. "The Mystery of Walt Ruding: A Solution." *Antiquarian Book Monthly* 27.11 (Dec. 2000): 22–26.

New Women and Literature

Ardis, Ann. *New Women, New Novels: Feminism and Early Modernism*. New Brunswick: Rutgers UP, 1990.

Arnold, Ethel M. *Platonics*. 1894. Bristol: Thoemmes, 1995.

Cunningham, Gail. *The New Woman and the Victorian Novel*. New York: Barnes, 1978.

Egerton, George. *Discords. Keynotes and Discords*. London: Virago, 1983.

Heilmann, Ann. *New Woman Fiction: Women Writing First-Wave Feminism*. Basingstoke: Palgrave, 2000.

Ledger, Sally. *The New Woman: Fiction and Feminism at the fin de siècle*. Manchester: Manchester UP, 1997.

Ledger, Sally, and Roger Luckhurst, eds. *The Fin de Siècle: A Reader in Cultural History, c. 1880–1900*. Oxford: Oxford UP, 2000.

Ledger, Sally, and Scott McCracken, eds. *Cultural Politics at the Fin de Siècle*. Cambridge: Cambridge UP, 1995.

Miller, Jane Eldridge. *Rebel Women: Feminism, Modernism and the Edwardian Novel*. London: Virago, 1994.

Nelson, Carolyn Christensen, ed. *A New Woman Reader*. Peterborough: Broadview, 2000.

Pykett, Lyn. *The "Improper" Feminine: The Women's Sensation Novel and the New Woman Writing*. London: Routledge, 1992.

Richardson, Angelique. *Love and Eugenics in the Late Nineteenth*

Century: Rational Reproduction and the New Woman. Oxford: Oxford UP, 2003.

Richardson, Angelique, and Chris Willis, eds. *The New Woman in Fiction and in Fact: Fin-de-Siècle Feminisms*. 2001. Basingstoke: Palgrave, 2002.

Showalter, Elaine. *Sexual Anarchy: Gender and Culture at the Fin de Siècle*. New York: Viking, 1990.

—, ed. *Daughters of Decadence: Women Writers of the Fin-de-Siècle*. New Brunswick: Rutgers UP, 1993.

Stubbs, Patricia. *Women and Fiction: Feminism and the Novel, 1880–1920*. New York: Barnes, 1979.

Thompson, Nicola Diane, ed. *Victorian Women Writers and the Woman Question*. Cambridge: Cambridge UP, 1999.

Women and Art

Chalmers, F. Graeme. *Women in the Nineteenth-Century Art World: Schools of Art and Design for Women in London and Philadelphia*. Westport: Greenwood, 1998.

Cherry, Deborah. *Painting Women: Victorian Women Artists*. London: Routledge, 1993.

Taylor, Hilary. "'If a Young Painter Be Not Fierce and Arrogant God ... Help Him': Some Women Art Students at the Slade, c. 1895–9," *Art History* 9 (1986): 232–44.

Women and Sexuality

Castle, Terry. *The Apparitional Lesbian: Female Homosexuality and Modern Culture*. New York: Columbia UP, 1993.

Cvetkovich, Ann. "Sexual Trauma/Queer Memory: Incest, Lesbianism, and Therapeutic Culture." *Incest and the Literary Imagination*. Ed. Elizabeth Barnes. Gainesville: UP of Florida, 2002. 329–57.

Faderman, Lillian. *Surpassing the Love of Men: Romantic Friendship and Love between Women from the Renaissance to the Present*. New York: Morrow, 1981.

Grosskurth, Phyllis. *Havelock Ellis: A Biography*. New York: Knopf, 1980.

Jackson, Louise A. *Child Sexual Abuse in Victorian England*. London: Routledge, 2000.

Kincaid, James R. *Child-Loving: The Erotic Child and Victorian Culture*. New York: Routledge, 1994.

Putzell-Korab, Sara. "Passion between Women in the Victorian

Novel." *Sexuality and Victorian Literature*. Ed. Don Richard
Cox. Knoxville: U of Tennesse P, 1984. 180–95.

Russell, Diana E.H. *The Secret Trauma: Incest in the Lives of Girls
and Women*. Rev. ed. New York: Basic, 1999.

Smith-Rosenberg, Carroll. "The Female World of Love and
Ritual: Relations between Women in Nineteenth-Century
America." *Signs* 1 (1975): 1–29.

Swanson, Diana L. "Safe Space or Danger Zone? Incest and the
Paradox of Writing in Woolf's Life." *Creating Safe Space: Vio-
lence and Women's Writing*. Ed. Tomoko Kuribayashi and Julie
Tharp. Albany: State U of New York P, 1998. 79–99.

Vicinus, Martha. "Distance and Desire: English Boarding-
School Friendships." *Signs* 9 (1984): 600–22.

——. *Intimate Friends: Women Who Loved Women, 1778-1928*.
Chicago: U of Chicago P, 2004.

Walkowitz, Judith R. *City of Dreadful Delight: Narratives of
Sexual Danger in Late-Victorian London*. Chicago: U of
Chicago P, 1992.

Works Cited by Stoddard

Hassal, Mary. *Secret History, or, The Horrors of St. Domingo*.
Philadelphia: Bradford & Inskeep, 1808.

Hilliard d'Auberteuil, Michel-René. *Considérations sur l'état
présent de la colonie française de Saint-Domingue*. 2 vols. Paris:
Grangé, 1776–77.

Mills, Herbert Elmer. *The Early Years of the French Revolution in
San Domingo*. Diss. Cornell U, 1889. Poughkeepsie: Haight,
1892.

Moreau de Saint-Méry, M.L.E. *Description topographique,
physique, civile, politique et historique de la partie française de
l'isle Saint-Domingue*. 2 vols. Philadelphia, 1797–98.

Vaissière, Pierre de. *Saint-Domingue*. Paris: Perrin, 1909.

Wimpffen, Alexandre-Stanislas, baron de. *A Voyage to Saint
Domingo, in the Years 1788, 1789, and 1790*. London: Cadell
and Davies, 1797.